Night Before
CHRISTMAS

One
Night Before
CHRISTMAS

JANICE
MAYNARD

ROBYN
GRADY

KATHIE
DeNOSKY

& MILLS
BOON

Published in Great Britain 2016
By Mills & Boon, an imprint of HarperCollins*Publishers*
1 London Bridge Street, London, SE1 9GF

ONE NIGHT BEFORE CHRISTMAS © 2016 Harlequin Books S.A.

A Billionaire for Christmas © 2013 Janice Maynard
One Night, Second Chance © 2014 Robyn Grady
It Happened One Night © 2013 Kathie DeNosky

ISBN: 978-0-263-92716-0

9-1116

Our policy is to use papers that are natural, renewable and recyclable products and made from wood grown in sustainable forests.
The logging and manufacturing processes conform to the legal environmental regulations of the country of origin.

Printed and bound in Spain
by CPI, Barcelona

A BILLIONAIRE
FOR CHRISTMAS

JANICE MAYNARD

For my mother, Pat Scott, who loved Christmas as much as anyone I have ever known.

USA TODAY bestselling author **Janice Maynard** loved books and writing even as a child. But it took multiple rejections before she sold her first manuscript. Since 2002, she has written over thirty-five books and novellas. Janice lives in east Tennessee with her husband, Charles. They love hiking, travelling and spending time with family.

You can connect with Janice at
www.twitter.com/janicemaynard,
www.facebook.com/janicemaynardreaderpage,
www.wattpad.com/user/janicemaynard,
and www.instagram.com/janicemaynard.

One

Leo Cavallo had a headache. In fact, his whole body hurt. The drive from Atlanta to the Great Smoky Mountains in East Tennessee hadn't seemed all that onerous on the map, but he'd gravely miscalculated the reality of negotiating winding rural roads after dark. And given that the calendar had flipped only a handful of days into December, he'd lost daylight a long time ago.

He glanced at the clock on the dashboard and groaned as he registered the glowing readout. It was after nine. He still had no idea if he was even close to his destination. The GPS had given up on him ten miles back. The car thermometer read thirty-five degrees, which meant that any moment now the driving rain hammering his windshield might change over to snow, and he'd really be screwed. Jags were not meant to be driven in bad weather.

Sweating beneath his thin cotton sweater, he reached into the console for an antacid. Without warning, his brother's voice popped into his head, loud and clear.

"I'm serious, Leo. You have to make some changes. You had a heart attack, for God's sake."

Leo scowled. *"A mild cardiac event. Don't be so dramatic. I'm in excellent physical shape. You heard the doctor."*

"Yes, I did. He said your stress levels are off the charts. And he preached heredity. Our father died before he hit forty-two. You keep this up, and I'll be putting you in the ground right beside him..."

Leo chewed the chalky tablet and cursed when the road suddenly changed from ragged pavement to loose gravel. The wheels of his vehicle spun for purchase on the uneven surface. He crept along, straining his eyes for any signs of life up ahead.

On either side, steep hillsides boxed him in. The headlights on his car picked out dense thickets of rhododendron lining the way. Claustrophobic gloom swathed the vehicle in a cloying blanket. He was accustomed to living amidst the bright lights of Atlanta. His penthouse condo offered an amazing view of the city. Neon and energy and people were his daily fuel. So why had he agreed to voluntary exile in a state whose remote corners seemed unwelcoming at best?

Five minutes later, when he was almost ready to turn around and admit defeat, he saw a light shining in the darkness. The relief he felt was staggering. By the time he finally pulled up in front of the blessedly illuminated house, every muscle in his body ached with tension. He hoped the porch light indicated some level of available hospitality.

Pulling his plush-lined leather jacket from the backseat, he stepped out of the car and shivered. The rain had slacked off...finally. But a heavy, fog-wrapped drizzle accompanied by bone-numbing chill greeted him. For the moment, he would leave his bags in the trunk. He didn't know exactly where his cabin was located. Hopefully, he'd be able to park closer before he unloaded.

Mud caked the soles of his expensive leather shoes as he made his way to the door of the modern log structure. It looked as if it had been assembled from one of those kits that well-heeled couples bought to set up getaway homes in the mountains. Certainly not old, but neatly put together.

From what he could tell, it was built on a single level with a porch that wrapped around at least two sides of the house.

There was no doorbell that he could see, so he took hold of the bronze bear-head knocker and rapped it three times, hard enough to express his growing frustration. Additional lights went on inside the house. As he shifted from one foot to the other impatiently, the curtain beside the door twitched and a wide-eyed female face appeared briefly before disappearing as quickly as it had come.

From inside he heard a muffled voice. "Who is it?"

"Leo. Leo Cavallo," he shouted at the door. Grinding his teeth, he reached for a more conciliatory tone. "May I come in?"

Phoebe opened her front door with some trepidation. Not because she had anything to fear from the man on the porch. She'd been expecting him for the past several hours. What she dreaded was telling him the truth.

Backing up to let him enter, she winced as he crossed the threshold and sucked all the air out of the room. He was a big man, built like a lumberjack, broad through the shoulders, and tall, topping her five-foot-nine stature by at least four more inches. His thick, wavy chestnut hair gleamed with health. The glow from the fire that crackled in the hearth picked out strands of dark gold.

When he removed his jacket, running a hand through his disheveled hair, she saw that he wore a deep blue sweater along with dark dress pants. The faint whiff of his aftershave mixed with the unmistakable scent of the outdoors. He filled the room with his presence.

Reaching around him gingerly, she flipped on the overhead light, sighing inwardly in relief when the intimacy of firelight gave way to a less cozy atmosphere. Glancing down at his feet, she bit her lip. "Will you please take off your shoes? I cleaned the floors this morning."

Though he frowned, he complied. Before she could say another word, he gave her home a cursory glance, then settled his sharp gaze on her face. His übermasculine features were put together in a pleasing fashion, but the overall impression was intensely male. Strong nose, noble forehead, chiseled jaw and lips made for kissing a woman. His scowl grew deeper. "I'm tired as hell, and I'm starving. If you could point me to my cabin, I'd like to get settled for the night, Ms....?"

"Kemper. Phoebe Kemper. You can call me Phoebe." Oh, wow. His voice, low and gravelly, stroked over her frazzled nerves like a lover's caress. The faint Georgia drawl did nothing to disguise the hint of command. This was a man accustomed to calling the shots.

She swallowed, rubbing damp palms unobtrusively on her thighs. "I have a pot of vegetable beef stew still warm on the stove. Dinner was late tonight." And every night, it seemed. "You're welcome to have some. There's corn bread, as well."

The aura of disgruntlement he wore faded a bit, replaced by a rueful smile. "That sounds wonderful."

She waved a hand. "Bathroom's down the hall, first door on the right. I'll get everything on the table."

"And afterward you'll show me my lodgings?"

Gulp. "Of course." Perhaps she shouldn't have insisted that he remove his shoes. There was something about a man in his sock feet that hinted at a level of familiarity. The last thing she needed at this juncture in time was to feel drawn to someone who was most likely going to be furious with her no matter how she tried to spin the facts in a positive light.

He was gone a very short time, but Phoebe had everything ready when he returned. A single place mat, some silverware and a steaming bowl of stew flanked by corn bread and a cheerful yellow gingham napkin. "I didn't know what you wanted to drink," she said. "I have decaf iced tea, but the weather's awfully cold tonight."

"Decaf coffee would be great…if you have it."

"Of course." While he sat down and dug into his meal, she brewed a fresh pot of Colombian roast and poured him a cup. He struck her as the kind of man who wouldn't appreciate his java laced with caramel or anything fancy. Though she offered the appropriate add-ons, Leo Cavallo took his coffee black and unsweetened. No fuss. No nonsense.

Phoebe puttered around, putting things away and loading the dishwasher. Her guest ate with every indication that his previous statement was true. Apparently, he *was* starving. Two large bowls of stew, three slabs of corn bread and a handful of the snickerdoodles she had made that morning vanished in short order.

As he was finishing his dessert, she excused herself. "I'll be back in just a moment." She set the pot on the table. "Help yourself to more coffee."

Leo's mood improved dramatically as he ate. He hadn't been looking forward to going back down that road to seek out dinner, and though his cabin was supposed to be stocked with groceries, he was not much of a cook. Everything he needed, foodwise, was close at hand in Atlanta. He was spoiled probably. If he wanted sushi at three in the morning or a full breakfast at dawn, he didn't have to look far.

When he finished the last crumb of the moist, delicious cookies, he wiped his mouth with his napkin and stood up to stretch. After the long drive, his body felt kinked and cramped from sitting in one position for too many hours. Guiltily, he remembered the doctor's admonition not to push himself. Truthfully, it was the only setting Leo had. Full steam ahead. Don't look back.

And yet now he was supposed to turn himself into somebody new. Even though he'd been irritated by the many people hovering over him—work colleagues, medical professionals and his family—in his heart, he knew the level of their concern was a testament to how much he had scared them all. One moment he had been standing at the head of a large conference table giving an impassioned pitch to a group of global investors, and the next, he'd been on the floor.

None of the subsequent few minutes were clear in his memory. He recalled not being able to breathe. And an enormous pressure in his chest. But not much more than that. Shaken and disturbed by the recollection of that day, he paced the confines of the open floor plan that incorporated the kitchen and living area into a pleasing whole.

As he walked back and forth, he realized that Phoebe Kemper had created a cozy nest out here in the middle of nowhere. Colorful area rugs cushioned his feet. The floor consisted of wide, honey-colored hardwood planks polished to a high sheen.

Two comfortable groupings of furniture beckoned visitors to sit and enjoy the ambience. Overhead, a three-tiered elk antler chandelier shed a large, warm circle of light. On the far wall, built-in bookshelves flanked the stacked stone fireplace. As he scanned Phoebe's collection of novels and nonfiction, he realized with a little kick of pleasure that he was actually going to have time to read for a change.

A tiny noise signaled his hostess's return. Whirling around, he stared at her, finally acknowledging, if only to himself, that his landlady was a knockout. Jet-black hair long enough to reach below her breasts had been tamed into a single thick, smooth braid that hung forward over her shoulder. Tall and slender and long-limbed, there was nothing frail or helpless about Phoebe Kemper. Yet he could imagine many men rushing to her aid, simply to coax a smile from those lush unpainted lips that were the color of pale pink roses.

She wore faded jeans and a silky coral blouse that brought out the warm tones in her skin. With eyes so dark they were almost black, she made him wonder if she claimed Cherokee blood. Some resourceful members of that tribe had hidden deep in these mountains to escape the Trail of Tears.

Her smile was teasing. "Feel better now? At least you don't look like you want to commit murder anymore."

He shrugged sheepishly. "Sorry. It was a hell of a day."

Phoebe's eyes widened and her smile faded. "And it's about to get worse, I'm afraid. There's a problem with your reservation."

"Impossible," he said firmly. "My sister-in-law handled all the details. And I have the confirmation info."

"I've been trying to call her all day, but she hasn't answered. And no one gave me your cell number."

"Sorry about that. My niece found my sister-in-law's phone and dropped it into the bathtub. They've been scrambling to get it replaced. That's why you couldn't reach her. But no worries. I'm here now. And it doesn't look like you're overbooked," he joked.

Phoebe ignored his levity and frowned. "We had heavy rains and high winds last night. Your cabin was damaged."

His mood lightened instantly. "Don't worry about a thing, Ms. Phoebe. I'm not that picky. I'm sure it will be fine."

She shook her head in disgust. "I guess I'll have to show you to convince you. Follow me, please."

"Should I move my car closer to the cabin?" he asked as he put on his shoes and tied them. The bottoms were a mess.

Phoebe scooped up something that looked like a small digital camera and tucked it into her pocket. "No need," she said. She shrugged into a jacket that could have been a twin to his. "Let's go." Out on the porch, she picked up a large, heavy-duty flashlight and turned it on. The intense beam sliced through the darkness.

The weather hadn't improved. He was glad that Luc and Hattie had insisted on packing for him. They had undoubtedly covered every eventuality if he knew his sister-in-law. Come rain, sleet, snow or hail, he'd be prepared. But for now, everything he'd brought with him was stashed in the trunk of his car. Sighing for the lost opportunity to carry a load, he followed Phoebe.

Though he would never have found it on his own in the inky, fog-blinding night, the path from Phoebe's cabin to the next closest one was easy to pick out with the flashlight. Far more than a foot trail, the route they followed was clearly an extension of the gravel road.

His impatience grew as he realized they could have driven the few hundred feet. Finally, he dug in his heels. "I should move the car," he said. "I'm sure I'll be fine."

At that very moment, Phoebe stopped so abruptly he nearly plowed into her. "We're here," she said bluntly. "And *that* is what's left of your two-month rental."

The industrial-strength flashlight was more than strong enough to reveal the carnage from the previous night's storm. An enormous tree lay across the midline of the house at a forty-five-degree angle. The force of the falling trunk had crushed the roof. Even from this vantage point, it was clear that the structure was open to the elements.

"Good Lord." He glanced behind him instinctively, realizing with sick dismay that Phoebe's home could have suffered a similar fate. "You must have been scared to death."

She grimaced. "I've had better nights. It happened about 3:00 a.m. The boom woke me up. I didn't try to go out then, of course. So it was daylight before I realized how bad it was."

"You haven't tried to cover the roof?"

She chuckled. "Do I look like Superwoman? I know

my own limitations, Mr. Cavallo. I've called my insurance company, but needless to say, they've been inundated with claims from the storm. Supposedly, an agent will be here tomorrow afternoon, but I'm not holding my breath. Everything inside the house got soaked when the tree fell, because it was raining so hard. The damage was already done. It's not like I could have helped matters."

He supposed she had a point. But that still left the issue of where he was expected to stay. Despite his grumblings to Luc and Hattie, now that he was finally here, the idea of kicking back for a while wasn't entirely unpleasant. Perhaps he could find himself in the great outdoors. Maybe even discover a new appreciation for life, which as he so recently had found out, was both fragile and precious.

Phoebe touched his arm. "If you've seen enough, let's go back. I'm not going to send you out on the road again in this miserable weather. You're welcome to stay the night with me."

They reversed their steps as Leo allowed Phoebe to take the lead. The steady beam of light led them without incident back to his car. The porch light was still on, adding to a feeling of welcome. Phoebe waved a hand at the cabin. "Why don't you go inside and warm up? Your sister-in-law told me you've been in the hospital. I'd be happy to bring in your luggage if you tell me what you'll need."

Leo's neck heated with embarrassment and frustration. Damn Hattie and her mother-hen instincts. "I can get my own bags," he said curtly. "But thank you." He added that last bit grudgingly. Poor Phoebe had no reason to know that his recent illness was a hot-button issue for him. He was a young man. Being treated like an invalid made him nuts. And for whatever reason, it was especially important to him that the lovely Phoebe see him as a competent, capable male, and not someone she had to babysit.

His mental meanderings must not have lasted as long

as he thought, because Phoebe was still at his side when he heard—very distinctly—the cry of a baby. He whirled around, expecting to see that another car had made its way up the narrow road. But he and Phoebe were alone in the night.

A second, less palatable possibility occurred to him. He'd read that a bobcat's cry could emulate that of an upset infant's. And the Smoky Mountains were home to any number of those nocturnal animals. Before he could speculate further, the sound came again.

Phoebe shoved the flashlight toward him. "Here. Keep this. I've got to go inside."

He took it automatically, and grinned. "So you're leaving me out here alone with a scary animal stalking us?"

She shook her head. "I don't know what you're talking about."

"The bobcat. Isn't that what we're hearing?"

Phoebe laughed softly, a pleasing sensual sound that made the hair on his arms stand up even more than the odd noise had. "Despite your interesting imagination," she said with a chuckle, "no." She reached in her pocket and removed the small electronic device he had noticed earlier. Not a camera, but a monitor. "The noise you hear that sounds like a crying baby is *actually* a baby. And I'd better get in there fast before all heck breaks loose."

Two

Leo stood there gaping at her even after the front door slammed shut. It was only the realization his hands were in danger of frostbite that galvanized him into motion. In short order he found the smaller of the two suitcases he had brought. Slinging the strap across one shoulder, he then reached for his computer briefcase and a small garment bag.

Locking the car against any intruders, human or otherwise, he walked up the steps, let himself in and stopped dead in his tracks when he saw Phoebe standing by the fire, a small infant whimpering on her shoulder as she rubbed its back. Leo couldn't quite sort out his emotions. The scene by the hearth was beautiful. His sister-in-law, Hattie, wore that same look on her face when she cuddled her two little ones.

But a baby meant there was a daddy in the picture somewhere, and though Leo had only met this particular Madonna and child today, he knew the feeling in the pit of his stomach was disappointment. Phoebe didn't wear a wedding ring, but he could see a resemblance between mother and child. Their noses were identical.

Leo would simply have to ignore this inconvenient attraction, because Phoebe was clearly not available. And though he adored his niece and nephew, he was not the kind of man who went around bouncing kids on his knee and playing patty-cake.

Phoebe looked up and smiled. "This is Teddy. His full name is Theodore, but at almost six months, he hasn't quite grown into it yet."

Leo kicked off his shoes for the second time that night and set down his luggage. Padding toward the fire, he mustered a smile. "He's cute."

"Not nearly as cute at three in the morning." Phoebe's expression as she looked down at the baby was anything but aggravated. She glowed.

"Not a good sleeper?"

She bristled at what she must have heard as implied criticism. "He does wonderfully for his age. Don't you, my love?" The baby had settled and was sucking his fist. Phoebe nuzzled his neck. "Most evenings he's out for the count from ten at night until six or seven in the morning. But I think he may be cutting a tooth."

"Not fun, I'm sure."

Phoebe switched the baby to her left arm, holding him against her side. "Let me show you the guest room. I don't think we'll disturb you even if I have to get up with him during the night."

He followed her down a short hallway past what was obviously Phoebe's suite all the way to the back right corner of the house. A chill hit him as soon as they entered the bedroom.

"Sorry," she said. "The vents have been closed off, but it will warm up quickly."

He looked around curiously. "This is nice." A massive king-size bed made of rough timbers dominated the room. Hunter-green draperies covered what might have been a large picture window. The attached bathroom, decorated in shades of sand and beige, included a Jacuzzi tub and a roomy shower stall. Except for the tiled floor in the bath-

room, the rest of the space boasted the same attractive hardwood he'd seen in the remainder of the house, covered here
and there by colorful rugs.

Phoebe hovered, the baby now asleep. "Make yourself
at home. If you're interested in staying in the area, I can
help you make some calls in the morning."

Leo frowned. "I paid a hefty deposit. I'm not interested
in staying anywhere else."

A trace of pique flitted across Phoebe's face, but she answered him calmly. "I'll refund your money, of course. You
saw the cabin. It's unlivable. Even with a speedy insurance
settlement, finding people to do the work will probably be
difficult. I can't even guesstimate how long it will be before everything is fixed."

Leo thought about the long drive from Atlanta. He hadn't
wanted to come here at all. And yesterday's storm damage
was his ticket out. All he had to do was tell Luc and Hattie,
and his doctor, that circumstances had conspired against
him. He could be back in Atlanta by tomorrow night.

But something—stubbornness maybe—made him contrary. "Where is Mr. Kemper in all this? Shouldn't he be
the one worrying about repairing the other cabin?"

Phoebe's face went blank. "Mr. Kemper?" Suddenly,
she laughed. "I'm not married, Mr. Cavallo."

"And the baby?"

A small frown line appeared between her brows. "Are
you a traditionalist, then? You don't think a single female
can raise a child on her own?"

Leo shrugged. "I think kids deserve two parents. But
having said that, I do believe women can do anything they
like. I can't, however, imagine a woman like you needing
to embrace single parenthood."

He'd pegged Phoebe as calm and cool, but her eyes
flashed. "A woman like me? What does that mean?"

Leaning his back against one of the massive bedposts,

he folded his arms and stared at her. Now that he knew she wasn't married, all bets were off. "You're stunning. Are all the men in Tennessee blind?"

Her lips twitched. "I'm pretty sure that's the most clichéd line I've ever heard."

"I stand by my question. You're living out here in the middle of nowhere. Your little son has no daddy anywhere in sight. A man has to wonder."

Phoebe stared at him, long and hard. He bore her scrutiny patiently, realizing how little they knew of each other. But for yesterday's storm, he and Phoebe would likely have exchanged no more than pleasantries when she handed over his keys. In the weeks to come, they might occasionally have seen each other outside on pleasant days, perhaps waved in passing.

But fate had intervened. Leo came from a long line of Italian ancestors who believed in the power of *destino* and *amore*. Since he was momentarily banned from the job that usually filled most of his waking hours, he was willing to explore his fascination with Phoebe Kemper.

He watched as she deposited the sleeping baby carefully in the center of the bed. The little boy rolled to his side and continued to snooze undisturbed. Phoebe straightened and matched her pose to Leo's. Only instead of using the bed for support, she chose to lean against the massive wardrobe that likely held a very modern home entertainment center.

She eyed him warily, her teeth nibbling her bottom lip. Finally she sighed. "First of all, we're not in the middle of nowhere, though it must seem that way to you since you had to drive up here on such a nasty night. Gatlinburg is less than ten miles away. Pigeon Forge closer than that. We have grocery stores and gas stations and all the modern conveniences, I promise. I like it here at the foot of the mountains. It's peaceful."

"I'll take your word for it."

"And Teddy is my nephew, not my son."

Leo straightened, wondering what it said about him that he was glad the woman facing him was a free agent. "Why is he here?"

"My sister and her husband are in Portugal for six weeks settling his father's estate. They decided the trip would be too hard on Teddy, and that cleaning out the house would be much easier without him. So I volunteered to let him stay with me until they get home."

"You must like kids a lot."

A shadow crossed her face. "I love my nephew." She shook off whatever mood had momentarily stolen the light. "But we're avoiding the important topic. I can't rent you a demolished cabin. You have to go."

He smiled at her with every bit of charm he could muster. "You can rent me *this* room."

Phoebe had to give Leo Cavallo points for persistence. His deep brown eyes were deceptive. Though a woman could sink into their warmth, she might miss entirely the fact that he was a man who got what he wanted. If he had been ill recently, she could find no sign of it in his appearance. His naturally golden skin, along with his name, told her that he possessed Mediterranean genes. And in Leo's case, that genetic material had been spun into a ruggedly handsome man.

"This isn't a B and B," she said. "I have an investment property that I rent out to strangers. That property is currently unavailable, so you're out of luck."

"Don't make a hasty decision," he drawled. "I'm housebroken. And I'm handy when it comes to changing lightbulbs and killing creepy-crawlies."

"I'm tall for a woman, and I have monthly pest control service."

"Taking care of a baby is a lot of work. You might enjoy having help."

"You don't strike me as the type to change diapers."

"Touché."

Were they at an impasse? Would he give up?

She glanced at Teddy, sleeping so peacefully. Babies were an important part of life, but it was a sad day when a grown woman's life was so devoid of male companionship that a nonverbal infant was stimulating company. "I'll make a deal with you," she said slowly, wondering if she were crazy. "You tell me why you really want to stay, and I'll consider your request."

For the first time, she saw discomfort on Leo's face. He was one of those consummately confident men who strode through life like a captain on the bridge of his ship, everyone in his life bowing and scraping in his wake. But at the moment, a mask slipped and she caught a glimpse of vulnerability. "What did my sister-in-law tell you when she made the reservation?"

A standard ploy. Answering a question with a question. "She said you'd been ill. Nothing more than that. But in all honesty, you hardly look like a man at death's door."

Leo's smile held a note of self-mockery. "Thank God for that."

Curiouser and curiouser. "Now that I think about it," she said, trying to solve the puzzle as she went along, "you don't seem like the kind of man who takes a two-month sabbatical in the mountains for any reason. Unless, of course, you're an artist or a songwriter. Maybe a novelist? Am I getting warm?"

Leo grimaced, not quite meeting her gaze. "I needed a break," he said. "Isn't that reason enough?"

Something in his voice touched her…some note of discouragement or distress. And in that moment, she felt a kinship with Leo Cavallo. Hadn't she embraced this land

and built these two cabins for that very reason? She'd been disillusioned with her job and heartbroken over the demise of her personal life. The mountains had offered healing.

"Okay," she said, capitulating without further ado. "You can stay. But if you get on my nerves or drive me crazy, I am well within my rights to kick you out."

He grinned, his expression lightening. "Sounds fair."

"And I charge a thousand dollars a week more if you expect to share meals with me."

It was a reckless barb, an attempt to get a rise out of him. But Leo merely nodded his head, eyes dancing. "Whatever you say." Then he sobered. "Thank you, Phoebe. I appreciate your hospitality."

The baby stirred, breaking the odd bubble of intimacy that had enclosed the room. Phoebe scooped up little Teddy and held him to her chest, suddenly feeling the need for a barrier between herself and the charismatic Leo Cavallo. "We'll say good night, then."

Her houseguest nodded, eyes hooded as he stared at the baby. "Sleep well. And if you hear me up in the night, don't be alarmed. I've had a bit of insomnia recently."

"I could fix you some warm milk," she said, moving toward the door.

"I'll be fine. See you in the morning."

Leo watched her leave and felt a pinch of remorse for having pressured her into letting him invade her home. But not so much that he was willing to leave. In Atlanta everyone had walked on eggshells around him, acting as if the slightest raised voice or cross word would send him into a relapse. Though his brother, Luc, tried to hide his concern, it was clear that he and Hattie were worried about Leo. And as dear as they both were to him, Leo needed a little space to come to terms with what had happened.

His first instinct was to dive back into work. But the

doctor had flatly refused to release him. This mountain getaway was a compromise. Not an idea Leo would have embraced voluntarily, but given the options, his only real choice.

When he exited the interstate earlier that evening, Leo had called his brother to say he was almost at his destination. Though he needed to escape the suffocating but well-meaning attention, he would never *ever* cause Luc and Hattie to worry unnecessarily. He would do anything for his younger brother, and he knew Luc would return the favor. They were closer than most siblings, having survived their late teen and early-adult years in a foreign land under the thumb of their autocratic Italian grandfather.

Leo yawned and stretched, suddenly exhausted. Perhaps he was paying for years of burning the candle at both ends. His medical team *and* his family had insisted that for a full recovery, Leo needed to stay away from work and stress. Maybe the recent hospital stay had affected him more than he realized. But whatever the reason, he was bone tired and ready to climb into that large rustic bed.

Too bad he'd be sleeping alone. It was oddly comforting when his body reacted predictably to thoughts of Phoebe. Something about her slow, steady smile and her understated sexuality really did it for him. Though his doctor had cleared Leo for exercise and sexual activity, the latter was a moot point. Trying to ignore the erection that wouldn't be seeing any action tonight, he reached for his suitcase, extracted his shaving kit and headed for the shower.

To Phoebe's relief, the baby didn't stir when she laid him in his crib. She stood over him for long moments watching the almost imperceptible movements of his small body as he breathed. She knew her sister was missing Teddy like crazy, but selfishly, Phoebe herself was looking forward to having someone to share Christmas with.

Her stomach did a little flip as she realized that Leo might be here, as well. But no. Surely he would go home at the holidays and come back to finish out his stay in January.

When she received the initial reservation request, she had researched Leo and the Cavallo family on Google. She knew he was single, rich and the CFO of a worldwide textile company started by his grandfather in Italy. She also knew that he supported several charities, not only with money, but with his service. He didn't need to work. The Cavallo vaults, metaphorically speaking, held more money than any one person could spend in a lifetime. But she understood men like Leo all too well. They thrived on challenge, pitting themselves repeatedly against adversaries, both in business and in life.

Taking Leo into her home was not a physical risk. He was a gentleman, and she knew far more about him than she did about many men she had dated. The only thing that gave her pause was an instinct that told her he needed help in some way. She didn't need another responsibility. And besides, if the cabin hadn't been demolished, Leo would have been on his own for two months anyway.

There was no reason for her to be concerned. Nevertheless, she sensed pain in him, and confusion. Given her own experience with being knocked flat on her butt for a long, long time, she wouldn't wish that experience on anyone. Maybe she could probe gently and see why this big mountain of a man, who could probably bench-press more than his body weight, seemed lost.

As she prepared for bed, she couldn't get him out of her mind. And when she climbed beneath her flannel sheets and closed her eyes, his face was the image that stayed with her through the night.

Three

Leo awoke when sunlight shining through a crack in the drapes hit his face. He yawned and scrubbed his hands over his stubbly chin, realizing with pleased surprise that he had slept through the night. Perhaps there was something to this mountain retreat thing after all.

Most of his stuff was still in the car, so he dug out a pair of faded jeans from his overnight case and threw on his favorite warm cashmere sweater. It was a Cavallo product... of course. The cabin had an efficient heat system, but Leo was itching to get outside and see his surroundings in the light of day.

Tiptoeing down the hall in case the baby was sleeping, he paused unconsciously at Phoebe's door, which stood ajar. Through the narrow crack he could see a lump under the covers of a very disheveled bed. Poor woman. The baby must have kept her up during the night.

Resisting the urge to linger, he made his way to the kitchen and quietly located the coffeepot. Phoebe was an organized sort, so it was no problem to find what he needed in the cabinet above. When he had a steaming cup brewed, strong and black, he grabbed a banana off the counter and went to stand at the living room window.

Supposedly, one of his challenges was to acquire the habit of eating breakfast in the morning. Normally, he had neither the time nor the inclination to eat. As a rule, he'd be at the gym by six-thirty and at the office before eight. After that, his day was nonstop until seven or later at night.

He'd never really thought much about his schedule in the past. It suited him, and it got the job done. For a man in his prime, *stopping to smell the roses* was a metaphor for growing old. Now that he had been admonished to do just that, he was disgruntled and frustrated. He was thirty-six, for God's sake. Was it really time to throw in the towel?

Pulling back the chintz curtains decorated with gamboling black bears, he stared out at a world that glistened like diamonds in the sharp winter sun. Every branch and leaf was coated with ice. Evidently, the temperatures had dropped as promised, and now the narrow valley where Phoebe made her home was a frozen wonderland.

So much for his desire to explore. Anyone foolish enough to go out at this moment would end up flat on his or her back after the first step. *Patience, Leo. Patience.* His doctor, who also happened to be his racquetball partner on the weekends, had counseled him repeatedly to take it easy, but Leo wasn't sure he could adapt. Already, he felt itchy, needing a project to tackle, a problem to solve.

"You're up early."

Phoebe's voice startled him so badly he spun around and managed to slosh hot coffee over the fingers of his right hand. "Ouch, damn it."

He saw her wince as he crossed to the sink and ran cold water over his stinging skin.

"Sorry," she said. "I thought you heard me."

Leo had been lost in thought, but he was plenty alert now. Phoebe wore simple knit pj's that clung to her body in all the right places. The opaque, waffle-weave fabric was pale pink with darker pink rosebuds. It faithfully outlined firm high breasts, a rounded ass and long, long legs.

Despite his single-minded libido, he realized in an instant that she looked somewhat the worse for wear. Her long braid had frayed into wispy tendrils and dark smudges underscored her eyes.

"Tough night with the baby?" he asked.

She shook her head, yawning and reaching for a mug in the cabinet. When she did, her top rode up, exposing an inch or two of smooth golden skin. He looked away, feeling like a voyeur, though the image was impossible to erase from his brain.

After pouring herself coffee and taking a long sip, Phoebe sank into a leather-covered recliner and pulled an afghan over her lap. "It wasn't the baby this time," she muttered. "It was me. I couldn't sleep for thinking about what a headache this reconstruction is going to be, especially keeping track of all the subcontractors."

"I could pitch in with that," he said. The words popped out of his mouth, uncensored. Apparently old habits were hard to break. But after all, wasn't helping out a fellow human being at least as important as inhaling the scent of some imaginary rose that surely wouldn't bloom in the dead of winter anyway? Fortunately, his sister-in-law wasn't around to chastise him for his impertinence. She had, in her sweet way, given him a very earnest lecture about the importance of not making work his entire life.

Of course, Hattie was married to Luc, who had miraculously managed to find a balance between enjoying his wife and his growing family and at the same time carrying his weight overseeing the R & D department. Luc's innovations, both in fabric content and in design, had kept their company competitive in the changing world of the twenty-first century. Worldwide designers wanted Cavallo textiles for their best and most expensive lines.

Leo was happy to oblige them. For a price.

Phoebe sighed loudly, her expression glum. "I couldn't ask that of you. It's my problem, and besides, you're on vacation."

"Not a vacation exactly," he clarified. "More like an involuntary time-out."

She grinned. "Has Leo been a naughty boy?"

Heat pooled in his groin and he felt his cheeks redden. He really had to get a handle on this urge to kiss her senseless. Since he was fairly sure that her taunt was nothing more than fun repartee, he refrained from saying what he really thought. "Not naughty," he clarified. "More like too much work and not enough play."

Phoebe swung her legs over the arm of the chair, her coffee mug resting on her stomach. For the first time he noticed that she wore large, pink Hello Kitty slippers on her feet. A less seductive female ensemble would be difficult to find. And yet Leo was fascinated.

She pursed her lips. "I'm guessing executive-level burnout?"

Her perspicacity was spot-on. "You could say that." Although it wasn't the whole story. "I'm doing penance here in the woods, so I can see the error of my ways."

"And who talked you into this getaway? You don't seem like a man who lets other people dictate his schedule."

He refilled his cup and sat down across from her. "True enough," he conceded. "But my baby brother, who happens to be part of a disgustingly happy married couple, thinks I need a break."

"And you listened?"

"Reluctantly."

She studied his face as though trying to sift through his half-truths. "What did you think you would do for two months?"

"That remains to be seen. I have a large collection of

detective novels packed in the backseat of my car, a year of *New York Times* crossword puzzles on my iPad and a brand-new digital camera not even out of the box yet."

"I'm impressed."

"But you'll concede that I surely have time to interview prospective handymen."

"Why would you want to?"

"I like keeping busy."

"Isn't that why you're here? To be *not* busy? I'd hate to think I was causing you to fall off the wagon in the first week."

"Believe me, Phoebe. Juggling schedules and workmen for your cabin repair is something I could do in my sleep. And since it's not my cabin, there's no stress involved."

Still not convinced, she frowned. "If it weren't for the baby, I'd never consider this."

"Understood."

"And if you get tired of dealing with it, you'll be honest." He held up two fingers. "Scout's honor."

"In that case," she sighed, "how can I say no?"

Leo experienced a rush of jubilation far exceeding the appropriate response to Phoebe's consent. Only at that moment did he realize how much he had been dreading the long parade of unstructured days. With the cabin renovation to give him focus each morning, perhaps this rehabilitative exile wouldn't be so bad.

Guiltily, he wondered what his brother would say about this new turn of events. Leo was pretty sure Luc pictured him sitting by a fire in a flannel robe and slippers reading a John Grisham novel. While Leo enjoyed fiction on occasion, and though Grisham was a phenomenal author, a man could only read so many hours of the day without going bonkers.

Already, the idleness enforced by his recent illness had

made the days and nights far too long. The doctor had cleared him for his usual exercise routine, but with no gym nearby, and sporting equipment that was useless in this environment, it was going to require ingenuity on his part to stay fit and active, especially given that it was winter.

Suddenly, from down the hall echoed the distinct sound of a baby who was awake and unhappy.

Phoebe jumped to her feet, nearly spilling her coffee in the process. "Oh, shoot. I forgot to bring the monitor in here." She clunked her mug in the sink and disappeared in a flash of pink fur.

Leo had barely drained his first cup and gone to the coffeepot for a refill when Phoebe reappeared, this time with baby Teddy on her hip. The little one was red-faced from crying. Phoebe smoothed his hair from his forehead. "Poor thing must be so confused not seeing his mom and dad every morning when he wakes up."

"But he knows you, right?"

Phoebe sighed. "He does. Still, I worry about him day and night. I've never been the sole caregiver for a baby, and it's scary as heck."

"I'd say you're doing an excellent job. He looks healthy and happy."

Phoebe grimaced, though the little worried frown between her eyes disappeared. "I hope you're right."

She held Teddy out at arm's length. "Do you mind giving him his bottle while I shower and get dressed?"

Leo backed up half a step before he caught himself. It was his turn to frown. "I don't think either Teddy or I would like that. I'm too big. I scare children."

Phoebe gaped. Then her eyes flashed. "That's absurd. Wasn't it you, just last night, who was volunteering to help with the baby in return for your keep?"

Leo shrugged, feeling guilty but determined not to show it. "I was thinking more in terms of carrying dirty diapers out to the trash. Or if you're talking on the phone, listening to the monitor to let you know when he wakes up. My hands are too large and clumsy to do little baby things."

"You've never been around an infant?"

"My brother has two small children, a boy and a girl. I see them several times a month, but those visits are more about kissing cheeks and spouting kudos as to how much they've grown. I might even bounce one on my knee if necessary, but not often. Not everyone is good with babies."

Little Teddy still dangled in midair, his chubby legs kicking restlessly. Phoebe closed the distance between herself and Leo and forced the wiggly child to Leo's chest. "Well, you're going to learn, because we had a deal."

Leo's arms came up reflexively, enclosing Teddy in a firm grip. The wee body was warm and solid. The kid smelled of baby lotion and some indefinable nursery scent that was endemic to babies everywhere. "I thought becoming your renovation overseer got me off the hook with Teddy."

Phoebe crossed her arms over her chest, managing to emphasize the fullness of her apparently unconfined breasts. "*It. Did. Not.* A deal is a deal. Or do I need a written contract?"

Leo knew when he was beaten. He'd pegged Phoebe as an easygoing, Earth Mother type, but suddenly he was confronted with a steely-eyed negotiator who would as soon kick him to the curb as look at him. "I'd raise my hands in surrender if I were able," he said, smiling, "But I doubt your nephew would like it."

Phoebe's nonverbal response sounded a lot like *humph*. As Leo watched, grinning inwardly, she quickly prepared a serving of formula and brought it to the sofa where Leo sat with Teddy. She handed over the bottle. "He likes it sitting up. Burp him halfway through."

"Yes, ma'am."

Phoebe put her hands on her hips. "Don't mock me. You're walking on thin ice, mister."

Leo tried to look penitent, and also tried not to take note of the fact that her pert nipples were at eye level. He cleared his throat. "Go take your shower," he said. "I've got this under control. You can trust me."

Phoebe nibbled her bottom lip. "Yell at my bedroom door if you need me."

Something about the juxtaposition of *yell* and *bedroom door* and *need* rekindled Leo's simmering libido. About the only thing that could have slowed him down was the reality of a third person in the cabin. Teddy. Little innocent, about-to-get-really-hungry Teddy.

"Go," Leo said, taking the bottle and offering it to the child in his lap. "We're fine."

As Phoebe left the room, Leo scooted Teddy to a more comfortable position, tucking the baby in his left arm so he could offer the bottle with his right hand. It was clear that the kid was almost capable of feeding himself. But if he dropped the bottle, he would be helpless.

Leo leaned back on the comfy couch and put his feet on the matching ottoman, feeling the warmth and weight of the child, who rested so comfortably in his embrace. Teddy seemed content to hang out with a stranger. Presumably as long as the food kept coming, the tyke would be happy. He did not, however, approve when Leo withdrew the bottle for a few moments and put him on his shoulder to burp him.

Despite Teddy's pique, the new position coaxed the desired result. Afterward, Leo managed to help the kid finish the last of his breakfast. When Teddy sucked on nothing but air, Leo set aside the bottle and picked up a small, round teething ring from the end table flanking the sofa. Teddy chomped down on it with alacrity, giving Leo the opportunity to examine his surroundings in detail.

He liked the way Phoebe had furnished the place. The

cabin had a cozy feel that still managed to seem sophisticated and modern. The appliances and furniture were top-of-the-line, built to last for many years, and no doubt expensive because of that. The flooring was high-end, as well.

The pale amber granite countertops showcased what looked to be handcrafted cabinetry done in honey maple. He saw touches of Phoebe's personality in the beautiful green-and-gold glazed canister set and in the picture of Phoebe, her sister and Teddy tacked to the front of the fridge with a magnet.

Leo looked down at Teddy. The boy's big blue eyes stared up at him gravely as if to say, *What's your game?* Leo chuckled. "Your auntie Phoebe is one beautiful woman, my little man. Don't get me in trouble with her and you and I will get along just fine."

Teddy's gaze shifted back to his tiny hands covered in drool.

Leo was not so easily entertained. He felt the pull of Atlanta, of wondering what was going on at work, of needing to feel in control…at the helm. But something about cuddling a warm baby helped to freeze time. As though any considerations outside of this particular moment were less than urgent.

As he'd told Phoebe, he wasn't a complete novice when it came to being around kids. Luc and Hattie adopted Hattie's niece after they married last year. The little girl was almost two years old now. And last Valentine's Day, Hattie gave birth to the first "blood" Cavallo of the new generation, a dark-haired, dark-eyed little boy.

Leo appreciated children. They were the world's most concrete promise that the globe would keep on spinning. But in truth, he had no real desire to father any of his own. His lifestyle was complicated, regimented, full. Children deserved a healthy measure of their parents' love and attention. The Cavallo empire was Leo's baby. He knew on any given day what the financial bottom line was. During hard financial times, he wrestled the beast that was their investment and sales strategy and demanded returns instead of losses.

He was aware that some people called him hard...unfeeling. But he did what he did knowing how many employees around the world depended on the Cavallos for their livelihoods. It irked the hell out of him to think that another man was temporarily sitting in his metaphorical chair. The vice president Luc had chosen to keep tabs on the money in Leo's absence was solid and capable.

But that didn't make Leo feel any less sidelined.

He glanced at his watch. God in heaven. It was only ten-thirty in the morning. How was he going to survive being on the back burner for two months? Did he even want to try becoming the man his family thought he could be? A balanced, laid-back, easygoing guy?

He rested his free arm across the back of the sofa and closed his eyes, reaching for something Zen. Something peaceful.

Damn it, he didn't want to change. He wanted to go home. At least he had until he met Phoebe. Now he wasn't sure what he wanted.

Hoping that the boy wasn't picking up on his frustration and malcontent thoughts, Leo focused on the only thing capable of diverting him from his problems. Phoebe. Tall, long-legged Phoebe. A dark-haired, dark-eyed beauty with an attitude.

If Phoebe could be lured into an intimate relationship, then this whole recuperative escape from reality had definite possibilities. Leo sensed a spark between them. And he was seldom wrong about things like that. When a man had money, power and reasonably good looks, the female sex swarmed like mosquitoes. That wasn't ego speaking. Merely the truth.

As young men in Italy, he and Luc had racked up a number of conquests until they realized the emptiness of being wanted for superficial reasons. Luc had finally found his soul mate in college. But things hadn't worked out, and it had been ten years before he achieved happiness with the same woman.

Leo had never even made it that far. Not once in his life had he met a female who really cared about who he was as a person. Would-be "Mrs. Cavallos" saw the external trappings of wealth and authority and wanted wedding rings. And the real women, the uncomplicated, good-hearted ones, steered clear of men like Leo for fear of having their hearts broken.

He wasn't sure which category might include Phoebe Kemper. But he was willing to find out.

Four

Phoebe took her time showering, drying her hair and dressing. If Leo wasn't going to live up to his end of the bargain, she wanted to know it now. Leaving Teddy in his temporary care was no risk while she enjoyed a brief respite from the demands of surrogate parenthood. Despite Leo's protestations to the contrary, he was a man who could handle difficult situations.

It was hard to imagine that he had been ill. He seemed impervious to the things that lesser mortals faced. She envied him his confidence. Hers had taken a serious knock three years ago, and she wasn't sure if she had ever truly regained it. A younger Phoebe had taken the world by storm, never doubting her own ability to craft outcomes to her satisfaction.

But she had paid dearly for her hubris. Her entire world had crumbled. Afterward, she had chosen to hide from life, and only in the past few months had she finally begun to understand who she was and what she wanted. The lessons had been painful and slow in coming.

Unfortunately, her awakening had also made her face her own cowardice. Once upon a time she had taken great pleasure in blazing trails where no other women had gone.

Back then, she would have seen a man like Leo as a challenge, both in business and in her personal life.

Smart and confident, she had cruised through life, never realizing that on any given day, she—like any other human being—was subject to the whims of fate. Her perfect life had disintegrated in the way of a comet shattering into a million pieces.

Things would never be as they were. But could they be equally good in another very different way?

She took more care in dressing than she did normally. Instead of jeans, she pulled out a pair of cream corduroy pants and paired them with a cheery red scoop-necked sweater. Christmas was on the way, and the color always lifted her mood.

Wryly acknowledging her vanity, she left her hair loose on her shoulders. It was thick and straight as a plumb line. With the baby demanding much of her time, a braid was easier. Nevertheless, today she wanted to look nice for her guest.

When she finally returned to the living room, Teddy was asleep on Leo's chest, and Leo's eyes were closed, as well. She lingered for a moment in the doorway, enjoying the picture they made. The big, strong man and the tiny, defenseless baby.

Her chest hurt. She rubbed it absently, wondering if she would always grieve for what she had lost. Sequestering herself like a nun the past few years had given her a sort of numb peace. But that peace was an illusion, because it was the product of not living.

Living hurt. If Phoebe were ever going to rejoin the human race, she would have to accept being vulnerable. The thought was terrifying. The flip side of great love and joy was immense pain. She wasn't sure the first was worth risking the prospect of the last.

Quietly she approached the sofa and laid a hand on Leo's

arm. His eyes opened at once as if he had perhaps only been lost in thought rather than dozing. She held out her arms for the baby, but Leo shook his head.

"Show me where to take him," he whispered. "No point in waking him up."

She led the way through her bedroom and bathroom to a much smaller bedroom that adjoined on the opposite side. Before Teddy's arrival she had used this space as a junk room, filled with the things she was too dispirited to sort through when she'd moved in.

Now it had been tamed somewhat, so that half the room was full of neatly stacked plastic tubs, while the other half had been quickly transformed into a comfy space for Teddy. A baby bed, rocking chair and changing table, all with matching prints, made an appealing, albeit temporary, nursery.

Leo bent over the crib and laid Teddy gently on his back. The little boy immediately rolled to his side and stuck a thumb in his mouth. Both adults smiled. Phoebe clicked on the monitor and motioned for Leo to follow her as they tiptoed out.

In the living room, she waved an arm. "Relax. Do whatever you like. There's plenty of wood if you feel up to building us a fire."

"I told you. I'm not sick."

The terse words had a bite to them. Phoebe flinched inwardly, but kept her composure. Something had happened to Leo. Something serious. Cancer maybe. But she was not privy to that information. So conversation regarding the subject was akin to navigating a minefield.

Most men were terrible patients. Usually because their health and vigor were tied to their self-esteem. Clearly, Leo had been sent here or had agreed to come here because he needed rest and relaxation. He didn't want Phoebe hovering or commenting on his situation. Okay. Fine. But she was still going to keep an eye on him, because whatever had given him a wallop was serious enough to warrant a two-month hiatus from work.

That in itself was telling. In her past life, she had interacted with lots of men like Leo. They were alpha animals, content only with the number one spot in the pack. Their work was their life. And even if they married, familial relationships were kept in neatly separated boxes.

Unfortunately for Phoebe, she possessed some of those same killer instincts...or she had. The adrenaline rush of an impossible-to-pull-off business deal was addictive. The more you succeeded, the more you wanted to try again. Being around Leo was going to be difficult, because like a recovering alcoholic who avoided other drinkers, she was in danger of being sucked into his life, his work issues, whatever made him tick.

Under no circumstances could she let herself be dragged back into that frenzied schedule. The world was a big, beautiful place. She had enough money tucked away to live simply for a very long time. She had lost herself in the drive to achieve success. It was better now to accept her new lifestyle.

Leo moved to the fireplace and began stacking kindling and firewood with the precision of an Eagle Scout. Phoebe busied herself in the kitchen making a pot of chili to go with sandwiches for their lunch. Finally, she broke the awkward silence. "I have a young woman who babysits for me when I have to be gone for a short time. It occurred to me that I could see if she is free and if so, she could stay here in the house and watch Teddy while you and I do an initial damage assessment on the other cabin."

Leo paused to look over his shoulder, one foot propped on the raised hearth. "You sound very businesslike about this."

She shrugged. "I used to work for a big company. I'm accustomed to tackling difficult tasks."

He lit the kindling, stood back to see if it would catch, and then replaced the fire screen, brushing his hands together to remove the soot. "Where did you work?"

Biting her lip, she berated herself inwardly for bringing up a subject she would rather not pursue. "I was a stockbroker for a firm in Charlotte, North Carolina."

"Did they go under? Is that why you're here?"

His was a fair assumption. But wrong. "The business survived the economic collapse and is expanding by leaps and bounds."

"Which doesn't really answer my question."

She grimaced. "Maybe when we've known each other for more than a nanosecond I might share the gory details. But not today."

Leo understood her reluctance, or he thought he did. Not everyone wanted to talk about his or her failures. And rational or not, he regarded his heart attack as a failure. He wasn't overweight. He didn't smoke. Truth be told, his vices were few, perhaps only one. He was type A to the max. And type A personalities lived with stress so continuously that the condition became second nature. According to his doctor, no amount of exercise or healthy eating could compensate for an inability to unwind.

So maybe Leo was screwed.

He joined his hostess in the kitchen, looking for any excuse to get closer to her. "Something smells good." *Smooth, Leo. Real smooth.*

Last night he had dreamed about Phoebe's braid. But today…wow. Who knew within that old-fashioned hairstyle was a shiny waterfall the color of midnight?

Phoebe adjusted the heat on the stove top and turned to

face him. "I didn't ask. Do you have any dietary restrictions? Any allergies?"

Leo frowned. "I don't expect you to cook for me all the time I'm here. You claimed that civilization is close by. Why don't I take you out now and then?"

She shot him a pitying look that said he was clueless. "Clearly you've never tried eating at a restaurant with an infant. It's ridiculously loud, not to mention that the chaos means tipping the server at least thirty percent to compensate for the rice cereal all over the floor." She eyed his sweater. "I doubt you would enjoy it."

"I know kids are messy." He'd eaten out with Luc and Hattie and the babies a time or two. Hadn't he? Or come to think of it, maybe it was always at their home. "Well, not that then, but I could at least pick up a pizza once a week."

Phoebe smiled at him sweetly. "That would be lovely. Thank you, Leo."

Her genuine pleasure made him want to do all sorts of things for her...and *to* her. Something about that radiant smile twisted his insides in a knot. The unmistakable jolt of attraction was perhaps inevitable. They were two healthy adults who were going to be living in close proximity for eight or nine weeks. They were bound to notice each other sexually.

He cleared his throat as he shoved his hands into his pockets. "Is there a boyfriend who won't like me staying here?"

Again, that faint, fleeting shadow that dimmed her beauty for a moment. "No. You're safe." She shook her head, giving him a rueful smile. "I probably should say yes, though. Just so you don't get any ideas."

He tried to look innocent. "What ideas?" All joking aside, he was a little worried about having sex for the first time since... Oh, hell. He had a hard time even saying it in his head. Heart attack. There. He wasn't afraid of two stupid words.

The doctor had said *no restrictions,* but the doctor hadn't seen Phoebe Kemper in a snug crimson sweater. She reminded Leo of a cross between Wonder Woman and Pocahontas. Both of whom he'd fantasized about as a preteen boy. What did that say about his chances of staying away from her?

She shooed him with her hands. "Go unpack. Read one of those books. Lunch will be ready in an hour."

Leo enjoyed Phoebe's cooking almost as much as her soft, feminine beauty. If he could eat like this all the time, maybe he wouldn't skip meals and drive through fast-food places at nine o'clock at night. Little Teddy sat in his high chair playing with a set of plastic keys. It wasn't time for another bottle, so the poor kid had to watch the grown-ups eat.

They had barely finished the meal when Allison, the babysitter, showed up. According to Phoebe, she was a college student who lived at home and enjoyed picking up extra money. Plus, she adored Teddy, which was a bonus.

Since temperatures had warmed up enough to melt the ice, Leo went out to the car for his big suitcase, brought it in and rummaged until he found winter gear. Not much of it was necessary in Atlanta. It did snow occasionally, but rarely hung around. Natives, though, could tell hair-raising stories about ice storms and two-week stints without power.

When he made his way back to the living room, Allison was playing peekaboo with the baby, and Phoebe was slipping her arms into a fleece-lined sheepskin jacket. Even the bulky garment did nothing to diminish her appeal.

She tucked a notepad and pen into her pocket. "Don't be shy about telling me things you see. Construction is not my forte."

"Nor mine, but my brother and I did build a tree house once upon a time. Does that count?"

He followed her out the door, inhaling sharply as the icy wind filled his lungs with a jolt. The winter afternoon enwrapped them, blue-skied and damp. From every corner echoed the sounds of dripping water as ice gave way beneath pale sunlight.

Lingering on the porch to take it all in, he found himself strangely buoyed by the sights and sounds of the forest. The barest minimum of trees had been cleared for Phoebe's home and its mate close by. All around them, a sea of evergreen danced in the brisk wind. Though he could see a single contrail far above them, etched white against the blue, there was little other sign of the twenty-first century.

"Did you have these built when you moved here?" he asked as they walked side by side up the incline to the other cabin.

Phoebe tucked the ends of her fluttering scarf into her coat, lifting her face to the sun. "My grandmother left me this property when she died a dozen years ago. I had just started college. For years I held on to it because of sentimental reasons, and then much later…"

"Later, what?"

She looked at him, her eyes hidden behind dark sunglasses. Her shoulders lifted and fell. "I decided to mimic Thoreau and live in the woods."

Phoebe didn't expand on her explanation, so he didn't push. They had plenty of time for sharing confidences. And besides, he was none too eager to divulge all his secrets just yet.

Up close, and in the unforgiving light of day, the damage to the cabin was more extensive than he had realized. He put a hand on Phoebe's arm. "Let me go first. There's no telling what might still be in danger of crumbling."

They were able to open the front door, but just barely. The tree that had crushed the roof was a massive oak, large enough around that Leo would not have been able to encircle it with his arms. The house had caved in so dramatically that the floor was knee-deep in rubble—insulation, roofing shingles, branches of every size and, beneath it all, Phoebe's furnishings.

She removed her sunglasses and craned her neck to look up at the nonexistent ceiling as she followed Leo inside. "Not much left, is there?" Her voice wobbled a bit at the end. "I'm so grateful it wasn't *my* house."

"You and me, both," he muttered. Phoebe or Teddy or both could have been killed or badly injured…with no one nearby to check on them. The isolation was peaceful, but he wasn't sure he approved of a defenseless woman living here. Perhaps that was a prehistoric gut feeling. Given the state of the structure in which they were standing, however, he did have a case.

He just didn't have any right to argue it.

Taking Phoebe's hand to steady her, they stepped on top of and over all the debris and made their way to the back portion of the cabin. The far left corner bedroom had escaped unscathed…and some pieces of furniture in the outer rooms were okay for the moment. But if anything were to be salvaged, it would have to be done immediately. Dampness would lead to mildew, and with animals having free rein, further damage was a certainty.

Phoebe's face was hard to read. Finally she sighed. "I might do better to bulldoze it and start over," she said glumly. She bent down to pick up a glass wildflower that had tumbled from a small table, but had miraculously escaped demolition. "My friends cautioned me to furnish the rental cabin with inexpensive, institutional stuff that would not be a big deal to replace in case of theft or carelessness on the part of the tenants. I suppose I should have listened."

"Do you have decent insurance?" He was running the numbers in his head, and the outcome wasn't pretty.

She nodded. "I don't remember all the ins and outs of the policy, but my agent is a friend of my sister's, so I imagine he made sure I have what I need."

Phoebe's discouragement was almost palpable.

"Sometimes things work out for a reason," he said, wanting to reassure her, but well aware that she had no reason to lean on him. "I need something to do to keep me from going crazy. You have a baby to care for. Let me handle this mess, Phoebe. Let me juggle and schedule the various contractors. Please. You'd be doing me a favor."

Five

Phoebe was tempted. So tempted. Leo stood facing her, legs planted apart in a stance that said he was there to stay. Wearing an expensive quilted black parka and aviator sunglasses that hid his every emotion, he was an enigma. Why had a virile, handsome, vigorous male found his way to her hidden corner of the world?

What was he after? Healing? Peace? He had the physique of a bouncer and the look of a wealthy playboy. Had he really been sick? Would she be committing a terrible sin to lay this burden on him from the beginning?

"That's ridiculous," she said faintly. "I'd be taking advantage of you. But I have to confess that I find your offer incredibly appealing. I definitely underestimated how exhausting it would be to take care of a baby 24/7. I love Teddy, and he's not really a fussy child at all, but the thought of adding all this…" She flung out her arm. "Well, it's daunting."

"Then let me help you," he said quietly.

"I don't expect you to actually do the work yourself."

He pocketed his sunglasses and laughed, making his rugged features even more attractive. "No worries there. I'm aware that men are known for biting off more than they can chew, but your cabin, or what's left of it, falls into the category of catastrophe. That's best left to the experts."

She stepped past him and surveyed the large bed with the burgundy-and-navy duvet. "This was supposed to be your room. I know you would have been comfortable here." She turned to face him. "I'm sorry, Leo. I feel terrible about shortchanging you."

He touched her arm. Only for a second. The smile disappeared, but his eyes were warm and teasing. "I'm pretty happy where I ended up. A gorgeous woman. A cozy cabin. Sounds like I won the jackpot."

"You're flirting," she said, hearing the odd and embarrassingly breathless note in her voice.

His gaze was intent, sexy...leaving no question that he was interested. "I've been admonished to stop and smell the roses. And here you are."

Removing her coat that suddenly felt too hot, she leaned against the door frame. The odd sensation of being inside the house but having the sunlight spill down from above was disconcerting. "You may find me more of a thorn. My sister says that living alone up here has made me set in my ways." It was probably true. Some days she felt like a certified hermit.

Once a social animal comfortable at cocktail parties and business lunches, she now preferred the company of chipmunks and woodpeckers and the occasional fox. Dull, dull, dull...

Leo kicked aside a dangerously sharp portion of what had been the dresser mirror. "I'll take my chances. I've got nowhere to go and nobody to see, as my grandfather used to say. You and Teddy brighten the prospect of my long exile considerably."

"Are you ever going to tell me why you're here?" she asked without censoring her curiosity.

He shrugged. "It's not a very interesting story...but maybe...when it's time."

"How will you know?" This odd conversation seemed to have many layers. Her question erased Leo's charmingly flirtatious smile and replaced it with a scowl.

"You're a pain in the butt," he said, the words a low growl.

"I told you I'm no rose."

He took her arm and steered her toward the front door. "Then pretend," he muttered. "Can you do that?"

Their muted altercation was interrupted by the arrival of the insurance agent. The next hour was consumed with questions and photographs and introducing Leo to the agent. The two men soon had their heads together as they climbed piles of rubble and inspected every cranny of the doomed cabin.

Phoebe excused herself and walked down the path, knowing that Allison would be ready to go home. As she opened the door and entered the cabin, Teddy greeted her with a chortle and a grin. Envy pinched her heart, but stronger still was happiness that the baby recognized her and was happy to see her.

Given Phoebe's background, her sister had been torn about the arrangement. But Phoebe had reassured her, and eventually, her sister and brother-in-law gave in. Dragging a baby across the ocean was not an easy task in ideal circumstances, and facing the disposal of an entire estate, they knew Teddy would be miserable and they would be overwhelmed.

Still, Phoebe knew they missed their small son terribly. They used FaceTime to talk to him when Phoebe went into town and had a decent phone signal, and she sent them constant, newsy updates via email and texts. But they were so far away. She suspected they regretted their decision to leave him. Probably, they were working like fiends to take care of all the estate business so they could get back to the U.S. sooner.

When Allison left, Phoebe held Teddy and looked out the window toward the other cabin. Leo and the insurance agent were still measuring and assessing the damage. She rubbed the baby's back. "I think Santa has sent us our present early, my little man. Leo is proving to be a godsend. Now all I have to do is ignore the fact that he's the most attractive man I've seen in a long, long time, and that he makes it hard to breathe whenever I get too close to him, and I'll be fine."

Teddy continued sucking his thumb, his long-lashed eyelids growing heavy as he fought sleep.

"You're no help," she grumbled. His weight was comfortable in her arms. Inhaling his clean baby smell made her womb clench. What would it be like to share a child with Leo Cavallo? Would he be a good father, or an absent one?

The man in question burst through the front door suddenly, bringing with him the smell of the outdoors. "Honey, I'm home." His humor lightened his face and made him seem younger.

Phoebe grinned at him. "Take off your boots, *honey.*" She was going to have to practice keeping him at arm's length. Leo Cavallo had the dangerous ability to make himself seem harmless. Which was a lie. Even in a few short hours, Phoebe had recognized and assessed his sexual pull.

Some men simply oozed testosterone. Leo was one of them.

It wasn't just his size, though he was definitely a bear of a man. More than that, he emanated a gut-level masculinity that made her, in some odd way, far more aware of her own carnal needs. She would like to blame it on the fact that they were alone together in the woods, but in truth, she would have had the same reaction to him had they met at the opera or on the deck of a yacht.

Leo was a man's man. The kind of male animal who caught women in his net without even trying. Phoebe had thought herself immune to such silly, pheromone-driven impulses, but with Leo in her house, she recognized an appalling truth. She needed sex. She wanted sex. And she had found just the man to satisfy her every whim.

Her face heated as she pretended to be occupied with the baby. Leo shed his coat and pulled a folded piece of paper from his pocket. "Here," he said. "Take a look. I'll hold the kid."

Before Phoebe could protest, Leo scooped Teddy into his arms and lifted him toward the ceiling. Teddy, who had been sleepy only moments before, squealed with delight. Shaking her head at the antics of the two males who seemed in perfect accord, Phoebe sank into a kitchen chair and scanned the list Leo had handed her.

"Ouch," she said, taking a deep breath for courage. "According to this, I was probably right about the bulldozer."

Leo shook his head. "No. I realize the bottom line looks bad, but it would be even worse to build a new cabin from the ground up. Your agent thinks the settlement will be generous. All you have to provide is an overabundance of patience."

"We may have a problem," she joked. "That's not my strong suit."

Teddy's shirt had rucked up. Leo blew a raspberry against the baby's pudgy, soft-skinned stomach. "I'll do my best to keep you out of it. Unless you want to be consulted about every little detail."

Phoebe shuddered. "Heavens, no. If you're foolish enough to offer me the chance to get my property repaired without my lifting a finger, then far be it from me to nitpick."

Teddy wilted suddenly as Leo cuddled him. What was it about the sight of a big, strong man being gentle with a baby that made a woman's heart melt? Phoebe told herself she shouldn't be swayed by such an ordinary thing, but she couldn't help it. Seeing Leo hold little Teddy made her insides mushy with longing. She wanted it all. The man. The baby. Was that too much to ask?

Leo glanced over at her, hopefully not noticing the way her eyes misted over.

"You want me to put him in his bed?" he asked.

"Sure. He takes these little forty-five-minute catnaps on and off instead of one long one. But he seems happy, so I go with the flow."

Leo paused in the hallway. "How long have you had him?"

"Two weeks. We've settled into a routine of sorts."

"Until I came along to mess things up."

"If you're fishing for compliments, forget it. You've already earned your keep, and it hasn't even been twenty-four hours yet."

He flashed her a grin. "Just think how much you'll love me when you get to know me."

Her knees went weak, and she wasn't even standing. "Go put him down, Leo, and behave."

He kissed the baby's head, smiling down at him. "She's a hard case, kiddo. But I'll wear her down."

When Leo disappeared from sight, Phoebe exhaled loudly. She'd been holding her breath and hadn't even realized it. Rising to her feet unsteadily, she went from window to window closing the curtains. Darkness fell early in this mountain *holler,* as the old generation called it. Soon it would be the longest night of the year.

Phoebe had learned to dread the winter months. Not just the snow and ice and cold, gray days, but the intense loneliness. It had been the season of Christmas one year when she lost everything. Each anniversary brought it all back. But even before the advent of Leo, she had been determined to make this year better. She had a baby in the house. And now a guest. Surely that was enough to manufacture holiday cheer and thaw some of the ice that had kept her captive for so long.

Leo returned, carrying his laptop. He made himself at home on the sofa. "Do you mind giving me your internet password?" he asked, opening the computer and firing it up.

Uh-oh. "Um…" She leaned against the sink for support. "I don't have internet," she said, not sure there was any way to soften that blow.

Leo's look, a cross between horror and bafflement, was priceless. "Why not?"

"I decided I could live my life without it."

He ran his hands through his hair, agitation building. His neck turned red and a pulse beat in his temple. "This is the twenty-first century," he said, clearly trying to speak calmly. "*Everybody* has internet." He paused, his eyes narrowing. "This is either a joke, or you're Amish. Which is it?"

She lifted her chin, refusing to be judged for a decision that had seemed entirely necessary at the time. "Neither. I made a choice. That's all."

"My sister-in-law would never have rented me a cabin that didn't have the appropriate amenities," he said stubbornly.

"Well," she conceded. "You're right about that. The cabin I rent out has satellite internet. But as you saw for yourself, everything was pretty much demolished, including the dish."

She watched Leo's good humor evaporate as he absorbed the full import of what she was saying. Suddenly he pulled his smartphone from his pocket. "At least I can check email with this," he said, a note of panic in his voice.

"We're pretty far back in this gorge," she said. "Only one carrier gets a decent signal and it's—"

"Not the one I have." He stared at the screen and sighed. "Unbelievable. Outposts in Africa have better connectivity than this. I don't think I can stay somewhere that I have to be out of touch from the world."

Phoebe's heart sank. She had hoped Leo would come to appreciate the simplicity of her life here in the mountains. "Is it really that important? I have a landline phone you're welcome to use. For that matter, you can use *my* cell phone. And I do have a television dish, so you're welcome to add the other service if it's that important to you." If he were unable to understand and accept the choices she had made, then it would be foolish to pursue the attraction between them. She would only end up getting hurt.

Leo closed his eyes for a moment. "I'm sorry," he said at last, shooting her a look that was half grimace, half apology. "It took me by surprise, that's all. I'm accustomed to having access to my business emails around the clock."

Was that why he was here? Because he was *too* plugged in? Had he suffered some kind of breakdown? It didn't seem likely, but she knew firsthand how tension and stress could affect a person.

She pulled her cell phone from her pocket and crossed the room to hand it to him. "Use mine for now. It's not a problem."

Their fingers brushed as she gave him the device. Leo hesitated for a moment, but finally took it. "Thank you," he said gruffly. "I appreciate it."

Turning her back to give him some privacy, she went to the kitchen to rummage in the fridge and find an appealing dinner choice. Now that Leo was here, she would have to change her grocery buying habits. Fortunately, she had chicken and vegetables that would make a nice stir-fry.

Perhaps twenty minutes passed before she heard a very ungentlemanly curse from her tenant. Turning sharply, she witnessed the fury and incredulity that turned his jaw to steel and his eyes to molten chocolate. "I can't believe they did this to me."

She wiped her hands on a dish towel. "What, Leo? What did they do? Who are you talking about?"

He stood up and rubbed his eyes with the heels of his hands. "My brother," he croaked. "My black-hearted, devious baby brother."

As she watched, he paced, his scowl growing darker by the minute. "I'll kill him," he said with far too much relish. "I'll poison his coffee. I'll beat him to a pulp. I'll grind his wretched bones into powder."

Phoebe felt obliged to step in at that moment. "Didn't you say he has a wife and two kids? I don't think you really want to murder your own flesh and blood…do you? What could he possibly have done that's so terrible?"

Leo sank into an armchair, his arms dangling over the sides. Everything about his posture suggested defeat. "He locked me out of my work email," Leo muttered with a note of confused disbelief. "Changed all the passwords. Because he didn't trust me to stay away."

"Well, it sounds like he knows you pretty well, then. 'Cause isn't that exactly what you were doing? Trying to look at work email?"

Leo glared at her, his brother momentarily out of the crosshairs. "Whose side are you on anyway? You don't even know my brother."

"When you spoke of him earlier…he and your sister-in-law and the kids…I heard love in your voice, Leo. So that tells me he must love you just as much. Following that line of reasoning, he surely had a good reason to do what he did."

A hush fell over the room. The clock on the mantel ticked loudly. Leo stared at her with an intensity that made the hair on the back of her neck stand up. He was pissed. Really angry. And since his brother wasn't around, Phoebe might very well be his default target.

She had the temerity to inch closer and perch on the chair opposite him. "Why would he keep you away from work, Leo? And why did he and your sister-in-law send you here? You're not a prisoner. If being with me in this house is so damned terrible, then do us both a favor and go home."

Six

Leo was ashamed of his behavior. He'd acted like a petulant child. But everything about this situation threw him off balance. He was accustomed to being completely in charge of his domain, whether that be the Cavallo empire or his personal life. It wasn't that he didn't trust Luc. He did. Completely. Unequivocally. And in his gut, he knew the business wouldn't suffer in his absence.

Perhaps that was what bothered him the most. If the company he had worked all of his adult life to build could roll along just fine during his two-month hiatus, then what use was Leo to anyone? His successes were what he thrived on. Every time he made an acquisition or increased the company's bottom line, he felt a rush of adrenaline that was addictive.

Moving slot by slot up the Fortune 500 was immensely gratifying. He had made more money, both for the company and for himself, by the time he was thirty than most people earned in a lifetime. He was damned good at finance. Even in uncertain times, Leo had never made a misstep. His grandfather even went so far as to praise him for his genius. Given that eliciting a compliment from the old dragon was as rare as finding unicorn teeth, Leo had been justifiably proud.

But without Cavallo…without the high-tech office… without the daily onslaught of problems and split-second decisions…who was he? Just a young man with nowhere to go and nothing to do. The aimlessness of it all hung around his neck like a millstone.

Painfully aware that Phoebe had observed his humiliating meltdown, he stood, grabbed his coat from the hook by the door, shoved his feet in his shoes and escaped.

Phoebe fixed dinner with one ear out for the baby and one eye out the window to see if Leo was coming back. His car still sat parked out front, so she knew he was on foot. The day was warm, at least by December standards. But it *was* possible to get lost in these mountains. People did it all the time.

The knot in her stomach eased when at long last, he reappeared. His expression was impossible to read, but his body language seemed relaxed. "I've worked up an appetite" he said, smiling as if nothing had happened.

"It's almost ready. If we're lucky we'll be able to eat our meal in peace before Teddy wakes up."

"He's still asleep?"

She nodded. "I can never predict his schedule. I guess because he's still so small. But since I'm flexible, I'm fine with that."

He held out a chair for her and then joined her at the table. Phoebe had taken pains with the presentation. Pale green woven place mats and matching napkins from a craft cooperative in Gatlinburg accentuated amber stoneware plates and chunky handblown glass goblets that mingled green and gold in interesting swirls.

She poured each of them a glass of pinot. "There's beer in the fridge if you'd prefer it."

He tasted the wine. "No. This is good. A local vintage?"
"Yes. We have several wineries in the area."

Their conversation was painfully polite. Almost as awkward as a blind date. Though in this case there was nothing of a romantic nature to worry about. No *will he* or *won't he* when it came time for a possible good-night kiss at the front door.

Even so, she was on edge. Leo Cavallo's sexuality gave a woman ideas, even if unintentionally. It had been a very long time since Phoebe had kissed a man, longer still since she had felt the weight of a lover's body moving against hers in urgent passion. She thought she had safely buried those urges in her subconscious, but with Leo in her house, big and alive and so damned sexy, she was in the midst of an erotic awakening.

Like a limb that has gone to sleep and then experienced the pain of renewed blood flow, Phoebe's body tingled with awareness. Watching the muscles in his throat as he swallowed. Inhaling the scent of him, warm male and crisp outdoors. Inadvertently brushing his shoulder as she served him second helpings of chicken and rice. Hearing the lazy tempo of his speech that made her think of hot August nights and damp bodies twined together beneath a summer moon.

All of her senses were engaged except for taste. And the yearning to do just that, to kiss him, swelled in her chest and made her hands shake. The need was as overwhelming as it was unexpected. She fixated on the curve of his lips as he spoke. They were good lips. Full, but masculine. What would they feel like pressed against hers?

Imagining the taste of his mouth tightened everything inside her until she felt faint with arousal. Standing abruptly, she put her back to him, busying herself at the sink as she rinsed plates and loaded the dishwasher. Suddenly, she felt him behind her, almost pressing against her.

"Let me handle cleanup," he said, the words a warm breath of air at her neck. She froze. Did he sense her jittery nerves, her longing?

She swallowed, clenching her fingers on the edge of the counter. "No. Thank you. But a fire would be nice." She was already on fire. But what the heck...in for a penny, in for a pound.

After long seconds when it seemed as if every molecule of oxygen in the room vaporized, he moved away. "Whatever you want," he said. "Just ask."

Leo was neither naive nor oblivious. Phoebe was attracted to him. He knew, because he felt the same inexorable pull. But he had known her for barely a day. Perhaps long enough for an easy pickup at a bar or a one-night stand, but not for a relationship that was going to have to survive for a couple of months.

With a different woman at another time, he would have taken advantage of the situation. But he was at Phoebe's mercy for now. One wrong move, and she could boot him out. There were other cabins...other peaceful getaways. None of them, however, had Phoebe. And he was beginning to think that she was his talisman, his lucky charm, the only hope he had of making it through the next weeks without going stark raving mad.

The fire caught immediately, the dry tinder flaming as it coaxed the heavier logs into the blaze. When he turned around, Phoebe was watching him, her eyes huge.

He smiled at her. "Come join me on the sofa. We're going to be spending a lot of time together. We might as well get to know each other."

At that very moment, Teddy announced his displeasure with a noisy cry. The relief on Phoebe's face was almost comical. "Sorry. I'll be back in a minute."

While she was gone, he sat on the hearth, feeling the heat

from the fire sink into his back. Beneath his feet a bearskin pelt covered the floor. He was fairly certain it was fake, but the thick, soft fur made him imagine a scenario that was all too real. Phoebe...nude...her skin gilded with firelight.

The vivid picture in his mind hardened his sex and dried his mouth. Jumping to his feet, he went to the kitchen and poured himself another glass of wine. Sipping it slowly, he tried to rein in his hunger. Something might develop during this time with Phoebe. They could become friends. Or even more than that. But rushing his fences was not the way to go. He had to resist the temptation to bring sex into the picture before she had a chance to trust him.

Regardless of Phoebe's desires, or even his own, this was a situation that called for caution. Not his first impulse, or even his last. But if he had any hope of making her his, he'd bide his time.

His mental gyrations were interrupted by Phoebe's return. "There you are," he said. "I wondered if Teddy had kidnapped you."

"Poopy diaper," she said with a grimace. She held the baby on her hip as she prepared a bottle. "He's starving, poor thing. Slept right through dinner."

Leo moved to the sofa and was gratified when Phoebe followed suit. She now held the baby as a barricade between them, but he could wait. The child wasn't big enough to be much of a problem.

"So tell me," he said. "What did you do with yourself before Teddy arrived?"

Phoebe settled the baby on her lap and held the bottle so he could reach it easily. "I moved in three years ago. At first I was plenty busy with decorating and outfitting both cabins. I took my time and looked for exactly what I wanted. In the meantime, I made a few friends, mostly women I met at the gym. A few who worked in stores where I shopped."

"And when the cabins were ready?"

She stared down at the baby, rubbing his head with a wistful smile on her face. He wondered if she had any clue how revealing her expression was. She adored the little boy. That much was certain.

"I found someone to help me start a garden," she said. "Buford is the old man who lives back near the main road where you turned off. He's a sweetheart. His wife taught me how to bake bread and how to can fruits and vegetables. I know how to make preserves. And I can even churn my own butter in a pinch, though that seems a bit of a stretch in this day and age."

He studied her, trying to get to the bottom of what she wasn't saying. "I understand all that," he said. "And if I didn't know better, I'd guess you were a free spirit, hippie-commune, granola-loving Earth Mother. But something doesn't add up. How did you get from stockbroker to this?"

Phoebe understood his confusion. None of it made sense on paper. But was she willing to expose all of her painful secrets to a man she barely knew? No…not just yet.

Picking her words carefully, she gave him an answer. Not a lie, but not the whole truth. "I had some disappointments both personally and professionally. They hit me hard…enough to make me reconsider whether the career path I had chosen was the right one. At the time, I didn't honestly know. So I took a time-out. A step backward. I came here and decided to see if I could make my life simpler. More meaningful."

"And now? Any revelations to report?"

She raised an eyebrow. "Are you mocking me?"

He held up his hands. "No. I swear I'm not. If anything, I have to admire you for being proactive. Most people simply slog away at a job because they don't have the courage to try something new."

"I wish I could say it was like that. But to be honest,

it was more a case of crawling in a hole to hide out from the world."

"You don't cut yourself much slack, do you?"

"I was a mess when I came here."

"And now?"

She thought about it for a moment. No one had ever asked her straight-out if her self-imposed exile had borne fruit. "I think I have a better handle on what I want out of life. And I've forgiven myself for mistakes I made. But do I want to go back to that cutthroat lifestyle? No. I don't."

"I know this is a rude question, but I'm going to ask it anyway. What have you done for money since you've been out of work?"

"I'm sure a lot of people wonder that." She put the baby on her shoulder and burped him. "The truth is, Leo. I'm darned good at making money. I have a lot stashed away. And since I've been here, my weekly expenses are fairly modest. So though I can't stay here forever, I certainly haven't bankrupted myself."

"Would you say your experience has been worth it?"

She nodded. "Definitely."

"Then maybe there's hope for me after all."

Phoebe was glad to have Teddy as a buffer. Sitting with Leo in a firelit room on a cold December night was far too cozy. But when Teddy finished his bottle and was ready to play, she had no choice but to get down on the floor with him and let him roll around on the faux bearskin rug. He had mastered flipping from his back to his tummy. Now he enjoyed the increased mobility.

She was truly shocked when Leo joined them, stretching out on his right side and propping his head on his hand. "How long 'til he crawls?"

"Anytime now. He's already learned to get his knees up under him, so I don't think it will be too many more weeks." Leo seemed entirely relaxed, while Phoebe was in danger of hyperventilating. Anyone watching them might assume they were a family…mom, dad and baby. But the truth was, they were three separate people who happened to be occupying the same space for the moment.

Teddy was her nephew, true. But he was on loan, so to speak. She could feed him and play with him and love him, but at the end of the day, he wasn't hers. Still, what could it hurt to pretend for a while?

She pulled her knees to her chest and wrapped her arms around her legs. Ordinarily, she would have lain down on her stomach and played with Teddy at his level. But getting horizontal with Leo Cavallo was not smart, especially since he was in touching distance. She'd give herself away, no doubt. Even with a baby between them, she couldn't help thinking how nice it would be to spend an unencumbered hour with her new houseguest.

Some soft music on the radio, another bottle of wine, more logs on the fire. And after that…

Her heartbeat stuttered and stumbled. Dampness gathered at the back of her neck and in another, less accessible spot. Her breathing grew shallow. She stared at Teddy blindly, anything to avoid looking at Leo. Not for the world would she want him to think she was so desperate for male company that she would fall at his feet.

Even as she imagined such a scenario, he rolled to his back and slung an arm across his face. Moments later, she saw the steady rise and fall of his chest as he gave in to sleep.

Teddy was headed in the same direction. His acrobatics had worn him out. He slumped onto his face, butt in the air, and slept.

Phoebe watched the two males with a tightness in her chest that was a combination of so many things. Yearning for what might have been. Fear of what was yet to come.

Hope that somewhere along the way she could have a family of her own.

Her sleepless night caught up with her, making her eyelids droop. With one wary look at Leo to make sure he was asleep, she eased down beside her two companions and curled on her side with Teddy in the curve of her body. Now she could smell warm baby and wood smoke, and perhaps the faint scent of Leo's aftershave.

Closing her eyes, she sighed deeply. She would rest for a moment....

Seven

Leo awoke disoriented. His bed felt rock-hard, and his pillow had fallen on the floor. Gradually, he remembered where he was. Turning his head, he took in the sight of Phoebe and Teddy sleeping peacefully beside him.

The baby was the picture of innocence, but Phoebe… He sucked in a breath. Her position, curled on her side, made the neckline of her sweater gape, treating him to an intimate view of rounded breasts and creamy skin. Her hair tumbled around her face as if she had just awakened from a night of energetic sex. All he had to do was extend his arm and he could stroke her belly beneath the edge of her top.

His sex hardened to the point of discomfort. He didn't know whether to thank God for the presence of the kid or to curse the bad timing. The strength of his desire was both surprising and worrisome. Was he reacting so strongly to Phoebe because he was in exile and she was the only woman around, or had his long bout of celibacy predisposed him to want her?

Either way, his hunger for her was suspect. It would be the height of selfishness to seduce her because of boredom or propinquity. Already, he had taken her measure. She was loving, generous and kind, though by no means a pushover.

Even with training in what some would call a nonfeminine field, she nevertheless seemed completely comfortable with the more traditional roles of childcare and homemaking.

Phoebe was complicated. That, more than anything else, attracted him. At the moment a tiny frown line marked the space between her brows. He wanted to erase it with a kiss. The faint shadowy smudges beneath her eyes spoke of her exhaustion. He had been around his brother and sister-in-law enough to know that dealing with infants was harrowing and draining on the best of days.

He also knew that they glowed with pride when it came to their children, and he could see in Phoebe the same self-sacrificial love. Even now, in sleep, her arms surrounded little Teddy, keeping him close though he was unaware.

Moving carefully so as not to wake them, he rolled to his feet and quietly removed the screen so he could add wood to the smoldering fire. For insurance, he tossed another handful of kindling into the mix and blew on it gently. Small flames danced and writhed as he took a medium-size log and positioned it across the coals.

The simple task rocked him in an indefinable way. How often did he pause in his daily schedule to enjoy something as elemental and magical as an honest-to-God wood fire? The elegant gas logs in his condo were nothing in comparison.

As he stared into the hearth, the temperature built. His skin burned, and yet he couldn't move away. Phoebe seemed to him more like this real fire than any woman he had been with in recent memory. Energetic…messy… mesmerizing. Producing a heat that warmed him down to his bones.

Most of his liaisons in Atlanta were brief. He spent an enormous amount of time, perhaps more than was warranted, growing and protecting the Cavallo bottom line. Sex was good and a necessary part of his life. But he had never been tempted to do what it took to keep a woman in his bed night after night.

Kneeling, he turned and looked at Phoebe. Should he wake her up? Did the baby need to be put to bed?

Uncharacteristically uncertain, he deferred a decision. Snagging a pillow from the sofa, he leaned back against the stone hearth, stretched out his legs and watched them sleep.

Phoebe awoke slowly, but in no way befuddled. Her situation was crystal clear. Like a coward, she kept her eyes closed, even though she knew Leo was watching her. Apparently, her possum act didn't fool him. He touched her foot with his. "Open your eyes, Phoebe."

She felt at a distinct disadvantage. There was no graceful way to get up with him so close. Sighing, she obeyed his command and stared at him with as much chutzpah as she could muster. Rolling onto her back, she tucked her hands behind her head. "Have I brought a voyeur into my home?" she asked with a tart bite in her voice. It would do no good to let him see how much he affected her.

Leo yawned and stretched, his eyes heavy-lidded. "It's not my fault you had too much wine at dinner."

"I did not," she said indignantly. "I'm just tired, because the baby—"

"Gotcha," he said smugly, his eyes gleaming with mischief.

She sat up and ran her hands through her hair, crossing her legs but being careful not to bump Teddy. "Very funny. How long was I out?"

He shrugged. "Not long." His hot stare told her more clearly than words what he was thinking. They had rocketed from acquaintances to sleeping partners at warp speed. It was going to be difficult to pretend otherwise.

Her breasts ached and her mouth was dry. Sexual tension

shimmered between them like unseen vines drawing them ever closer. The only thing keeping them apart was a baby.

A baby who was her responsibility. That reality drew her back from the edge, though the decision to be clear-headed was a painful one. "I think we'll say good-night," she muttered. "Feel free to stay up as long as you like. But please bank the fire before you go to bed."

His gaze never faltered as she scooped up Teddy and gathered his things. "We have to talk about this," he said, the blunt words a challenge.

It took a lot, but she managed to look him straight in the eyes with a calm smile. "I don't know what you mean. Good night, Leo."

At two o'clock, he gave up the fight to sleep. He was wired, and his body pulsed with arousal, his sex full and hard. Neither of which condition was conducive to slumber. The *New York Times* bestseller he had opened failed to hold his attention past the first chapter. Cursing as he climbed out of his warm bed to pace the floor, he stopped suddenly and listened.

Faintly, but distinctly, he heard a baby cry.

It was all the excuse he needed. Throwing a thin, gray wool robe over his navy silk sleep pants, he padded into the hall, glad of the thick socks that Hattie had packed for him. Undoubtedly she had imagined him needing them if it snowed and he wore his boots. But they happened to be perfect for a man who wanted to move stealthily about the house.

In the hallway, he paused, trying to locate his landlady. There was a faint light under her door, but not Teddy's. The kid cried again, a fretful, middle-of-the-night whimper. Without weighing the consequences, Leo knocked.

Seconds later, the door opened a crack. Phoebe peered

out at him, her expression indiscernible in the gloom. "What's wrong? What do you want?"

Her stage whisper was comical given the fact that Teddy was clearly awake.

"You need some backup?"

"I'm fine." She started to close the door, but he stuck his foot in the gap, remembering at the last instant that he wasn't wearing shoes.

She pushed harder than he anticipated, and his socks were less protection than he expected. Pain shot up his leg. He groaned, jerking backward and nearly falling on his ass. Hopping on one foot, he pounded his fist against the wall to keep from letting loose with a string of words definitely not rated for kid ears.

Now Phoebe flung the door open wide, her face etched in dismay. "Are you hurt? Oh, heavens, of course you are. Here," she said. "Hold him while I get ice."

Without warning, his arms were full of a squirmy little body that smelled of spit-up and Phoebe's light floral scent. "But I…" He followed her down the hall, wincing at every step, even as Teddy's grumbles grew louder.

By the time he made it to the living room, Phoebe had turned on a couple of lamps and filled a dish towel with ice cubes. Her fingers curled around his biceps. "Give me the baby and sit down," she said, sounding frazzled and ir-ritated, and anything but amorous. She pushed him toward the sofa. "Put your leg on the couch and let me see if you broke anything."

Teddy objected to the jostling and cried in earnest. Leo lost his balance and flopped down onto the sofa so hard that the baby's head and Leo's chin made contact with jar-ring force.

"Damn it to hell." He lay back, half-dazed, as Phoebe plucked Teddy from his arms and sat at the opposite end of the sofa. Before he could object, she had his leg in her lap and was peeling off his sock.

When slim, cool fingers closed around the bare arch of his foot, Leo groaned again. This time for a far different reason. Having Phoebe stroke his skin was damned arousing, even if he was in pain. Her thumb pressed gently, moving from side to side to assess the damage.

Leo hissed, a sharp involuntary inhalation. Phoebe winced. "Sorry. Am I hurting you too badly?"

She glanced sideways and her eyes grew big. His robe had opened when he lost his balance. Most of his chest was bare, and it was impossible to miss the erection that tented his sleep pants. He actually saw the muscles in her throat ripple as she swallowed.

"It feels good," he muttered. "Don't stop."

But Teddy shrieked in earnest now, almost inconsolable.

Phoebe dropped Leo's foot like it was a live grenade, scooting out from under his leg and standing. "Put the ice on it," she said, sounding breathless and embarrassed. "I'll be back."

Phoebe sank into the rocker in Teddy's room, her whole body trembling with awareness. The baby curled into her shoulder as she rubbed his back and sang to him quietly. He wasn't hungry. She had given him a bottle barely an hour ago. His only problem now was that his mouth hurt. She'd felt the tiny sharp edge of a tooth on his bottom gum and knew it was giving him fits. "Poor darling," she murmured. Reaching for the numbing drops, she rubbed a small amount on his sore mouth.

Teddy sucked her fingertip, snuffled and squirmed, then gradually subsided into sleep. She rocked him an extra five minutes just to make sure. When he was finally out, she laid him in his crib and tiptoed out of the room.

Her bed called out to her. She was weaving on her feet,

wrapped in a thick blanket of exhaustion. But she had told Leo she would come back. And in truth, nothing but cowardice could keep her from fulfilling that promise.

When she returned to the living room, it was filled with shadows, only a single lamp burning, though Leo had started another fire in the grate that gave off some illumination. He was watching television, but he switched it off as soon as she appeared. She hovered in the doorway, abashed by the sexual currents drawing her to this enigma of a man. "How's the foot?"

"See for yourself."

It was a dare, and she recognized it as such. Her legs carried her forward, even as her brain shouted, *Stop. Stop.* She wasn't so foolish this time as to sit down on the sofa. Instead, she knelt and removed the makeshift ice pack, setting it aside on a glass dish. Leo's foot was bruising already. A thin red line marked where the sharp corner of the door had scraped him.

"How does it feel?" she asked quietly.

Leo sat up, wincing, as he pulled his thick wool sock into place over his foot and ankle. "I'll live."

When he leaned forward with his forearms resting on his knees, he was face-to-face with her. "Unless you have an objection," he said, "I'm going to kiss you now." A lock of hair fell over his forehead. His voice was husky and low, sending shivers down her spine. The hour was late, that crazy time when dawn was far away and the night spun on, seemingly forever.

She licked her lips, feeling her nipples furl tightly, even as everything else in her body loosened with the warm flow of honey. "No objections," she whispered, wondering if he had woven some kind of spell over her while she was sleeping.

Slowly, gently, perhaps giving her time to resist, he cupped her cheeks with his hands, sliding his fingers into her hair and massaging her scalp. His thumbs ran along her jawline, pausing when he reached the little indentation beneath her ear.

"God, you're beautiful," he groaned, resting his forehead against hers. She could feel the heat radiating from his bare chest. All on their own, her hands came up to touch him, to flatten over his rib cage, to explore miles of warm, smooth skin. Well-defined pectoral muscles gave way to a thin line of hair that led to a flat belly corded with more muscles.

She felt drunk with pleasure. So long…it had been so long. And though she had encountered opportunities to be intimate with men during the past three years, none of them had been as tempting as Leo Cavallo. "What are we doing?" she asked raggedly, almost beyond the point of reason.

He gathered handfuls of her hair and played with it, pulling her closer. "Getting to know each other," he whispered. His mouth settled over hers, lips firm and confident. She opened to him, greedy for more of the hot pleasure that built at the base of her abdomen and made her shift restlessly.

When his tongue moved lazily between her lips, she met it with hers, learning the taste of him as she had wanted to so badly, experimenting with the little motions that made him shudder and groan. He held her head tightly now, dragging her to him, forcing her neck to arch so he could deepen the kiss. He tasted of toothpaste and determination.

Her hands clung to his wrists. "You're good at this," she panted. "A little too good."

"It's you," he whispered. "It's you." He moved down beside her so that they were chest to chest. "Tell me to stop, Phoebe." Wildly he kissed her, his hands roving over her back and hips. They were so close, his erection pressed into her belly.

She was wearing her usual knit pajamas, nothing sexy about them. But when his big hands trespassed beneath the elastic waistband and cupped her butt, she felt like a desirable woman. It had been so long since a man had touched her. And this wasn't just any man.

It was Leo. Big, brawny Leo, who looked as if he could move mountains for a woman, and yet paradoxically touched her so gently she wanted to melt into him and never leave his embrace. "Make love to me, Leo. Please. I need you so much…."

He dragged her to her feet and drew her closer to the fireplace. Standing on the bearskin rug, he pulled her top over her head. As he stared at her breasts, he cradled one in each hand, squeezing them carefully, plumping them with an expression that made her feel wanton and hungry.

At last looking at her face, he rubbed her nipples lightly as he kissed her nose, her cheeks, her eyes. His expression was warmly sensual, wickedly hot. "You make a man weak," he said. "I want to do all sorts of things to you, but I don't know where to start."

She should have felt awkward or embarrassed. But instead, exhilaration fizzed in her veins, making her breathing choppy. His light touch was not enough. She twined her arms around his neck, rubbing her lower body against his. "Does this give you any ideas?"

Eight

Leo was torn on a rack of indecision. Phoebe was here… in his arms…willing. But some tiny shred of decency in his soul insisted on being heard. The timing wasn't right. *This* wasn't right.

Cursing himself inwardly with a groan of anguish for the effort it took to stop the train on the tracks, he removed her arms from around his neck and stepped back. "We can't," he said. "I won't take advantage of you."

Barely able to look at what he was saying no to, he grabbed her pajama top and thrust it toward her. "Put this on."

Phoebe obeyed instantly as mortification and anger colored her face. "I'm not a child, Leo. I make my own decisions."

He wanted to comfort her, but touching her again was out of the question. An explanation would have to suffice. He hoped she understood him. "A tree demolished one of your cabins. You're caring for a teething baby, who has kept you up big chunks of the past two nights. Stress and exhaustion are no basis for making decisions." He of all people should know. "I don't want to be that man you regret when the sun comes up."

She wrapped her arms around her waist, glaring at him with thinly veiled hurt. "I should toss you out on your ass," she said, the words holding a faint but audible tremor.

His heart contracted. "I hope you won't." There were things he needed to tell her before they became intimate, and if he wasn't ready to come clean, then he wasn't ready to have sex with Phoebe. He hurt just looking at her. With her hair mussed and her protective posture, she seemed far younger than he knew her to be. Achingly vulnerable.

She lifted her chin. "We won't do this again. You keep to yourself, and I'll keep my end of the bargain. Good night, Leo." Turning on her heel, she left him.

The room seemed cold and lonely in her absence. Had he made the most colossal mistake of his life? The fire between the two of them burned hot and bright. She was perfection in his arms, sensual, giving, as intuitive a lover as he had ever envisaged.

Despite his unfilled passion, he knew he had done the right thing. Phoebe wasn't the kind of woman who had sex without thinking it through. Despite her apparent willingness tonight to do just that, he knew she would have blamed both herself and him when it was all over.

What he wanted from her, if indeed he had a chance of ever getting close to her again, was trust. He had secrets to share. And he suspected she did, as well. So he could wait for the other, the carnal satisfaction. Maybe….

Phoebe climbed into her cold bed with tears of humiliation wetting her cheeks. No matter what Leo said, tonight had been a rejection. What kind of man could call a halt when he was completely aroused and almost at the point of penetration? Only one who wasn't fully involved or committed to the act of lovemaking.

Perhaps she had inadvertently stimulated him with her foot massage. And maybe the intimacy of their nap in front of the fire had given him a buzz. But in the end, Phoebe simply wasn't who or what he wanted.

The fact that she could be badly hurt by a man she had met only recently gave her pause. Was she so desperate? So lonely? Tonight's debacle had given her some painful truths to examine.

But self-reflection would have to wait, because despite her distress, she could barely keep her eyes open....

Leo slept late the next morning. Not intentionally, but because he had been up much of the night pacing the floor. Sometime before dawn he had taken a shower and pleasured himself, but it had been a hollow exercise whose only purpose was to allow him to find oblivion in much-needed sleep.

The clock read almost ten when he made his way to the front of the house. He liked the open floor plan of the living room and kitchen, because it gave fewer places for Phoebe to hide.

Today, however, he was dumbstruck to find that she was nowhere in the house. And Teddy's crib was empty.

A twinge of panic gripped him until he found both of them out on the front porch chatting with the man who had come to remove the enormous fallen oak tree. When he stepped outside, Phoebe's quick disapproving glance reminded him that he had neither shaved nor combed his hair.

The grizzled workman who could have been anywhere from fifty to seventy saluted them with tobacco-stained fingers and headed down the lane to where he had parked his truck.

"I'm sorry," Leo said stiffly. "I was supposed to be handling this."

Phoebe's lips smiled, but her gaze was wintry. "No problem. Teddy and I dealt with it. If you'll excuse me, I have to get him down for his morning nap."

"But I—"

She shut the door in his face, leaving him out in the cold…literally.

He paused on the porch to count to ten, or maybe a hundred. Then, when he thought he had a hold on his temper, he went back inside and scavenged the kitchen for a snack to hold him until lunch. A couple of pieces of cold toast he found on a plate by the stove would have to do. He slathered them with some of Phoebe's homemade strawberry jam and sat down at the table. When Phoebe returned, he had finished eating and had also realized that he needed a favor. Not a great time to ask, but what the heck.

She ignored him pointedly, but he wasn't going to let a little cold shoulder put him off. "May I use your phone?" he asked politely.

"Why?"

"I'm going to order a new phone from your carrier since mine is virtually useless, and I also want to get internet service going. I'll pay the contract fees for a year, but when I leave you can drop it if you want to."

"That's pretty expensive for a short-term solution. It must be nice to be loaded."

He ground his teeth together, reminding himself that she was still upset about last night. "I won't apologize for having money," he said quietly. "I work very hard."

"Is it really that important to stay plugged in? Can't you go cold turkey for two months?" Phoebe was pale. She looked at him as if she would put him on the first plane out if she could.

How had they become combatants? He stared at her until her cheeks flushed and she looked away. "Technology and business are not demons," he said. "We live in the information age."

"And what about your recovery?"

"What about it?"

"I got the impression that you were supposed to stay away from business in order to rest and recuperate."

"I can do that and still have access to the world."

She took a step in his direction. "Can you? Can you really? Because from where I'm standing, you look like a guy who is determined to get what he wants when he wants it. Your doctor may have given you orders. Your brother may have, as well. But I doubt you respect them enough to really do what they've asked."

Her harsh assessment hit a little too close to home. "I'm following doctor's orders, I swear. Though it's really none of your business." The defensive note in his voice made him cringe inwardly. Was he honestly the ass she described?

"Do what you have to do," she said, pulling her phone from her pocket and handing it to him. Her expression was a mix of disappointment and resignation. "But I would caution you to think long and hard about the people who love you. And why it is that you're here."

At that moment, Leo saw a large delivery truck pull up in front of the cabin. Good, his surprise had arrived. Maybe it would win him some brownie points with Phoebe. And deflect her from the uncomfortable subject of his recuperation.

She went to the door as the bell rang. "But I didn't order anything," she protested when the man in brown set a large box just inside the door.

"Please sign here, ma'am," he said patiently.

The door slammed and Phoebe stared down at the box as if it possibly contained dynamite.

"Open it," Leo said.

Phoebe couldn't help being a little anxious when she tore into the package. It didn't have foreign postage, so it was not from her sister. She pulled back the cardboard flaps and stared in amazement. The box was full of food—an expensive ham, casseroles preserved in freezer packs, desserts, fresh fruit, the list was endless.

She turned to look at Leo, who now lay sprawled on the sofa. "Did you do this?"

He shrugged, his arms outstretched along the back of the couch. "Before I lost my temper yesterday about my work email, I scrolled through my personal messages and decided to contact a good buddy of mine, a cordon bleu chef in Atlanta who owes me a favor. I felt bad about you agreeing to cook for me all the time, so I asked him to hook us up with some meals. He's going to send a box once a week."

Her mind reeled. Not only was this a beautifully thoughtful gesture, it was also incredibly expensive. She stared at the contents, feeling her dismal mood slip away. A man like Leo would be a lovely companion for the following two months, even if all he wanted from her was friendship.

Before she could lose her nerve, she crossed the room, leaned down and kissed him on the cheek. His look of shock made her face heat. "Don't worry," she said wryly. "That was completely platonic. I merely wanted to say thank-you for a lovely gift."

He grasped her wrist, his warm touch sending ripples of heat all the way up her arm. "You're welcome, Phoebe. But of course, it's partially a selfish thing. I get to enjoy the bounty, as well." His smile could charm the birds off the trees. In repose, Leo's rugged features seemed austere, even intimidating. But when he smiled, the force of his charisma increased exponentially.

Feeling something inside her soul ease at the cessation of hostilities, she returned the smile, though she pulled away and put a safe distance between them. It was no use being embarrassed or awkward around Leo. She wasn't so heartless as to throw him out, and truthfully, she didn't want to. Teddy was a sweetheart, but having another adult in the house was a different kind of stimulation.

Suddenly, she remembered what she had wanted to ask Leo before last night when everything ended so poorly. "Tell me," she said. "Would you object to having Christmas decorations in the house?"

"That's a strange segue, but why would I object?" he asked. "I'm not a Scrooge."

"I never thought you were, but you might have ethnic or religious reasons to abstain."

"No problems on either score," he chuckled. "Does this involve a shopping trip?"

"No. Actually, I have boxes and boxes of stuff in the attic. When I moved here, I wasn't in the mood to celebrate. Now, with Teddy in the house, it doesn't seem right to ignore the holiday. I wasn't able to take it all down on my own. Do you mind helping? I warn you…it's a lot of stuff."

"Including a tree?"

She smiled beseechingly. "My old one is artificial, and not all that pretty. I thought it might be fun to find one in the woods."

"Seriously?"

"Well, of course. I own thirty acres. Surely we can discover something appropriate."

He lifted a skeptical eyebrow. *"We?"*

"Yes, we. Don't be so suspicious. I'm not sending you out in the cold all on your own. I have one of those baby carrier things. Teddy and I will go with you. Besides, I don't think men are the best judge when it comes to locating the perfect tree."

"You wound me," he said, standing and clutching his chest. "I have excellent taste."

"This cabin has space limitations to consider. And admit it. Men always think bigger is better."

"So do women as a rule."

His naughty double entendre was delivered with a straight face, but his eyes danced with mischief. Phoebe knew her cheeks had turned bright red. She felt the heat. "Are we still talking about Christmas trees?" she asked, her throat dry as the Sahara.

"You tell me."

"I think you made yourself pretty clear last night," she snapped.

He looked abashed. "I never should have let things go that far. We need to take baby steps, Phoebe. Forced proximity makes for a certain intimacy, but I respect you too much to take advantage of that."

"And if *I* take advantage of you?"

She was appalled to hear the words leave her mouth. Apparently her libido trumped both her pride and her common sense.

Leo's brows drew together in a scowl. He folded his arms across his broad chest. With his legs braced in a fighting stance, he suddenly seemed far more dangerous. Today he had on old jeans and a cream wool fisherman's sweater.

Everything about him from his head to his toes screamed wealth and privilege. So why hadn't he chosen some exclusive resort for his sabbatical? A place with tennis courts and spas and golf courses?

He still hadn't answered her question. The arousal swirling in her belly congealed into a small knot of embarrassment. Did he get some kind of sadistic kick out of flirting with women and then shutting them down?

"Never mind," she said, the words tight. "I understand."

He strode toward her, his face a thundercloud. "You don't understand a single damn thing," he said roughly. Before she could protest or back up or initiate any other of a dozen protective moves, he dragged her to his chest, wrapped one arm around her back and used his free hand to anchor her chin and tip her face up to his.

His thick-lashed brown eyes, afire with emotion and seemingly able to peer into her soul, locked on hers and dared her to look away. "Make no mistake, Phoebe," he said. "I want you. And Lord willing, I'm going to have you. When we finally make it to a bed—or frankly any flat surface, 'cause I'm not picky—I'm going to make love to you until we're both too weak to stand. But in the meantime, *you're* going to behave. *I'm* going to behave. Got it?"

Time stood still. Just like in the movies. Every one of her senses went on high alert. He was breathing hard, his chest rising and falling rapidly. When he grabbed her, she had braced one hand reflexively on his shoulder, though the idea of holding him at bay was ludicrous. She couldn't manage that even if she wanted to. His strength and power were evident despite whatever illness had plagued him.

Dark stubble covered his chin. He could have been a pirate or a highwayman or any of the renegade heroes in the historical novels her sister read. Phoebe was so close she could inhale the warm scent of him. A great bear of a man not long from his bed.

She licked her lips, trembling enough that she was glad of his support. "Define *behave*." She kissed his chin, his wrist, the fingers caressing her skin.

Leo fought her. Not outwardly. But from within. His struggle was written on his face. But he didn't release her. Not this time.

The curse he uttered as he gave in to her provocation was heartfelt and earthy as he encircled her with both arms and half lifted her off her feet. His mouth crushed hers, taking…giving no quarter. His masculine force was exhilarating. She was glad she was tall and strong, because it gave her the ability to match him kiss for kiss.

Baby steps be damned. She and Leo had jumped over miles of social convention and landed in a time of desperation, of elemental reality. Like the prehistoric people who had lived in these hills and valleys centuries before, the base human instinct to mate clawed its way to the forefront, making a mockery of soft words and tender sentiments.

This was passion in its most raw form. She rubbed against him, desperate to get closer. "Leo," she groaned, unable to articulate what she wanted, what she needed. "Leo…"

Nine

He was lost. Months of celibacy combined with the uncertainty of whether his body would be the same after his attack walloped him like a sucker punch. In his brain he repeated a frenzied litany. *Just a kiss. Just a kiss, just a kiss...*

His erection was swollen painfully, the taut skin near bursting. His lungs had contracted to half capacity, and black dots danced in front of his eyes. Phoebe felt like heaven in his arms. She was feminine and sinfully curved in all the right places, but she wasn't fragile. He liked that. No. Correction. He loved that. She kissed him without apology, no half measures.

Her skin smelled like scented shower gel and baby powder. This morning her hair was again tamed in a fat braid. He wrapped it around his fist and tugged, drawing back her head so he could nip at her throat with sharp love bites.

The noise she made, part cry, part moan, hit him in the gut. He lifted her, grunting when her legs wrapped around his waist. They were fully clothed, but he thrust against her, tormenting them both with pressure that promised no relief.

Without warning, Phoebe struggled to get away from him. He held her more tightly, half crazed with the urge to take her hard and fast.

She pushed at his chest. "Leo. I hear the baby. He's awake."

Finally, her breathless words penetrated the fog of lust that chained him. He dropped her to her feet and staggered backward, his heart threatening to pound through the wall of his chest.

Afraid of his own emotions, he strode to the door where his boots sat, shoved his feet into them, flung open the door and left the cabin, never looking back.

Phoebe had never once seen Teddy's advent into her life as anything but a blessing. Until today. Collecting herself as best she could, she walked down the hall and scooped him out of his crib. "Well, that was a short nap," she said with a laugh that bordered on hysteria. Teddy, happy now that she had rescued him, chortled as he clutched her braid. His not-so-nice baby smell warned her that he had a messy diaper, probably the reason he had awakened so soon.

She changed him and then put him on a blanket on the floor while she tidied his room. Even as she automatically carried out the oft-repeated chores, her mind was attuned to Leo's absence. He had left without a coat. Fortunately, he was wearing a thick sweater, and thankfully, the temperature had moderated today, climbing already into the low fifties.

She was appalled and remorseful about what had happened, all of it her fault. Leo, ever the gentleman, had done his best to be levelheaded about confronting their attraction amidst the present situation. But Phoebe, like a lonely, deprived spinster, had practically attacked him. It was no wonder things had escalated.

Men, unless they were spoken for—and sometimes not even then—were not physically wired to refuse women who threw out such blatant invitations. And that's what

Phoebe had done. She had made it abysmally clear that she was his for the taking.

Leo had reacted. Of course. What red-blooded, straight, unattached male wouldn't? *Oh, God.* How was she going to face him? And how did they deal with this intense but ill-timed attraction?

A half hour later she held Teddy on her hip as she put away the abundance of food Leo's chef friend had sent. She decided to have the chimichangas for lunch. They were already prepared. All she had to do was thaw them according to the directions and then whip up some rice and salad to go alongside.

An hour passed, then two. She only looked out the window a hundred times or so. What if he was lost? Or hurt? Or sick? Her stomach cramped, thinking of the possibilities.

Leo strode through the forest until his legs ached and his lungs gasped for air. It felt good to stretch his physical limits, to push himself and know that he was okay. Nothing he did, however, erased his hunger for Phoebe. At first he had been suspicious of his immediate fascination. His life had recently weathered a rough patch, and feminine companionship hadn't even been on his radar. That was how he rationalized his response to Phoebe, even on the day they'd met.

But he knew it was more than that. She was a virus in his blood, an immediate, powerful affliction that was in its own way as dangerous as his heart attack. Phoebe had the power to make his stay here either heaven or hell. And if it were the latter, he might as well cut and run right now.

But even as he thought it, his ego *and* his libido shouted a vehement *hell, no.* Phoebe might be calling the shots as his landlady, but when it came to sex, the decision was already made. He and Phoebe were going to be lovers. The only question was when and where.

His head cleared as he walked, and the physical exertion gradually drained him to the point that he felt able to go back. He had followed the creek upstream for the most part, not wanting to get lost. In some places the rhododendron thickets were so dense he was forced to climb up and around. When he finally halted, he was partway up the mountainside. To his surprise, he could see a tiny section of Phoebe's chimney sticking up out of the woods.

Perhaps Luc had been right. Here, in an environment so antithetical to Leo's own, he saw himself in a new light. His world was neither bad nor good in comparison to Phoebe's. But it was different.

Was that why Phoebe had come here? To get perspective? And if so, had she succeeded? Would she ever go back to her earlier life?

He sat for a moment on a large granite boulder, feeling the steady pumping of his heart. Its quiet, regular beats filled him with gratitude for everything he had almost lost. Perhaps it was the nature of humans to take life for granted. But now, like the sole survivor of a plane crash, he felt obliged to take stock, to search for meaning, to tear apart the status quo and see if it was really worthy of his devotion.

Amidst those noble aspirations, he shamefully acknowledged if only to himself that he yearned to be back at his desk. He ran a billion-dollar company, and ran it well. He was Leo Cavallo, CFO of a textile conglomerate that spanned the globe. Like a recovering addict, his hands itched for a fix…for the pulse-pumping, mentally stimulating, nonstop schedule that he understood so intimately.

He knew people used *workaholic* as a pejorative term, often with a side order of pitying glances and shakes of the head. But, honest to God, he didn't see anything wrong with having passion for a job and doing it well. It irritated the hell out of him to imagine all the balls that were being dropped in his absence. Not that Luc and the rest of the team weren't as smart as he was...it wasn't that.

Leo, however, gave Cavallo his everything.

In December, the prep work began for year-end reports. Who was paying attention to those sorts of things while Leo was AWOL? It often became necessary to buy or sell some smaller arms of the business for the appropriate tax benefit. The longer he thought about it, the more agitated he became. He could feel his blood pressure escalating.

As every muscle in his body tensed, he had to force himself to take deep breaths, to back away from an invisible cliff. In the midst of his agitation, an inquisitive squirrel paused not six inches from Leo's boot to scrabble in the dirt for an acorn. Chattering his displeasure with the human who had invaded his territory, the small animal worked furiously, found the nut and scampered away.

Leo smiled. And in doing so, felt the burden he carried shift and ease. He inhaled sharply, filling his lungs with clean air. As a rule, he thrived on the sounds of traffic and the ceaseless hum of life in a big city. Yet even so, he found himself noticing the stillness of the woods. The almost imperceptible presence of creatures who went about their business doing whatever they were created to do.

They were lucky, Leo mused wryly. No great soul-searching for them. Merely point A to point B. And again. And again.

He envied them their singularity of purpose, though he had no desire to be a hamster on a wheel. As a boy, his teachers had identified him as gifted. His parents had enrolled him in special programs and sent him to summer camps in astrophysics and geology and other erudite endeavors.

All of it interested and engaged him, but he never quite fit in anywhere. His size and athletic prowess made him a target of suspicion in the realm of the nerds, and his academic successes and love for school excluded him from the jock circle.

His brother became, and still was, his best friend. They squabbled and competed as siblings did, but their bond ran deep. Which was why Leo was stuck here, like a storybook character, lost in the woods. Because Luc had insisted it was important. And Leo owed his brother. If Luc believed Leo needed this time to recover, then it was probably so.

Rising to his feet and stretching, he shivered hard. After his strenuous exercise, he had sat too long, and now he was chilled and stiff. Suddenly, he wanted nothing more than to see Phoebe. He couldn't share his soul-searching and his minor epiphanies with her, because he hadn't yet come clean about his health. But he wanted to be with her. In any way and for any amount of time fate granted him.

Though it was not his way, he made an inward vow to avoid the calendar and to concentrate on the moment. Perhaps there was more to Leo Cavallo than met the eye. If so, he had two months to figure it out.

Phoebe couldn't decide whether to cry or curse when Leo finally came through the door, his tall, broad silhouette filling the doorway. Her giddy relief that he was okay warred with irritation because he had disappeared for so long without an explanation. Of course, if he had been living in his own cabin, she would not have been privy to his comings and goings.

But this was different. He and Phoebe were cohabiting. Which surely gave her some minimal rights when it came to social conventions. Since she didn't have the guts to chastise him, her only choice was to swallow her pique and move forward.

As he entered and kicked off his muddy boots, he smiled sheepishly. "Have you already eaten?"

"Yours is warming in the oven." She returned the smile,

but stayed seated. It wasn't necessary to hover over him like a doting housewife. Leo was a big boy.

Teddy played with a plastic straw while Phoebe enjoyed a second cup of coffee. As Leo joined her at the table, she nodded at his plate. "Your friend is a genius. Please thank him for me. Though I'm sure I'll be ruing the additional calories."

Leo dug into his food with a gusto that suggested he had walked long and hard. "You're right. I've even had him cater dinner parties at my home. Makes me very popular, I can tell you."

As he finished his meal, Phoebe excused herself to put a drooping Teddy down for his nap. "I have a white noise machine I use sometimes in his room, so I think we'll be able to get the boxes down without disturbing him," she said. "And if he takes a long afternoon nap like he sometimes does, we can get a lot of the decorating done if you're still up for it."

Leo cocked his head, leaning his chair back on two legs. "I'm definitely *up* for it," he said, his lips twitching.

She couldn't believe he would tease about their recent insanity. "That's not funny."

"You don't have to tell me." He grinned wryly. "I realize in theory that couples with young children have sex. I just don't understand how they do it."

His hangdog expression made Phoebe burst into laughter, startling Teddy, who had almost fallen asleep on her shoulder. "Well, you don't have to worry about it," she said sharply, giving him a look designed to put him in his place. "All I have on the agenda this afternoon is decking the halls."

Leo had seldom spent as much time alone with a woman as he had with Phoebe. He was beginning to learn her expressions and to read them with a fair amount of accuracy.

When she reappeared after settling the baby, her excitement was palpable.

"The pull-down steps to the attic are in that far corner over there." She dragged a chair in that direction. "I'll draw the cord and you get ready to steady the steps as they come down."

He did as she asked, realizing ruefully that this position put him on eye level with her breasts. Stoically, he looked in the opposite direction. Phoebe dragged on the rope. The small framed-off section of the ceiling opened up to reveal a very sturdy set of telescoping stairs.

Leo grabbed the bottom section and pulled, easing it to the floor. He set his foot on the first rung. "What do you want me to get first?"

"The order doesn't really matter. I want it all. Except for the tree. That can stay. Here," she said, handing him a flashlight from her pocket. "I almost forgot."

Leo climbed, using the heavy flashlight to illuminate cobwebs so he could swat them away. Perhaps because the cabin was fairly new, or maybe because Phoebe was an organized sort, her attic was not a hodgepodge of unidentified mess. Neatly labeled cardboard cartons and large plastic tubs had been stacked in a tight perimeter around the top of the stairs within easy reach.

Some of the containers were fairly heavy. He wondered how she had managed to get them up here. He heard a screech and bent to stick his head out the hole. "What's wrong?"

Phoebe shuddered. "A spider. I didn't think all this stuff would have gotten so icky in just three years."

"Shall I stop?"

She grimaced. "No. We might as well finish. I'll just take two or three showers when we're done."

He tossed her a small box that was light as a feather. In neat black marker, Phoebe had labeled *Treetop Angel*.

When she caught it, he grinned at her. "I'd be glad to help with that body check. I'll search the back of your hair for creepy-crawlies."

"I can't decide if that's revolting or exciting. Seems like you made a similar offer when you were convincing me to let you stay. Only then, you promised to kill *hypothetical* bugs."

"Turns out I was right, doesn't it?" He returned to his task, his body humming with arousal. He'd never paid much attention to the holidays. But with Phoebe, suddenly all the chores surrounding Christmas took on a whole new dimension.

By the time he had brought down the last box and stored away the stairs, Phoebe was elbows-deep into a carton of ornaments.

She held up a tiny glass snowman. "My grandmother gave me this when I was eight."

He crouched beside her. "Is she still alive?"

"No. Sadly."

"And your parents?" He was close enough to brush his lips across the nape of her neck, but he refrained.

Phoebe sank back on her bottom and crossed her legs, working to separate a tangle of glittery silver beads. "My parents were hit by a drunk driver when my sister and I were in high school. A very kind foster family took us in and looked after us until we were able to graduate and get established in college."

"And since then?"

"Dana and I are very close."

"No significant others in your past?"

She frowned at the knot that wouldn't give way. "What about your family, Leo?"

He heard the unspoken request for privacy, so he backed off. "Oddly enough, you and I have that in common. Luc and I were seventeen and eighteen when we lost our parents. Only it was a boating accident. My father loved his nautical toys, and he was addicted to the adrenaline rush of speed. We were in Italy visiting my grandfather one spring break. Dad took a friend's boat out, just he and my mom. On the way back, he hit a concrete piling at high speed as they were approaching the dock."

"Oh, my God." Her hands stilled. "How dreadful."

He nodded, the memory bleak even after all this time. "Grandfather insisted on having autopsies done. My mother wasn't wearing a life jacket. She drowned when she was flung into the water. I took comfort in the fact that she was probably unconscious when she died, because she had a severe head wound."

"And your father?"

Leo swallowed. "He had a heart attack. That's what caused him to lose control of the boat." Repeating the words stirred something dark and ugly in his gut. To know that he was his father's son had never pained him more than in the past few months.

Phoebe put a hand on his arm. "But wasn't he awfully young?"

"Forty-one."

"Oh, Leo. I'm so very sorry."

He shrugged. "It was a long time ago. After the funerals, Grandfather took Luc and I back to Italy to live with him. He insisted we attend college in Rome. Some would say we were lucky to have had such an education, but we were miserable for a long time. Our grief was twofold, of course. On top of that, Grandfather is not an easy man to love." He hesitated for a moment. "I don't tell many people that story, but you understand what it feels like to have the rug ripped out from under your feet."

"I do indeed. My parents were wonderful people. They always encouraged Dana and me to go for any goal we wanted. Never any question of it being *too hard* or *not a girl thing.* Losing them changed our lives."

Silence fell like a pall. Leo tugged at her braid. "Sorry. I didn't mean to take us down such a dismal path."

She rested her head against his hand. "It's hard not to think of family at this time of year, especially the ones we've lost. I'm glad you're here, Leo."

Ten

She wasn't sure who initiated the intimate contact. Their lips met briefly, sweetly. The taste of him was as warm and comfortable as a summer rain. She felt the erotic river of molten lava hidden just beneath the surface, but as if by unspoken consent, the kiss remained soft and easy.

Leaning into him, she let herself be bolstered by his strength. One big arm supported her back. He was virile and sexy. She couldn't be blamed for wanting more. "Leo," she muttered.

All she said was his name, but she felt the shudder that ran through him. "What?" he asked hoarsely. "What, Phoebe?"

A million different answers hovered at the tip of her tongue. *Undress me. Touch my bare skin. Make love to me.* Instead, she managed to be sensible. "Let me put some music on to get us in the mood for decorating."

"I *am* in the mood," he grumbled. But he smiled when he said it and kissed the tip of her nose. Then he sobered. "To be absolutely clear, I want you in my bed, tonight, Phoebe. When the little man is sound asleep and not likely to interrupt us."

His eyes were dark chocolate, sinful and rich and designed to make a woman melt into their depths. She stared at him, weighing the risks. As a financial speculator, she played hunches and often came out on top. But taking Leo as a lover was infinitely more dangerous.

He was here only for a short while. And though Phoebe had made peace with her demons and embraced her new lifestyle, she was under no illusions that Leo had done the same. He was anxious to return home. Coming to the mountains had been some sort of penance for him, a healing ritual that he accepted under protest.

Leo would never be content to stagnate. He had too much energy, too much life.

She touched his cheek, knowing that her acquiescence was a forgone conclusion. "Yes. I'd like that, too. And I'm sorry that we can't be more spontaneous. A new relationship should be hot and crazy and passionate." *Like this morning when you nearly took me standing up.* Her pulse tripped and stumbled as her thighs tightened in remembrance.

Leo cupped her hand to his face with one big palm. "It will be, Phoebe, darlin'. Don't you worry about that."

To Phoebe's surprise and delight, the afternoon became one long, drawn-out session of foreplay. Leo built a fire so high and hot they both had to change into T-shirts to keep cool. Phoebe found a radio station that played classic Christmas songs. She teased Leo unmercifully when she realized he never remembered any of the second verses, and instead made up his own words.

Together, they dug out a collection of balsam-scented candles, lit them and set them on the coffee table. During the summer, the trapped heat in the attic had melted the wax a bit, so the ones that were supposed to be Christmas trees looked more like drunken bushes.

Phoebe laughed. "Perhaps I should just throw them away."

Leo shook his head. "Don't do that. They have *character*."

"If you say so." She leaned down and squinted at them. "They look damaged to me. Beyond repair."

"Looks can be deceiving."

Something in his voice—an odd note—caught her attention. He was staring at the poor trees as if all the answers to life's great questions lay trapped in green wax.

What did Leo Cavallo know about being damaged? As far as Phoebe could see, he was at the peak of his physical strength and mental acuity. Sleek muscles whispered of his ability to hold a woman...to protect her. And in a contest of wits, she would need to stay on her toes to best him. Intelligence crackled in his eyes and in his repartee.

Leo was the whole package, and Phoebe wanted it all.

Gradually, the room was transformed. With Leo's assistance, Phoebe hung garland from the mantel and around the doorways, intertwining it with tiny white lights that sparkled and danced even in the daytime. She would have preferred fresh greenery. But with a baby to care for and a cabin to repair, she had to accept her limits.

Leo spent over an hour tacking silver, green and gold snowflakes to the ceiling. Far more meticulous than she would have been, he measured and arranged them until every glittering scrap of foil was perfectly placed. The masculine satisfaction on his face as he stood, neck craned, and surveyed his handiwork amused her, but she was quick to offer the appropriate accolades.

In addition to the misshapen candles, the coffee table now sported a red wool runner appliquéd in reindeer. The *Merry Christmas* rug she remembered from her home in Charlotte now lay in front of a new door. The kitchen table boasted dark green place mats and settings of Christmas china.

At long last, Leo flopped down on the sofa with a groan. "You *really* like Christmas, don't you?"

She joined him, curling into his embrace as naturally as if they were old friends. "I lost the spirit for a few years, but with Teddy here, this time I think it will be pretty magical." Weighing her words, she finally asked the question she had been dying to have him answer. "What about you, Leo? Your sister-in-law made your reservation for two months. But you'll go home for the holidays, won't you?"

Playing lazily with the ends of her braid, he sighed. "I hadn't really thought about it. Many times in the past six or eight years, Luc and I flew to Italy to be with Grandfather for Christmas. But when Luc and Hattie married the year before last, Grandfather actually came over here, though he swore it wouldn't be an annual thing, because the trip wore him out. Now, with two little ones, I think Luc and Hattie deserve their own family Christmas."

"And what about you?"

Leo shrugged. "I'll have an invitation or two, I'm sure."

"You could stay here with Teddy and me." Only when she said the words aloud did she realize how desperately she wanted him to say yes.

He half turned to face her. "Are you sure? I wouldn't want to intrude."

Was he serious? She was a single woman caring for a baby that wasn't hers in a lonely cabin in the woods. "I think we can make room," she said drily. Without pausing to think of the ramifications, she ran a hand through his thick hair. The color, rich chestnut shot through with dark gold, was far too gorgeous for a man, not really fair at all.

Leo closed his eyes and leaned back, a smile on his face, but fine tension in his body. "That would be nice…." he said, trailing off as though her gentle scalp massage was making it hard to speak.

She put her head on his chest. With only a thin navy

T-shirt covering his impressive upper physique, she could hear the steady *ka-thud, ka-thud, ka-thud* of his heart. "Perhaps we should wait and see how tonight goes," she muttered. "I'm out of practice, to be honest." Better he know now than later.

Moving so quickly that she never saw it coming, he took hold of her and placed her beneath him on the sofa, his long, solid frame covering hers as he kissed his way down her throat. One of his legs lodged between her thighs, opening her to the possibility of something reckless. She lifted her hips instinctively. "Don't stop," she pleaded.

He found her breasts and took one nipple between his teeth, wetting the fabric of her shirt and bra as he tormented her with a bite that was just short of pain. Fire shot from the place where his mouth touched her all the way to her core. Shivers of pleasure racked her.

Suddenly, Leo reared back, laughing and cursing.

Blankly, she stared up at him, her body at a fever pitch of longing. "What? Tell me, Leo."

"Listen. The baby's awake."

When a knock sounded at the door minutes later, Leo knew he and Phoebe had narrowly escaped embarrassment on top of sexual frustration. She was out of sight tending to Teddy, so Leo greeted the man at the door with a smile. "Can I help you?"

The old codger in overalls looked him up and down. "Name's Buford. These sugared pecans is from my wife. She knowed they were Miss Phoebe's favorite, so she made up an extra batch after she finished the ones for the church bazaar. Will you give 'em to her?"

Leo took the paper sack. "I'd be happy to. She's feeding the baby a bottle, I think, but she should be finished in a moment. Would you like to come in?"

"Naw. Thanks. Are you the fella that was going to rent the other cabin?"

"Yes, sir, I am."

"Don't be gettin' any ideas. Miss Phoebe's pretty popular with the neighbors. We look out fer her."

"I understand."

"You best get some extra firewood inside. Gonna snow tonight."

"Really?" The afternoon sunshine felt more like spring than Christmas.

"Weather changes quicklike around here."

"Thanks for the warning, Buford."

With a tip of his cap, the guy ambled away, slid into a rust-covered pickup truck and backed up to turn and return the way he had come.

Leo closed the door. Despite feeling like a sneaky child, he unfolded the top of the sack and stole three sugary pecans.

Phoebe caught him with his hand in the bag…literally. "What's that?" she asked, patting Teddy on the back to burp him.

Leo chewed and swallowed, barely resisting the urge to grab another handful of nuts. "Your farmer friend, Buford, came by. How old is he anyway?"

"Buford is ninety-eight and his wife is ninety-seven. They were both born in the Great Smoky Mountains before the land became a national park. The house Buford and Octavia now live in is the one he built for her when they married in the early 1930s, just as the Depression was gearing up."

"A log cabin?"

"Yes. With a couple of rambling additions. They still used an actual outhouse up until the mid-eighties when their kids and grandkids insisted that Buford and Octavia were getting too old to go outside in the dead of winter to do their business."

"What happened then?"

"The relatives chipped in and installed indoor plumbing."

"Good Lord." Leo did some rapid math. "If they married in the early thirties, then—"

"They'll be celebrating their eightieth anniversary in March."

"That seems impossible."

"She was seventeen. Buford one year older. It happened all the time."

"Not their ages. I mean the part about eighty years together. How can anything last that long?"

"I've wondered that myself. After all, even a thirty-five-year marriage is becoming harder to find among my peers' parents."

Leo studied Phoebe, trying to imagine her shoulders stooped with age and her beautiful skin lined with wrinkles. She would be lovely still at sixty, and even seventy. But closing in on a hundredth birthday? Could any couple plan on spending 85 percent of an entire life looking at the same face across the breakfast table every morning? It boggled the mind.

Somehow, though, when he really thought about it, he *was* able see Phoebe in that scenario. She was strong and adaptable and willing to step outside her comfort zone. He couldn't imagine ever being bored by her. She had a sharp mind and an entertaining sense of humor. Not to mention a body that wouldn't quit.

Leo, himself, had never fallen in love even once. Relationships, good ones, took time and effort. Until now, he'd never met a woman capable of making him think long term.

Phoebe was another story altogether. He still didn't fully understand the decision that had brought her to the mountains, but he planned on sticking around at least long enough to find out. She intrigued him, entertained him and aroused him. Perhaps it was their isolation, but he felt a connection that transcended common sense and entered the realm of the heart. He was hazy about what he wanted from her in the long run. But tonight's agenda was crystal clear.

He desired Phoebe. Deeply. As much and as painfully as a man could hunger for a woman. Barring any unforeseen circumstances, she was going to be his.

To Phoebe's eyes, Leo seemed to zone out for a moment. She didn't feel comfortable demanding an explanation, not even a joking "Penny for your thoughts." Instead, she tried a distraction. "Teddy is fed and dry and rested at the moment. If we're going to get a tree, the time is right."

Leo snapped out of his fog and nodded, staring at the baby. "You don't think it will be too cold?"

"I have a snowsuit to put on him. That should be plenty of insulation for today. I'll get the two of us ready. If you don't mind going out to the shed, you can get the ax. It's just inside the door."

"You have an ax?" He was clearly taken aback.

"Well, yes. How else would we cut down a tree?"

"But you told me you haven't had a Christmas tree since you've been here. Why do you need an ax?"

She shrugged. "I split my own wood. Or at least I did in the pre-Teddy days. Now I can't take the chance that something might happen to me and he'd be in the house helpless. So I pay a high school boy to do it."

"I'm not sure how wise it is for you to be so isolated and alone. What if you needed help in an emergency?"

"We have 911 access. And I have the landline phone in addition to my cell. Besides, the neighbors aren't all that far away."

"But a woman on her own is vulnerable in ways a man isn't."

She understood what he wasn't saying. And she'd had those same conversations with herself in the beginning. Sleeping had been difficult for a few months. Her imagination had run wild, conjuring up rapists and murderers and deviants like the Unabomber looking for places to hide out in her neck of the woods.

Eventually, she had begun to accept that living in the city carried the same risks. The only difference being that they were packaged differently.

"I understand what you're saying," Phoebe said. "And yes, there have been nights, like the recent storm for instance, when I've questioned my decision to live here. But I decided over time that the benefits outweigh the negatives, so I've stayed."

Leo looked as if he wanted to argue the point, but in the end, he shook his head, donned his gear and left.

It took longer than she expected to get the baby and herself ready to brave the outdoors. That had been the biggest surprise about keeping Teddy. Everything about caring for him was twice as complicated and time-consuming as she had imagined. Finally, though, she was getting the hang of things, and already, she could barely remember her life without the little boy.

Eleven

It was the perfect day for an excursion. Since men were still working at the cabin removing the last of the tree debris and getting ready to cover the whole structure with a heavy tarp, Phoebe turned in the opposite direction, walking side by side with Leo back down the road to a small lane which turned off to the left and meandered into the forest.

She had fastened Teddy into a sturdy canvas carrier with straps that crisscrossed at her back. Walking was her favorite form of exercise, but it took a quarter mile to get used to the extra weight on her chest. She kept her hand under Teddy's bottom. His body was comfortable and warm nestled against her.

Leo carried the large ax like it weighed nothing at all, when Phoebe knew for a fact that the wooden-handled implement was plenty heavy. He seemed pleased to be out of the house, whistling an off-key tune as they strode in amicable silence.

The spot where she hoped to find the perfect Christmas tree was actually an old home site, though only remnants of the foundation and the chimney remained. Small weather-roughened headstones nearby marked a modest family cemetery. Some of the writing on the stones was still legible, including several that read simply, Beloved Baby. It pained her to think of the tragic deaths from disease in those days.

But she had suffered more than her share of hurt. She liked to think she understood a bit of what those families had faced.

Leo frowned, seeing the poignant evidence of human lives loved and lost. "Does this belong to you?" The wind soughed in the trees, seeming to echo chattering voices and happy laughter of an earlier day.

"As much as you can own a graveyard, I guess. It's on my property. But if anyone ever showed up to claim this place, I would give them access, of course. If descendants exist, they probably don't even know this is here."

One of the infant markers caught his attention. "I can't imagine losing a child," he said, his expression grim. "I see how much Luc and Hattie love their two, and even though I'm not a parent, sometimes it terrifies me to think of all the things that happen in the world today."

"Will you ever want children of your own?" Her breath caught in her throat as she realized that his answer was very important to her.

He squatted and brushed leaves away from the base of the small lichen-covered stone. "I doubt it. I don't have the time, and frankly, it scares the hell out of me." Looking up at her, his smile was wry. But despite the humor, she realized he was telling the absolute truth.

Her stomach tightened in disappointment. "You're still young."

"The business is my baby. I'm content to let Luc carry on the family lineage."

Since she had no answer to that, the subject lapsed, but she knew she had been given fair warning. Not from any intentional ultimatum on Leo's part. The problem was, Phoebe had allowed her imagination to begin weaving fantasies. Along the way, her heart, once broken but well on the way to recovery, had decided to participate.

The result was an intense and sadly dead-end infatuation with Leo Cavallo.

She stroked Teddy's hair, smiling to see the interest he demonstrated in his surroundings. He was a happy, inquisitive baby. Since the day he was born, she had loved him terribly. But this time alone, just the two of them, and now with Leo, had cemented his place in her heart. Having to return him to his parents was going to be a dreadful wrench. The prospect was so dismal, she forced the thought away. Much more of this, and she was going to start quoting an infamous Southern belle. *I'll think about that tomorrow.*

Leo stood and stretched, rolling his shoulders, the ax on the ground propped against his hip. "I'm ready. Show me which one."

"Don't be silly. We have to make a careful decision."

"This is the world's biggest Christmas tree farm. I'd say you won't have too much trouble. How about that one right there?" He pointed at a fluffy cedar about five feet tall.

"Too small and the wrong variety. I'll know when I see it."

Leo took her arm and steered her toward a grouping of evergreens. "Anything here grab your fancy?"

She and Leo were both encased in layers of winter clothes. But she fancied she could feel the warmth of his fingers on her skin. A hundred years ago, Leo would have worked from dawn to dusk, providing for his family. At night, when the children were asleep in the loft, she could see him making love to his wife on a feather tick mattress in front of the fire. Entering *her,* Phoebe, with a fire, a passion he had kept banked during the daylight hours. Saving those special moments of intimacy for the dark of night.

Wishing she could peel out of her coat, she stripped off her gloves and removed her scarf. The image of a more primitive Leo was so real, her breasts ached for his touch. She realized she had worn too many clothes. The day was warm for a winter afternoon. And thoughts of Leo's expertise in bed made her feel as if she had a fever.

She cleared her throat, hoping he wouldn't notice the hot color that heated her neck and cheeks. "Give me a second." Pretending an intense interest in the grouping of trees, she breathed deeply, inhaling the scent of the fresh foliage. "This one," she said hoarsely, grabbing blindly at the branches of a large Fraser fir.

At her back, Leo stood warm and tall. "I want you to have your perfect Christmas, Phoebe. But as the voice of reason I have to point out that your choice is a little on the big side." He put his hands on her shoulders, kissing her just below the ear. "If it's what you want, though, I'll trim it or something."

She nodded, her legs shaky. "Thank you."

He set her aside gently, and picked up the ax. "Move farther back. I don't know how far the wood chips will fly."

Teddy had dozed off, his chubby cheeks a healthy pink. She kept her arms around him as Leo notched the bottom of the tree trunk and took a few practice chops. At the last minute, he shed his heavy parka, now clad above the waist in only a thermal weave shirt, green to match his surroundings.

It was ridiculous to get so turned on by a Neanderthal exhibition of strength. But when Leo took his first powerful swing and the ax cut deeply into the tree, Phoebe felt a little faint.

Leo was determined to make Phoebe happy. The trunk of this particular fir was never going to fit into a normal-size tree stand. He'd have to cobble something together with a large bucket and some gravel. Who knew? At the moment, his first task was to fell the sucker and drag it home.

At his fifth swing, he felt a twinge in his chest. The feeling was so unexpected and so sharp, he hesitated half a second, long enough for the ax to lose its trajectory and land out of target range. Now, one of the lower branches was about two feet shorter than it had been.

Phoebe, standing a good ten feet away, called out to him. "What's wrong?"

"Nothing," he said, wiping his brow with the back of his hand. Tree chopping was damned hard work. Knowing that her eyes were on him, he found his stride again, landing four perfect strikes at exactly the same spot. The pain in his chest had already disappeared. Probably just a muscle. His doctor had reassured him more than once that Leo's health was perfect. Trouble was, when a man had been felled by something he couldn't see, it made him jumpy.

Before severing the trunk completely, he paused before the last swing and tugged the tree to one side. The fragrance of the branches was alluring. Crisp. Piquant. Containing memories of childhood days long forgotten. Something about scent leaped barriers of time and place.

Standing here in the forest with sap on his hands and his muscles straining from exertion, he felt a wave of nostalgia. He turned to Phoebe. "I'm glad you wanted to do this. I remember Christmases when I begged for a real tree. But my dad was allergic. Our artificial trees were always beautiful—Mom had a knack for that—but just now, a whiff of the air brought it all back. It's the smell of the holidays."

"I'm glad you approve," she said with a charming grin. Standing as she was in a splash of sunlight, her hair glistened with the sheen of a raven's wing. The baby slept against her breast. Leo wondered what it said about his own life that he envied a little kid. Phoebe's hand cradled Teddy's head almost unconsciously. Every move she made to care for her sister's child spoke eloquently of the love she had for her nephew.

Phoebe should have kids of her own. And a husband. The thought hit him like a revelation, and he didn't know why it was startling. Most women Phoebe's age were looking to settle down and start families. But maybe she wasn't. Because, clearly, she had hidden herself away like the unfortunate heroine in Rapunzel's castle. Only in Phoebe's case, the incarceration was voluntary.

Why would a smart, attractive woman isolate herself in an out-of-the-way cabin where her nearest neighbors were knocking on heaven's door? When was the last time she'd had a date? Nothing about Phoebe's life made sense, especially since she had admitted to working once upon a time in a highly competitive career.

A few thin clouds had begun to roll in, dropping the temperature, so he chopped one last time and had the satisfaction of hearing the snap that freed their prize. Phoebe clapped softly. "Bravo, Paul Bunyan."

He donned his coat and lifted an eyebrow. "Are you making fun of me?"

She joined him beside the tree and reached up awkwardly to kiss his cheek, the baby tucked between them. "Not even a little. You're my hero. I couldn't have done this on my own."

"Happy to oblige." Her gratitude warmed him. But her next words gave him pause.

"If we eat dinner early, we can probably get the whole thing decorated before bedtime."

"Whoa. Back up the truck. I thought we had *plans* for bedtime." He curled a hand behind her neck and stopped her in her tracks by the simple expedient of kissing her long and slow. Working around the kid was a challenge, but he was motivated.

Phoebe's lashes fluttered downward as she leaned into him. "We do," she whispered. The fact that she returned his kiss was noteworthy, but even more gratifying was her enthusiasm. She went up on tiptoes, aligned their lips perfectly and kissed him until he shuddered and groaned. "Good Lord, Phoebe."

She smoothed a strand of hair behind his ear, her fingers warm against his chilled skin. "Are you complaining, Mr. Cavallo?"

"No," he croaked.

"Then let's get crackin'."

Even though Phoebe carried a baby, and had been for some time, Leo was equally challenged by the difficulty of dragging the enormous tree, trunk first, back to the house. He walked at the edge of the road in the tall, dead grass, not wanting to shred the branches on gravel. By the time they reached their destination, he was breathing hard. "I think this thing weighs a hundred pounds."

Phoebe looked over her shoulder, her smile wickedly teasing. "I've seen your biceps, Leo. I'm sure you can bench-press a single measly tree." She unlocked the front door and propped it open. "I've already cleared a spot by the fireplace. Let me know if you need a hand."

Phoebe couldn't remember the last time she'd had so much fun. Leo was a good sport. Chopping down the large tree she had selected was not an easy task, but he hadn't complained. If anything, he seemed to get a measure of satisfaction from conquering *O Tannenbaum*.

Phoebe unashamedly used Teddy as a shield for the rest of the day. It wasn't that she didn't want to be alone with Leo. But there was something jarring about feeling such wanton, breathless excitement for a man when she was, at the same time, cuddling a little baby.

It would probably be different if the child were one they shared. Then, over Teddy's small, adorable head, she and Leo could exchanges smiles and loving glances as they remembered the night they created this precious bundle of joy. With no such scenario in existence, Phoebe decided her feelings were fractured…much like the time she'd had a high school babysitting job interrupted by the arrival of her boyfriend. That long-ago night as a sixteen-year-old, it had been all she could do to concentrate on her charges.

Almost a decade and a half later, with Leo prowling the interior of the cabin, all grumpy and masculine and gorgeous, she felt much the same way. Nevertheless, she focused on entertaining her nephew.

Fortunately, the baby was in an extremely good mood. He played in his high chair while Phoebe threw dinner together. Thanks to the largesse of Leo's buddy—which Leo no doubt cofunded—it was no trouble to pick and choose. Chicken Alfredo. Spinach salad. Fruit crepes for dessert. It would be easy to get spoiled by having haute cuisine at her fingertips with minimal effort. She would have to resist, though. Because, like Leo's presence in her life, the four-star meals were temporary.

Leo, after much cursing and struggling, and with a dollop of luck, finally pronounced himself satisfied with the security of their Christmas pièce de résistance. After changing the baby's diaper, Phoebe served up two plates and set them on the table. "Hurry, then. Before it gets cold."

Leo sat down with a groan. "Wouldn't matter to me. I'm starving."

She ended up sitting Teddy in his high chair and feeding him his bottle with one hand while she ate with the other. At the end of the meal, she scooped Teddy up and held him out to Leo. "If you wouldn't mind playing with him on the sofa for a little while, I'll clean up the kitchen, and we can start on the tree."

A look of discomfort crossed Leo's face. "I'm more of an observer when it comes to babies. I don't think they like me."

"Don't be silly, Leo. And besides, you did offer to help with Teddy when I let you stay. Remember?"

He picked up his coat. "Buford says it's going to snow tonight. I need to move half of that pile of wood you have out by the shed and stack it on the front porch. If it's a heavy snow, we might lose power." Before Phoebe could protest, he bundled up in his winter gear and was gone.

Phoebe felt the joy leach out of the room. She wanted Leo to love Teddy like she did, but that was silly. Leo had his own family, a brother, a sister-in-law, a niece, a nephew and a grandfather. Besides, he'd been pretty clear about not wanting kids. Some people didn't get all warm and fuzzy when it came to infants.

Still, she felt a leaden sense of disappointment. Leo was a wonderful man. Being squeamish about babies was hardly a character flaw.

She put Teddy back in the high chair. "Sorry, kiddo. Looks like it's you and me on KP duty tonight. I'll be as quick as I can, and then I'll read you a book. How about that?"

Teddy found the loose end of the safety strap and chewed it. His little chortling sounds and syllables were cute, but hardly helpful when it came to the question of Leo.

Tonight was a big bridge for Phoebe to cross. She was ready. She wanted Leo, no question. But she couldn't help feeling anxiety about the future. In coming to the mountains, she had learned to be alone. Would agreeing to be Leo's lover negate all the progress she had made? And would ultimately losing him—as she surely would—put her back in that dark place again?

Even with all her questions, tonight's outcome was a forgone conclusion. Leo was her Christmas present to herself.

Twelve

Leo pushed himself hard, carrying five or six heavy logs at a time. He took Buford's warning seriously, but the real reason he was out here was because staying in the cabin with Phoebe was torture. It was one thing to casually say, "We'll wait until bedtime." It was another entirely to keep himself reined in.

Every time she bent over to do something with the baby or to put something in the oven, her jeans cupped a butt that was the perfect size for a man's hands to grab hold of. The memory of her naked breasts lodged in his brain like a continuous, R-rated movie reel.

Earlier, he had called Luc, explaining the isolation of Phoebe's cabin and promising to stay in touch. His new phone should arrive in the morning, and the satellite internet would be set up, as well. By bedtime *tomorrow* night, Leo would be plugged in, all of his electronic devices at his fingertips. A very short time ago, that notion would have filled him with satisfaction and a sense of being on track. Not today. Now he could think of nothing but taking Phoebe to bed.

When he had a healthy stack of logs tucked just outside the front door in easy reach, he knew it was time to go in and face the music. His throat was dry. His heart pounded far harder than warranted by his current task. But the worst part was his semipermanent erection. He literally ached all over…wanting Phoebe. *Needing* her with a ferocious appetite that made him grateful to be a man with a beating heart.

He told himself he was close to having everything he craved. All he had to do was make it through the evening. But he was jittery with arousal. Testosterone charged through his bloodstream like a devil on his shoulder. Urging him on to stake a claim. Dismissing the need for gentleness.

Phoebe was his for the taking. She'd told him as much. A few more hours, and everything he wanted would be his.

Phoebe moved the portable crib into the living room near the fireplace, on the opposite side from the tree. Her hope was that Teddy would amuse himself for a while. He'd been fed, changed, and was now playing happily with several of his favorite teething toys.

When Leo came through the door on a blast of cold air, her stomach flipped. She'd given herself multiple lectures on remaining calm and cool. No need for him to know how agitated she was about the evening to come. Her giddiness was an odd mixture of anticipation and reservation.

Never in her life had she been intimate with a man of whom she knew so little. And likewise, never had she contemplated sex with someone for recreational purposes. She and Leo were taking advantage of a serendipitous place and time. Neither of them made any pretense that this was more. No passionate declarations of love. No tentative plans for the future.

Just sex.

Did that cheapen what she felt for him?

As he removed his coat and boots, she stared. The look in his eyes was hot and predatory. A shiver snaked down her spine. Leo was a big man, both in body and in personality. His charisma seduced her equally as much as his honed, masculine body.

She licked her lips, biting the lower one. "Um…there's hot chocolate on the stove. I made the real stuff. Seemed appropriate."

He rubbed his hands together, his cheeks ruddy from the cold. "Thanks."

The single syllable was gruff. Phoebe knew then, beyond the shadow of a doubt, that Leo was as enmeshed in whatever was happening between them as she was. The knowledge settled her nerves. She had been afraid of seeming gauche or awkward. Leo's intensity indicated that he was perhaps as off balance as she felt.

As he poured his drink, she expected him to come sit on the sofa. Instead, he lingered in the kitchen. She dragged a large red plastic tub nearer the tree. "If you'll do the lights, I'll sort through the ornaments and put hangers on them so that part will go quickly."

He set his mug in the sink. "Lights?"

She shot him an innocent look. "It's the man's job. Always."

"And if there were no man around?"

"I'd have to handle it. But I'm sure the tree would not look nearly as pretty."

Finally, he joined her, his body language somewhat more relaxed. "You are so full of it," he said with a fake glower as he bent and picked up the first strand. "You realize, don't you, that many people buy pre-lit trees these days."

"True." She plugged in the extension cord and handed him the end. "But not live ones. Think how proud you're going to be when we're finished, how satisfied with a job well done."

Tugging her braid, he deliberately brushed the backs of his fingers down her neck. "I'm a long way from satisfied."

His chocolate-scented breath was warm on her cheek. If she turned her head an inch or two, their lips would meet.

She closed her eyes involuntarily, her body weak with longing. Leo had to know what he was doing to her. And judging by the smirk on his face when she finally managed to look at him, he was enjoying her discomfiture.

Turnabout was fair play. "Good things come to those who wait," she whispered. She stroked a hand down the middle of his rib cage, stopping just above his belt buckle.

Leo sucked in a sharp breath as his hands clenched on her shoulders. "Phoebe…"

"Phoebe, what?" Toying with the hem of his shirt, she lifted it and touched his bare skin with two fingertips. Teasing him like this was more fun than she could have imagined. Her long-buried sensual side came out to play. Taking one step closer so that their bodies touched chest to knee, she laid her cheek against him, hearing the steady, though rapid, beat of his heart.

Between them, she felt the press of his erection, full and hard, at her stomach. For so long she had hidden from the richness of life, afraid of making another tragic misstep. But one lesson she had learned well. No matter how terrible the mistake and how long the resultant fall, the world kept on turning.

Leo might well be her next blunder. But at least she was living. Feeling. Wanting. Her emotions had begun to thaw with the advent of Teddy. Leo's arrival in the midst of her reawakening had been fortuitous. Six months ago, she would not have had the courage to act on her attraction.

Now, feeling the vestiges of her grief slide into the realm of the past, her heart swelled with joy in the realization that the Phoebe Kemper she had once known was still alive. It had been a long road. And she didn't think she would ever want to go back and reclaim certain remnants of that woman's life.

But she was ready to move forward. With Leo.

He set her away from him, his expression strained. "Give me the damn lights."

Leo was at sixes and sevens, his head muddled with a million thoughts, his body near crippled with desire. Fortunately for him, Phoebe was the meticulous sort. There were no knots of wire to untangle. Every strand of lights had been neatly wrapped around pieces of plywood before being stored away. He sensed that this Christmas decorating ritual was far more important to Phoebe than perhaps he realized. So despite his mental and physical discomfort, he set his mind to weaving lights in amongst the branches.

Phoebe worked nearby, unwrapping tissue-wrapped ornaments, discarding broken ones, tending to Teddy now and again. Music played softly in the background. One tune in particular he recognized. He had always enjoyed the verve and tempo of the popular modern classic by Mariah Carey. But not until this exact minute had he understood the songwriter's simple message.

Some things were visceral. It was true. He needed no other gift but Phoebe. When a man was rich enough to buy anything he wanted, the act of exchanging presents took on new meaning. He had always given generously to his employees. And he and Luc knew each other well enough to come up with the occasional surprise gift that demonstrated thought and care.

But he couldn't remember a Christmas when he'd been willing to strip the holiday down to its basic component. Love.

His mind shied away from that thought. Surely a man of his age and experience and sophistication didn't believe in love at first sight. The heart attack had left him floundering, grasping at things to stay afloat in a suddenly changing world. Phoebe was here. And it was almost Christmas.

He wanted her badly. No need to tear the situation apart with questions.

He finished the last of the lights and dragged one final tub over to the edge of the coffee table so he could sit and sift through the contents. Though the tree was large, he wasn't sure they were going to be able to fit everything on the limbs.

Spying a small, unopened green box, he picked it up and turned it over. Visible through the clear plastic covering was a sterling sliver rocking horse with the words *Baby's First Christmas* engraved on the base. And a date. An old date. His stomach clenched.

When he looked up, Phoebe was staring at the item in his hands, her face ashen. Cursing himself for not moving more quickly to tuck it out of sight, he stood, not knowing what to say. A dozen theories rushed through his mind. But only one made sense.

Tears rolled from Phoebe's huge pain-darkened eyes, though he was fairly certain she didn't know she was crying. It was as if she had frozen, sensing danger, not sure where to run.

He approached her slowly, his hands outstretched. "Phoebe, sweetheart. Talk to me."

Her eyes were uncomprehending…even when she wiped one wet cheek with the back of her hand.

"Let me see it," she whispered, walking toward the tub of ornaments.

He put his body in front of hers, cupping her face in his hands. "No. It doesn't matter. You're shaking." Wrapping his arms around her and holding her as tightly as he could, he tried to still the tremors that tore through her body cruelly.

Phoebe never weakened. She stood erect, not leaning into him, not accepting his comfort. He might as well have been holding a statue. At last, he stepped back, staring into her eyes. "Let me get you a drink."

"No." She wiped her nose.

Leo reached into his pocket for a handkerchief and handed it to her. He was torn, unsure if talking about it would make things better or worse. As he stood there, trying to decide how to navigate the chasm that had opened at his feet, the fraught moment was broken by a baby's cry.

Phoebe whirled around. "Oh, Teddy. We were ignoring you." She rushed to pick him up, holding him close as new tears wet her lashes. "It's your bedtime, isn't it, my sweet? Don't worry. Aunt Phoebe is here."

Leo tried to take the boy. "You need to sit down, Phoebe." He was fairly certain she was in shock. Her hands were icy cold and her lips had a blue tinge.

Phoebe fought him. "No. You don't like babies. I can do it."

The belligerence in her wild gaze shocked him, coming as it did out of nowhere. "I never said that." He spoke softly, as though gentling a spooked animal. "Let me help you."

Ignoring his plea, she exited the room, Teddy clutched to her chest. He followed the pair of them down the hall and into the baby's nursery cum storage room. He had never seen this door open. Phoebe always used her own bedroom to access Teddy's.

She put the child on the changing table and stood there. Leo realized she didn't know what to do next.

Quietly, not making a fuss, he reached for the little pair of pajamas hanging from a hook on the wall nearby. The diapers were tucked into a cheerful yellow plastic basket at the boy's feet. Easing Phoebe aside with nothing more than a nudge of his hip, he unfastened what seemed like a hundred snaps, top and bottom, and drew the cloth up over Teddy's head. Teddy cooed, smiling trustingly as Leo stripped him naked. The baby's skin was soft, his flailing arms and legs pudgy and strong.

The diaper posed a momentary problem, but only until Leo's brain clicked into gear and he saw how the assembly worked. Cleaning the little bottom with a baby wipe, he gave thanks that he was only dealing with a wet diaper, not a messy one.

Phoebe hadn't moved. Her hands were clenched on the decorative edge of the wooden table so hard that her knuckles were white.

Leo closed up the diaper, checked it for structural integrity, and then held up the pajamas. He couldn't really see much difference between these pj's and the daytime outfits the kid wore, but apparently there was one. This piece of clothing was even more of a challenge, because the snaps ran from the throat all the way down one leg. It took him three tries to get it right.

Through it all, Phoebe stood unaware. Or at least it seemed that way.

Cradling the child in one arm, Leo used his free hand to steer Phoebe out of the room. "You'll have to help me with the bottle," he said softly, hoping she was hearing him.

Her brief nod was a relief.

Leo installed Phoebe in a kitchen chair. Squatting in front of her, he waited until her eyes met his. "Can you hold him?"

She took the small, squirmy bundle and bowed her head, teardrops wetting the front of the sleeper. "I have a bottle ready," she said, the words almost inaudible. "Put it in a bowl of hot water two or three times until the formula feels warm when you sprinkle it on your wrist."

He had seen her perform that task several times, so it was easy to follow the instructions. When the bottle was ready, he turned back to Phoebe. Her grip on Teddy was firm. The child was in no danger of being dropped. But Phoebe had ceased interacting with her nephew.

Leo put a hand on her shoulder. "Would you like to feed him, or do you want me to do it? I'm happy to."

Long seconds ticked by. Phoebe stood abruptly, handing him the baby. "You can. I'm going to my room."

He grabbed her wrist. "No. You're not. Come sit with us on the sofa."

Thirteen

Phoebe didn't have the emotional energy to fight him. Leo's gaze was kind but firm. She followed him to the living room and sat down with her legs curled beneath her. Leo sat beside her with Teddy in his arms. Fortunately, Teddy didn't protest the change in leadership. He took his bottle from Leo as if it were an everyday occurrence.

Despite the roaring fire that Leo had built, which still leaped and danced vigorously, she felt cold all over. Clenching her jaw to keep her teeth from chattering, she wished she had thought to pick up an afghan. But the pile neatly folded on the hearth was too far away. She couldn't seem to make her legs move.

Trying to distract her thoughts, she studied Leo out of the corner of her eye. The powerful picture of the big man and the small baby affected her at a gut-deep level. Despite Leo's professed lack of experience, he was doing well. His large hands were careful as he adjusted Teddy's position now and again or moved the bottle to a better angle.

Beyond Leo's knee she could see the abandoned ornaments. But not the little green box. He must have shoved it out of sight beneath the table. She remembered vividly the day she'd purchased it. After leaving her doctor's office, she was on her way back to work. On a whim, she stopped by the mall to grab a bite of lunch and to walk off some of her giddy euphoria.

It was September, but a Christmas shop had already opened its doors in preparation for the holidays. On a table near the front, a display of ornaments caught her eyes. Feeling crazily joyful and foolishly furtive, she picked one out and paid for it.

Until this evening she had suppressed that memory. In fact, she didn't even realize she had kept the ornament and moved it three years ago.

Leo wrapped an arm around her shoulders, pulling her closer to his side. "Lean on me," he said.

She obeyed gladly, inhaling the scent of his aftershave and the warm "man" smell of him. Gradually, lulled by the fire and the utter security of Leo's embrace, she closed her eyes. Pain hovered just offstage, but she chose not to confront it at the moment. She had believed herself to be virtually healed. As though all the dark edges of her life had been sanded away by her sojourn in the woods.

How terribly unfair to find out it wasn't true. How devastating to know that something so simple could trip her up.

Perhaps because the afternoon and evening had been so enjoyable, so delightfully *homey,* the harshness of being thrust into a past she didn't want to remember was all the more devastating.

Teddy drained the last of the bottle, his little eyelashes drooping. Leo coaxed a muffled burp from him and then put a hand on Phoebe's knee. "Is it okay for me to lay him down? Anything I need to know?"

"I'll take him," she said halfheartedly, not sure if she could make the effort to stand up.

He squeezed her hand. "Don't move. I'll be right back."

She stared into space, barely even noticing when he returned and began moving about the kitchen with muffled sounds. A few minutes later he handed her a mug of cocoa. She wrapped her fingers around the warm stoneware, welcoming the heat against her frozen skin.

Leo had topped her serving with whipped cream. She sipped delicately, wary of burning her tongue.

He sat down beside her and smiled. "You have a mustache," he teased. Using his thumb, he rubbed her upper lip. Somewhere deep inside her, regret surfaced. She had ruined their sexy, fun-filled evening.

Leo appeared unperturbed. He leaned back, his legs outstretched, and propped his feet on the coffee table. With his mug resting against his chest, he shot her a sideways glance. "When you're ready, Phoebe, I want you to tell me the story."

She nodded, her eyes downcast as she studied the pale swirls of melted topping in the hot brown liquid. It was time. It was beyond time. Even her sister didn't know all the details. When the unthinkable had happened, the pain was too fresh. Phoebe had floundered in a sea of confused grief, not knowing how to claw her way out.

In the end, her only choice had been to wait until the waves abated and finally receded. Peace had eventually replaced the hurt. But her hard-won composure had been fragile at best. Judging by today, she had a long way to go.

Leo got up to stoke the fire and to add more music to the stereo. She was struck by how comfortable it felt to have him in her cabin, in her life. He was an easy man to be with. Quiet when the occasion demanded it, and drolly amusing when he wanted to be.

He settled back onto the couch and covered both of them with a wool throw. Fingering the cloth, he wrinkled his nose. "We should burn this," he said with a grin. "Imported fabric, cheap construction. I could hook you up with something far nicer."

"I'll put it on my Christmas list." She managed a smile,

not wanting him to think she was a total mental case. "I'm sorry I checked out on you," she muttered.

"We're all entitled now and then."

The quiet response took some of the sting out of her embarrassment. He was being remarkably patient. "I owe you an explanation."

"You don't *owe* me anything, sweet Phoebe. But it helps to talk about it. I know that from experience. When our parents were killed, Grandfather was wise enough to get us counseling almost immediately. We would never have shown weakness to him. He was and still is a sharp-browed, blustering tyrant, though we love him, of course. But he knew we would need an outlet for what we were feeling."

"Did it work?"

"In time. We were at a vulnerable age. Not quite men, but more than boys. It was hard to admit that our world had come crashing down around us." He took her hand. She had twisted one piece of blanket fringe so tightly it was almost severed. Linking their fingers, he raised her hand to his lips and kissed it. "Is that what happened to you?"

Despite her emotional state, she was not above being moved by the feel of his lips against her skin. Hot tears stung her eyes, not because she was so sad, but in simple recognition of his genuine empathy. "You could say that."

"Tell me about your baby."

There was nothing to be gained from denial. But he would understand more if she began elsewhere. "I'll go back to the beginning if you don't mind."

"A good place to start." He kissed her fingers again before tucking her hand against his chest. The warmth of him, even through his clothing, calmed and comforted her.

"I told you that I was a stockbroker in Charlotte."

"Yes."

"Well, I was good, really good at my job. There were a half dozen of us, and competition was fierce. Gracious for the most part, but inescapable. I had a knack for putting together portfolios, and people liked working with me, because I didn't make them feel stupid or uninformed about their money. We had a number of very wealthy clients with neither the time nor the inclination to grow their fortunes, so we did it for them."

"I'm having a hard time reconciling *killer* Phoebe with the woman who bakes her own bread."

His wry observation actually made her laugh. "I can understand your confusion. Back then I focused on getting ahead in my profession. I was determined to be successful and financially comfortable."

"Perhaps because losing your parents left you feeling insecure in so many other ways."

His intuitive comment was impressive. "You should hang out a shingle," she said. "I'm sure people would pay for such on-the-mark analysis."

"Is that sarcasm I hear?"

"Not at all."

"I can't take too much credit. You and I have more in common than I realized. Getting the foundations knocked out from under you at a time when most young people are getting ready to step out into the big wide world breeds a certain distrust in the system. Parents are supposed to help their children with the shift into adulthood."

"And without them, everything seems like a scary gamble at best."

"Exactly. But there's more, isn't there?"

She nodded, fighting the lump in her throat. "I was engaged," she croaked. "To another broker. We had an ongoing battle to see who could bring in the most business. I thought we were a team, both professionally *and* personally, but it turns out I was naive."

"What happened?"

Taking a deep breath, she ripped off the Band-Aid of her

old wound and brought it all back to life…to ugly life. "We had plans to get married the following year, but no specific date. Then—in the early fall—I found out I was pregnant."

"Not planned, I assume?"

"Oh, gosh, no. I assumed that motherhood, if it ever rolled around, was sometime *way* in the future. But Rick and I—that was his name—well…once we got over the shock, we started to be happy about it. Freaked-out, for sure. But happy nevertheless."

"Did you set a date then for a wedding?"

"Not at first. We decided to wait a bit, maybe until we knew the sex of the baby, to tell our coworkers. I thought everything was rocking along just fine, and then Rick began dropping subtle and not-so-subtle hints that I should think about taking a leave for a while."

"Why? It wasn't a physically demanding job, was it?"

"No. But he kept bringing up the stress factor. How my intensity and my long hours could be harmful to the baby. At first, I was confused. I honestly didn't see any problem."

"And was there?"

"Not the one he was trying to sell to me. But the truth was, Rick knew he could be top dog at the company if I were gone. And even when I came back after maternity leave, he would have made so much progress that I would never catch up."

"Ouch."

She grimaced. "It was a nasty smack in the face. We had a huge fight, and he accused me of being too ambitious for my own good. I called him a sexist pig. Things degenerated from there."

"Did you give the ring back?"

"How could I? Even if I now knew that my fiancé was a jerk, he was the father of my baby. I decided I had no choice but to make it work. But no matter how hard I tried, things only got worse."

"Did you have an abortion?"

Leo's quiet query held no hint of judgment, only a deep compassion. From where he was standing, that assumption made perfect sense.

She swallowed. The trembling she had managed to squelch started up again. "No. I wanted the baby by then. Against all odds. I was three and a half months along, and then…" Her throat tightened. Leo rubbed her shoulder, the caress comforting rather than sexual.

"What happened, Phoebe?"

Closing her eyes, she saw the moment as if it had been yesterday. "I started bleeding at work one day. Terribly. They rushed me to the hospital, but I lost the baby. All I could think about when I was lying in that bed, touching my empty belly, was that Rick had been right."

"You were young and healthy. I can't imagine there was a reason you shouldn't have been working."

"That's what my doctor said. She tried to reassure me, but I wasn't hysterical. Just cold. So cold. They told me the baby had developed with an abnormality. I would never have carried it to term. One of those random, awful things."

She didn't cry again. The emptiness was too dry and deep for that…a dull, vague feeling of loss.

Leo lifted her onto his lap, turning her sideways so her cheek rested on his chest. His arms held her tightly, communicating without words his sympathy and his desire to comfort her. He brushed a stray hair from her forehead. "I'm so sorry, Phoebe."

She shrugged. "Lots of people lose babies."

"But usually not a fiancé at the same time. You lost everything. And that's why you came here."

"Yes. I was a coward. I couldn't bear people staring at me with pity. And with Rick still working at the company, I knew I was done. My boss wasn't happy about it. I think he would have liked to fire Rick and keep me, but you can't terminate a guy for being a selfish, self-absorbed bastard."

"I would have." The three words encompassed an icy intensity that communicated his anger toward a man he had never met. "Your boss shouldn't have been so spineless. You were good at your job, Phoebe. If you had stayed, you might have recovered from your loss much sooner. The work would have been a healthy distraction. Perhaps even fulfilling in a new way."

Here was the crux of the matter. "The thing is," she said slowly. "I have my doubts. Looking back, I can see that I had all the makings of a workaholic. It's bad enough when a man falls into that trap. But women are traditionally the caregivers, the support system for a spouse or a family. So even though the doctor told me I had done nothing wrong, I felt as if I had betrayed my child by working nonstop."

Leo's arms tightened around her, his chest heaving in a startled inhalation. "Good Lord, Phoebe. That's totally irrational. You were an unencumbered woman on the upswing of your career. Female pioneers have fought for decades so you could be exactly where you were."

"And yet we still have battles within the sisterhood between stay-at-home moms and those who work outside the home. I've seen both groups sneer at each other as though one choice is more admirable than the other."

"I'll give you that one. In reality, though, I assume women work for many reasons. Fulfillment. Excitement. Or in some cases, simply to put food on the table."

"But it's about balance, Leo. And I had none. It's not true that women can have it all. Life is about choices. We only have twenty-four hours in a day. That never changes. So if I don't learn how to fit *work* into a box of the appropriate size, I don't know that I'll ever be able to go back."

"That's it, then? You're never going to be employed

again? Despite the fact that you've been gifted with financial talents and people skills?"

"I'd like to have a family someday. And even more importantly, find peace and contentment in the way I live my life. Is that so wrong?"

"How are you supposed to accomplish that by hiding out? Phoebe, you're not doing what you're good at…and borrowing a baby from your sister isn't exactly going after what you want."

"I don't know if I'm ready yet. It sounds like a cliché, but I've been trying to find myself. And hopefully in the process learning something about balance."

"We all have to live in the real world. Most of the life lessons I've learned have come via failure."

"Well, that's depressing."

"Not at all. You have to trust yourself again."

"And if I crash and burn?"

"Then you'll pick yourself up and start over one more time. You're more resilient than you think."

Fourteen

Leo was more bothered by Phoebe's soul-searching than he should have been. Her self-evaluation proved her to be far more courageous than he was in facing up to painful truths. But in his gut, he believed she was missing the bigger picture. Phoebe had clearly excelled in her previous career. And had loved the work, even with overt competition...perhaps *because* of it.

She was lucky to have had the financial resources to fund her long sabbatical. In the end, though, how would she ever know if it was time to leave the mountains? And what if she decided to stay? She had proved her independence. And in her eyes and in her home he saw peace. Did that mean she couldn't see herself finding happiness—and perhaps a family—anywhere but here?

He played with her hair, removing the elastic band that secured her braid. Gently, he loosened the thick ropes, fanning out the dark, shiny tresses until they hung down her back, covering his hand in black silk. Holding her in his arms as a friend and not a lover was difficult, but he couldn't push her away.

Phoebe saw herself as a coward, but that was far from the truth. Though she had been at the top of her game, she had wanted the baby that threatened to disrupt her life. Even in the face of disappointment, knowing that her fiancé was not the man she thought he was, she had been prepared to work at the relationship so they could be a family.

Leo admired her deeply.

Her eyes were closed, her breathing steady. It had been a long, busy day, and an emotional one for her. Leo knew their timing was off. Again. Even with Teddy sleeping soundly, Phoebe was in no shape to initiate a sexual relationship with a new partner. Perhaps if they had been a couple for a long time, Leo could have used the intimacy of sex to comfort and reassure her. As it was, his role would have to be that of protector.

A man could do worse when it came to Phoebe Kemper.

He stood, prepared to carry her to her room. Phoebe stirred, her long lashes lifting to reveal eyes that were still beautiful, though rimmed in red. "What are you doing?"

"You need to be in bed. Alone," he clarified, in case there was any doubt about his intentions.

She shook her head, a stubborn expression he had come to know all too well painting her face with insistence. "I want to sleep in here so I can see the tree. I'll keep the monitor with me. You go on to bed. I'm fine."

He nuzzled her nose with his, resisting the urge to kiss her. Her aching vulnerability held him back. "No," he said huskily. "I'll stay with you." He set her on her feet and went to his room to get extra blankets and a pillow. The bearskin rug in front of the fire would be a decent enough bed, and from there, he'd be able to keep the fire going. He brushed his teeth and changed into his pajama pants and robe.

By the time he returned, Phoebe had made the same preparations. It was colder tonight. Instead of her knit pj's, she had donned a high-necked flannel nightgown that made her look as if she had stepped right out of the pages of *Little*

House on the Prairie. The fabric was pale ivory with little red reindeer cavorting from neck to hemline.

The old-fashioned design should have made her look as asexual as a nun. But with her hair spilling around her shoulders and her dark eyes heavy-lidded, all Leo could think about was whether or not she had on panties beneath that fortress of a garment.

If the utilitarian cloth and enveloping design was meant to discourage him, Phoebe didn't know much about men. When the castle was barricaded, the knights had to fight all the harder to claim their prize.

She clutched a pillow to her chest, her cheeks turning pink. "You don't have to stay with me. I'm okay...really."

"What if I want to?" The words came out gruffer than he intended.

Her eyes widened. He could swear he saw the faint outline of pert nipples beneath the bodice of her nightwear. She licked her lips. "You've been very sweet to me, Leo. I'm sorry the night didn't go the way we planned. But maybe it's for the best. Perhaps we were rushing into this."

"You don't want me?" He hadn't meant to ask it. Hated the way the question revealed his need.

Phoebe's chin wobbled. "I don't know. I mean, yes. Of course I want you. I think that's painfully obvious. But we're not..."

"Not what?" He took the pillow from her and tossed it on the couch. Gathering her into his arms, he fought a battle of painful scale. It seemed as if he had wanted her for a lifetime. "Only a fool would press you now...when you've dealt with so much tonight. But make no mistake, Phoebe. I'm going to have you. No matter how long the wait." He stroked his hands down her back, pulling her hips to his, establishing once and for all that she was *not* wearing underwear.

Had he detected any resistance at all on her part, he

would have been forced to release her. But she melted into him, her body warm and soft and unmistakably feminine through the negligible barrier of her gown. He had belted his robe tightly before leaving his bedroom, not wanting to give any appearance of carnal intent.

To his intense shock and surprise, a small hand made its way between the thin layers of cashmere and found his bare chest. Within seconds his erection lifted and thickened. His voice locked in his throat. He was positive that if he spoke, the words would come out wrong.

Phoebe's hand landed over his heart and lingered as if counting the beats. Could she hear the acceleration? Did she feel the rigidity of his posture? He gulped, his breathing shallow and ragged. There was no way she could miss his thrusting sex, even through her pseudo armor.

The woman in his arms sighed deeply. "You should go to your room," she whispered. "The floor will be too hard."

"I'll manage." He thrust her away, hoping the maneuver wasn't as awkward as it felt. Turning his back, he added logs to the fire and then prepared his makeshift bed.

In his peripheral vision he saw Phoebe ready the sofa with a pile of blankets and her own pillow. When she sat down, removed her slippers and swung her legs up onto the couch, he caught one quick glimpse of bare, slender thighs. *Holy hell.*

A shot of whiskey wouldn't come amiss, but Phoebe's fridge held nothing stronger than beer. Quietly, keeping a wide perimeter between himself and temptation, he went about the cabin turning off lights. Soon, only the glow of the fire and the muted rainbow colors of the tree illuminated the room.

He checked the lock on the front door and closed a gap in the drapes. When he could think of nothing else as a distraction, he turned reluctantly and surveyed the evocative scene Phoebe's love of Christmas had created. Even the most hardened of "Scrooge-ish" hearts surely couldn't resist the inherent emotion.

Peace. Comfort. Home. All of it was there for anyone with eyes to see. Had his luxurious condo in Atlanta ever been as appealing?

Phoebe's eyes were closed, a half smile on her lips. She lay like a child with one hand tucked beneath her cheek. He didn't know if she was already asleep or simply enjoying the smell of the outdoors they had managed to capture in a tree. Perhaps it was the sound of the fire she savored, the same life-affirming heat that popped and hissed as it had for generations before.

Exhaustion finally overrode his lust-addled brain and coaxed him toward sleep. He fashioned his bed in front of the hearth and climbed in. It wasn't the Ritz-Carlton, but for tonight, there was nowhere he would rather be. After no more than five minutes, he realized that his robe was going to be far too warm so close to the fire.

Shrugging out of it, he tossed it aside and lay back in the covers with a yawn. A month ago if anyone had told him he'd be camping out on a hard floor in dangerous proximity to a fascinating woman he wanted desperately, he'd have laughed. Of course, he would have had a similar reaction if that same someone had told him he'd have a heart attack at thirty-six.

He had to tell Phoebe the truth about why he had come to the Smoky Mountains…to her cabin in the woods. She had bared her soul to him. Perhaps tomorrow he would find the opportunity and the words to reveal the truth. The prospect made him uneasy. He hated admitting weakness. Always had. But his pride should not stand in the way of his relationship to a woman he had come to respect as much or more than he desired her.

He shifted on the furry pallet, searching for a position that was comfortable. With Phoebe in the same room, he didn't even have the option of taking his sex in hand and finding relief. Hours passed, or so it seemed, before he slept....

Phoebe jerked awake, her heart pounding in response to some unremembered dream. It took her several seconds to recognize her surroundings. In the next instant, she glanced at the baby monitor. Reassurance came in the form of a grainy picture. Teddy slept in his usual position.

Sighing shakily as adrenaline winnowed away, she glanced at the clock on the far wall. Two in the morning. The fire burned brightly, so Leo must have been up tending to it recently. The room was warm and cozy. Despite her unaccustomed bed and the late hour, she felt momentarily rested and not at all sleepy.

Warily, she lifted her head a couple of inches, only enough to get a clear view of Leo over the top of the coffee table. Her breath caught at the picture he made. Sprawled on his back on the bearskin rug, he lay with one arm flung outward, the other bent and covering his eyes.

He was bare-chested. Firelight warmed skin that was deep gold dusted with a hint of dark hair that ran down the midline of his rib cage. Smooth muscles gave definition to a torso that was a sculptor's dream.

Arousal swam in her veins, sluggish and sweet, washing away any vestige of sadness from earlier in the evening. A wave of yearning tightened her thighs. Moisture gathered in her sex, readying her for his possession. Leo would never have made a move on her this evening in light of what she had shared with him.

Which meant that Phoebe had to take the initiative.

Telling herself and her houseguest that intimacy between them wasn't a good idea was as realistic as commanding the moon not to rise over the mountain. She *wanted* Leo. She trembled with the force of that wanting. It had been aeons since she had felt even the slightest interest in a man, longer still since she had paid any attention to the sexual needs of her body.

It was foolish to miss this chance that might never come her way again. Leo was not only physically appealing, he was also a fascinating and complex man. She was drawn to him with a force that was as strong as it was unexpected. Some things in life couldn't be explained. Often in her old life, she had picked stocks based on hunches. Nine times out of ten she was right.

With Leo, the odds might not be as good. Heartbreak and loss were potential outcomes. But at this barren time in her life, she was willing to take that chance.

Before she could change her mind, she drew her gown up and over her head. Being naked felt wanton and wicked, particularly in the midst of winter. Too long now she had bundled herself up in every way…mentally…emotionally. It was time to face life and be brave again.

She knelt beside him and sat back on her haunches, marveling at the beauty of his big, elegant body. His navy sleep pants hung low on his hips, exposing his navel. The tangle of bedding, blankets and all, reached just high enough to conceal his sex. Though she was pushing her limits, she didn't quite have the courage to take a corner of the sheet and pull.

Would he reject her, citing her emotional distress and bad timing? Or was Leo's need as great as hers? Did he want her enough to ignore all the warning signs and go for it regardless of possible catastrophe?

There was only one way to find out. Slipping her hand beneath the blanket, she encountered silk warmed by his skin. Carefully, she stroked over the interesting mound that was his sex. She had no more than touched him when he began to swell and harden.

Fifteen

Leo was having the most amazing dream. One of Phoebe's hands touched him intimately, while the other moved lightly over his chest, toying with his navel, teasing his nipples with her thumb. He groaned in his sleep, trying not to move so the illusion wouldn't shatter.

He sensed her leaning over him, her hair brushing his chest, his shoulders, his face, as she found his mouth. The kiss tasted sweet and hot. Small, sharp teeth nipped his bottom lip. He shuddered, bound in thrall to a surge of arousal that left him weak and gasping for breath. His chest heaved as he tried to pull air into his lungs.

His heart pounded like the hooves of a racehorse in the last turn. For a split second, a dash of cold fear dampened his enthusiasm. He hadn't had sex since his heart attack. All medical reassurances to the contrary, he wasn't sure what would happen when he was intimate with a woman. His hand—and the process of self-gratification—he trusted. Would the real deal finish him off?

But this was a dream. No need for heartburn. He laughed inwardly at his own pun. Nothing mattered but hanging onto the erotic fantasy and enjoying it until the end.

He felt Phoebe slide his loose pants down his legs and

over his feet. In the next second she was up on her knees straddling him. Grabbing one smooth, firm thigh, he tugged, angling her leg over his shoulder so he could pleasure her with his mouth. When he put his tongue at her center and probed, he shot from the realm of slumber to delicious reality in a nanosecond. The taste of Phoebe's sweet, hot sex was all too authentic.

His hands cupped her ass to hold her steady, even as his brain struggled to catch up. "Phoebe?" The hoarse word was all he could manage. Blinking to clear his sleep-fogged eyes, he looked up and found himself treated to the vision of soft, full breasts half hidden in a fall of silky black hair. Curvy hips nipped into a narrow waist.

Phoebe's wary-eyed gaze met his. She licked her lips, uncertainty in every angle of her body. "I didn't ask," she said, looking delightfully guilty.

"Trust me, honey. There's not a man living who would object. But you should have woken me up sooner. I don't want to miss anything." He loved the fact that she had taken the initiative in their coming together, because it told him she was as invested in this madness as he was. He scooted his thumb along the damp crevice where her body was pink and perfect. When he concentrated on a certain spot, Phoebe moaned.

Inserting two fingers, he found her swollen and wet. *Sweet Lord.* The driving urge he had to take her wildly and immediately had to be subdued in favor of pleasuring such an exquisite creature slowly. Making her yearn and burn and ultimately reach the same razor-sharp edge of arousal on which he balanced so precariously.

"Put your hair behind your shoulders," he commanded.

Phoebe lifted her arms and obeyed.

"Link your hands behind your back."

A split second of hesitation and then compliance. The

docile acquiescence gave him a politically incorrect rush of elation. She was his. She was his.

Watching her face for every nuance of reaction, he played with her sex…light, teasing strokes interspersed with firmer pressure. Her body bloomed for him, the spicy sent of her making him drunk with hunger. Keeping his thumb on the little bud that encompassed her pleasure center, he entered her with three fingers this time, stretching her sheath.

Phoebe came instantly, with a keening cry. He actually felt the little flutters inside her as she squeezed. Imagining what that would feel like on his shaft made him dizzy.

When the last ripple of orgasm released her, he sat up, settling Phoebe in his lap and holding her tightly. His eager erection bumped up against her bottom. Her thighs were draped over his, her ankles linked at his back.

Emotions hit him hard and fast. The one he hadn't anticipated was regret. Not for touching her, never that. But sorrow that they hadn't met sooner. And fear that she would be dismissive of their intimacy because their time together had been so brief.

He waited as long as he could. At least until her breathing returned to normal. Then he pulled back and searched her face. "Don't think for a minute that we're almost done. That was only a tiny prelude. I'm going to devote myself to making you delirious with pleasure."

Her smile was smug. "Been there, done that, bought the T-shirt."

Leo knew that if things were to progress he had to get up. But knowing and doing were two different matters. "Can I ask you a very important question, my Phoebe?"

She rested her forehead on his shoulder. "Ask away."

"If I go fetch a bushel of condoms, will you change your mind about this while I'm gone?"

He felt her go still. "No." The voice was small, but the sentiment seemed genuine.

"And if Teddy wakes at an inopportune moment, will that be an excuse? Or even a sign from the universe that we should stop?"

She lifted her head, her eyes searching his. For what? Encouragement? Sincerity? "If that happens," she said slowly, "we'll settle him back to sleep and pick up where we left off."

"Good." He told himself to release her. Until he rustled up some protection, he couldn't take her the way he wanted to. But holding her like this was unutterably sweet. A real conundrum, because he couldn't ever remember feeling such a thing with another lover. This mix of shivering need and overwhelming tenderness.

Phoebe smiled. "Shall I go get them?"

He shook his head. "No. Just give me a minute." The actual fire had died down, and he needed to take care of that, as well.

While he sat there, desperately trying to find the will to stand up, Phoebe reached behind her bottom and found his shaft, giving it a little tug. The teasing touch was almost more than he could stand. The skin at the head was tight and wet with fluid that had leaked in his excitement.

Her fingers found the less rigid part of his sex and massaged him gently. "Don't. Ah, God, don't," he cried. But it was too late. He came in a violent climax that racked him with painful, fiery release. Gripping Phoebe hard enough to endanger her ribs, he groaned and shuddered, feeling the press of her breasts against his chest.

In the pregnant silence that followed, the witch had the temerity to laugh. "Perhaps we should quit while we're ahead. I don't think you're going to make it down the hall anytime soon."

He pinched her ass, gasping for breath. "Impertinent hussy."

"Well, it's true. I suppose I should have thought through all the ramifications before I jumped your bones."

"You *were* a tad eager," he pointed out, squeezing her perfectly plump butt cheeks.

Phoebe wriggled free and wrapped a blanket around her shoulders. "Go, Leo. Hurry. I'm getting cold."

Dragging himself to his feet, he yawned and stretched. Just looking at her had his erection bobbing hopefully again. *Down, boy.* He removed the fire screen, threw on a couple of good-size logs and poked the embers until they blazed up again. "Don't go anywhere," he ordered. "I'll be right back."

Phoebe watched him walk away with stars in her eyes. This was bad. This was very bad. Leo in the buff was one spectacular sight. Aside from his considerable *assets,* the view from the rear was impressive, as well. Broad shoulders, trim waist, taut buttocks, nicely muscled thighs. Even his big feet were sexy.

Despite everything they had done in the last forty-five minutes, her body continued to hum with arousal. She still couldn't believe she had stripped naked and attacked him in his sleep. That was something the old Phoebe might have done. But only if the man in question were Leo. He had the ability to make a woman throw caution to the wind.

She tidied the pile of bedding and smoothed out the wrinkles. Just like a cavewoman preparing for the return of her marauding spouse. It struck her as funny that Leo really had provided food for her. Not by clubbing anything over the head, but still…

Now that he was gone, she felt a bit bashful. She had seen the size of his sex. Wondering how things would fit together made her nipples furl in anticipation.

His return was rapid and startling. From his hand dangled a long strip of connected condom packages. She licked her lips. "I don't think the night is that long."

Dropping down beside her, he bit her shoulder. "Trust me, sweetheart."

He took her chin in his hand, the lock of hair falling across his forehead making him look younger and more carefree. "I'm thinking we'll go hard and fast the first time and then branch out into variations."

As he cupped her breast, her eyelids fluttered shut all of their own accord. Despite the fact that he had paraded nude through the house, his skin was as warm as ever. She burrowed closer. "Merry Christmas to me," she muttered.

"Look at me, Phoebe."

When she obeyed, she saw that every trace of his good humor had fled. His face was no more than planes and angles, painted by firelight to resemble an ancient king. Eyes so dark they appeared black. Still he held her chin. "I'm looking," she quipped with deliberate sass. "What am I supposed to see?" His intensity aroused and agitated her, but she wouldn't let him know how his caveman antics affected her. Not yet.

He flipped her onto her back without warning, her brief fall cushioned by the many-layered pallet. Instead of answering her provocative question, he *showed* her. Kneeling between her thighs, he yanked a single packet free, ripped it open with his teeth and extracted the contents. Making sure she watched him—by the simple expedient of locking her gaze to his—he rolled the condom over his straining erection.

She doubted he meant for her to see him wince. But the evidence of his arousal lit a fire low in her belly. Leo was in pain. Because of her. He wanted her so badly his hands were shaking. That meant he was more vulnerable than she had imagined. And knowing she was not the only one falling apart calmed her nerves.

Clearly, Leo did not see her as one in a line of faceless women. Whatever their differences in lifestyle, or world view, or even sexual experience, tonight was special.

She grabbed his wrist. "Tell me what you're going to do to me." She breathed the words on a moan as his legs tangled with hers and he positioned the head of his sex at her opening.

Still he didn't smile. His expression was a mask of frayed control…jaw clenched, teeth ground together. "I'm going to take you, my sweet. To heaven and back."

At the first push of his rigid length, she lost her breath. Everything in the room stood still. Her body strained to accommodate him. Though she was more than ready, she had been celibate a long time, and Leo was a big man.

He paused, though the effort brought beads of perspiration to his forehead. "Too much?" he asked, his voice raw.

"No." She concentrated on relaxing, though everything inside her seemed wound tight. "I want all of you."

Her declaration made him shudder as though the mental picture was more stimulating than the actual joining of their flesh. Steadily, he forced his way in. Phoebe felt his penetration in every inch of her soul. She knew in that instant that she had been deceiving herself. Leo was more than a mere fling. He was the man who could make her live again.

When he was fully seated, he withdrew with a hoarse shout and slammed into her, making her grab the leg of the coffee table as a brace. "I don't want to hurt you," he rasped.

"Then don't stop, Leo. I can handle whatever you have to give."

Sixteen

Leo was out of control. In some sane corner of his mind, he knew it. But Phoebe…God, Phoebe…she milked the length of him every time he withdrew, and on the downstroke arched her back, taking him a centimeter deeper with each successive thrust.

Her legs had his waist in a vise. Her cloud of night-dark hair fanned out around them. He buried his face in it at one point, stilling his frantic motions, desperately trying to stave off his release. She smelled amazing. Though he couldn't pinpoint the fragrance, he would have recognized her scent in a pitch-black room.

Her fingernails dug into his back. He relished the stinging discomfort…found his arousal ratcheting up by a degree each time she cried out his name and marked his flesh.

But nothing prepared him for the feel of her climax as she tightened on his shaft and came apart in release. He held her close, feeling the aftershocks that quivered in her sex like endless ripples of sensation.

When he knew she was at peace, he lost it. Slamming into her without finesse or reason, he exploded in a white-hot flash of lust. He lost a few seconds in the aftermath, his mouth dry and his head pounding.

Barely conscious, he tried to spare her most of his weight. He had come twice in quick succession, and his brain was muddled, incredulous that he wanted her still.

Phoebe stirred restlessly. "We should get some sleep." Her words were barely audible, but he caught the inference.

No way. She wasn't leaving him. No way in hell. Rolling onto his side, he scooped her close, spooning her with a murmur of satisfaction. Though her soft bottom pressed into the cradle of his thighs, his arousal was a faint whisper after two incredible climaxes. The need he felt was more than physical.

Her head pillowed on his arm, he slept.

He couldn't mark the moment consciousness returned, but he knew at once that he was alone. Sunlight peeked in around the edges of the drapes, the reflection strangely bright. He could hear the furnace running, and although the fire had long since burned out, he was plenty warm.

Sitting up with a groan, he felt muscle twinges that came from a night of carnal excess. Thinking about it made him hard. He cursed, well aware that any repeat of last night's sexual calisthenics was hours in the future.

Phoebe had put away all the bedding she had used on the sofa. But on the kitchen counter he saw a pot of coffee steaming. He stood up, feeling as if he'd been on a weekend bender. Grabbing his robe that had gotten wedged beneath the edge of the sofa, he slid his arms into the sleeves and zeroed in on the life-saving caffeine.

After two cups he was ready to go in search of his landlady. He found her and Teddy curled up on Phoebe's bed reading books. She sat up when she saw him, her smile warm but perhaps tinged with reserve. "I hope we didn't wake you."

He put his hands on top of the door frame and stretched

hard, feeling the muscles loosen bit by bit. "I didn't hear a thing. Has he been up long?"

"An hour maybe. I gave him his bottle in here."

They were conversing like strangers. Or perhaps a married couple with nothing much to say.

He sat down on the edge of the bed and took her hand. "Good morning, Phoebe."

Hot color flushed her cheeks and reddened her throat. "Good morning."

He dragged her closer for a scorching kiss. "It sure as hell is."

That surprised a laugh from her, and immediately he felt her relax. "Have you looked outside?" she asked.

He shook his head. "No. Why? Did it snow?"

She nodded. "We got three or four inches. Buford's grandson will plow the driveway by midmorning. I know you were expecting some deliveries."

Shock immobilized him. It had been hours since he had checked his email on Phoebe's phone or even sent his brother a text. Never in his adult life could he remember going so long without his electronic lifelines. Yet with Phoebe, tucked away from the world, he had gradually begun to accept the absence of technology as commonplace.

Not that she was really rustic in her situation. She had phones and television. But beyond that, life was tech-free. He frowned, not sure he was comfortable with the knowledge that she had converted him in a matter of days. It was the sex. That's all. He'd been pleasantly diverted. Didn't mean he wanted to give up his usual M.O. on a permanent basis.

Smiling to cover his unease, he released her. "I'm going to take a shower. I can play with the kid after that if you want to clean up."

* * *

Phoebe watched him go, her heart troubled. Something was off, but she couldn't pinpoint it. Maybe nothing more than a bad case of *morning after*.

By the time both adults were clean and dressed, the sound of a tractor echoed in the distance. Soon the driveway was passable, and in no time at all, vehicles began arriving. A truck dealing with Leo's satellite internet. The express delivery service with his new phone. A large moving van that somehow managed to turn and back up to the damaged cabin.

With the felled tree completely gone now, a small army of men began carrying out everything salvageable to place into storage until the repairs were complete. Leo didn't even linger for breakfast. He was out the door in minutes, wading into the midst of chaos...coordinating, instructing, and generally making himself indispensable. Phoebe wasn't sure what she would have done without his help. If she had not been laden with the responsibility of Teddy, she would have managed just fine. But caring for a baby and trying to deal with the storm damage at the same time would have made things extremely difficult.

She was amazed that she could see a difference in the baby in two weeks. He was growing so quickly and his personality seemed more evident every day. This morning he was delighting himself by blowing bubbles and babbling nonsense sounds.

After tidying the kitchen, Phoebe picked him up out of his high chair and carried him over to the tree. "See what Leo and I did, Teddy? Isn't it pretty?" The baby reached for an ornament, and she tucked his hand to her cheek. "I know. It isn't fair to have so many pretty baubles and none of them for you to play with."

Teddy grabbed a strand of her hair that had escaped her braid and yanked. She'd been in a hurry that morning after her shower and had woven her hair in its usual style with less than her usual precision. It was beginning to be clear to her why so many young mothers had simple hairstyles. Caring for an infant didn't leave much time for primping.

In another half hour Teddy would be ready for a nap. Already his eyes were drooping. After last night's excess, Phoebe might try to sneak in a few minutes of shut-eye herself. Thinking about Leo made her feel all bubbly inside. Like a sixteen-year-old about to go to prom with her latest crush.

Even in the good days with her fiancé, sex had never been like that. Leo had devoted himself to her pleasure, proving to her again and again that she had more to give and receive. Her body felt sensitized…energized…eager to try it all over again.

She walked the baby around the living room, humming Christmas carols, feeling happier than she had felt in a long time.

When the knock sounded at the front door, she looked up in puzzlement. Surely Leo hadn't locked himself out. She had made sure to leave the catch undone when he left. Before she could react, the door opened and a familiar head appeared.

"Dana!" Phoebe eyed her sister with shock and dismay. "What's wrong? Why are you here?"

Leo jogged back to the cabin. He was starving, but more than that, he wanted to see Phoebe. He didn't want to give her time to think of a million reasons why they shouldn't be together. When he burst through the front door, he ground to a halt, immediately aware that he had walked into a tense situation. He'd seen an unfamiliar car outside, but hadn't paid much attention, assuming it belonged to one of the workmen.

Phoebe's eyes met his across the room. For a split second, he saw into her very soul. Her anguish seared him, but the moment passed, and now her expression seemed normal. She smiled at him. "You're just in time. My sister, Dana, arrived unexpectedly. Dana, this is Leo."

He shook hands with the other woman and tried to analyze the dynamic that sizzled in the room. Dana was a shorter, rounder version of her sister. At the moment, she seemed exhausted and at the point of tears.

Phoebe held Teddy on her hip. "What are you doing here, Dana? Why didn't you let me know you were coming? I would have picked you up at the airport. You look like you haven't slept in hours."

Dana plopped onto the sofa and burst into tears, her hands over her face. "I knew you would try to talk me out of it," she sobbed. "I know it's stupid. I've been on a plane for hours, and I have to be back on a flight at two. But I couldn't spend Christmas without my baby. I thought I could, but I can't."

Leo froze, realizing at once what was happening. Phoebe…dear, beautiful, strong Phoebe put whatever feelings she had aside and went to sit beside her sister. "Of course you can't. I understand. Dry your eyes and take your son." She handed Teddy over to his mother as though it were the most natural thing in the world.

Leo knew it was breaking her heart.

Dana's face when she hugged her baby to her chest would have touched even the most hardened cynic. She kissed the top of his head, nuzzling the soft, fuzzy hair. "We found a lady in the village who speaks a little English. She's agreed to look after him while we work."

Phoebe clasped her hands in her lap as if she didn't know what to do with them. "How are things going with your father-in-law's estate?"

Dana made a face. "It's a mess. Worse than we thought. So stressful. The house is chock-full of junk. We have to go through it all so we don't miss anything valuable. I know it doesn't make sense to take Teddy over there, but if I can just have him in the evenings and be able to see him during the day when we take breaks, I know I'll feel so much better."

Phoebe nodded. "Of course you will."

Dana grabbed her sister's wrist. "You don't know how much we love you and appreciate all you've done for Teddy. I have an extra ticket on standby if you want to come back with me...or even in a day or two. I don't want you to be alone at Christmas, especially because it was that time of year when you lost—" She clapped her hand over her mouth, her expression horrified. "Oh, God, honey. I'm sorry. I'm exhausted and I don't know what I'm saying. I didn't mean to mention it."

Phoebe put an arm around the frazzled woman and kissed her cheek. "Take a deep breath, Dana. Everything's fine. I'm fine. If you're really on such a time crunch, let's start packing up Teddy's things. He'll nap in the car while you drive."

Phoebe paused in the back hallway, leaning against the wall and closing her eyes. Her smile felt frozen in place. Leo wasn't fooled. She could see his concern. But the important thing was for Dana not to realize what her unexpected arrival had done to Phoebe's plans for a cozy Christmas.

In less than an hour from start to finish, Dana came and went, taking Teddy with her. The resultant silence was painful. The only baby items left behind were the high chair in the kitchen and the large pieces of furniture in Teddy's room. Without asking, Leo took the high chair, put it in with the other stuff and shut the door. Phoebe watched him, her heart in pieces at her feet.

When he returned, she wrapped her arms around her

waist, her mood as flat as a three-day-old helium balloon. "I knew he wasn't my baby."

"Of course you did."

Leo's unspoken compassion took her close to an edge she didn't want to face. "Don't be nice to me or I may fall apart."

He grinned, taking her in his arms and resting his cheek on her head. "I'm very proud of you, Phoebe."

"For what?"

"For being such a good sister and aunt. For not making Dana feel guilty. For doing what had to be done."

"I was looking forward to Christmas morning," she whispered, her throat tight with unshed tears. "His presents are all wrapped." She clung to Leo, feeling his warm presence like a balm to her hurting spirit.

He squeezed her shoulders. "I have an idea to cheer you up."

She pulled back to look at him, only slightly embarrassed that her eyes were wet. "Having recently participated in some of your ideas, I'm listening," she said.

He wiped the edge of her eye with his thumb. "Get your mind out of the gutter, Ms. Kemper. I wanted to propose a trip."

"But you just arrived."

Putting a finger over her lips, he drew her to the sofa and sat down with her, tucking her close to his side. "Let me get it all out before you interrupt."

Phoebe nodded. "Okay."

"You asked me earlier about my plans for Christmas, and I had pretty much decided to stay here with you and Teddy. But I did feel a twinge of sadness and guilt to be missing some things back home. This weekend is the big Cavallo Christmas party for all our employees and their families. We have it at Luc's house. I'd like you to go with me."

She opened her mouth to speak, but he shushed her.

"Hear me out," he said. "I have an older friend who retired from Cavallo ten years ago, but he likes to keep busy. So now and again when the need arises, he does jobs for me. I know he would jump at the chance to come up here and oversee your cabin renovation. I trust him implicitly. He could stay in my room if it's okay with you. What do you think?"

"So I'm allowed to speak now?" She punched his ribs.

He inclined his head. "You have my permission."

"Where would *I* stay?"

"You mean in Atlanta?"

She nodded. "Yes."

"I was hoping you'd be at my place. But I can put you up at a nice hotel if you'd rather do that."

She scooted onto his lap, facing him, her hands on his shoulders. "But what about all my decorations and the tree?"

He pursed his lips. "Well, we could replicate the ambience at my place. You *do* like decorating. But I was also thinking that maybe you and I could come back here in time for Christmas Eve. Just the two of us. I know it won't be the same without Teddy, so if that's a bad idea, you can say so."

Seventeen

Leo held his breath, awaiting her answer. The fact that she felt comfortable enough with him to be sitting as she was reassured him. Last night a noticeable dynamic between them had shifted. She felt a part of him now. In ways he couldn't quite explain.

It had killed him to know she was so hurt this morning. Yet in the midst of her pain, she had handled herself beautifully, never once letting her sister realize how much Phoebe had been counting on Christmas with her nephew. By Phoebe's own admission, this was the first time in three years she had felt like celebrating. Yet when everything seemed to be going her way, she was blindsided by disappointment and loss.

Not a tragedy or a permanent loss, but deeply hurtful nevertheless.

Phoebe ran her fingers across his scalp, both hands... messing up his hair deliberately. "Do I have to decide now?"

"You mean about Christmas Eve?"

"Yes."

"I think that can wait. But does that mean you'll go with me?"

"I suppose I'll need a fancy dress." She traced the outer edges of his ears, making him squirm restlessly.

"Definitely. Is that a problem?" Holding her like this was a torment he could do without at the moment. He heard too much activity going on outside to be confident of no interruptions. When she slid a hand inside his shirt collar, he shivered. His erection was trapped uncomfortably beneath her denim-clad butt.

"No problem at all," she said breezily, unfastening the top two buttons of his shirt. "I have a whole closet full of nice things from my gainfully employed days."

"Define nice…."

She kissed him softly, sliding her tongue into his mouth and making him crazy. "Backless," she whispered. "Not much of a front. Slit up the leg. How does that sound?"

He groaned. "Lord, have mercy." He wasn't sure if he was talking about the dress or about the way her nimble fingers were moving down his chest. "Phoebe," he said, trying to sound more reasonable and less desperate. "Was that a *yes?*"

She cupped his face in her hands, her expression suddenly sweet and intense. "Thank you, Leo. You've saved Christmas for me. As hard as it was to say goodbye to little Teddy, you're the only other male of my acquaintance who could make me want to enjoy the season. So yes. I'd love to go with you to Atlanta."

He had to talk fast, but he managed to convince her they should leave that afternoon. Already he was fantasizing about making love to her in his comfy king-size bed. Last night's spontaneous lunacy had been mind-blowing, but there was something to be said for soft sheets and a firm mattress. Not to mention the fact that he wanted to wine and dine her and show her that the big city had its own appeal.

When she finally emerged from her bedroom, he stared.

Phoebe had one large suitcase, two smaller ones and a garment bag.

He put his hands on his hips, cocking his head. "You did understand that this was a *brief* visit…right?"

She was hot and flushed and wisps of hair stood out from her head like tiny signals saying, *Don't mess with me!* Dumping the bags at his feet, she wiped her forehead with the back of her hand. "I want to be prepared for any eventuality."

He nudged the enormous bag with his toe. "The NASA astronauts weren't *this* prepared," he joked. But inside he was pleased that the sparkle was back in her eyes. "Anything else I should know about? You do know I drive a Jag."

Phoebe smiled sweetly. "We could take my van."

He shuddered theatrically. "Leo Cavallo has a reputation to uphold. No, thank you."

While Phoebe went through the cabin turning off lights and putting out fresh sheets and towels, Leo studied the phone he had ordered. No point in taking it with him. He would only need it if he came back. If. Where had that thought come from? His reservation was fixed until the middle of January with a possible two-week extension.

Simply because he and Phoebe were going to make an appearance at the Christmas party didn't mean that his doctor and Luc were going to let him off the hook. He was painfully aware that he still hadn't told Phoebe the truth. And the reasons were murky.

But one thing stood out. Vanity. He didn't want her to see him as weak or broken. It was a hell of a thing to admit. But would she think of him differently once she knew?

By the time the car was loaded and they had dropped off the keys at Buford's house, Leo was starving. In blissful disregard of the calendar date, Phoebe had packed a picnic. To eat in the car, she insisted.

Instead of the way he had come in before, Phoebe suggested another route. "If you want to, we can take the scenic route, up over the mountains to Cherokee, North Carolina, and then we'll drop south to Atlanta from there. The road was closed by a landslide for a long time, but they've reopened it."

"I'm game," he said. "At least this time it will be daylight."

Phoebe giggled, tucking her legs into the car and waiting for him to shut the door. "You were so grumpy that night."

"I thought I was never going to get here. The rain and the fog and the dark. I was lucky I didn't end up nose deep in the creek."

"It wasn't that bad."

He shook his head, refusing to argue the point. Today's drive, though, was the complete opposite of his introduction to Phoebe's home turf. Sun shone down on them, warming the temperatures nicely. The winding two-lane highway cut through the quaint town of Gatlinburg and then climbed the mountain at a gentle grade. The vistas were incredible. He'd visited here once as a child, but it had been so long ago he had forgotten how peaceful the Smokies were... and how beautiful.

The trip flew by. Part of the time they talked. At other moments, they listened to music, comparing favorite artists and arguing over the merits of country versus pop. If driving to Tennessee had initially seemed like a punishment, today was entirely the opposite. He felt unreasonably lucky and blessed to be alive.

As they neared the city, he felt his pulse pick up. This was where he belonged. He and Luc had built something here, something good. But what if the life he knew and loved wasn't right for Phoebe?

Was it too soon to wonder such a thing?

All day he had been hyperaware of her…the quick flash of her smile, her light flowery scent, the way she moved her hands when she wanted to make a point. He remained in a state of constant semi-arousal. Now that they were almost at their destination, he found himself subject to a surprising agitation.

What if Phoebe didn't like his home?

She was silent as they pulled into the parking garage beneath his downtown high-rise building and slowed to a halt beside the kiosk. "Hey, Jerome," he said, greeting the stoop-shouldered, balding man inside the booth with a smile. "This is where we get out, Phoebe." He turned back to Jerome. "Do you mind asking one of the boys to unload the car and bring up our bags?"

"Not at all, Mr. Cavallo. We'll get them right up."

Leo took Phoebe's elbow and steered her toward the elevator, where he used his special key to access and press the penthouse button. "Jerome's a retired army sergeant. He runs this place with an iron fist."

Phoebe clutched her purse, her expression inscrutable. Because the video camera in this tiny space was recording everything they said, Leo refrained from personal chitchat. He preferred to keep his private life private.

Upstairs, they stepped out into his private hallway. He generally took the recessed lighting and sophisticated decor for granted, but Phoebe looked around with interest. Once inside, he tossed his keys on a console table and held out a hand. "Would you like the tour?"

Phoebe felt like Alice in Wonderland. To go from her comfortable though modest cabin to this level of luxury was the equivalent of situational whiplash. She had realized on an intellectual level that Leo must be wealthy. Though she hadn't known him personally before he arrived on her doorstep, she was well aware of the Cavallo empire and the pricey goods it offered to high-end consumers. But somehow, she hadn't fully understood *how* rich Leo really was.

The floors of his penthouse condo, acres of them it seemed, were laid in cream-colored marble veined with gold. Expensive Oriental rugs in hues of cinnamon and deep azure bought warmth and color to what might otherwise have been too sterile a decorating scheme.

Incredible artwork graced the walls. Some of the paintings, to Phoebe's inexperience gaze, appeared to be priceless originals. Two walls of the main living area were made entirely of glass, affording an unparalleled view of Atlanta as far as the eye could see. Everything from the gold leaf–covered dome of the Capitol building to the unmistakable outline of Stone Mountain in the far distance.

A variety of formal armchairs and sofas were upholstered in either pale gold velvet or ecru leather. Crimson and navy pillows beckoned visitors to sit and relax. Overhead, a massive modern chandelier splayed light to all corners of the room.

Undoubtedly, all of the fabrics were of Italian Cavallo design. Phoebe, who had always adored vivid color and strong statements in decor, fell in love with Leo's home immediately. She turned in a circle. "I'm speechless. Should I take off my shoes?"

He stepped behind her, his hands on her shoulders. Pushing aside her hair, left loose for a change, he kissed her neck just below her ear. "It's meant to be lived in. May I say how glad I am that you're here?"

She turned to face him, wondering if she really knew him at all. At her old job, she had earned a comfortable living. But in comparison to all this, she was a pauper. How did Leo know she was not interested in him for his money? Unwilling to disclose her unsettling thoughts, she linked her arms around his neck. "Thank you for inviting me."

She tugged at his bottom lip with the pad of her thumb. "Surely there are bedrooms I should see."

His eyes darkened. "I didn't want to rush you."

Her hand brushed the front of his trousers. "I've noticed this fellow hanging around all day."

The feel of her slim fingers, even through the fabric of his pants, affected him like an electric shock. "Seems to be a permanent condition around you."

"Then I suppose it's only fair if I offer some…um…"

His grin was a wicked flash of white teeth. "While you're thinking of the appropriate word, my sweet," Leo said, scooping her into his arms, "I could show you my etchings."

She tweaked his chin. "Not in here, I presume?"

"Down the hall." He held her close to his chest, his muscular arms bearing her weight as if she were no more than a child.

Being treated like Scarlett O'Hara seemed entirely appropriate here in the Peach State. Leo's power and strength seduced her almost as much as the memory of last night's erotic play. "The sofa is closer," she whispered, noting the shadow of his stubble and the way his golden-skinned throat moved when he spoke huskily.

He nodded his head, hunger darkening his eyes. "I like the way you think." He kissed her cheek as he strode across the room.

"No one knows you're home, right?"

"Correct."

"And there's no one else on this floor?"

He shook his head, lowering her onto the soft cushions. "No."

"So I can be as loud as I like?"

He stared at her in shock as her outrageous taunt sank in. "Good God Almighty." Color crept from his throat to his hairline. "I thought you were a sweet young thing when I first met you. But apparently I was wrong."

"Never judge a book by its cover, Mr. Cavallo." She ripped her sweater off over her head. "Please tell me you have some more of those packets."

Leo seemed fixated on the sight of her lace-covered breasts, but he recovered. "Damn it." His expression leaned toward desperation.

"What's wrong?"

"All of our luggage is downstairs."

"Your bathroom. Here?"

"Well, yes, but somebody will be coming up that elevator any moment now."

"Leo…" she wailed, not willing to wait another second. "Call them back. Tell them we're in the shower."

"Both of us?" He glanced at the door and back at her, frustration a living, breathing presence between them. An impressive erection tented his slacks. "It won't be long. Fifteen minutes tops."

The way she felt at the moment, five minutes was too long. She wanted Leo. Now.

Fortunately for both of them, a quiet chime sounded, presumably a doorbell, though it sounded more like a heavenly harp. Leo headed for the entrance and stared back at her. "You planning on staying like that?"

Her jaw dropped. She was half naked and the doorknob was turning in Leo's hand. With a squeak, she clutched her sweater to her breasts and ran around the nearest wall, which happened to conceal the kitchen. Not even bothering to envy the fabulous marble countertops and fancy appliances, she listened with bated breath as Leo conversed with the bellman. At long last, she heard the door close, and the sound of footsteps.

As she hovered amidst gourmet cookware and the scent of unseen spices, Leo appeared. "He's gone." In his hand he held a stack of condoms. "Is this what you wanted?"

Eighteen

Leo had never particularly considered his kitchen to be a sexy place. In truth, he spent little time here. But with Phoebe loitering half naked, like a nymph who had lost her way, he suddenly began to see about a zillion possibilities.

He leaned a hip against the counter. "Take off the rest of your clothes." Would she follow his lead, or had he come on too strong?

When perfect white teeth mutilated her bottom lip, he couldn't decide if she was intending to drive him crazy by delaying or if she was perhaps now a bit shy. Without responding verbally, she tugged off her knee-length boots and removed her trim black slacks. The only article of clothing that remained, her tiny panties, was a perfect match to her blush-pink bra.

"The floor is cold," she complained as she kicked aside the better part of her wardrobe.

His hands clenched the edge of the counter behind him. Lord, she was a handful. And gorgeous to boot. "You're not done," he said with far more dispassion than he felt.

Phoebe thrust out her bottom lip and straightened her shoulders. "I don't know why you have to be so bossy."

"Because you like it." He could see the excitement building in her wide-eyed stare as she reached behind her back and unfastened her bra. It fell to the floor like a wispy pink cloud. Though she hesitated for a brief moment, she continued disrobing, stepping out of her small undies with all the grace of a seasoned stripper.

She twirled the panties on the end of her finger. "Come and get me."

He literally saw red. His vision hazed and he felt every molecule of moisture leach from his mouth. Quickly, with razor-sharp concentration that belied the painful ache in his groin, he assessed the possibilities. Beside the refrigerator, some genius architect had thought to install a desk that matched the rest of the kitchen. The marble top was the perfect height for what Leo had in mind.

Forget the sofa or the bedroom or any other damned part of his house. He was going to take her here.

He could barely look at Phoebe without coming apart at the seams. Young and strong and healthy, she was the epitome of womanhood. Her dark hair fell over one shoulder, partially veiling one raspberry nipple. "You're beautiful, Phoebe."

The raw sincerity in his strained voice must have told her that the time for games was over. Surprised pleasure warmed her eyes. "I'm glad you think so." She licked her lips. "Do you plan on staying over there forever?"

"I don't know," he said in all seriousness. "The way I feel at the moment, I'm afraid I'll take you like a madman."

Her lips curved. "Is that a bad thing?"

"You tell me." Galvanized at last into action by a yearning that could no longer be denied, he picked her up by the waist and sat her on the desk. Phoebe yelped when the cold surface made contact with her bottom, but she exhaled on a long, deep sigh as the sensation subsided.

He ripped at his zipper and freed his sex. He was as hard as the marble that surrounded them, but far hotter. Sheathing himself with fumbling hands, he stepped between her legs. "Prop your feet on the desk, honey."

Phoebe's cooperation was instant, though her eyes rounded when she realized what he was about to do.

He positioned himself at the opening of her moist pink sex and shoved, one strong thrust that took him all the way. He held her bottom for leverage and moved slowly in and out. Phoebe's arms linked around his neck in a stranglehold. Her feet lost their purchase and instead, she linked her ankles behind his waist.

It would be embarrassing if she realized that his legs were trembling and his heart was doing weird flips and flops that had nothing to do with his recent health event. Phoebe made him forget everything he thought was important and forced him to concentrate on the two of them. Not from any devious machinations on her part, but because she was so damned cute and fun.

Even as he moved inside her, he was already wondering where they could make love next. Heat built in his groin, a monstrous, unstoppable force. "I'm gonna come," he groaned.

She had barely made a sound. In sudden dismay, he leaned back so he could see her face. "Talk to me, Phoebe." Reaching down, he rubbed gently at the swollen nub he'd been grazing again and again with the base of his sex. When his fingers made one last pass, Phoebe arched her back and cried out as she climaxed. Inside, her body squeezed him with flutters that threatened to take off the top of his head because the feeling was so intense.

With his muscles clenched from head to toe, he held back his own release so he could relish every moment of her shuddering finale. As she slumped limp in his embrace, he cursed and thrust wildly, emptying himself until he was wrung dry. With one last forceful thrust, he finished, but as he did, his forehead met the edge of the cabinet over Phoe-be's head with enough force to make him stagger backward.

"Hell…" His reverse momentum was halted by the large island in the center of the kitchen. He leaned there, dazed.

Phoebe slid to her feet. "Oh, Leo. You're bleeding." Her face turned red, and she burst out laughing. Mortification and remorse filled her eyes in addition to concern, but she apparently couldn't control her mirth, despite the fact that he had been injured in battle.

Okay. So it *was* a little funny. His lips quirking, he put a hand to his forehead and winced when it came away streaked in red. "Would you please put some clothes on?" he said, trying not to notice the way her breasts bounced nicely when she laughed.

Phoebe rolled her eyes. "Take them off. Put them on. You're never satisfied."

He looked down at his erection that was already pre-paring for duty. "Apparently not." When she bent over to step into her underwear and pants, it was all he could do not to take her again.

Only the throbbing in his head held him back. When she was decent, he grimaced. "We're going to a party tomor-row night. How am I going to explain this?"

Phoebe took his hand and led him toward the bedrooms. "Which one is yours?" she asked. When he pointed, she kept walking, all the way to his hedonistic bathroom. "We'll put some antibiotic ointment on it between now and then. Plus, there's always makeup."

"Great. Just great."

She opened the drawer he indicated and gathered the needed supplies. "Sit on the stool."

He zipped himself back into his trousers, more to avoid temptation than from any real desire to be dressed. "Is this going to hurt?"

"Probably."

The truth was the truth. When she moistened a cotton ball with antiseptic and dabbed at the cut, it stung like fire. He glanced in the mirror. The gash, more of a deep scrape really, was about two inches long. And dead in the center of his forehead. Now, every time he saw his reflection for the next week or so, all he would remember was debauching Phoebe in his kitchen.

She smeared a line of medicated cream along the wound and tried covering it with two vertical Band-Aids. Now he looked like Frankenstein.

Their eyes met in the large mahogany-framed mirror. Phoebe put a hand over her mouth. "Sorry," she mumbled. But she was shaking all over, and he wasn't fooled. Her mirth spilled out in wet eyes and muffled giggles.

"Thank God you didn't go into nursing," he groused. He stood up and reached for a glass of water to down some ibuprofen. "Are you hungry, by any chance?" The kitchen episode had left him famished. Maybe it was the subliminal message in his surroundings.

Phoebe wiped her eyes and nodded. "That picnic food was a long time ago."

"In that case, let me show you to your room and you can do whatever you need to do to get ready. The place I want to take you is intimate, but fairly casual. You don't really have to change if you don't want to. But I'll drag your three dozen suitcases in there to be on the safe side."

Phoebe wasn't sure what to think about the opulent suite that was apparently hers for the duration of her visit. It was amazing, of course. Yards of white carpet. French country furniture in distressed white wood. A heavy cotton bedspread that had been hand embroidered with every wildflower in the world. And a bathroom that rivaled Leo's. But in truth, she had thought she would be sleeping with him.

Nevertheless, when Leo disappeared, she wasted no time

in getting ready. She took a quick shower, though she made sure to keep her hair dry. It had grown dramatically in three years, far longer than she had ever worn it. Once wet, it was a pain to dry. She brushed it quickly and bound it loosely at the back of her neck with a silver clasp.

Given Leo's description of their destination, she chose black tights and black flats topped with a flirty black skirt trimmed at the hem in three narrow layers of multicolored chiffon. With a hot-pink silk chemise and a waist-length black sweater, she looked nice, but not too over-the-top.

She had forgotten how much fun it was to dress up for a date. Fastening a silver chain around her neck, she fingered the charm that dangled from it. The letter *P* was engraved on the silver disc in fancy cursive script. Her mother's name had started with the same letter as Phoebe's. And Phoebe had decided that if her baby was a girl, she wanted to name her Polly. An old-fashioned name maybe, but one she loved.

It was hard to imagine ever being pregnant again. Would she be terrified the entire nine months? The doctor had insisted there was no reason her next pregnancy shouldn't be perfectly normal. But it would be hard, so hard, not to worry.

Pregnancy was a moot point now. There was no man in her life other than Leo. And the two of them had known each other for no time at all. Even if the relationship were serious—which it definitely was not—Leo wasn't interested in having kids. It hadn't been difficult to pick up on that.

He clearly loved his niece and nephew, and he had been great with Teddy. But he was not the kind of guy to settle for home and hearth. Running the Cavallo conglomerate required most of his devotion. He loved it. Was proud of it. And at the level of responsibility he carried, having any substantive personal life would be tricky.

His brother, Luc, seemed to have mastered the art of balance, from what Leo had said. But maybe Luc wasn't quite as single-mindedly driven as his intense brother.

When she was content with her appearance, she returned to the living room. Leo was standing in front of the expanse of glass, his hands clasped behind his back. He turned when he heard her footsteps. "That was quick."

He looked her over from head to toe. "I'll be the envy of every guy in the restaurant."

She smiled, crossing the room to him and lightly touching his forehead. "You okay?"

"A little headache, but I'll live. Are you ready?"

She nodded. "Perhaps we should stop by a pharmacy and grab some tiny Band-Aids so you don't scare children."

"Smart-ass." He put an arm around her waist and steered her toward the door.

"I'm serious."

"So am I...."

Nineteen

After a quick stop for medical supplies, they arrived at a small bistro tucked away in the heart of downtown Atlanta. The maître d' recognized Leo and escorted them to a quiet table in the corner. "Mr. Cavallo," he said. "So glad to see you are well."

An odd look flashed across Leo's face. "Thank you. Please keep our visit quiet. I hope to surprise my brother tomorrow."

"At the Christmas party, yes?" The dumpy man with the Italian accent nodded with a smile. "My nephew works in your mail room. He is looking forward to it."

"Tell him to introduce himself if he gets a chance."

Leo held Phoebe's chair as she was seated and then joined her on the opposite side of the table. He handed her a menu. "I have my favorites, but you should take a look. They make everything from scratch, and it's all pretty amazing."

After they ordered, Phoebe cocked her head and stared at him with a smile. "Does everyone in Atlanta know who you are?"

"Hardly. I'm just the guy who writes the checks."

"Modest, but suspect."

"It's true," he insisted. "I'm not a player, if that's what you're thinking."

"You don't have the traditional little black book full of names?"

"My phone is black. And a few of the contacts are women."

"That's not an answer."

"I'll plead the Fifth Amendment."

Phoebe enjoyed the dinner immensely. Leo was wearing a beautiful navy-and-gray tweed blazer with dark slacks. Even battle-scarred, he was the most impressive man in the room. Despite his size, he handled his fragile wineglass delicately, his fingers curled around the stem with care.

Thinking about Leo's light touch made Phoebe almost choke on a bite of veal. When she had drained her water glass and regained her composure, Leo grinned. "I don't know what you were thinking about, but your face is bright red."

"You're the one with the sex injury," she pointed out.

"Fair enough." His lips twitched, and his gaze promised retribution later for her refusal to explain.

On the way home, it started to rain. Phoebe loved the quiet swish of the wipers and the fuzzy glow of Christmas decorations in every window. Leo turned down a side street and parked at the curb. He stared through the windshield, his expression oddly intent, his hands clenched on the steering wheel.

"What is it?" she asked. "What's wrong?"

He glanced at her, eyes hooded. "Nothing's *wrong*. Would you mind if we go up to my office?"

She craned her neck, for the first time seeing the Cavallo name on the building directory. "Of course not." He was acting very strangely.

Leo exited the car, opened an umbrella and came around the car to help her out. Fortunately her shoes were not expensive, because her feet tripped through the edge of a puddle as they accessed the sidewalk.

She shivered while he took a set of keys from his pocket and opened the main door. The plate glass clunked shut behind them. "Over there," Leo said. Again, using his private keys, they entered a glossy-walled elevator.

Phoebe had seen dozens of movies where lovers used a quick ride to sneak a passionate kiss. Leo clearly didn't know the plot, because he leaned against the wall and studied the illuminated numbers as they went higher and higher. Cavallo occupied the top twelve floors.

When they arrived at their destination, Phoebe was not surprised to see all the trappings of an elite twenty-first-century business. A sleek reception area decorated for the season, secretarial cubicles, multiple managerial offices and, at the far end of the floor on which they entered, an imposing door with Leo's name inscribed on a brass panel.

Another key, another entry. They skirted what was obviously the domain of an executive assistant and walked through one last door.

Leo stopped so suddenly, she almost ran into his back. She had a feeling he had forgotten her presence. He moved forward slowly, stopping to run a hand along the edge of what was clearly *his* desk. The top was completely bare, the surface polished to a high sheen.

Leo turned to her suddenly, consternation on his face. "Make yourself comfortable," he said, pointing to a leather chair and ottoman near the window. "That's where I like to sit when I have paperwork to read through. I won't be long."

She did as he suggested, noting that much like his sophisticated home, his place of business, arguably the epicenter of his life, had two transparent walls. The dark, rainy night beyond the thick glass was broken up by a million pinpoints of light, markers of a city that scurried to and fro.

As she sat down and propped her feet on the ottoman,

she relaxed into the soft, expensive seat that smelled of leather and Leo's distinctive aftershave. The faint aroma made her nostalgic suddenly for the memory of curling up with him on her sofa, enjoying the Christmas tree and watching the fire.

Leo prowled, tension in the set of his shoulders. He opened drawers, shuffled papers, flicked the leaves of plants on the credenza. He seemed lost. Or at the very least confused.

Hoping to give him the semblance of privacy, she picked up a book from the small table at her elbow. It was a technical and mostly inaccessible tome about third-world economies. She read the first two paragraphs and turned up her nose. Not exactly escape reading.

Next down the pile was a news magazine. But the date was last month's, and she was familiar with most of the stories. Finally, at the bottom, was a collection of Sunday newspapers. Someone had taken great care to stack them in reverse order. Again, they were out of date, but that same someone had extracted the "Around Town" section of the most recent one and folded it to a story whose accompanying photograph she recognized instantly. It was Leo.

Reading automatically, her stomach clenched and her breathing grew choppy. No. This had to be a mistake.

She stood up, paper in her hand, and stared at him. Disbelief, distress and anger coursed through her veins in a nauseating cocktail. "You had a heart attack?"

Leo froze but turned around to face her, his shoulders stiff and his whole body tensed as if facing an enemy. "Who told you that?"

She threw the paper at him, watching it separate and rain down on the thick pile carpet with barely a sound. "It's right there," she cried, clutching her arms around her waist. Prominent Atlanta Businessman Leo Cavallo, Age 36, Suffers Heart Attack. "My God, Leo. Why didn't you tell me?"

He opened his mouth to speak, but she interrupted him with an appalled groan. "You carried wood for me. And chopped down a tree. I made you drag heavy boxes from the attic. Damn it, Leo, how could you not tell me?"

"It wasn't that big a deal." His expression was blank, but his eyes burned with an emotion she couldn't fathom.

She shivered, her mind a whirl of painful thoughts. He could have died. He could have died. He could have died. And she would never have known him. His humor. His kindness. His incredibly sexy and appealing personality. His big, perfect body.

"Trust me," she said slowly. "When a man in his thirties has a heart attack, it's a big freaking deal."

He shoved his hands into his pockets, the line of his mouth grim. "I had a very mild heart attack. A minor blockage. It's a hereditary thing. I'm extraordinarily healthy. All I have to do now is keep an eye on certain markers."

As she examined the days in the past week, things kept popping up, memories that made her feel even worse. "Your father," she whispered. "You said he had a heart attack. And that's why the boat crashed."

"Yes."

"That's it. Just *yes?* Did it ever occur to you when you were screwing me that your medical history was information I might have wanted to know? Hell, Leo, I gave you every intimate detail of my past and you couldn't be bothered to mention something as major as a heart attack?" She knew she was shouting and couldn't seem to stop. Her heart slammed in her chest.

"I've never heard you curse. I don't like it."

"Well, that's just too damn bad." She stopped short, appalled that she was yelling like a shrew. Hyperventilation threatened. "That's why you came to my cabin, isn't it? I thought maybe you'd had a bad case of the flu. Or complications from pneumonia. Or even, God forbid, a mental breakdown of some sort. But a heart attack..." Her legs gave out, and she sank back into the chair, feeling disappointed and angry and, beneath it all, so scared for him. "Why didn't you tell me, Leo? Why couldn't you trust me with the truth? Surely I deserved that much consideration."

But then it struck her. He hadn't shared the intimate details of his illness with her because she didn't matter. The bitter realization sat like a stone in her stomach. Leo had kept his secrets, because when all was said and done, Phoebe was nothing more than a vacation romance of sorts. Leo wasn't serious about any kind of a future with her. He fully planned to return to his old life and take up where he left off. As soon as his doctor gave permission.

He came to her then, sat on the ottoman and put a hand on her leg. "It wasn't something I could easily talk about, Phoebe. Try to understand that. I was a young man. One minute I was standing in a room, doing my job, and the next I couldn't breathe. Strangers were rushing me out to an ambulance. It was a hellish experience. All I wanted to do was forget."

"But you didn't want to come to the mountains."

"No. I didn't. My doctor, who happens to be a good friend, and my brother, who I consider my *best* friend, gave me no choice. I was supposed to learn how to control my stress levels."

She swallowed, wishing he wasn't touching her. The warmth of his hand threatened to dissolve the fragile hold she had on her emotions. "We had *sex,* Leo. To me, that's pretty intimate. But I can see in retrospect that I was just a piece of your convalescent plan, not dictated by your doctor friend, I'm sure. Did it even cross your mind to worry about *that?*"

He hesitated, and she knew she had hit a nerve.

She saw him swallow. He ran a hand through his hair, unintentionally betraying his agitation. "The first time I was with you…in that way, I hadn't had sex since my heart attack. And to be honest, not for several months before that. Do you want me to tell you I was scared shitless? Is that going to make you feel better?"

She knew it was the nature of men to fear weakness. And far worse was having someone witness that vulnerability. So she even understood his angry retort to some extent. But that didn't make her any less despairing. "You haven't taken any of this seriously, have you, Leo? You think you're invincible and that your exile to Tennessee was just a momentary inconvenience. Do you even want to change your ways?" Coming to the office tonight said louder than words what he was thinking.

"It's not that easy."

"Nothing important ever is," she whispered, her throat almost too tight for speech. She stood up and went to the window, blinking back tears. If he couldn't admit that he needed a life outside of work, and if he couldn't be honest with himself *or* with her, then he wasn't ready for the kind of relationship she wanted.

In that moment, she knew that any feeble hope she had nurtured for intimacy with Leo, even in the short term, was futile. "May we leave now?" she asked, her emotions at the breaking point. "I'm tired. It's been a long day."

Twenty

Leo knew he had hurt Phoebe. Badly. But for the life of him, he couldn't see a way to fix things. She disappeared into her room as soon as they got home from his office. The next day, they barely spoke. He fooled around on the internet and watched MSNBC and CNN, particularly the financial pundits.

Being in his office last night had unsettled him. The room had been cold and clinically clean, as if the last occupant had died and the desk was awaiting a new owner.

Somehow he'd thought he might get some kind of revelation about his life if he could stand where he'd once stood. As though in the very air itself he would be able to make sense of it all.

If he had gone straight home from the restaurant, he and Phoebe would no doubt have spent the night in bed dreaming up one way after another to lose themselves in pleasure.

Instead, his impulsive action had ruined everything.

He didn't blame her for being upset. But if he had it to do over again, he still wouldn't have told her about his heart attack. It wasn't the kind of news a man shared with the woman he wanted to impress.

And there it was. He wanted to impress Phoebe. With

his intellect, his entrepreneurial success, his life in general. As if by comparison she could and would see that her hermitlike retreat was not valid. That she was the one with lessons to learn.

As he remembered his brief time in Phoebe's magical mountain home, suddenly, everything clicked into focus. The reason his office had seemed sterile and empty last night was not because Leo had been gone for several weeks. The odd feelings he had experienced were a reluctant recognition of the difference between his work domain and the warm, cheerful home Phoebe had created.

In the midst of her pain and heartbreak, she hadn't become a bitter, angry woman. Instead, she had stretched her wings. She'd had the courage to step out in faith, trusting that she would find the answers she needed. Her solitude and new way of life had taught her valuable lessons about what was important. And she'd been willing to share her wisdom with Leo. But he had been too arrogant to accept that her experience could in any way shed light on his own life.

What a jackass he had been. He had lied to her by omission and all along had been patronizing about her simple existence. Instead of protecting his macho pride, he should have been begging her to help him make a new start.

He *needed* to find balance in his life. His brother, Luc, had managed that feat. Surely Leo could follow his example. And even beyond that, Leo needed Phoebe. More than he could ever have thought possible. But by his selfish actions, he had lost her. Perhaps forever. It would take every ounce of genius he possessed to win back her trust.

The magnitude of his failure was humbling. But as long as there was life, there was hope.

At his request, she consented to stay for the party. He knew she had booked a flight home for the following morning, because he had eavesdropped unashamedly at her door while she made the reservation.

When she appeared in the foyer at a quarter 'til seven that evening, his heart stopped. But this time he recognized the interruption. A lightning bolt of passion or lust or maybe nothing more complicated than need shattered his composure.

She wore a dress that many women would avoid for fear they couldn't carry it off. The fabric was red. An intense crimson that spoke for itself. And Phoebe hadn't been teasing when she described it. Cut low in the back and the front and high on the leg, it fit her as if it had been created with exactly her body in mind.

Stiletto heels in matte black leather put her almost on eye level with him. As equals.

Her hair was stunning. She had braided two tiny sections from the front and wound them at her crown. The rest cascaded in a sleek fall halfway down her back. On her right upper arm she wore a three-inch wide hammered silver band. Matching earrings dangled and caught the light.

He cleared his throat. "You look sensational."

"Thank you." Her expression was as remote as the Egyptian queen she resembled.

He had hoped tonight to strengthen the connection between them by showing her a slice of his life. His family. His employees. The way the company was built on trust and integrity. But now there was this chasm between Phoebe and him.

He hated the emotional distance, but he would use their physical attraction to fight back, to get through to her, if he had to. She had accused him of not taking his recovery seriously, but by God, he was serious now. His future hung in the balance. Everything he had worked for up until this point was rendered valueless. Without Phoebe's love and trust, he had nothing.

* * *

Fortunately his brother's home was close...on West Paces Ferry Road, an old and elegant established neighborhood for Atlanta's wealthy and powerful. But Luc and Hattie had made their home warm and welcoming amidst its elegant personality, a place where children could run and play, though little Luc Jr. was still too small for that.

Leo handed the keys of his Jag to the attendant and helped Phoebe out of the car. The college kid's eyes glazed over as he caught a glimpse of Phoebe's long, toned legs. Glaring at the boy, Leo wrapped her faux fur stole around her shoulders and ushered her toward the house.

Every tree and bush on the property had been trimmed in tiny white lights. Fragrant greenery festooned with gold bows wrapped lampposts and wrought-iron porch rails.

Phoebe paused on the steps, taking it all in. "I love this place," she said simply. "It feels like a classy Southern lady."

"Luc and Hattie will probably be at the door greeting their guests, but perhaps we can sit down with them later and catch up." The timing was off. Phoebe was leaving in the morning, and their relationship was dead in the water, but he still wanted her to meet his brother.

As it turned out, Leo was correct. His dashing brother took one look at Leo and wrestled him into a long bear hug that brought tears to Phoebe's eyes. Leo's sister-in-law wore the very same expression as she watched the two men embrace. Both brothers wore classic formal attire, and in their tuxes, they were incredibly dashing, almost like old film stars with their chiseled features.

Luc shook Phoebe's hand as they were introduced. "I wasn't sure Leo was going to come back for the holidays, or even if he should. I'm happy to see he has such a lovely woman looking after him."

Leo's jaw tightened, though his smile remained. "Phoebe's my date, not my nurse."

Phoebe saw from Luc's abashed expression that he knew he had stepped in it. Hattie whispered something in his ear, and he nodded.

Other people crowded in behind them, but Leo lingered for a moment longer. "Can we see the kids?"

Hattie touched his cheek, her smile warm and affectionate. "We have them asleep upstairs with a sitter, but you're welcome to take a peek." She smiled at Phoebe. "Leo dotes on our babies. Lord help us when he has some of his own. I've never known a man with a softer heart."

"Hey," Luc said, looking indignant. "I'm standing right here."

Hattie kissed his cheek. "Don't worry, sweetheart. I'll always love you best."

On the cloud of laughter that followed, Leo and Phoebe moved into the thick of the party. It was soon clear to her that Leo Cavallo was popular and beloved. Despite his reputation as a hard-hitting negotiator in the boardroom, everyone under Luc's roof treated Leo not only with respect, but with genuine caring and concern.

After an hour, though, she sensed that his patience was wearing thin. Perhaps he hadn't anticipated the many questions about his recovery. At any rate, she recognized his growing tension. She hated the unmistakable awkwardness between them as the evening progressed, but despite her hurt, she couldn't stop wanting to help him. Even if he couldn't be hers, she wanted him to be happy.

In a lull between conversations, she touched his arm. "Do you want to go upstairs and see your niece and nephew?"

He nodded, relief in his harried gaze.

Luc and Hattie's home was far different than Leo's, but spectacular in its own right. Phoebe experienced a frisson of envy for the couple who had created such a warm and nurturing family environment. The little girl's room was done in peach and cream with Disney fairies. The baby boy's nursery sported a delightful zoo animal theme.

Leo stroked his nephew's back and spoke to him softly, but he stayed the longest in Deedee's room. His eyes were somber as he watched the toddler sleep. "She's not their biological child, you know. When Hattie's sister died, Hattie took her baby to raise, and then after the wedding, Luc and Hattie adopted her."

"Has your brother been married long?"

"Less than two years. He and Hattie were pretty serious back in college. The relationship didn't work out, but they were lucky enough to find their way back to each other."

Phoebe stared at Leo's bent head as he sat carefully on the corner of the bed and touched his niece's hand. He took her tiny fingers in his and brought them to his lips. It would have been clear to a blind man that Leo was capable of great love and caring. He felt about these two little ones the way Phoebe did about Teddy.

He turned his head suddenly and caught her watching him, probably with her heart in her eyes. "Will you take a walk with me?" he asked gravely.

"Of course."

Tiny flurries of snow danced around them when they exited the back of the house. Leo had retrieved her wrap, but even so, the night was brisk. In the center of the upper terrace a large, tiled fire pit blazed with vigor, casting a small circle of warmth. Other than the old man adding logs now and again, Leo and Phoebe were alone. Apparently no one else was eager to brave the cold.

A wave of sadness, deep and poignant, washed over Phoebe. If only she and Leo had met under other circumstances. No pain and heartache in her past. No devastating illness in his. Just two people sharing a riveting attraction.

They could have enjoyed a sexual relationship that might have grown into something more.

Now, they stood apart, when only twenty-four hours ago, give or take, Leo had been turning her world upside down with his lovemaking. Their recent fight echoed in her mind. She had accused Leo of not wanting to change, but wasn't she just as cowardly? She had gone from one extreme to the other. Workaholic to hermit. Such a radical swing couldn't be considered balance at all.

In the faces of the crowd tonight, she saw more than the bonhomie of the season. She saw a kinship, a trust that came from working side by side. That was what she had given up, and she realized that she missed it. She missed all of it. The hard challenges, the silly celebrations, the satisfaction of a job well done.

So lost in her thoughts was she, that she jumped when Leo took her by the shoulders and turned her to face him. Again, as at her cabin, firelight painted his features. His eyes were dark, unfathomable. "I have a proposition for you, Phoebe, so hear me out before you say anything."

Her hands tightened on her wrap. "Very well." A tiny piece of gravel had found its way into her shoe. And she couldn't feel her toes. But not even a blizzard could have made her walk away.

He released her as though he couldn't speak freely when they were touching. She thought she understood. Passion had flared so hot and so quickly between them when they first met, its veracity was suspect given the length of their acquaintance.

"First of all," he said quietly, "I'm sorry I didn't tell you about the heart attack. It was an ego thing. I didn't want you to think less of me."

"But I…" She bit her lip and stopped, determined to listen as he had requested.

He ran a hand across the back of his neck. "I was angry

and bitter and confused when I met you. I'd spent a week at the hospital, a week here at Luc's, and then to top it all, they exiled me to Tennessee."

"Tennessee is a very nice state," she felt bound to point out.

A tiny smile flickered across his lips. "It's a lovely state, but that's not the point. I looked at you and saw a desirable woman. You had your hang-ups. We all do. But I didn't want you to look too closely at mine. I wanted you to see me as a strong, capable man."

"And I did."

"But you have to admit the truth, Phoebe. Last night in my office. You stared at me and saw something else." The defeat in his voice made her ill with regret.

"You don't understand," she said, willing him to hear her with an open mind. "I was upset, yes. It terrified me that you had been in such a dangerous situation. And I was angry that you didn't trust me enough to share that with me. But it never changed the way I saw you. If you felt that, then you were wrong."

He paced in silence for several long minutes. She wondered if he believed her. Finally, he stopped and lifted a hand to bat away the snowflakes that were increasing in size and frequency. "We jumped too far ahead," he said. "I want to say things to you that are too soon, too serious."

Her heart sank, because she knew he was right. "So that's it?" she asked bleakly. "We just chalk this up to bad timing and walk away?"

"Is that what you want?" He stood there…proud, tall and so alone her heart broke for him.

"No. That's not what I want at all," she said, daring to be honest with so much at stake. "So if you have a plan, I'm listening."

He exhaled noisily as if he'd been holding his breath. "Well, okay, then. Here it is. I propose that we go back to your place and spend Christmas Eve together when it rolls around. I'll stay with you for the remainder of the time I have reserved and work on learning how not to obsess about business."

"Is that even possible?" She said it with a grin so he would know she was teasing. Mostly.

"God, I hope so. Because I want you in my life, Phoebe. And you deserve a man who will not only make a place for you, but will put you front and center."

One hot tear rolled down her cheek. "Is there more?"

"Yes. And this is the scary part. At the end of January, assuming we haven't killed each other or bored each other to death, I want you to come back to Atlanta and move in with me...as my fiancée. Not now," he said quickly. "As of this moment, we are simply a man and a woman who are attracted to each other."

"Very attracted," Phoebe agreed, her heart lifting to float with the snowflakes.

She took a step in his direction, but he held up a hand. "Not yet. Let me finish."

His utter seriousness and heartfelt sincerity gave her hope that what had begun as a serendipitous fling might actually have substance and a solid foundation. Cautious elation fluttered inside her chest. But she kept her cool... barely. "Go on."

"I'm not criticizing you, Phoebe, but you have to admit— you have issues with balance, too. Work is valid and important. But when you left Charlotte, you cut off that part of yourself."

She grimaced, feeling shame for the holier-than-thou way she had judged his life. "You're right. I did. But I'm not sure how to step back in the opposite direction."

A tiny smile lifted the corners of his mouth. "When we get back to Atlanta, I want you to work for Cavallo. I could use someone with your experience and financial instincts.

Not only that, but it would make me very happy for us to share that aspect of who we are. I understand why you ran away to the mountains. I do. And I strongly suspect that knowing each of us, we'll need your cabin as an escape when work threatens to become all-encompassing."

Anxiety dampened her burgeoning joy. "I'm afraid, Leo. I messed things up so badly before."

He shook his head. "You had a man who didn't deserve you and you lost your baby, a miscarriage that was one of those inexplicable tragedies of life. But it's time to live again, Phoebe. I want that for both of us. It's not wrong to have a passion for work. But we can keep each other grounded. And I think together we can find that balance and peace that are so important." He paused. "There's one more thing."

She was shaking more on the inside than she was on the outside. Leo was so confident, so sure. Could she take another chance at happiness? "What is it?" she asked.

At last, he took her in his arms, warming her with his big, solid frame. He cupped her cheeks in his hands, his gaze hot and sweet. "I want to make babies with you, Phoebe. I thought my life was great the way it was. But then I had the heart attack, and I met you, and suddenly I was questioning everything I had ever known about myself. Watching you with Teddy did something to me. And now tonight, with Luc and Hattie's babies upstairs asleep, I see it all clearly. You and I, Phoebe, against all odds…we have a shot at the brass ring. Having the whole enchilada. I think you were wrong about that, my love. I think with the right person, life can be just about perfect."

He bent his head and took her mouth in a soft, firm kiss that was equal parts romance and knee-weakening passion. "Will you be my almost-fiancée?" he whispered, his voice hoarse and ragged. His hands slid down the silky fabric of her dress all the way to her hips. Dragging her closer still, he buried his face in her neck. She could feel him trembling.

Emotions tumbled in her heart with all the random patterns of the snowflakes. She had grieved for so long, too long in fact. Cowardice and the fear of being hurt again had constrained her equally as much as Leo's workaholic ways had hemmed him in.

The old man tending the fire had gone inside, probably to get warm. Phoebe gasped when Leo used the slit in her skirt to his advantage, placing a warm palm on her upper thigh. His fingers skated perilously close to the place where her body ached for him.

Teasing her with outrageous caresses, he nibbled her ear, her neck, the partially exposed line of her collarbone. "I need an answer, my love. Please."

Heat flooded her veins, negating the winter chill. Her body felt alive, spectacularly alive. Leo held her tightly, as if he were afraid she might run. But that was ludicrous, because there was no place she would rather be.

She gave herself a moment to say goodbye to the little child she would never know. So many hopes and dreams she had cherished had been ripped away. But the mountains had taught her much about peace, and in surviving, she had been given another chance. A wonderful, exciting, heart-pounding second chance.

Laying her cheek against Leo's crisp white shirt, feeling the steady beat of his wonderfully big heart, she nodded. "Yes, Leo Cavallo. I believe I will."

Epilogue

Leo paced the marble floor, his palms damp. "Hurry, Phoebe. They'll be here in a minute." He was nervous about his surprise, and if Phoebe lollygagged too much longer, it would be ruined. He gazed around his familiar home, noting the addition this year of a gigantic Christmas tree, its branches heavy with ornaments. In the chandelier overhead, tiny clumps of mistletoe dangled, tied with narrow red velvet ribbons.

His body tightened and his breath quickened as he recalled the manner in which he and Phoebe had christened that mistletoe, making love on the rug beneath. In truth, they had christened most of his condo in such a way. Including a repeat of what he liked to call "the kitchen episode."

He tugged at his bow tie, feeling much too hot all of a sudden.

At long last, his beloved wife appeared, her usual feminine stride hampered by a certain waddling movement. She grimaced. "This red dress makes me look like a giant tomato."

He pulled her in close for a kiss, running his hand over the fascinating swell of her large abdomen. "Red is my new favorite color. And besides, it's Christmas." Feeling the life growing inside his precious Phoebe tightened his throat and wet his eyes. So many miracles in his life. So much love.

She returned the kiss with passion. The force that drew them together in the beginning had never faded. In fact, it grew deeper and more fiery with each passing month.

This evening, though, they were headed for a night out on the town with Luc and Hattie. Dinner, followed by a performance of *The Nutcracker*.

Phoebe rubbed her back. "I hope I'm going to fit into a seat at the theater."

He grinned broadly. "Quit fishing for compliments. You know you're the sexiest pregnant woman in the entire state. But sit down, my love. I have something I want to give you before they get here."

Phoebe eased into a comfy armchair with a grimace. "It's five days 'til Christmas."

"This is an *early* present."

From his jacket pocket he extracted a ruby velvet rectangle. Flipping it open, he handed it to her. "I had it made especially for you."

Phoebe took the box from him and stared. Inside, nestled on a bed of black satin, was an exquisite necklace. Two dozen or more tiny diamond snowflakes glittered with fire on a delicate platinum chain. She couldn't speak for the emotion that threatened to swamp her with hormonal tears.

Leo went down on one knee beside her, removed the jewelry from the box and gently fastened it around her neck.

She put a hand to her throat, staring at his masculine beauty, feeling the tangible evidence of his boundless, generous love. "Thank you, Leo. It's perfect."

He wrapped a hand in her hair and fingered it. "I could have waited until our anniversary. But tonight is special to me. It was exactly a year ago that you stood in the snow and gave me a new life. A wonderful life."

Running one hand through his hair, she cupped his neck with the other and pulled him back for another kiss. "Are you channeling Jimmy Stewart now?" she teased, her heart full to bursting.

He laid a hand on her round belly, laughing softly when their son made an all too visible kick. "Not at all, my dear Phoebe. I'm merely counting my blessings. And I always count you twice."

* * * * *

ONE NIGHT, SECOND CHANCE

ROBYN GRADY

This book is dedicated to Holly Brooke.
I'm so very proud of you, baby.
Aim for the stars!

Robyn Grady's books feature regularly on best-sellers lists and at award ceremonies, including the National Readers Choice Awards, the Booksellers Best Awards, Cataromance Reviewers Choice Awards and Australia's prestigious Romantic Book of the Year.

Robyn lives on Australia's gorgeous Sunshine Coast where she met and married her real-life hero. When she's not tapping out her next story, she enjoys the challenges of raising three very different daughters, going to the theatre, reading on the beach and dreaming about bumping into Stephen King during a month-long Mediterranean cruise.

Robyn knows that writing romance is the best job on the planet and she loves to hear from her readers! You can keep up with news on her latest releases at www.robyngrady.com.

Prologue

Turning her back on the wall-to-wall mirror, Grace Munroe unzipped and stepped out of her dress. She slipped off her heels—matching bra and briefs, too—before wrapping herself in a soft, scented towel. But when she reached the bathroom door, a chill rippled through her, pulling her up with a start.

She sucked down a breath—tried to get enough air.

I'm an adult. I want this.

So relax.

Let it go.

A moment later, she entered a room that was awash with the glow from a tall corner lamp. She crossed to the bed, drew back the covers and let the towel drop to her feet. She was slipping between the sheets when a silhouette filled the doorway and a different sensation took hold. She hadn't been in this kind of situation before—and never would be again. But right now, how she wanted this.

How she wanted *him*.

Moving forward, he shucked off his shirt, undid his belt. When he curled over her, the tip of his tongue rimmed one nipple and her senses flew into a spin.

His stubble grazed her as he murmured, "I'd like to know your name."

She didn't wince—only smiled.

"And I'd like us under this sheet."

This evening had begun with a walk to clear her thoughts; since returning to New York, she'd been plagued by memories and regrets.

Passing a piano bar, she was drawn by the strains of a baby grand and wandered in to take a seat. A man stopped beside her. Distinctly handsome, he filled out his tailored jacket in a way that turned women's heads. Still, Grace was ready to flick him off. She hadn't wanted company tonight.

To her surprise, he only shared an interesting detail about the tune being played before sipping his drink and moving on. But something curious about his smile left its mark on her. She felt a shift beneath her ribs—a pleasant tug—and her thinking did a one-eighty.

Calling him back, she asked if he'd like to join her. Ten minutes. She wasn't staying long. Slanting his head, he began to introduce himself, but quickly she held up a hand; if it was all the same to him, she'd rather not get into each other's stories. Each other's lives. She saw a faint line form between his brows before he agreed with a salute of his glass.

For twenty minutes or so, they each lost themselves in the piano man's music. At the end of the break, when she roused herself and bid him good-night, her stranger said he ought to leave, too. It seemed natural for them to walk together, discussing songs and sports, and then food and the theater. He was so easy to talk to and laugh with... There was almost something familiar about his smile, his voice. Then they were passing his building and, as if they'd known each other for years, he asked if she'd like to come up. Grace didn't feel obliged. Nor did she feel uncertain.

Now, in this bedroom with his mouth finding hers, she wasn't sorry, either. But this experience was so far from her norm. Was it progress or simply escape?

A year ago, she'd been in a relationship. Sam was a decorated firefighter who respected his parents—valued the community. Nothing was too much for his family or friends. He had loved her deeply and, one night, had proposed. Twelve months on, a big part of Grace still felt stuck in that time.

But not right now. Not one bit.

As her stranger's tongue pushed past her lips, the slow-working rhythm fed a hunger that stretched and yawned up inside of her. When he broke the kiss, rather than wane, the steady beating at her core only grew. She was attracted to this man in a way she couldn't explain—physically, intellectually...and on a different level, too. She would have liked to see him again. Unfortunately, that wasn't possible. This was all about impulse, sexual attraction—a fusion of combustible forces.

A one-night stand.

And that's how it needed to stay.

One

"Beautiful, isn't she?"

Wynn Hunter gave the older man standing beside him a wry grin. "Hate to tell you, but that bridesmaid's a little young for you."

"I would hope so." Brock Munroe's proud shoulders shucked back. "She's my daughter."

Wynn froze; his scalp tingled. Then he remembered to breathe. As his mind wheeled to fit all the pieces together, he swallowed and then pushed out the words. Brock had three daughters. Now it struck Wynn which one this was.

"That's *Grace*?"

"All grown up."

Brock didn't need to know just *how* grown up.

Had Wynn suspected the connection three nights ago, he would never have taken her back to his Upper East Side apartment—not so much out of respect for Brock, who was a friend of his father, Australian media mogul and head of Hunter Enterprises Guthrie Hunter, but because Wynn had despised Grace Munroe when they were kids. She'd made his blood boil. His teeth grind.

How could he have enjoyed the single best evening of sex in his life with that girl—er, woman?

"Grace gets her looks from her mother, like the other two," Brock went on as music and slow-spinning lights drifted around the Park Avenue ballroom, which was decked out for tonight's wedding reception. "Remember the vacation we all spent together? That Colorado Christmas sure was a special one."

Brock had met Guthrie as a Sydney University graduate vacationing at the newly opened Vail Resort. Over the years, they'd kept in touch. When the Munroes and Hunters had got together two decades later, Wynn had turned eight. Whenever he and his older brothers had built a snowman outside of the chalet the two families had shared, Grace and Wynn's younger sister Teagan had conspired to demolish it. Back then, Wynn's angel of a mother had still been alive. She'd explained that the six-year-olds had simply wanted to join in. Be included.

Now Wynn ran Hunter Publishing, the New York-based branch of Hunter Enterprises. Until recently, he had always prided himself on being an affable type. But that Christmas day, when Grace had tripped him up then doubled over with laughter as his forehead had smacked the snow—and the rock hidden underneath—he'd snapped. While she'd scurried inside, pigtails flying, Wynn's brother Cole had struggled to hold him back.

So many years had passed since then and yet, in all his life, Wynn doubted anyone had riled him more than that pug-nosed little brat.

But since then, her mousey pigtails had transformed into a shimmering wheat-gold fall. And her lolly-legs in kiddies' jeans had matured into smooth, endless limbs. He recalled that pest from long ago who had relentlessly poked and teased, and then remembered his mouth working over hers that amazing night they'd made love. When they'd struck up a conversation at that Upper East Side piano bar, Grace couldn't possibly have known who he was.

Could she?

"How's your father and that situation back in Australia?" Brock asked as Grace continued to dance with her partnered groomsman and other couples filled the floor. "We spoke a couple of months back. All that business about someone trying to kill him? Unbelievable." Brock crossed his tuxedo-clad arms and shook his head. "Are the authorities any closer to tracking down the lowlife responsible?"

With half an eye on Grace's hypnotic behind as she swayed around in that sexy red cocktail number, Wynn relayed some details.

"A couple of weeks after my father's vehicle was run off the road, someone tried to shoot him. Thankfully the gunman missed. When Dad's bodyguard chased him on foot, the guy ran out in front of a car. Didn't survive."

"But wasn't there another incident not long after that?"

"My father was assaulted again, yes." Remembering the phone call he'd received from a livid Cole, Wynn's chest tightened. "The police are on the case but my brother also hired a P.I. friend to help."

Brandon Powell and Cole went back to navy-cadet days. Now Brandon spent his time cruising around Sydney on a Harley and running his private-investigation and security agency. He was instinctive, thorough and, everyone agreed, the right man for the job.

As one song segued into another, the music tempo increased and the lights dimmed more. On the dance floor, Grace Munroe was limbering up. Her moves weren't provocative in the strictest sense of the word. Still, the way she arranged her arms and bumped those hips... Well, hell, she stood out. And Wynn saw that he wasn't alone in that impression; her first dance partner had been replaced by a guy who could barely keep his hands to himself.

Wynn downed the rest of his drink.

Wynn didn't think Grace had noticed him yet among the three hundred guests. Now that he was aware of their shared background, there was less than no reason to hang around until she did. It was way too uncomfortable.

Wynn gestured toward the exit and made his excuse to Brock "Better get going. Early meeting tomorrow."

The older man sucked his cheeks in. "On a Sunday? Then again, you must be run off your feet since Hunter Publishing acquired La Trobes two years ago. Huge distribution."

Brock was being kind. "We've also shut down four publications in as many years." As well as reducing leases on foreign and national bureaus.

"These are difficult times." Brock grunted. "Adapt or die. God knows, advertising's in the toilet, too."

Brock was the founding chairman of Munroe Select Advertising, a company with offices in Florida, California and New York. Whether members of the Munroe family helped run the firm, Wynn couldn't say. The night he and Grace had got together, they hadn't exchanged personal information...no phone numbers, employment details. Obviously no names. Now curiosity niggled and Wynn asked.

"Does Grace work for your company?"

"I'll let her tell you. She's on her way over."

Wynn's attention shot back to the floor. When Grace recognized him, her smile vanished. But she didn't turn tail and run. Instead, she carefully pressed back her bare shoulders and, tacking up a grin, continued over, weaving her way through the partying crowd.

A moment later, she placed a dainty hand on Brock's sleeve and craned to brush a kiss on his cheek. Then she turned her attention toward Wynn. With her head at an angle, her wheat-gold hair cascaded to one side. Wynn recalled the feel of that hair beneath his fingers. The firm slide of his skin over hers.

"I see you've found a friend," she said loud enough to be heard over the music.

Brock gave a cryptic smile. "You've met before."

Her focus on Wynn now, Grace's let's-keep-a-secret mask held up. "Really?"

"This is Wynn," her father said. "Guthrie Hunter's third boy."

Her entrancing eyes—a similar hue to her hair—blinked twice.

"Wynn?" she croaked. "Wynn *Hunter*?"

"We were reminiscing," Brock said, setting his empty champagne flute on a passing waiter's tray. "Remembering the time we all spent Christmas together in Colorado."

"That was a long time ago." Gathering herself, Grace pegged out one shapely leg and arched a teasing brow. "I don't suppose you build snowmen anymore?"

Wynn deadpanned. "Way too dangerous."

"Dangerous…" Her puzzled look cleared up after a moment. "Oh, I remember. You were out in the yard with your brothers that Christmas morning. You hit your head."

He rubbed the ridge near his temple. "Never did thank you for the scar."

"Why would you do that?"

Seriously?

"You tripped me."

"The way I recall it, you fell over your laces. You were always doing that."

When Wynn opened his mouth to disagree—six-year-old Grace had stuck out her boot, plain and simple—Brock stepped in.

"Grace has been friends with the bride since grade school," the older man offered.

"Jason and I were at university together in Sydney," Wynn replied, still wanting to set straight that other point.

"Linley and Jason have been a couple for three years," Grace said. "I've never heard either one mention you."

"We lost touch." Wynn added, "I didn't expect an invitation."

"Seems the world is full of surprises."

While Wynn held Grace's wry look, Brock picked up a less complicated thread.

"Wynn runs the print arm of Hunter Enterprises here in New York now." He asked Wynn, "Is Cole still in charge of your broadcasting wing in Australia?"

Wynn nodded. "Although he stepped back a bit. He's getting married."

"Cole was always so committed to the company. A workaholic, like his dad." Brock chuckled fondly. "Glad he's settling down. Just goes to show—there's someone for everyone."

It seemed that before he could catch himself, Brock slid a hesitant look his daughter's way. Grace's gaze immediately dropped. He made a point of evaluating the room before sending a friendly salute over to a circle of friends nearby.

"I see the Dilshans. Should go catch up." Brock kissed his daughter's cheek. "I'll leave you two to get reacquainted."

As Brock left, Wynn decided to let them both off the hook. As much as this meeting was awkward, their interactions three nights ago had felt remarkably right. Details of that time had also been private and, as far as he was concerned, would remain that way.

"Don't worry," he said, tipping a fraction closer. "I won't let on that you and I were already reintroduced."

She looked amused. "I didn't think you'd blurt out the fact that we picked each other up at a bar."

She really didn't pull any punches.

"Still don't want to get into each other's stories?" he asked.

"As it turns out, we already know each other, remember?"

"I didn't mean twenty years ago. I'm talking about now."

Her grin froze before she lifted her chin and replied. "Probably best that we don't."

He remembered her father's comment about there being a person for everyone and Grace's reaction. He recalled how she'd wanted to keep their conversation superficial that night. His bet? Grace Munroe had secrets.

None of his business. Hell, he had enough crap of his own going down in his life. Still, before they parted again, he was determined to clear something up.

"Tell me one thing," he said. "Did you have any idea who I was that night?"

She laughed. "There, see? You *do* have a sense of humor."

As she turned away, he reached and caught her wrist. An electric bolt shot up his arm as her hair flared out and her focus snapped back around. She almost looked frightened. Not his intention at all.

"Dance with me," he said.

Those honeyed eyes widened before she tilted her chin again. "I don't think so."

"You don't want the chance to trip me up again?"

She grinned. "Admit it. You were a clumsy kid."

"You were a brat."

"Be careful." She eyed the fingers circling her wrist. "You'll catch girl germs."

"I'm immune."

"Don't be so sure."

"Trust me. I'm sure."

He shepherded her toward the dance floor. A moment later, when he took her in his arms, Wynn had to admit that though he'd never liked little Gracie Munroe, he sure approved of the way this older version fit so well against him. Surrounded by other couples, he studied her exquisite but indolent face before pressing his palm firmly against the small of her back.

Dancing her around in a tight, intimate circle, he asked, "How you holding up?"

"Not nauseous…yet."

"No driving desire to curl your ankle around the back of mine and push?"

"I'll keep you informed."

He surrendered a grin. He just bet she would.

"Where's your mother tonight?"

Her cheeky smile faded. "Staying with my grandmother. She hasn't been well."

"Nothing serious, I hope."

"Pining. My grandfather passed away not long ago. He was Nan's rock." Her look softened more. "I remember my parents going to your mother's funeral a few years back."

His stomach gave a kick. Even now, memories of his father failing due to lack of sleep from his immeasurable loss left a lump in Wynn's throat the size of an egg. The word *saint* had been tailor-made for his mom. She would never be forgotten. Would always be missed.

But life had gone on.

"My father married again."

She nodded, and he remembered her parents had attended the wedding. "Is he happy?"

"I suppose."

A frown pinched her brow as she searched his eyes. "You're not convinced."

"My stepmother was one of my mother's best friend's daughters."

"Wow. Sounds complicated."

That was one way to put it.

Cole and Dex, Guthrie's second-oldest son, had labeled their father's second wife a gold digger, and worse. Wynn's motto had always been Right Is Right. But not everything about Eloise Hunter was black or white. Eloise was, after all, his youngest brother Tate's mom. With his father's stalker still on the loose, little Tate didn't need one ounce more trouble in his life, particularly not nasty gossip concerning one of his parents running around.

Out of all his siblings, Wynn loved Tate the best. There was a time when he'd imagined having a kid just like him one day.

Not anymore.

Wynn felt a tap on his shoulder. A shorter man stood waiting, straightening his bow tie, wearing a stupid grin.

"Mind if I cut in?" the man asked.

Wynn gave a curt smile. "Yeah, I do."

With pinpricks of light falling over the dance floor in slow motion, Grace tsked as he moved them along. "That wasn't polite."

Wynn only smiled.

"He's a friend," she explained.

What could he say? *Too bad*.

She looked at him more closely. "I'm confused. From what I've heard, Cole was the workaholic, Dex, the playboy. Aren't you supposed to be the Hunter brother with a conscience?"

"I grew up."

"Hardened up."

"And yet you're captivated by my charm."

Her lips twitched. "I wouldn't say that."

"So I dreamed that you came home with me three nights ago?"

She didn't blush. Not even close.

"I was feeling self-indulgent. Guess we connected."

"In case you hadn't noticed," his head angled closer, "we still do."

Her hand on his shoulder tightened even as she averted her gaze. "I've never been in that kind of situation before."

He admitted, "Neither have I."

"I can't regret the other night." She let out a breath. "But, I'm not interested in pursuing anything…rekindling any flames. It's not a good time."

He felt his smile waver before firming back up.

"I don't recall asking."

"So, that hand sliding toward my behind, pressing me in against the ridge in your pants… I kind of took that as a hint." Her smile was thin. "I'm not after a relationship, Wynn. Not right now. Not of any kind."

He'd asked her to dance to prove, well, something. Now he wasn't sure what. Three nights ago, he'd been attracted by her looks. Intrigued by her wit. Drawn by her touch. Frankly, she was right. The way he felt this minute wasn't a whole lot different from that.

However, Grace Munroe had made her wishes known. On a less primal level, he agreed. At the edge of the dance floor, he released her and stepped away.

"I'll let you get back to your party."

A look—was it respect?—faded up in her eyes. "Say hi to Teagan and your brothers for me."

"Will do."

Although these days the siblings rarely saw each other. But Cole was set to tie the knot soon with Australian television producer Taryn Quinn, which meant a family gathering complete with wily stepmother, stalked father and, inevitably, questions surrounding the altered state of Wynn's own personal life.

Until recently, he—not Cole or Dex—had been the brother destined for marriage. Of course, that was before the former love of his life, Heather Matthews, had informed the world that actually, she'd made other plans. When the bomb had hit, he'd slogged through the devastated stage, the angry phase. Now, he was comfortable just cruising along. So comfortable, in fact, he had no desire to ever lay open his heart to anyone again for any reason, sexy Grace Munroe included.

Wynn found the bride and groom, did the right thing and wished them nothing but happiness. On his way out of the room, which was thumping with music now, he bumped into Brock again. Wynn had a feeling it wasn't by accident.

"I see you shared a dance with my daughter," Brock said.

"For old time's sake."

"She might have told you…Grace left New York twelve months ago. She's staying on in Manhattan for a few days, getting together with friends." He mentioned the name of the prestigious hotel. "If you wanted to call in, see how she's doing… Well, I'd appreciate it. Might help keep some bad memories at bay." Brock lowered his voice. "She lost someone close to her recently."

"She mentioned her grandfather—"

"This was a person around her age." The older man's mouth twisted. "He was a firefighter. A good man. They were set to announce their engagement before the accident."

The floor tilted beneath Wynn's feet. Concentrating, he rubbed his temple—that scar.

"Grace was engaged?"

"As good as. The accident happened a year ago last week here in New York."

Wynn had believed Grace when she'd said that their night was a one-off—that she'd never gone home with a man before on a whim. Now the pieces fit. On that unfortunate anniversary, Grace had drowned out those memories by losing herself in Wynn's company. He wasn't upset by her actions; he understood them better than most. Hadn't he found solace—oblivion—in someone else's arms, too?

"She puts on a brave face." Brock threw a weary glance around the room. "But being here at one of her best friends' weddings, in front of so many others who know... She should have been married herself by now." Brock squared his heavy shoulders. "No one likes to be pitied. No one wants to be alone."

Brock wished Wynn the best with his make-believe meeting in the morning. Wynn was almost at the door when the music stopped and the DJ announced, "Calling all eligible ladies. Gather round. The bride is ready to throw her bouquet!"

Wynn cast a final glance back. He was interested to see that Grace hadn't positioned herself for the toss; she stood apart and well back from the rest.

A drumroll echoed out through the sound system. In her fluffy white gown, the beaming bride spun around. With an arm that belonged in the majors, she lobbed the weighty bunch well over her head. A collective gasp went up as the bouquet hurtled through the air, high over the outstretched arms of the nearest hopefuls. Over outliers' arms, as well. It kept flying and flying.

Straight toward Grace.

As the bouquet dropped from the ceiling, Grace realized at the last moment that she was in the direct line of fire. Rather than catch it, however, she stepped aside and petals smacked the polished floor near her feet. Then, as if wrenched by an invisible cord, the bouquet continued to slide. It stopped dead an inch from Wynn's shoes. The room stilled before all eyes shot from the flowers to Grace.

The romantically minded might have seen this curious event as an omen. Might have thought that the trajectory of the bouquet as it slid along the floor from Grace to Wynn meant they ought to get together. Only most guests here would know. Grace didn't want a fiancé.

She was still grieving the one she had lost.

As he and Grace stared at each other, anticipation vibrated off the walls and Wynn felt a stubborn something creak deep inside him. An awareness that had lain frozen and unfeeling these past months thawed a degree, and then a single icicle snapped and fell away from his soul.

Hunkering down, he collected the flowers. With their audience hushed and waiting, he headed back to Grace.

When he stopped less than an arm's distance away, he inspected the flowers—red and white roses with iridescent fern in between. But he didn't hand over the bouquet. Rather, he circled his arm around Grace's back and, in front of the spellbound crowd, slowly—deliberately—lowered his head over hers.

Two

As he drew her near, two things flashed through Grace's mind.

What in God's name is Wynn Hunter doing?

The other thought evaporated into a deep, drugging haze when the remembered heat of his mouth captured hers. At the same instant her limbs turned to rubber, her fingertips automatically wound into his lapels. Her toes curled and her core contracted, squeezing around a kernel of mindless want.

This man's kiss was spun from dreams. The hot, strong feel of him, the taste…his scent…

From the time she'd left his suite that night, she had wondered. The hours she'd spent in his bed had seemed so magical, perhaps she'd only dreamed them up. But this moment was real, and now she only wanted to experience it all again—his lips drifting over her breasts, his hands stroking, hips rocking.

When his lips gradually left hers, the burning feel of

him remained. With her eyes closed, she focused on the
hard press of his chest against her bodice…her need to
have him kiss her again. Then, from the depths of her kiss-
induced fog, Grace heard a collective sigh go up in the
room. With her head still whirling, she dragged open heavy
eyes. Wynn's face was slanted over hers. He was smiling
softly.

In a matter of seconds, he had made her forget about
everything other than this. But the encounter three nights
ago had been a mutually agreed upon, ultraprivate affair.
This scene had been played out in front of an audience.
Friends, and friends of friends, who knew what had happened last year.

Or thought that they knew.

Grace kept her unsteady voice hushed. "What are you
doing?"

"Saying goodbye properly." With his arm still a strong
band around her, he took a step back. "Are you all right
to stand?"

She shook off more of her stupor. "Of course I can
stand." But as she moved to disengage herself, she almost
teetered.

With a knowing grin, he handed over the bouquet, which
she mechanically accepted at the same time the DJ's voice
boomed through the speakers.

"How about that, folks! What do you say? Is that our
next bride-to-be?"

The applause was hesitant at first before the show of
support went through the roof. Grace cringed at the attention. On another level, it also gave a measure of relief. Anything—including a huge misunderstanding—was better
than the sea of pitying faces she'd had to endure that day.

"If you want," Wynn murmured, "I can stay longer."

With her free hand, she smoothed down her skirt—

and gathered the rest of her wits. "I'm sure you've done enough."

His gaze filtered over her face, lingering on her lips, still moist and buzzing from his kiss. Then, looking as hot as any Hollywood hunk, he turned and sauntered away.

A heartbeat later, the lights faded, music blared again and Amy Calhoun caught ahold of Grace's hand. As Amy dragged her to a relatively quiet corner, out of general view, her red ringlets looked set to combust with excitement.

"Who was *that*?" she cried.

Still lightheaded, Grace leaned back against the wall. "You don't want to know."

"I saw you two dancing. Did you only meet tonight? I mean, you don't have to say a word. I'm just curious, like friends are." Amy squeezed Grace's hand. "It's so good to see you happy."

"I look happy?" She felt spacey. Agitated.

In need of a cold shower.

"If you want to know, you look swept off your feet." The plump lips covering Amy's overbite twitched. "I actually thought that's what he'd do. Lift you up into his arms and carry you away."

Amy was an only child. She and Grace had grown up tight, spending practically every weekend at each other's places on Long Island—dressing up as princesses, enjoying the latest Disney films. Amy still lived and espoused a Cinderella mentality; a happily-ever-after would surely come if only a girl believed. An optimistic mindset was never a bad thing. However, with regard to this situation, Amy's sentimental nature was a bust.

"Wynn and I had met before tonight. It happened." Grace tossed the flowers aside on a table. "It's over."

"Okay." Amy's pearl chocker bobbed as she swallowed. "So, when you say *it* happened, you mean *it* as in…"

"As in intercourse. One night of amazing, mind-blowing, unforgettable sex." Grace groaned out a breath. God, it felt good to get that off her chest.

"Wow." Amy held her brow as if her head might be spinning. "Mind-blowing, huh? That's great. *Fantastic.* I'm just a little—"

"Shocked?"

"In a good way," Amy gave her a sympathetic look. "We've all been so worried."

As that familiar sick feeling welled up inside her, Grace flinched. "No one needs to be."

"I'm sure everyone knows that now. Sam was a great guy...a decorated firefighter from an awesome family. We all loved him. And he loved you—so much. But you needed something to push you to move on."

Those last words pulled Grace up.

But Wynn's invitation to this wedding was based on a lapsed friendship with the groom. He wasn't in the loop, and it was a stretch to think that someone had mentioned a bridesmaid's tragic personal situation over coffee and wedding cake.

Unless her father had said something.

Except the bouquet sliding from her feet across to his had been pure fluke. If not for that, he would never have had the opportunity to... How had he put it? Say goodbye properly. No way had he kissed her to simply show them all that she wasn't as fragile and alone as they might think.

And Wynn certainly wouldn't have swooped in to play superhero if he'd had any inkling of what had transpired the night of that accident a year ago. But the truth had to come out sometime. She only needed to find the right time.

Puzzle it out the right way.

Three days later, as his workday drew to a close, Wynn answered a conference call from his brothers on Skype.

"Bad time?"

Wynn smiled at Dex's laid-back expression and smooth voice. He was the epitome of a Hollywood producer ever since he'd taken over the family's movie unit in L.A.

"I have an easy four o'clock then I'm out of here," Wynn said.

"Off early, mate."

Skyping in from Sydney, Cole looked particularly tan after his sojourn with his fiancée Taryn Quinn on their yacht in the Pacific.

"Good to hear, bro," Dex said. "We all need time to chill."

"How's Dad?" Standing behind his chair, Wynn slipped one arm then the other into his jacket sleeves. That interview with Christopher Riggs—a job interview, and likely placement, based on a recommendation from Wynn's father—shouldn't take long. He'd get ready now to zip out the door as soon as he was done.

"No more attempts on his life since we spoke last," Cole replied, "and thank God for that."

"He's wondering if Tate should come home," Dex said.

"But Brandon thinks it's best to keep him out of harm's way," Cole explained, "at least until he can chase up some leads on that van."

Months back, during the stalker's last attack, Tate had almost been abducted along with his dad. Until the situation was sorted out and guilty parties thrown behind bars, the family had decided to place the youngest Hunter in a safer environment. Tate had spent time with the sweetheart/renegade of the family, Teagan, who lived in Seattle. And right now he was bunking down in Los Angeles with Dex. Tate had been happy with his movie-boss brother, and Dex had been happy with the boy's babysitter, Shelby Scott—in fact, she had recently become Dex's fiancée.

But now that there were leads on the van that had been

involved in that last assault, they might have a break in the case. Tate might soon be able to go home. Excellent.

"Brandon pinned down some snaps taken by a speed camera," Cole went on, "the same day Dad was attacked."

"Don't tell me after all this time he discovered the license plates were legit?" That they'd tracked down the assailant as easily as through a registration number.

Dex groaned. "Unfortunately, this creep isn't that stupid."

"But the traffic shots show the driver pulled over with a flat," Cole added.

"You have a description?" Wynn asked.

"Dark glasses, fake beard," Cole said. "Other than general height and weight, no help. But Brandon did a thorough survey of the area. A woman walking her Pomeranian remembers the van *and* the man. She also recalls him dropping his keys."

Dex took over. "She scooped them up. Before handing them back, she took note of the rental tag."

Leaning toward the screen, Wynn set both palms flat on the desk. "Weren't all the rental companies checked out?"

"The company concerned is a fly-by-nighter from another state," Dex explained.

"Brandon found the guy who ran it," Cole added. "Other than simply hiring out the car, he doesn't appear to be involved. But getting corresponding records was like pulling teeth."

"Until Brandon threatened to bring in the authorities, criminal as well as tax," Dex said. "The guy's got until tomorrow to cough up."

"Great work. So, Tate's staying with you in the meantime, Dex?"

"He and Shelby are as thick as thieves. He loves her cooking. I do, too. You should taste her cupcakes." Sitting back, ex-playboy Dex rested his hands on his stomach and licked his chops. "We're looking at taking the plunge some-time in the New Year. The wedding will most likely be in Mountain Ridge, Oklahoma, her hometown."

"Oh, I can see you now, riding up to the minister on matching steeds like something out of a '40s Western."

Wynn grinned at Cole's ribbing.

"Laugh if you dare," Dex said. "I bought a property that used to belong to Shelby's dad." Dex's tawny-colored gaze grew reflective. "One day we might settle out there for good."

"Away from the hype and glitter of Hollywood?" Wynn found that hard to believe.

"If it means being with Shelby," Dex assured them both, "I'd live in a tar shack."

Wynn was pleased for both brothers' happiness, even if he no longer possessed a romantic thought or inclina-tion in his body.

Barring the other night.

He felt for Grace and her situation. Covert glances and well-intentioned pity over past relationships that hadn't ended well... Painful to endure. Far better to give people something to really talk about. And so, with the entire room's eyes upon them, he'd kissed her—no half measures. After the shock had cleared, however, she'd looked ready to slap his face rather than thank him. It was a shame, be-cause after another taste of Grace Munroe's lips, he'd only wanted more.

Remembering that interview with Riggs, Wynn checked the time. "Guys, I need to sign off. Dad rang a couple of weeks back about giving a guy a job. Background in pub-lishing. Apparently great credentials and, quote, 'a finger on the pulse of solutions for challenges in this digital age.' Dad thought I could use him."

"Sounds great," Dex said. "Should help take some pres-sure off."

Wynn frowned. "I'm not under pressure." Or wouldn't be half so much when the merger deal he'd been working on was in the bag. For now, however, that arrangement was tightly under wraps—he hadn't even told his father about the merger plans.

"Well, it'll be strictly fun and games when you guys come out for the wedding." Pride shone from Cole's face. "You and Dex are my best men."

Wynn straightened. That was the first he'd heard of it. "I'm honored." Then his thoughts doubled back. "Can a groom have two best men?"

"It's the 21st century." Dex laughed. "You can do any damn thing you want."

"So, Wynn," Cole went on, "you're definitely coming?"

Dex's voice lowered. "You're okay after that breakup now, right?"

Wynn wanted to roll his eyes. He'd really hoped he'd get through this conversation without anyone bringing that up.

"*The breakup…*" He forced a grin. "Sounds like the title of some soppy book."

"Movie, actually," Dex countered.

"Well, you'll all be relieved to know that I've moved on."

"Mentally or physically?" Dex asked.

"Both."

"Really?" Cole said at the same time Dex asked, "Anyone we know?"

"As a matter of fact…remember Grace Munroe?"

Cole blinked twice. "You don't mean Brock Munroe's girl?"

"*Whoa.* I remember," Dex said. "The little horror who crushed on you that Christmas in Colorado when we were all kids."

"That's back to front." Wynn set them straight. "I wanted to crush her—under my heel."

"And now?" Dex asked.

"We caught up."

"So, we can put her name down beside yours for the wedding?" Cole prodded.

"I said I've moved on." Lifting his chin, Wynn adjusted his tie's Windsor knot. "No one's moving in."

In the past, these two had nudged each other, grinning over Wynn's plans to settle down sooner rather than later. Now Cole and Dex were the ones jabbed by Cupid's arrow and falling over themselves to commit while Wynn had welcomed the role of dedicated bachelor. Once bit and twice shy. He didn't need the aggravation.

The men signed off. Wynn could see his personal assistant Daphne Cranks down the hall trying to get his attention. She pushed her large-framed glasses up her nose before flicking her gaze toward a guest. A man dressed in an impeccable dark gray suit got up from his chair with an easy smile. Christopher Riggs was almost as tall as Wynn. He had a barrel chest like a buff character from a comic strip. When Wynn joined him, they shook hands, introduced themselves and headed for the boardroom.

"My father seems impressed by your credentials," Wynn said, pulling in his chair.

"He's a fascinating man."

"He worked hard to build Hunter Enterprises into the force it is today."

"I believe it was very much a local Australian concern when Guthrie took over from your grandfather."

"My father ran the company with my uncle for a short while. Two strong wills. Different ideas of how the place ought to run. I'm afraid it didn't work out." Wynn unbuttoned his jacket and sat back. "That was decades ago."

"Hopefully I'll have the chance to contribute something positive moving forward."

They discussed where the company was positioned at the moment, and went on to speak about publishing in general.

Christopher handed over his résumé and then volunteered information about his background. Guthrie had already mentioned that, until recently, Christopher's family had owned a notable magazine in Australia. Like so many businesses, the magazine had suffered in these harsh economic times. The Riggses had found a business partner who had buoyed the cash flow for a time before pulling the plug. The magazine had gone into receivership.

Christopher had a degree, a background in reporting and good references in marketing. Alongside that, he could talk rings around Wynn with regard to web presence statistics and methods, as well as social media strategies aimed at optimizing potential market share.

While they spoke, Wynn tried to look beyond the smooth exterior, deep into the man's clear mint-green eyes. No bad vibes. Christopher Riggs was the epitome of a composed professional. Even in his later years, Guthrie Hunter possessed an uncanny ability to sniff out true talent. Wynn could see Christopher well-placed in his marketing and tech team.

They discussed and then agreed on remuneration and benefits.

"Come in tomorrow." Wynn pushed to his feet. "Daphne can set you up in an office."

The men shook again and, with a bounce in his step, Christopher Riggs headed out.

After collecting his briefcase, Wynn came back into his private reception area. When he said good-night, Daphne held him up.

"These tickets arrived a few minutes ago." She gave him an embossed envelope. "A gift from the producer."

He was about to say that he wasn't interested in Broadway tonight—she was welcome to the tickets—but then he reconsidered.

Daphne was the most efficient personal assistant he'd

ever had. Always on top of things, constantly on his heels…
a bit of a puppy, he'd sometimes thought. Behind the Mr.
Magoo glasses and dull hairdo, she was probably attractive; however, from what he could gather, she was very
much single. He wasn't certain she even had friends. If he
left those tickets behind, chances were they'd be dropped
in the trash when five o'clock rolled around.

So he took the envelope as his thoughts swung to another
woman who was his assistant's opposite in every sense of
the word—except for the being single part.

Brock had mentioned Grace was in town for a few days.
Her hotel was around the corner. As he entered the elevator,
Wynn thought it over. Perhaps Grace had left New York by
now. And hadn't she made herself clear? She didn't regret
that night spent in his bed but she wasn't after an encore.
Grace didn't want to see him again.

As he slid the envelope into his inside breast pocket and
the elevator doors closed, Wynn hesitated, and then, remembering their last kiss, slowly grinned.

What the hell. He had nothing on tonight. Maybe he
could change her mind.

Three

Exiting the hotel elevator, Grace headed across the foyer and then pulled up with a start. Cutting a dynamite figure in a dark, tailored suit, Wynn Hunter stood at the reception counter, waiting to speak with someone behind the desk.

No need to assume he'd come to see her. There were a thousand other reasons he might be here tonight. Business. Friends. Another woman. An attractive, successful, single male like Wynn... Members of the opposite sex would flock to spend time with him.

She'd been on her way out to mull over a decision—whether or not to spend more time in New York before getting back to her job. Late last year she'd left New York to join a private practice in Florida as a speech-language pathologist. Providing tools to help both adults and children with communication disabilities was rewarding work. Just the other week, she'd got an update from a young mom who had needed additional support and advice on feeding her baby who'd been born with a cleft palate. The woman had wanted to let Grace know that the baby's first surgery, which included ear tubes to help with fluid buildup, had been a great success.

Grace had made good friends in Florida, too. Had a nice apartment in a great neighborhood. But she missed so much about New York—minus the memories surrounding Sam and his accident, of course, which seemed to pop up everywhere, constantly.

Except during that time she'd spent with Wynn.

Her lips still hummed and her body sang whenever she thought of the way they had kissed. She wasn't certain that, if she strolled over and started up a conversation with him now, one thing wouldn't lead to another. However, while the sex would be better than great, she'd already decided that their one-night stand should be left in the past. She wasn't ready to invite a man, and associated complications, into her life.

Best just to keep going without saying hi.

He seemed to wait until she was out in the open before rapping his knuckles on the counter and then absently turning around. In that instant, she felt his focus narrow and lock her in its sights. No choice now. She pulled up again.

He crossed over to her at a leisurely pace. People in his path naturally made way for him. In the three days since they'd spoken last, his raven's-wing hair had grown enough to lick his collar. The shadow on his jaw looked rougher, too. And his eyes seemed even darker—their message more tempting.

She remembered his raspy cheek grazing her flesh... the magic of his mouth on her thigh...his muscular frame bearing down again and again to meet her hips. And then he was standing in front of her and speaking in that deep, dreamy voice.

"You're on your way out?"

Willing her thumping heartbeat to slow, Grace nodded. "And you? Here on business?"

"Your father mentioned you were staying here for a few days." He waved an envelope. "I have tickets for a show. We could catch a bite first."

He was here to see her?

"Wynn, I'd really like to, but—"

"You have another date?"

She shook her head.

"You've already eaten?"

No, but suddenly she could taste the rich fudge ice-cream they'd devoured, eating off the same spoon that night when they had both needed to cool down.

Grace pushed the image aside. "I'm sorry. This doesn't work for me."

"Because it's not a good time."

For a relationship of any kind. She nodded. "That's right."

He seemed to weigh that up before asking, "When are you leaving New York?"

"I'm not sure. Soon."

"So, worst case scenario—we have a dog-awful time tonight and you won't need to bump into me again for another twenty years."

It sounded so harmless. And maybe it was.

Brock Munroe was a devoted father to all three of his daughters. He'd always been there, watching out for their best interests—doing what he could to help. Did that include organizing some male company to help divert her from unpleasant memories while she was back in town?

And if her father had gone so far as to suggest this get-together, what else had Wynn and her dad discussed? Had Sam been mentioned at all? To what extent? If Wynn had spoken with her mother, the subject of her past boyfriend would definitely have come up. Suzanne Munroe had thought of Sam as a son—always would—and she took every opportunity to let others know it.

There'll never be another Sam.

"Wynn, did my father put you up to this?" she asked.

Wynn's chin kicked up a notch. "Brock did mention it might be nice for us to catch up again while you were in town."

Grace sighed.

"I like to think of my father's smile if he found out his plan here had worked, but—"

"Grace, I'm not here because your father suggested it."

"It's okay. Honest. I—"

He laughed. "Come on now. I'm here because I want to be." When she hesitated, he went on. "We don't have to go to the show. But you have to eat. I know a great place on Forty-second."

She paused. "What place?"

He named a restaurant that she knew and loved.

"Great food," he added.

She agreed. "I remember."

"Their chocolate *panna cotta* is sensational."

"The mushroom risotto, too."

Wincing, he held his stomach. "Personally, I'm starved. I skipped lunch."

"I grabbed an apple-pie melt off a truck."

"I love apple-pie melts."

When he sent her a slanted smile, her heart gave a kick and, next thing she knew, she was nodding.

"All right," she said.

"So, that's a yes? To dinner, or dinner and the show? It's an opening night musical. The scores are supposed to be amazing."

Then he mentioned the name of the lead actor. Who said no to that? Only she wasn't exactly dressed for the theater.

"I need to go up and change first," she said.

But then, his gaze sharpened—almost gleamed—and Grace took stock again. Was he debating whether or not to suggest a drink in her room before heading out? Given the conflagration the last time they'd been alone together, no matter how great the songs or the food, she guessed he wouldn't complain if they ordered room service and bunked down in her bedroom for the night.

She was reconsidering the whole deal when his expression cleared and he waved the envelope toward a lounge adjoining the lobby.

"I'll wait over there," he said. "Take your time."

As he headed off, Grace blinked and then eased into a smile. No inviting himself up or flirty innuendoes. Perfect. Except...

If Wynn wasn't here at her father's behest, or to test the air for some no-strings-attached sex, that made tonight about a mutually attracted couple who wanted to enjoy some time together. In other words, a date.

Her first in a year.

"Some like it steamy." As he walked alongside her, Wynn gave her a puzzled look. Grace indicated a billboard across the street. "There," she explained. "It's the name of a new movie."

Wynn grinned. "Sounds like something my brother would dream up."

She and Wynn were heading back to the hotel. They'd enjoyed their meal and the show had been fantastic.

During dinner, she'd caught up on all the Hunter news. Apparently Cole and Dex had been at loggerheads for years. When their father had decided to split the company among the kids, workaholic Cole had expected more from Dex than he'd thought Mr. Casual could give. Dex had been happy to get away on his own to California to head Hunter Productions, which, after some challenges, was now doing well.

Teagan had got out of the family business altogether. She'd followed brother Dex to the States and had forged a successful health and fitness business in Seattle. Grace decided she really ought to get in touch with her old friend again.

As for the show, the staging had been spectacular and singing amazing; more than once, Grace had had to swallow past the lump in her throat. And Wynn's company had been as intoxicating as ever. Despite her reservations, she was glad he'd convinced her to go out.

"I know Cole's getting married," she said as her attention shifted from the billboard to take in Wynn's classic profile. "But isn't Dex engaged, too? I'm sure I saw an announcement somewhere."

"I get to meet both Dex's and Cole's love interests in a couple of weeks. Cole's wedding's back home in Sydney."

In Australia? She remembered wondering about his accent that first night; she'd thought possibly English but hadn't wanted to get into backgrounds. "A Hunter wedding. Set to be the social event of the season, I bet."

Grunting, he flipped his jacket's hem back to slot both hands in his pockets. "I wouldn't count on that."

The Hunters were wealthy, well connected. When Guthrie had remarried a few years ago, her parents had attended. Grace's mother had come home gushing over the extravagance of the reception as well as the invitation list—sporting legends, business magnates, some of the biggest names in Hollywood today. But it sounded as if Cole and his bride-to-be might be planning a more private affair.

Grace was about to ask more when a raindrop landed on her nose. She checked out the sky. A second and third raindrop smacked her forehead and her chin. Then the starless sky seemed to split wide apart.

As the deluge hit, Grace yelped. Wynn caught her hand, hauling her out of the downpour and into the cozy alcove of a handy shopfront.

"It'll pass soon," he said with an authoritative voice that sounded as if he could command the weather rather than predict it.

With his hair dripping and features cast in soft-edged shadows, he looked so assured. So handsome. Was it possible for a man to be *too* masculine? Too take-me-now sexy?

As he flicked water from his hands, his focus shifted from the rain onto her. As if he'd read her thoughts, his gaze searched hers before he carefully reached for her cheek. But he only swept away the wet hair that was plastered over her nose, around her chin.

"Are you cold?" he asked.

She thought for a moment then feigned a shiver and nodded.

He maneuvered her to stand with her back to him. He held open his silk-lined, wool-blend jacket and cocooned her against a wall of muscle and heat. *Heavenly.* Then his strong arms folded across her and tugged her in super close.

Surrendering, Grace let her eyes drift shut. She might not want to get involved, but she was human and, damn, this felt good.

His stubble grazed her temple. "Warm now?"

Grinning, she wiggled back against him. "Not yet."

When his palms flattened against her belly, slowly ironing up before skimming back down, she bit her lip to contain the sigh. Then his hug tightened at the same time his fingers fanned and gradually spread lower. She let her head rock back and rest against his shoulder.

"Better?" he asked against her ear.

"Not yet," she lied.

"If we keep it up," he murmured, "we might need to explain ourselves to the police in that patrol car over there."

"We're not exactly causing a scene."

"Not yet."

He nuzzled down beneath her scarf and dropped a lingering kiss on the side of her throat as one hand coasted higher, over her ribs, coming to rest beneath the slope of her breast. When his thumb brushed her nipple, back and forth three times, she quivered all over.

She felt his chest expand before he turned her around. In the shadows, she caught a certain glimmer in his eyes. Then his gaze zeroed in on her mouth as his grip tightened on her shoulders.

"Grace, precisely how much do you want to heat up?"

Her heartbeat began to race. No denying—they shared a chemistry, a connection, like two magnets meant to lock whenever they crossed paths. She'd had fun this evening. She knew he had, too. And the way he was looking at her now—as if he could eat her...

On a purely primal level, she wanted the flames turned up to high. But if she weakened and slept with Wynn again tonight, how would she feel about herself in the morning? Perhaps simply satisfied. Or would she wish that she'd remembered her earlier stand?

She liked Wynn. She adored the delicious way he made her feel. Still, it was best to put on the brakes.

Sometimes when she thought about Sam, the years they'd spent together, the night that he had died—it all seemed like a lifetime ago and yet still so "now." Before she could truly move forward and think about starting something new, she needed to make sense of what had come before.

The loss.

Her guilt.

Lowering her gaze, Grace turned to face the street. The display featured in the shop window next to them caught her eye. They were sheltering from the rain in a bookshop doorway. The perfect in for a change of subject.

"Does Hunter Publishing own bookstores?" she asked.

Wynn combed long fingers back through his hair then

shook out the moisture as if trying to shake off his steamier thoughts.

"We handle magazines and newspapers," he told her, "not novels."

"Everyone's supposed to have at least one story in them," she murmured, thinking aloud.

She certainly had one. Nothing she wanted professionally published, of course. But she knew that committing unresolved feelings to paper could be therapeutic.

"Have you got a flight booked back home?" he asked as the rain continued to fall.

"Actually I was thinking of taking a little more time off."

Hands in his pockets, Wynn leaned back against the shop door. "How much time?"

"A couple of weeks." Another experienced therapist had just started with the practice. Grace's boss had said, although she was relatively new, if she needed a bit more time off, it shouldn't be a problem.

His eyes narrowed as he gave her a cryptic grin. "You should come to Cole's wedding with me."

She blinked twice. "You're not serious."

"I am serious."

"You want me to jump on a plane and travel halfway around the world with you, just like that?" She pulled a face. "That's crazy."

"Not crazy. You know all the old crowd. I already told my brothers that we caught up."

Her heart skipped a beat. Exactly how much had he told them? "What did they say?" she asked.

"They said you had a crush on me when you were six."

"When you were such a dweeb?"

"I was focused."

She teased, "Focused, but clumsy."

She could attest to the fact that he'd outgrown the clumsy phase.

"Cole suggested it earlier today. I brushed it off, but after tonight…" He pushed off from the door and stood up straight. "It'll be fun."

The idea of catching up with his family was certainly tempting. After that Christmas, she and Teagan had been pen pals for a long while. Then Tea had that accident and was in and out of hospital with a string of surgeries. Tea's letters had dwindled to the point where they'd finally lost touch.

But foremost a trip to Australia would mean spending loads of time with Wynn, which didn't add up to slowing things down or giving herself the time she still needed to work through and accept her past with Sam.

She waved the suggestion off. "You don't need me."

"That's right. I *want* you."

Such a simple yet complicated statement—it took her aback.

She tried to make light. "You must have a mile-long list of women to choose from."

His brows knitted. "You have that wrong. Dex was the playboy. Never me."

When a group of boisterous women walked by the alcove, he stepped forward to gauge the prewinter night sky.

"Rain's stopped," he said. "Let's go before we get caught again."

As they walked side by side past puddles shimmering with light from the neon signs and streetlamps, Wynn thought back.

By age ten, he'd had a handle on the concept of delayed gratification. If he needed the blue ribbon in swim squad, he put in time at the pool. If he wanted to win his father's approval, he studied until he excelled. Reward for effort was the motto upon which he'd built his life, professional as well as private.

Then Heather had walked away and that particular view on life had changed.

On the night he and Grace had met again, Wynn had seen what he'd wanted and decided simply to take it. A few minutes ago, with her bundled against him in those shadows, the same thousand-volt arc had crackled between them. For however long it lasted, he wanted to enjoy it. More than gut said Grace wanted that, too, even if she seemed conflicted.

Hell, if she had time off, why not come to Australia? He could show her some sights. They could share a few laughs. No one needed to get all heavy and "forever" about it. He wasn't out to replace her ex. He understood certain scars didn't heal.

Maybe it would make a difference if he let her know that.

"Should we have a nightcap?" he asked as they entered the relative quiet of her hotel lobby a few minutes later. "I found a nice spot in that lounge earlier. No piano though."

She continued on, heading for the elevators. "I have to get up early."

When she didn't elaborate, Wynn adjusted his plan. He'd say his piece when he said good-night at her door. At the elevators, however, she cut down that idea, too.

"It's been a great night," she said, after he'd hit the Up key. "But I think I'll say good-night here."

He was forming words to reply when he heard a woman's laugh—throaty, familiar. All the muscles in his stomach clenched tight a second before he tracked down the source. Engaged in conversation with a jet-set rock'n'roll type, Heather Matthews was strolling across a nearby stretch of marble tiles.

Wynn's heart dropped.

Over eight million people and New York could still be a freaking small world.

At the same time his ex glanced in his direction, the el-

evator pinged and the doors slid open. He shepherded Grace
inside and stabbed a button. As the doors closed, the ice in
his blood began to thaw and the space between collar and
neck started to steam. It took a moment before he realized
Grace was studying him.

"Inviting yourself up?" she drawled.

"I'll say good-night at the door."

"Because of that woman you want to avoid?" She hit a
floor key. "Want to tell me who she is?"

His jaw clenched. "Not particularly."

She didn't probe, which he appreciated. Except, maybe
it would help if Grace knew that he'd recently lost someone, too, though in a different way.

He tugged at his tie, loosening the knot that was pressing on his throat. "That woman and I...we were together
for a few years. There was a time I thought we'd get married," he added. "Have a family. She didn't see it that way."

Her eyes rounded then filled with sympathy. The kind
of pity Wynn abhorred and, he thought, Grace knew well.

"Wynn...I'm sorry."

"It's in the past." Drawing himself up to his full height, he
shrugged. "I'm happy for Cole. For Dex, too. But I'm steering clear of that kind of—" heartache? "—commitment."

A bell pinged and the elevator doors opened. She stepped
out, and then, with a look, let him know he could follow.
She stopped outside a door midway down the corridor,
flipped her key card over the sensor. When the light blinked
on, she clicked open the door and, after an uncertain moment, faced him again. They were both damp from the rain.
Drops still glistened in her hair.

"For what it's worth," she said, "I think your ex missed
out."

Then she stepped forward and craned up on her toes.
When her lips brushed his cheek, time seemed to wind
down. She lingered there. If she was going to step away,

she wasn't in too much of a hurry. She had to get up early. Had wanted to say good-night. But if he wasn't mistaken, this was his cue.

His hands cupped her shoulders. As her face angled up, his head dropped down. When his mouth claimed hers, he held off a beat before winding one arm around her back. He felt more than heard the whimper in her throat. A heartbeat later, she relaxed and then melted.

As his tongue pushed past her lips, a thick molten stream coursed through his veins. The delicious surge…that visceral tug… And then her arms coiled around his neck and the connection started to sizzle.

He hadn't planned on taking Grace to bed tonight. He knew she hadn't planned this, either. But what could he say? Plans changed.

A muttering at his back seeped through the fog.

"For pity's sake, get a room."

Grace stiffened, and then pried herself away. Down the hall, a middle-aged couple were shaking their heads as they disappeared into a neighboring suite. Coming close again, Wynn slid a hand down her side.

Get a room.

"Maybe that's not such a bad idea," he murmured against her brow.

When she didn't respond, he drew back. A pulse was popping in her throat, but reason had returned to her eyes.

"Good night, Wynn."

"What about Sydney?"

"I'll let you know."

"Soon." He handed over a business card with his numbers.

Before her soft smile disappeared behind the crack in the door, she agreed. "Yes, Wynn. Soon."

Four

The next morning, Wynn arrived at the office early.

By seven, he was downstairs, speaking with his editor-in-chief about a plagiarism claim that was causing the legal department major grief. An hour and a half later, he was heading back upstairs and thinking about Grace. They had parted amicably, to say the least. He thought there was a chance she might even take him up on the invitation to accompany him to Cole's wedding.

He'd give her a day, and then try her at the hotel. Or he could get her cell number from Brock. Even if she decided not to go to Sydney, he wanted to take her out again. By the time he got back to the States, she would have left New York and gone back to her life in Florida.

Wynn made his way past Daphne's vacant desk; his assistant was running a little late. A moment later, when he swung open his office door, he was called back—but not by Daphne. Christopher Riggs was striding up behind him, looking as enthusiastic as he had the previous day at his interview.

"Hey, Wynn." Christopher ran a hand through his hair, pushing a dark wave off his brow. "Daphne wasn't at her desk. I thought I'd take a chance and see if you were in."

Wynn flicked a glance at his watch. His next meeting—an important one—wasn't far off. But he could spare a few minutes.

As they moved inside his office, Christopher's expression sharpened when something on Wynn's desk caught his eye—the interconnecting silver L and T of a publishing logo. "La Trobes," he said.

Leaning back against the edge of the desk, Wynn crossed his arms. "Impress me with your knowledge."

"I know La Trobes's publications have a respectable share of the marketplace."

"Keeping in mind that print share is shrinking."

"But there are other, even greater opportunities outside of print, if they're harnessed properly. I've given a lot of thought to out-of-the-box strategies and the implementation of facilities for digital readers to be compatible with innovative applications."

For the next few minutes, Wynn listened to an extended analysis of the digital marketplace. Obviously this guy knew his stuff. But now wasn't the time to get into a full-blown discussion.

After a few more minutes of Christopher sharing his ideas, Wynn got up from the desk and interrupted. "I have a meeting. We'll talk later."

A muscle in Christopher's jaw jumped twice. He was pumped, ready to let loose with a thousand initiatives. But he quickly reined himself in.

"Of course," he said, backing up. "I'll get out of your hair."

Christopher was headed out when Daphne appeared at the open door.

"Oh, sorry to interrupt," Daphne said. "I didn't realize—"

As she backed up, her elbow smacked the jamb. When her trusty gold-plated pen jumped from her hand, Christopher swooped to rescue it. As he returned the pen, Wynn didn't miss the wink he sent its owner. He also noted Daphne's blush and her preoccupation as Christopher vacated the room.

Rousing herself, she nudged those glasses back up her nose and, in the navy blue dress reserved for Thursdays, moved forward. As Wynn dragged in his seat, Daphne lowered into her regular chair on the other side of his desk. So—head back in the game. First up, before that meeting, he needed to make some arrangements.

"I'm flying to Sydney Monday."

Daphne crossed her legs and scribbled on her pad. "Returning when?"

"Keep it open."

"I'll organize a car to the airport." She scrunched her pert nose. "Will you need accommodation?"

"We're all staying at the family home. Guthrie wants us all in one place leading up to the big day."

If Grace decided to join him, he'd make additional arrangements. Lots of them.

As Daphne took notes, her owlish, violet-blue eyes sparkled behind their lenses. He couldn't be sure, but he suspected his assistant was a romantic. She liked the thought of a wedding. Not so long ago, she had really liked Heather.

The two women had met several times. Daphne had commented on how carefree, beautiful and friendly his partner was. The morning after Heather had left him sitting alone in that restaurant, he'd returned to his apartment and had lain like a fallen redwood on his couch. He'd let his phone ring and ring. He didn't eat. Didn't drink. When an urgent knocking had forced him to his feet, he'd found Daphne standing, fretting in his doorway. Looking pale, she'd announced, "I've been calling all day." For the first time in their history, her tone had been heated. Concerned.

He had groaned out his story and had felt a little better for it. Afterward, she'd made coffee and a sandwich he couldn't taste. Then she'd simply sat alongside of him, keeping him company without prying or hassling about the meetings he'd missed. They hadn't spoken about that day since, but he wasn't sorry she'd appeared on his doorstep and had seen that shattered man. He trusted her without reservation. He knew she would always be there for him, as a top assistant, even as an unlikely friend.

Now, like every weekday, he and Daphne went through the day's schedule.

"Midmorning," Daphne said, "you have a meeting with digital strategists."

To make existing online sites more efficient and user-friendly while increasing cross-promotional links between Hunter Publishing's properties.

"At two, a consultation with the financial heads," she went on.

To get down to the pins and tacks of whether his proposed partial merger with another publisher—Episode Features—was as viable as he believed.

Daphne glanced at the polished-steel wall clock. "In a few minutes," she said, "a meeting with Paul Lumos."

Episode's CEO. They were both anxious to finalize outstanding sticking points. Neither man wanted leaks to either the public, employees or, in Wynn's case, his family.

Normally, walls didn't exist between Hunter father and son. This was an exception. During a recent phone conversation, Wynn had brought up the subject of mergers. Guthrie had cut the conversation down with a single statement. "Not interested." His father's business model was built around buyouts and takeovers. He didn't agree with handing over *any* controlling interest. Even in these challenging times, this giant oak would not bend. But with the regularity of print-run schedules cut in half, both Lumos and Wynn saw critical benefits in sharing overheads relating to factory and delivery costs.

As Brock Munroe had said: adapt or die.

Daphne was leaving the office when Wynn's private line announced an incoming call. His father. Sitting back, Wynn checked his watch. Lumos was due any moment. He'd need to make this brief.

"Checking in," Guthrie said. "Making sure we'll see you next week."

Smiling, Wynn sat back. "The flight's booked."

"I just got off the phone with Dex and Tate." His father pushed out a weary breath. "This place feels so empty without that boy's smile."

Wynn read his father's thoughts. *Did I do the right thing sending my youngest son away?* He'd had no choice.

"We all agreed. While there's any risk of Tate being caught up again in that trouble, it's best he stay somewhere safe."

It had also been agreed that *all* the Hunters should return home for Cole's wedding. Since that last incident, where father and child had very nearly been abducted, additional security had been arranged. On conference calls, the older Hunter brothers had discussed with Brandon Powell how to increase those measures these coming weeks.

"Any news on that car rental company's records?" Wynn asked.

"The license plate was a fake," Guthrie confirmed. "After hiring the van, the plates were switched and switched again before dropping it back. If that woman Brandon interviewed hadn't caught sight of the rental company's name on the keys, we'd be clueless. Now at least we have some kind of description of the man."

"Was a sketch artist brought in?"

"Should have something on that soon." Guthrie exhaled. "God help me, I want to know what's behind all this."

Wynn imagined his father standing by the giant arched window in the second-story master suite of his magnificent Sydney house—the estate that Wynn and his brothers had called home growing up. The frustration, the fury, must be eating him alive.

"We're getting closer, Dad." Hopefully soon his father would have his life back and Tate could go home to Sydney for good.

Wynn changed the subject.

"Christopher Riggs started today."

His father sounded sure-footed again. "That boy has good credentials. Christopher's father worked for me years ago. Later, he bought a low distribution magazine that he built up. A recent merger turned out to be a death sentence. The family's interests were swallowed up and spat out."

Wynn's stomach tightened. But his father couldn't know about his meetings with Lumos or his merger plans for Hunter Publishing.

"Christopher's father is a good friend," Guthrie continued. "Someone I would trust with my life. When Tobias and I had our falling out, it was Vincent Riggs I turned to. I wanted to fold—give my brother any damn thing he wanted if he agreed to stay and help run the company—it was our father's dying wish. But Vincent helped clear my head. Tobias and I did things differently. Thought differently. Still do. We would have ended up killing each other if he'd stayed on. I'll always be grateful to Vincent for making me see that. Giving his only son this opportunity is the least I can do."

Wynn was sitting back, rubbing the scar on his forehead

as he stared at the portrait of his father hanging on the wall. He couldn't imagine how betrayed Guthrie would feel when he found out he'd gone behind his back organizing that deal.

"You there, son?"

Wynn cleared his throat. "Yeah. Sorry. I have a meeting in five."

"I won't hold you up."

His father muttered a goodbye and Wynn pushed out of his chair. When his gaze found the La Trobes folder on his desk, he remembered Guthrie's words and his chest burned again. His father had spoken of how, in his dealings with Uncle Tobias, he'd needed to accept that sometimes the answer to a problem is: there is no answer.

And now, Wynn had no option, either. He had to pursue this merger deal. No matter the casualties or hard feelings—he needed to keep his corner of the Hunter empire strong.

Five

"Well, now, this is a surprise."

At the sound of Wynn's greeting and sight of his intrigued smile, the nerves in Grace's stomach knotted up. Wearing a white business shirt, which stretched nicely across his chest, a crimson tie and dark suit pants that fit his long, strong legs to perfection, he looked so incredibly tasty, her mouth wanted to water.

"I was out doing a few things," she replied as he crossed his large private reception area. "When I passed your building, I thought I might catch you before you left for the day."

When Grace had arrived, the assistant had let Wynn know he had a visitor. Now, as the young woman packed up for the day, pushing to her feet and securing a massive handbag over her shoulder, Grace noticed the interested—*or was that protective?*—glance she sent Wynn's way. Wearing serious glasses and a dress that had submitted to the press of an iron one too many times, the woman looked more suited to court dictation than boardroom infatuation. But wasn't it always the quiet ones?

A moment later, Grace was following Wynn into his spacious office suite.

To the left, black leather settees were arranged in a *U* formation around a low Perspex occasional table stacked with three neat piles of magazines and newspapers. A spotless fireplace was built into the oak-paneled wall. To one side of the mantle sat a framed copy of a well-known Hunter magazine—on the other hung an identically framed copy of the *New York Globe*, Hunter Publishing's primary newspaper; their offices were located on a lower floor. But what drew her attention most was the view of Midtown visible beyond those wall-to-wall windows. It never got old.

From this vantage point, gazing out over Times Square toward Rockefeller Center, she felt settled, warm—as if she were swaddled in a cashmere wrap.

She wandered over and set a palm against the cool glass. "I've missed this."

A few seconds later, Wynn's voice rumbled out from behind her.

"Growing up," he said, "I remember my father being away a lot. He had good people in key positions here in New York, but he wanted to keep an eagle eye on things himself. When he said he trusted me enough to take on that gatekeeping role, I almost fell out of my chair. I was twenty-three when I started my grooming here."

The deep, rich sound of his voice, the comfort of his body heat warming her back... She really needed to say her piece and get out of here before her knees got any weaker.

As she turned to face him, however, her blouse brushed his shirtfront and that weak-kneed feeling gripped her doubly tight. The message in his gaze wasn't difficult to read. She was a confident, intelligent woman who had her act together for the most part, yet she felt like a sieve full of warm putty whenever Wynn Hunter looked at her that way.

She moistened her lips. "I've decided not to go to Sydney."

His eyebrows knitted before his gaze dipped to her mouth, then combed over one cheek. She felt the appraisal like a touch.

"That's a shame." With a curious grin hooking one side of his mouth, he edged a little closer. "Sure I can't convince you?"

"If we arrive and stay there together... Well, I just don't want to give anyone the wrong idea."

"What idea is that? That we're a couple?"

"Yes, actually."

"And that would make you uncomfortable. Make you feel disloyal to your ex." He explained, "Your dad mentioned what happened last year. It must've been hard."

Her stomach began to churn in that sick way it did whenever someone said those words to her.

"I'm working through it," she told him, crossing to his desk and stopping to one side of the big, high-backed chair.

"No one has to know any background," he said.

"Your family will ask questions."

"Trust me." He followed her. "They'll only be jazzed about seeing you again. Particularly Teagan."

She exhaled. He never gave up. "Wynn, we've known each other five minutes." *This time.*

"I'd like to get to know you more."

When his fingertips feathered the back of her hand, she eased away around the other side of the chair. "I'm not ready for this."

"I'm talking about soaking up gobs of therapeutic, subtropical sunshine. Have you any idea how soft a koala's fur feels beneath your fingertips?"

She narrowed her eyes at him. "Not fair."

He moved around the chair to join her. When his fingers slipped around hers, she was infused with his heat.

She wanted to move away again. Tell him that he couldn't talk her around. Only these toasty feelings were getting harder to ignore. She could so easily give in to the urge, tip forward.

Let go.

"I lay awake last night," he said, moving closer. "I was thinking about our evening together. About putting the past in the past for a couple of weeks."

She remembered again how candidly he'd spoken about his ex. She'd seen it in the shadows of his eyes. He'd been badly hurt, too.

In some ways, he understood. And Grace understood him.

She couldn't fix it with Sam, but Wynn was here, in her present. He'd been nothing but thoughtful toward her. And he wasn't looking to set up house or anything drastic. He was merely suggesting that they make the most of the time they had left before she returned to Florida.

And, of course, he was right—she didn't have to divulge anything to his family that she didn't want to. That was her conscience getting in the way, holding her back—same way it had all these months.

When the pad of Wynn's thumb brushed her palm, her fingers twitched.

"If you won't see me again," he said, "could I ask you to do just one thing?"

"What's that?"

"Leave me with a kiss."

Her breath caught. He was looking at her so intently.

"Just one?" she asked.

He brought her close. "You decide."

The moment his mouth covered hers, longing flooded her every cell. The night before, she had lain awake, too,

imagining he was there beside her, stroking and toying
and pleasing her the way only Wynn seemed to know how.
She'd reinvented the moment before she'd said good-night,
but rather than closing the door, she'd grabbed his tie and
dragged him inside.

Now, with his mouth working a slow-burn rhythm over
hers and that hot pulse at her core beginning to throb, she
felt boneless—beaten. *One kiss.* She didn't want to stop
at just one. But she hadn't lost her mind completely. This
wasn't the place or the time.

Breathless, she broke away. "Wynn, I need to go."

"I want you to stay." His lips grazed hers. "*You* want
to stay."

"Anyone could come in."

He strode across the room, locked the door, strode back.
No more words. He only brought her close, and as his mouth
captured hers and his embrace tightened, suddenly time
and place didn't matter.

He shifted his big hands and gripped her on either side
of her waist. He slowly lifted her and as her feet left the
floor, he made certain that he pressed her against him extra
close. Then their mouths slipped apart and rather than looking up at him, now she was looking down.

When he sat her on the desk, his mouth found hers
again—a scorching all-bets-are-off caress. His palms drove
all the way down her back, and as his hands wedged under
her behind, she blindly unbuttoned part of his shirt. Slipping a hand into the opening, she sighed at the feel of crisp
hair matted over hard, steamy flesh.

One hand slipped out from beneath her, slicing down the
back of her thigh until he gripped the back of that knee. As
the kiss deepened, she wrenched at the knot of his tie. When
collar buttons proved too stubborn, she tugged harder and
they popped off. She unraveled the shirt from his shoulders

at the same time he pushed against her, tilting her back, bringing her knee back, too.

When she lay flat on the desk, his mouth broke from hers. He shifted enough to peel the shirt off his back. As he moved forward, he pushed up her skirt. He positioned himself between her thighs and his mouth met hers again.

Arching up, she clutched at his chest while a big warm hand drove between them and found the front of her briefs. When she bucked, wanting more, the kiss intensified before two thick fingers slid lower between thin silk and warm skin. As he explored her slick folds, the pad of his thumb grazed the bead at the top of her cleft. She bit her lip to contain a sigh. *All those sizzling nerve endings.* Then he pressed that spot with just the right pressure and a burning arrow shot straight to her core.

She was clinging to his shoulders when he slipped his hand out from her briefs. She pushed up against him until she was sitting upright, her hands colliding with his in their race to unbutton her blouse. As he wrangled the sleeves off her shoulders, she scooted back more on the desk.

But then their eyes connected, and a hushed surreal moment passed. He drew down a breath and seemed to gather himself before he urged her back down. Finding her right leg, he raised it at an angle almost perpendicular to the desk. Taking his time, he slid off her high heel before his palms sailed down either side of her calf, her thigh. Then he slipped off the other heel and raised that leg, too. He dropped a lingering kiss on one instep and then repeated the caress on the other.

Holding her ankles on either side of his ears, he let his gaze travel all the way down her body. He studied her rumpled skirt and, higher, the swell of her breasts encased in two scraps of lace. Releasing her legs, he scooped one breast out from its cup. Between finger and thumb, he twirled the nipple, lightly plucked the tip. When the tingling, beautiful burn was almost too much to bear, she reached out, inviting him down.

His tongue circled her nipple, flicked around the edges, before teasing the tip. As his mouth covered the peak and he lightly sucked, she sighed and knotted her fingers in his hair. She murmured about how amazing he was—how incredible he made her feel—as the pulse in her womb beat stronger and the fuse linking pleasure to climax grew alarmingly short. She adored the suction, the careful graze of his teeth but, so much more now, she needed him to open her—to enter and to fill her.

He shifted his attention to scooping her other breast from the bra. As he turned his head and his mouth worked its magic there, his hands slid under her shoulders. When he drew her toward him, she was raised up and then off the desk to stand before him. His mouth left her nipple with a soft smacking sound before he unsnapped her bra and released her skirt's clasp. The skirt dropped at the same time she shrugged off her bra and he whipped open his belt, unzipped his pants and fell back into his big leather chair.

She was down to hold-up stockings and briefs. He tipped forward and two fingers slid under the elastic strips resting on each hip. He pressed a moist kiss high on her leg just shy of her sex before he dragged the silk triangle all the way down. The tip of his tongue drew a slow, moist path across her bikini line as a palm filed up over her belly, her abdomen and then high enough to weigh one breast. When his tongue trailed lower, fire shot through her body. Gripping the hand kneading her breast, she dropped her head to press kisses on each fingertip.

Reclining, he drew her along with him until she straddled his lap. She hadn't noticed until now but he'd already found a foil-wrapped condom. To give him room, she grabbed the back of the chair and pushed up on her knees—which relocated her sex at the level of his mouth.

As he rolled protection on, he dotted kisses on one side of her mound then the other. Then he guided her down until the tip of his length nudged at her opening and eased a little inside.

The rush was so direct, so entirely perfect, Grace shuddered from her crown to the tips of her still-stockinged feet. He held her in that position, hovering, as his lips trailed her throat and he told her how much he'd missed her, missed this. When she clasped his ears and planted her lips over his, he eased her down a little more.

He rotated her hips in a way that put pressure on an internal hot spot that already felt ready to combust. When he eased out and in again, deeper this time, a trail of effervescent sensations drifted through the expressways of her veins. Hands on her hips, he urged her up until the tip of his erection was cupped by her folds. Then he brought her down again, more firmly, filling her completely this time.

The slam hit her everywhere and all at once. Her walls squeezed at the same time her head dropped into his hair. She wanted to keep him there, buried deep inside of her. She needed to hold onto the fringes of this feeling that let her know she was already hanging so close to that edge. With each and every breath, the world dropped farther away. She'd become only the rhythm beating in her brain, ordering her movements, stoking those flames.

As his tempo increased, her breath came in snatches. When a thrust hit that hot spot again, she let go of the chair and pulled his face up to hers. Her fingers knotted in his hair as their tongues darted in and out.

And then his movements slowed to an intense, controlled grind. When his tongue probed deeper, everything started to close in.

As Wynn thrust forward, she flopped back, wrapping her legs around his hips. When he moved harder, faster, she couldn't hold on. The force of her orgasm threw her back more.

As she stiffened, he drew her toward him, his arms holding her like a vice. When his mouth closed over hers, it only pushed her higher. She came apart, every fiber, every thought. She felt as if she'd been released into the tightest, brightest place that had ever existed. Nothing could interrupt the energy, nothing could defuse the thrill. Nothing... except...

Except maybe...

She frowned.

That sound.

Who was knocking on the door?

With the throbs petering out, reality seeped back in. She was crouched over Wynn, naked but for stockings, one of which was pushed down below the knee. Wynn at least still had his pants on, even if they weren't covering what they normally would.

When the knock came again and a man called out, she looked to Wynn, who put a finger to her lips. A sound filtered back from the other side of the room—the knob rattling. With her eyes, she asked, *What do we do?* and he gave her a *don't worry* look. Then the rattling stopped.

After a long moment, he whispered, "Let's pretend that didn't happen—the interruption, I mean." He stole a deep kiss. "Not this."

When he leaned in close and flashed her his slanted smile again, she turned her head, let out a breath and gathered herself. The lights were so bright. Had the person at the door heard any telltale sighs or groans?

She held her damp brow. "We got carried away."

He was nibbling her shoulder. "Uh-huh." His mouth slid up her throat. "Let's do it again."

Pulling back, she gaped at him and almost laughed. "You're crazy."

"It's my office. My company." He dropped a kiss on her chin, on her jaw. "I can be crazy if I want."

He pulled her closer and she felt him still thick and rigid inside of her. She'd been so involved in her own responses, she hadn't thought about him, although now she got the impression he was dangerously close to climaxing, too. But what if that knocking came again? Wondering if someone was still hovering around out there wasn't so great for the mood.

As if reading her thoughts, he nodded toward a connecting door. "I have a suite through there I use if I've had a long day and feel too beat to drag myself home."

"Let me guess." She arched a brow. "There's a bed."

His lips grazed hers. "Coming right up."

Later, as she and Wynn lay in the adjoining suite's bed, her blood hummed with warmth, as if every drop were coated in soft golden light. She felt so high, she couldn't imagine enduring a less satisfied state. She wouldn't worry about whether this had been a dumb move or merely inevitable. Now that Wynn had finished to supreme satisfaction what had begun in his office, Grace only wanted to bask in the afterglow…although she did feel unsettled about one thing.

With his arm draped around her shoulders, Wynn was nuzzling her crown while Grace snuggled in and asked, "Any idea who knocked on the door?"

"Christopher Riggs. I put him on here at my father's recommendation. Guess he had something he wanted to share."

"Something urgent?"

"Right now, this takes priority."

When he leaned forward and grinned, she pushed up on an elbow. "It sounded urgent."

He lay back and cradled his head. "He's full of ideas. Good ones. But nothing that can't wait till tomorrow."

When Wynn rolled over and his mouth once again covered hers, thoughts of Christopher Riggs evaporated. All that mattered were the shimmering emotions wrapping around her body and her mind. She could lie here with Wynn like this all night, but she winced at the thought of slinking out of the building after dawn. He might not like it, either.

When his mouth gradually left hers, his strong arms bundled her closer still. "I'll book another ticket for Sydney."

Cupping his raspy jaw, she brushed her lips back and forth over his. "I haven't said yes yet."

"But you will," he said with a confidence that made her feel somehow safe.

Before they'd begun to make love outside in his office, yes, she had decided to change her mind and go with him. Naturally his family would be curious about her life, but she didn't need to answer any questions she felt uncomfortable with.

Wynn's hand trailed down over her hip. "And we could spend more time together," he murmured against her lips. "More time like this."

Mmm. So nice. "You've convinced me," she said, brushing her smile over his. "I'll go."

His dark eyes lit and his smile grew. "I'll let Cole know tomorrow. Teagan will be stoked, and you'll love Tate. I think he's the one I'm looking forward to seeing again most. Dad must be counting down the days."

Did Wynn mean *counting down the days to the wedding*, or, "Has Tate been away?"

He hesitated, frowned and then propped himself up. "There's been some trouble back home."

He relayed details surrounding the problems Guthrie Hunter had experienced with a stalker. Unbelievable, Hollywood thriller type stuff.

"Tate was with Dad the day he was assaulted," Wynn

said. "We all thought it best that he be removed from that situation until they catch the guy. He stayed with Teagan first. Now he's with Dex."

"But he's going back to Australia next week, right? So, the stalker's been caught?"

"Not yet."

The pieces of the puzzle began to slot into place. She thought back. "Last night, when I assumed your brother's wedding would be a huge event…"

"It was decided that a small and therefore more easily controlled ceremony would be wise."

"So where's the wedding being held?"

"At the family home. They have a huge mansion overlooking the harbor. Obviously security will be of the highest priority. We have a top gun in the security world on the job. Brandon Powell is the best."

"Does my dad know about all this?" She hadn't seen any reports in the news. Obviously the Hunters had worked to keep the whole ordeal as quiet as possible.

"We've tried to keep it out of the media, but our fathers have spoken about it. Brock and I touched on the subject the other night, too."

Clearly the problem was serious—serious enough for a father to ship his youngest halfway around the world. What lay behind it all?

Wynn eased out a breath. "It's been months since that last incident, and the investigation is still going strong. If anyone thought there was any possibility of danger, Tate wouldn't be coming home."

"So, he's staying home for good?"

Wynn hesitated. "Not decided yet." His hand wrapped around hers. "I'm looking forward to seeing all the family again together. It'll be good having you be a part of that, too."

An odd feeling crept into her stomach. The idea of some

psycho searching out Guthrie Hunter, intent on doing major harm… It chilled her to the bone. On the other hand, Wynn seemed so certain that everything was under control. Hopefully Brandon Powell would find some answers, and fast.

Six

Brock Munroe commuted to Manhattan from Long Island each weekday for work. However, rather than ask her father for a lift, Grace hired a car to drive herself to the French-inspired manor she'd once called home.

On returning to New York last week, Grace had, of course, arranged to drop by. That day she'd been welcomed by fifty of the family's closest friends. Everyone had been so careful not to mention Sam. Even her mother, perhaps his biggest fan, seemed to try. But Grace wouldn't run the risk of being swamped again. She'd decided that on subsequent visits, including this one, she'd show up unannounced.

Grace drove up the wide, graveled drive and took in the manicured lawns and the manor's grand provincial theme. A moment later, the Munroe's soaring front door was opened by a woman who had just joined the house staff earlier that year.

"Miss Munroe!" With a wide smile, the housekeeper

ushered her through. "Your mother will be pleased to see you."

"Thanks, Jenn." Grace stepped onto the white-oak hardwood flooring of the double-story foyer. Absorbing the familiar smells of cypress beams and jasmine-scented incense, she glanced around. "Where is she?"

"The sunroom. I need to consult on the dinner menu with your mother. I'll walk you through." Jenn headed down the hall. "Your sister's here."

"Tilly?"

The youngest Munroe girl was in her final year of high school. Popular as well as a brain, Tilly seemed to breeze through life, blithely knocking down whatever obstacle got in her way.

"Matilda's upstairs," Jenn said, "dancing to one of her routines, I expect." Pointing her rubber-soled toes, the housekeeper gave Grace a cheeky grin. "I learned dance when I was young." She looked ahead again. "Rochelle's here, too."

Grace's step faltered and she groaned. Guess she'd catch up with everyone, then.

A pattering of footfalls filtered down the hall before a little girl turned a corner and trundled into view, her mahogany curls bouncing in a cloud around her head. When Grace's five-year-old niece saw her, April squealed. Putting her head down, she ran in earnest, sending layers of play necklaces jangling and clinking around her neck. Laughing, Grace knelt and caught her niece as she ploughed into her open arms. April smacked a kiss on her cheek.

"The bell rang and Granma sent me." April held her aunt's face in tiny, dimpled hands. "We didn't know it'd be *you!*"

They rubbed noses. Then Grace pushed up to her full height and took her niece's hand.

"What've you been up to, princess?" Grace asked as they strolled on.

"Daddy's working hard. He has lots of people to fix."

"Your daddy's a surgeon. Very important job."

"Uh-huh. He's busy." Innocent brown eyes turned up to meet her aunt's. "Mommy says he has to stay away a while."

At the hospital? Or was Trey at a medical convention? No doubt, she'd hear the entire story from Rochelle soon— one more treat in her sister's chocolate box of "perfect married life" tales.

Nearing the sunroom, April skipped on ahead. "Gracie's here!" she called.

Looking exquisite in an apricot jersey dress, Suzanne Munroe pushed up from a white brocade sofa. Grace couldn't remember a time when her mother had looked anything other than exquisite. As a girl, Grace wanted to grow up to be just like her and had sought out her mother's approval in everything. If Mom suggested she tie ribbons in her hair, ribbons it would be. If her mother proposed singing lessons, Grace would do her best to reach those high notes. As she'd gotten older, she'd come to understand that she had her own identity and dreams to pursue.

The dynamics of their relationship had needed to change.

But apron strings made of steel weren't easy to break. As her mother crossed over, Grace imagined those same high-tensile tendrils reaching out to coil around her now. But at age twenty-six, whose fault was that—her mother's for not listening, or her own for not making herself heard?

Grace walked into an extra-long hug from her mother at the same time Suzanne Munroe instructed Jenn to come back with some suggestions for tonight's menu, which, she reminded the housekeeper, needed to be free of all nut and egg products. April was allergic. Then, pulling back, her mother gestured toward the stash of costume and kids' jewelry littering a coffee table. Lit by afternoon sunshine steaming in through a bank of picture windows, piles of red, green and yellow "diamonds" glittered like a children's book treasure.

Her mother explained. "April and I have been trying on our jewels."

Grace crouched beside April, who was holding up another bundle of necklaces in front of her pink pinafore bodice.

"When I was young, I loved dressing up," Grace told her niece.

"You had more costumes than regular clothes," her mom pointed out. "One minute you were a princess, then a mermaid...the next, a bride..."

On the surface, that last remark was harmless; however, Grace didn't miss the lamenting tone. The connection. Sam hadn't been the high-flying lawyer or doctor her upper-crust mother might have preferred for a son-in-law, but his family was extremely wealthy and, having saved two young boys from a raging inferno a couple of years ago, he'd been known as a hero. Before Sam's accident, how many times had her mother announced that she couldn't wait to see Grace in a white gown and veil? Couldn't wait for her to make them all happy as a bride?

"Your costumes...can I have the princess one?" April cupped the top of her head. "Does it have a crown?"

"That was a long time ago," Grace replied. It went way back to a time when she'd first known Wynn Hunter.

Her mother took Grace's hands. "I brought Nan back with me from Maine. She's been asking about you."

Grace remembered how frail her grandmother had looked three months ago, one hand resting on her husband's rose-strewn coffin, the other pressing a lace handkerchief to her cheek.

"How is she?" Grace asked.

"Still feeling lost." Her mother gave Grace a "you'd understand" look before flicking a glance toward the stairs. "She's napping."

"Nanna naps all the time," April lamented, slotting a multicarat "ruby" on her middle finger and then scooting off up the stairs, presumably to check.

"When she sees you," her mother went on, "I'm sure she'll perk up. You'll stay for dinner." She dropped her chin. "Now, I won't take no for an answer."

Grace was about to say that of course she'd stay—she also wanted to ask where Rochelle was hiding—but then two items resting on the mantle of the French limestone fireplace drew her attention and the words dried on her tongue. When her mother's attention shifted to the mantle, too, her shoulders slumped. Crossing to the fireplace, her mother studied the photos—one of Grandpa, the other of Sam.

"Last week, before you called in," her mother said, returning with Sam's photo in hand, "I put this away. Your father didn't think you needed reminding. Of course, I put it back out after you left." She smiled down at the picture and sighed. "He always looked so handsome in his uniform."

When she held the frame out to her, Grace automatically stepped away. Yes, Sam was kind and brave and handsome. He was a natural with kids, including April. But her father was right. She didn't need reminding. She lived with enough memories.

But she couldn't go back—change what had already played out. She could only move forward, and now seemed the time to let her mother know precisely that, and as plainly as she could.

"I'm going to Australia," Grace announced. "Leaving next week."

Her mother's brow pinched. "Why? With whom?"

"With Wynn Hunter."

While Grace's heart hammered against her ribs, her

mother blinked several times before a smile appeared, small and wry.

"Your father mentioned that he'd run into Wynn. But now, you're...what? Seeing each other?"

"His brother Cole's getting married in Sydney. Wynn asked if I'd like to go. It'll be nice to catch up with Teagan."

"I saw Wynn at his mother's funeral a few years back. At his father's subsequent wedding, too. He seemed to have grown into a fine young man." Her focus dipped to the photo again, and then she arched a brow. "Is it serious?"

Grace could truthfully admit, "Not serious at all."

"So, you're not having a...well," her voice dropped, "a relationship?"

Grace thought about it. "That would depend on your definition."

"I see. More a fling." Her mother's look was dry—*wounded*—as she crossed to slot the frame back on the mantle. "It's none of my business...." Then she took a breath and swung back around. "But, I'm sorry, Grace. I can't say I approve. Those types of affairs might seem like a harmless distraction. Except someone always gets hurt."

A movement near the stairs drew Grace's eye. Rochelle was wandering over. Her face was almost as pale as the white linen shirt she wore. With a fluid gait, her mother joined her.

"My God, Rochelle," Grace murmured, "what's wrong?"

When their mother asked, "Is April with Nan?" Rochelle found energy enough to nod and settle on the sofa. Sitting, too, Grace held her older sister's arm and examined her blotched complexion.

"Shell, you've been crying."

Rochelle shuddered out a defeated breath. "Trey's had an affair. He's gone."

The room seemed to tilt. Grace remembered April's comment about her daddy needing to stay away. So, he'd left the family home? Or had Rochelle kicked him out? But none of it made sense. Those two had the perfect marriage, the kind of union their parents held up as a shining example. The kind of relationship their mother wanted for all her girls. The kind of bond Grace had once tried to convince herself she'd had with Sam.

In the past, Rochelle's stories revolving around her sparkling life had grated. Still, Grace loved her sister. She adored her niece. Now, as tears filled Rochelle's desolate green eyes, Grace wanted to help if she could.

"Do you know the other woman?"

"A nurse. A friend." Rochelle set her vacant stare on the far wall. "I had no idea. She held April's hand while we all watched fireworks on Independence Day."

When a tear slid down Rochelle's cheek, Grace folded her sister in her arms; she couldn't imagine how dazed and sick to her stomach she must feel. And if Trey had confessed... Was the affair still on?

"Is Trey still seeing this woman?"

"Doesn't matter whether he is or not." Their mother's elegant fingers clutched her throat as she sniffed. "The damage is done."

Grace considered her mother's indignant look and made the leap: *this* was an example of a fling's dire consequences.

Another, younger voice boomed out across the room. "Yay! Gracie's here!"

With a hip-hop gait, Tilly entered the room. Given those shocks of black and burgundy hair, she might have stuck her finger in a power socket. Grace noted that Rochelle was swiping at her cheeks, putting on a brave face—the stoic Munroe way.

So, Tilly didn't know?

Tilly was blinking from one to the other. "What's up?"

Her mother busied herself tidying the jewels. "Everything's fine."

Tilly crossed her arms. "Doesn't look fine."

"Grace is staying for dinner." Taking control of the situation, as usual, their mother moved to slip an arm around her youngest daughter's waist. "Jenn can prepare a big roast with sweet potato rounds for appetizers. Oh, and how about a strawberry torte to finish?"

While Rochelle looked flattened, Tilly seemed confused and Grace couldn't help but recall: torte had been Sam's favorite.

When Brock Munroe arrived home that evening, Suzanne took him aside, presumably to relay the news regarding Trey's infidelity. During dinner, their father remained stony-faced, poor Nan and Rochelle barely spoke and Tilly quietly observed the whole scene. Their mother overcompensated with a slew of chatter—except when it came to the subject of Grace's visit to Sydney.

While her father patted her hand and said the trip sounded nice—he obviously didn't see a problem with regard to Guthrie Hunter's recent difficulties or her accompanying Wynn over there—the tension at the other end of the long table built.

After plates were cleared, Nan excused herself, April was put to bed and Grace decided some fresh air and alone time were in order.

She'd bought a notebook the day before. Now with that book and a rug tucked under one arm, she ventured out onto the back partly enclosed terrace, which overlooked the pool. She rested an elbow on the wicker chair's arm, tapped the pen against her chin and let her mind wind back. In these surroundings with her family—here and now seemed the best place to start.

Grace was a world away, adding to how events had unraveled the night of Sam's accident, when she was interrupted.

"What are you writing?"

Snapping back to the present, Grace focused on Rochelle, who had appeared beside a row of potted sculptured shrubs. She half fibbed. "Working on an exercise."

"For speech therapy?"

"It's definitely about getting a message clear."

Once she'd begun to jot down her thoughts, she'd experienced a kind of catharsis. Now she wondered why she hadn't thought to do this before.

"How're you feeling?" Grace asked, closing the notebook.

"Less shaken than I was earlier," Rochelle admitted. "April's eyes were itching before she nodded off."

"Allergies?"

"Maybe just tired. She's had a big day." She gestured toward a chair. "Can I join you?"

"I'd like that."

"I came from Tilly's room." Rochelle lowered into a chair. "She wanted to know what was wrong."

"You told her?"

"She might be seventeen but she's not a child. She said she'd come stay over the holidays if April and I needed company."

"Tilly's always been a good kid."

"And the only one in this family who Mom can't corral. That girl has the stubbornness of a mule."

"Of *ten* mules."

They both grinned before a distant look clouded Rochelle's eyes. Bowing her head, she studied her left hand. The enormous diamond on her third finger caught the artificial light, casting shifting prisms over her face.

"It's hard to believe it was all an illusion," Rochelle murmured. "That he doesn't really love me."

"Did Trey say that?"

"A person doesn't eat off another plate if he's happy

with the dish he has at home. This year, I wanted to try for another baby. Trey said to wait." Biting her lip, she let her head rock back. "I'm such an idiot."

"None of this is your fault. No one deserves that kind of betrayal."

"Mom didn't want Trey and I to get married. She thought he was a flirt. Women respond when he walks into a room." Rochelle's watery eyes blinked slowly as her mouth formed a bittersweet smile. "I felt lucky."

They sat in silence for a while, studying the shadows beyond the terrace, before Rochelle spoke again.

"I'm sorry I wasn't much of a help when Sam passed away. I liked him."

Yeah. "Everyone liked Sam."

"But you didn't love him, did you, Grace? Not deeply and with all your heart."

Grace froze as a surreal sensation swept through her body. She stared at her sister. "You knew?"

"He looked at you the same way I look at Trey—with adoration, and hope."

When Rochelle hugged herself, Grace threw one side of the rug over for her to share.

"If he hadn't died," Rochelle said, snuggling in, "do you think you'd have got married?"

"No." Grace shook her head. "Even if everyone else thought we should."

"I always wondered why Trey asked me."

"Maybe because you're smart and beautiful—"

"And filled with insecurities? You can't imagine how tiring it is, pretending everything's amazingly wonderful when you wonder if your husband thinks your hips are monstrous, or you're not witty enough, and it's a matter of time before someone finds out you're a big fat fraud."

Queen Rochelle had never thought she was good enough?

The stories about her fabulous life were all a front? Guess they weren't so different, after all.

"We all have insecurities," Grace admitted. "At some stage, we all pretend."

"All those late, long hours…" Rochelle's nostrils flared. "He's probably had other flings."

There was that word again. That jolt. But her situation with Wynn was a thousand times different from Rochelle's. No cheating was involved—although in some ways they were each still attached to other people: her to Sam's memory, and Wynn to his beautiful ex.

Wynn had said that woman was in his past and yet she'd seen the emotion in his eyes. His ex had broken it off. Had she cheated on him the way Trey had cheated on Rochelle? Sam would never have done such a thing. Wynn, either.

Surely not.

"When are you leaving for Australia?" Rochelle asked.

Grace was still shivering from that last thought. "Monday. Mom's not pleased about it."

"Daddy thinks it's a good idea. I do, too. It's been years but I liked Wynn Hunter, even if he seemed a little intense."

"He's still intense, but in a different, steady-simmer kind of way. There's something about him, Shell. Something… hypnotic." Grace's smile wavered. "Almost dangerous."

"Different from Sam, then?" Rochelle joked.

"In pretty much every way."

When Grace shifted, the notebook slipped. Rochelle caught it and handed it back. Thinking about the secret contained within those pages, Grace ran a fingertip over the cover. What would her family say if they knew the whole story? Given Wynn's past, what would *he* say?

"I'm still not one hundred percent sure about going to Sydney," she admitted. "Cole's getting married. Apparently Dex is besotted with his fiancée. Cupid's shooting arrows all over the place where the Hunters are concerned."

She thought of her friend Amy and her bubbling enthusiasm over Wynn's kiss the previous weekend.

"I know the kind of atmosphere weddings create," Grace said. "Everyone's in love with the idea of being in love, and I'm over fending off other people's expectations."

"I'm not the one to give advice here but, Gracie, don't worry about what anyone thinks. You're a different person from the girl who started dating Sam. Hell, I'm different from the person who fell head over heels seven years ago for Trey. Back then, I felt giddy—so happy. Now I feel as if I've fallen in some deep, dark pit."

Grace's heart squeezed for her sister. It had been hard losing Sam, but he wasn't the father of her child. Regardless of this bombshell, Rochelle had loved her husband. Still, Rochelle could find comfort in the knowledge that people cared about her, and would look after both her and April, no matter what.

Grace held her sister's gaze. "You'll be okay. You know that, right?"

"Yeah. I know." Finding a brave smile, Rochelle leaned her head on her little sister's shoulder. "We both will."

Seven

The following week, the Qantas airbus Grace and Wynn had boarded in New York landed safely at Sydney Airport. With luggage collected, the pair jumped into a luxury rental vehicle and headed for the Hunter mansion. Travelling over connecting roads with the convertible's soft top down, Grace sighed at the picture-perfect views.

Sydney's heart was its harbor, an enormous, mirror-blue expanse that linked town and suburbs via fleets of green-and-yellow ferries. Built on the capital's northeastern tip, the giant shells of the world-famous Sydney Opera House reflected the majesty of a city whose mix of skyscrapers and parkland said "smart and proud and new." The mint-fresh air and southern-hemisphere sunshine left Grace feeling clean and alive, even after a twenty-odd hour flight.

She'd been a little anxious over whether Wynn's wedding-focused family might cast rose petals in their path, or if that crazy stalker situation would prove to be less contained than Wynn hoped and believed; if some madman wanted to harm

Wynn's father, what better time to creep out from the shadows than when the entire family was together and off guard.

But with a warm breeze pulling through her hair and the promise of nothing but relaxation, mixed with some sight-seeing adventures, she was feeling good about her decision. Nevertheless, when the BMW swung into the Hunter mansion's massive circular drive, Grace found herself drawing down a deep breath.

A member of the house staff answered the door and they were shown to a lounge room that was filled with people. An older silver-haired man, whom Grace recognized as Guthrie Hunter, stepped forward and put his arms around Wynn in a brief but affectionate man-hug before stepping back to assess his son's face.

"You look well, Wynn."

"You, too."

Grace heard relief in Wynn's voice; given those escalating threats on his father's life, no doubt he expected the wear to show.

And then all eyes were on her. Grace tacked up her smile at the same time Wynn introduced her.

"Everyone, meet Grace Munroe." Grinning, he cocked a brow. "Or, should I say, meet her again?"

An attractive woman around Grace's age romped up to hug her, long and tight. With thick blond hair pulled back in a ponytail, she smelled of oatmeal shampoo. Her tanned arms were strong, her body superfit and lean in her hot pink exercise singlet. Grace let loose a laugh and pulled back.

"Teagan, you need to be on the cover of your own health and fitness magazine!"

"Blame the day job." Teagan mock flexed a biceps. "I can't wait to catch up on all your news." She slid a knowing glance Wynn's way. "That is, if my dear brother will let you out of his sight for a minute."

Grace waited for Wynn to somehow brush the remark

aside. Instead he looped an arm around her waist and gave everyone a lopsided smile—a kind of confirmation. Which felt nice, but also wrong. She hadn't wanted to give anyone that impression. They weren't dating. Or at least they didn't have any long-term agendas, and she didn't want to have to fend off any open speculation that they did.

But then Wynn gave her a squeeze and she read the message in his eyes. *Relax.* Guess she was looking up-tight. Overreacting.

A man stepped up, acknowledging her with an easy smile and tip of his head. He had hair dark and glossy like Wynn's, classically chiseled features and ocean-green eyes...

"You, I recognize," Grace exclaimed. "Cole, right?"

"The pigtails are gone," Cole joked, "but you haven't lost that cheeky grin." He beckoned someone over—a stunning woman with a waterfall of dark hair and eyes only for this man. She held out a hand—slender and manicured.

"I'm Taryn, Cole's blushing bride-to-be." Her Australian accent was pitch-perfect and welcoming. "We're so glad you could both make it."

"Wynn's excited about being here for the wedding, see-ing everyone," Grace admitted. "I am, too."

Another man sauntered up. This brother's hair was sun-streaked, and his expression was open for all who cared to see. Those tawny eyes—like a lion's—were unmistakable.

"I'm Dex," he said, "Let me introduce you to the love of my life."

Laughing, a statuesque redhead dressed in modest denim cut-offs stepped up and shook Grace's hand heart-ily. "Shelby Scott. Pleased to meet you."

Grace detected a hint of a twang. "Texas?"

"I was born in a real nice place in Oklahoma," Shelby said with pride.

"Mountain Ridge," Dex added. "Ranch country. You

should see her in a pair of spurs." With his strong arms linked around her, Shelby angled to give him a censoring look. Dex only snatched a kiss that lingered until a boy with Dex's same tawny-colored eyes and wearing a bright red T-shirt, broke through the wall of adults.

"Are you going to marry Wynn?" The boy's shoulders bobbed up and down. "All my brothers are getting hitched."

Dex ruffled the boy's hair. "Hey, buddy, rein it in a little. We don't want to scare Grace off just yet."

It seemed like a room full of curious eyes slid back toward Grace as the boy considered, and then asked again. "Well, are you?"

Wynn hunkered down. "Tate, when Grace and I first met, she was around your age. Crazy, huh?"

Shoving his hands into the back pockets of his shorts, Tate eyed Grace as if he truly did think it was mad, but also interesting. "I like dinosaurs," he told her. "Do you?"

Kneeling down, Grace tried to think. "I don't know any."

"That's okay." When Tate smiled, Grace saw he'd lost a tooth. "I have lots. I'll show you."

Taking her hand, Tate yanked but his father stopped him short. "Son, our latest guest hasn't met all the family yet."

Another woman—a *very* pregnant woman—entered the room. Her high cheekbones and large, thickly-lashed eyes bespoke classic beauty—or would have if not for the grimace, which seemed to have something to do with the way she held the small of her back. This must be Eloise, Grace thought. Wynn's stepmother, although she looked young enough to be a sister.

"I swear, if I don't have this child soon," Eloise said, "I'll collapse. I can't carry this twenty-pound bowling ball around inside of me much longer."

As Eloise ambled nearer, Cole's shoulders inched up. Taryn slipped an arm through her fiancé's, as if reminding him she was there, a support. Grace wondered.

What's that all about?

Stopping before the newly arrived couple, Eloise dredged up a put-upon smile and Wynn stepped forward to brush a kiss on his stepmom's cheek. As he drew away, Eloise looked to Grace as if she expected the same greeting from her. Grace only nodded hello before saying, "Thanks for having me in your home," and then, "Can I ask—do you know what you're having?"

"I've prayed for a daughter. Every woman wants one." Eloise's gaze flicked to Teagan, who was squatting, tying Tate's shoelace. "*Another* daughter, I mean." She set her weight on her other leg. "After that long trip, you both must need a good lie down. Your old room's all ready for you, honey," she said to Wynn.

"Barbecue's happening around five," Cole added.

"I'll bring a dinosaur," Tate said.

A moment later, Wynn was ushering Grace up a grand staircase, then down a corridor that led to a separate wing of the house. His "room" looked more like a penthouse suite. Standing in the center of the enormous space, which included a king-size bed, Grace set her hands on her hips.

"You had all this to yourself growing up?" she asked.

"Doesn't mean I sat around, bathing in milk and ringing the butler's bell."

"No?" She turned to face him.

"I worked very hard at my studies and sport."

She wandered over. "Wanna show me your trophies?"

"I wanna show you something."

His arms circled her and his mouth covered hers. It was a stirring kiss. Warm and good and…somehow different. Must be because of the surroundings. As his lips left hers, she let her eyes drift open and memories of the Hunters and that Colorado Christmas came flooding back. One memory in particular. She pressed her lips together to cover a laugh.

"I can still see you gnashing your teeth over that snow-man's hat not sitting straight."

He pretended to scowl. "Because you and Teagan kept messing with it when my back was turned."

She didn't cover her laugh this time. "You were so darn easy to stir."

When she bopped his nose, he jerked to take a bite at that finger. "You were lucky I remained a gentleman."

"I don't remember you behaving in a gentlemanly fash-ion. You'd go all stiff and mutter that I needed a good spanking."

His lips came close to graze up the slope of her throat. "I'm feeling and thinking the same thing now."

While his tongue tickled her earlobe, the zipper on the back of her dress whirred down. She felt the cool air, and then a warm palm slid in over her skin before skating down toward her rear. Closing her eyes, Grace let her head rock back.

"I thought we were going to rest before dinner," she said, "not play."

"Either way, we need to get out of these clothes."

He slid the dress off one shoulder, she handled the other shoulder, and the dress fell to the floor.

Since that evening in his office, they'd seen each other regularly. Whenever they got together, inevitably they would end up in bed, exploring each other's bodies, dis-covering what the other liked best, and then finding new ways to top that. Like that thing his mouth was doing now to the lower sweep of her neck. The gentle tug of his teeth on her skin felt light and yet deep enough to ignite a set of nerve endings directly connected to her core.

But today they'd been travelling around the clock. Her body was pleading for a warm shower and some rest.

She stepped out of the dress pooled around her ankles and headed for the dresser, stopping twice to slip off each shoe while unfastening her heavy necklace. Laying the necklace on top of the dresser, she caught Wynn's reflection in the mirror. His gaze was dark and fixed upon her hips, the back of her briefs. He didn't look tired at all.

When he slipped off his shoes and moved up behind her, Grace's insides began to squeeze. His palms sailed over her bare shoulders, down her arms. Leaning back against his muscled heat, she breathed in his musky scent as two sets of fingers drew lines across her ribs before arrowing down, running light grooves over her belly to her briefs. He plucked at the elastic and murmured, "These need to come off."

As his fingers dived lower to comb and lightly tug at her curls, liquid heat filled her.

For comfort's sake, she hadn't worn a bra on the flight. In the mirror, through half-lidded eyes she watched him scoop up a breast with one hand while, lower, his other worked beneath her briefs. When he lightly pinched and rolled her nipple, she shivered, sighed and let her head drop to one side. The palm covering her mound urged her closer, pushing her bottom back to mold against him.

Then, knees bending, he began to slide down. She savored the feel of his defined abdomen, his chest and then chin, riding lower down her spine. When she felt his breath warm the small of her back, a finger hooked into the rear of her briefs and the silk was eased down to her knees. He dropped a lazy kiss on a hip then the slope of her bare behind. At the same time, the stroking between her legs delved deeper, slipping a little inside of her. She couldn't see his reflection in the mirror anymore—she only felt his mouth as it explored one side of her tush before trailing across the small of her back to sample the other side.

When his lips traveled lower and he kissed the sensitive area under the curve of one cheek, she held on to the dresser for support. Between her thighs, his fingertip rode up until he grazed and circled that sensitive nub. When he applied perfect pressure to the spot, stars shot off in her head before falling in a tingling, fire-tipped rain. She brought up one knee. Her briefs dropped from that leg before falling to rest around the other ankle. Pushing to his feet, he turned her around.

As his teeth danced down the column of her throat and his hands cupped her rear—lifting her at the same time they scooped her in—she gripped his shoulders. Steamy heat came through the fabric of his shirt to warm her palms. She brushed her wicked grin through his hair.

"Am I the only one getting undressed here?"

He paused. "Well, now, that could work."

He backed up a few steps while his gaze drank her in. Feeling desirable—and a little vulnerable—she leaned back against the dresser as his chest expanded on a deeply satisfied breath.

"You're perfect," he said. "I could stand here and just look at you all day."

Her cheeks were burning, not because she was embarrassed but because his words, the honesty in his voice, touched her in a way that left her wanting to please and tease him this much all the time.

With his focus glued on her, he backed up until his legs met the bed. After he threw back the covers and sat on the edge of the mattress, he beckoned her with a single curl of a finger. He wanted her to walk over and, given the glimmer in his eyes, he wanted her to take her time.

She took a breath and set one foot in front of the other; the closer she got, the more his dark eyes gleamed. When she was close enough, he reached to cup her neck and draw her down.

Her hair fell forward as her lips touched his. The contact was teasing—deliberately light. Her tongue rimmed the upper and lower seam of his mouth before she nipped his bottom lip and gently sucked. That's when his mouth took hers. As a strong arm coiled around her back, drawing her toward him more, she let her lips slide down and away from his at the same time she lowered to kneel at his feet.

She was positioned between his opened thighs, her mouth inches away from his chest. Taking her time, she released a shirt button, two and then three. Each time, she twirled her tongue over the newly exposed skin.

She pulled the shirttails out from his jeans, and when his shirt lay wide open and the bronzed planes of his chest and stomach were completely revealed, she started on his pants. With him leaning back, his arms supporting his weight, she flicked the snap, unzipped his fly. As she tugged at his jeans, her head dropped down.

Her tongue drew a lazy circle around his navel before she dotted moist kisses along the trail of hair that led to his boxer briefs. When she grazed her teeth over the bulge waiting there, his chest gave an appreciative rumble and he leaned back more, propping his weight on his elbows. Her fingers curled inside his briefs.

She dug out his engorged shaft and whirled a finger around the naked tip before her head lowered and her mouth covered him—barely an inch. Gripping his length at its base, her fist squeezed up as her mouth came down. Relishing the taste of him—the scent—she repeated the move again and again, taking her time, building the heat. He started to curl his pelvis up each time she came down while she squeezed him harder, took him deeper.

Too soon, he was sweeping her up and over, so that she lay flat on the bed. He whipped the shirt off his back and then retrieved a condom from his wallet, all before she could say she wasn't finished with him yet. When he tore open the foil, she took the condom and rolled the rubber all the way on. After ditching the jeans, he came back to kiss her, first thoroughly and then in one hungry, savoring snatch after another.

They were tangled up around each other, breathing ragged and energy pumped, when he urged her onto her side and pressed in against her—his front to her back. As he nuzzled the side of her neck, he drew her leg back over his and entered her in a "no prisoners" kind of way.

When he slid her leg back more, she stretched and ground against him. His thigh felt like a steel pylon. His chest was a slab of thermal rock. She grazed her cheek against his biceps as he held her and moved, setting up a rhythm that fed the pulse thumping in her throat and in her womb.

With his palm pressed against her belly, his fingers toyed with her curls. With each sweep, he grazed that uber-sensitive nub. The contact was maddening—drugging and delicious. When she was balanced on a precipice, oh-so ready to let go, he used his weight to tip her over.

Her leg uncoiled from around his thigh and her knee dug into the mattress at the same time her cheek pressed against the pillow. Settling in behind her, he began moving again, his pace faster now—fast enough for the front of his thighs to slap the backs of hers. This different angle changed the way that he filled her, placing a different pressure on a sensitive spot inside. The pleasure was so fragile and yet fierce—too exquisite to get her whirling mind around.

As his thrusts went deeper, he slid a palm under her belly to lift and press her closer. A searing heat compressed her core. A few more thrusts and she cried out as her fingers curled into the sheet and contractions swept in.

A heartbeat later, he gripped her hips and his strangled growl of release filled her ears.

Eight

"We don't have to go down," Wynn murmured as he bundled her close. "Go back to sleep."

After making love in his former bedroom, he and Grace had crashed. When his watch alarm had beeped a moment ago, he'd been stirred from a vivid dream—and Wynn rarely dreamed.

They were kids again, back in Colorado that Christmas long ago. There was a snowman with a screwy felt hat, and Wynn's scar was a fresh wound on his brow. Rather than blame an annoying brat for the gash, Wynn wondered if he'd tripped over his lace. He'd gone on to invite Grace—a lively, pretty thing—back to his parents' home in Australia.

"My brain feels full of cottonwool," Grace murmured against his chest as she tangled her leg around his. Her toes tickled the back of his knee. "But everyone's expecting us."

Inhaling the remnants of floral perfume mixed with the more alluring scent of *woman,* he kissed her crown. "They'll understand."

She glanced up. A line formed between her brows as she pushed hair away from her face. "We're not spending all our time here, right?"

"You mean in bed?"

She grinned. "In Sydney, dummy."

"I do have a surprise or two planned."

"Then I want to spend as much time as I can with Teagan while we're here." Grace shifted to lean up against the headboard of the bed. Her hair was mussed and still flopped over one side of her brow. "Do you know if she's seeing anyone? Anyone special?"

"Dex said he thought that she might be. But the man who catches our Ms. Independence will need to be darn determined."

She concurred. "Doesn't work until a girl wants to be caught."

"Like this?"

Craning up, he exacted one very thorough kiss that he didn't want to end.

When his mouth finally left hers, her breathing was heavier. The sheet had slipped from under her arms. Sliding down, he took a warm nipple deep into his mouth. His tongue was teasing the tip and his hand was snaking down over her belly when she gathered herself and pushed at his shoulders.

"I need a shower."

He spoke around the nipple. "You really don't."

Grace eased off the mattress and he lost possession of that breast. Then she was on her feet, standing in front of him with fists on her hips, as if that could put him off. He would have hooked her around her waist and brought her back—only he had a better idea.

Pushing up on an elbow, he cradled his cheek in his palm and nudged his chin. "Bathroom's that way."

Her eyes narrowed as if she suspected he might suddenly pounce, but he only smiled.

Two minutes later, Grace had the shower running and Wynn was swinging open the glass door to join her. When she turned to face him—her hair wet and rivulets of foam trailing over her body—her expression was not surprised. As he stepped in, she threaded slippery arms up and around his neck. With her breasts sliding and brushing against his ribs, she grazed her lips up his throat to his chin.

"You are so predictable," she said.

Grinning, he reached for the soap. "Don't bet on it."

"It's about time!"

Standing alongside of Wynn in the Hunter mansion's manicured backyard, Grace tracked down the source of the remark.

Inside an extravagant pavilion, two house staff flipped and prodded food grilling on a barbecue. A third attendant, carrying a drinks tray, was headed for the resort-style bar. Music played—a current hit from the U.K.—while a half dozen people splashed around in an enormous pool. Australian time put the hour at six o'clock, but the sun's heat and angle said they had a couple more hours of daylight yet to enjoy.

Grace heard the male voice that had greeted them earlier call again from the pool. "We were getting ready to come up and drag you two out of bed," Dex said as he splashed water in their direction.

Grace's cheeks heated, but it was a harmless remark. No one knew what she and Wynn had gotten up to. Even if they had guessed, they were all adults, with one exception.

In the pool, Tate was balanced on Cole's shoulders. He had his legs wrapped around his big brother's neck and was kicking in excitement. With a grin, Grace wondered where the dinosaurs were.

"Wynn!" the little boy called out. "I got a beach ball. We're in teams. You're with me!"

"Us against those two clowns?" Wynn called back, making a face as he gestured toward Cole and Dex. "Hardly seems fair."

Wynn wore a pair of square-leg black trunks that, along with his impressive upper body and long, strong legs, made Grace want to pounce on him again. She wore a bikini the color of the pool water with a matching resort-style dress cover. Now, the arm around her waist brought her closer as he asked, "Are you game?"

To splash around in that enormous pool with four boys?

Taryn was already out of the water, wringing her long dark hair, and Shelby was wading up the last of the arced pool stairs, right behind her. Teagan must be around somewhere, too.

"I have a feeling a lot of splashing and dunking is about to go down." She pinched his scratchy chin. "I'll go hang with the girls."

She craned up to catch his light kiss before returning her attention to the women. Shelby was motioning her over.

As Wynn ran up to the pool edge and did a cannonball, creating one hell of a splash, Grace accepted a glass of juice from the help and joined Shelby and Taryn near an extravagant outdoor setting.

Grace eyed Taryn's tan and smiled. "Wynn mentioned you and Cole had been off sailing."

Taryn wrapped a towel around her hips and folded herself into a chair. "A leisurely sweep around some Pacific islands." She sighed. "Pure heaven."

"When are you going again?" Shelby asked, grabbing a plastic flute of orange juice off the table before reclining into a chair.

"If all goes according to plan, we'll be able to fit it in just after the wedding." Taryn sent an adoring look over to where her fiancé was spiking a ball at Wynn. "Cole wants to start a family straightaway. Me, too."

Shelby leaned across and wrapped an arm around her future sister-in-law. "That's fabulous, hon."

Grace didn't feel she knew Taryn well enough to hug her. She saluted with her glass of juice instead.

Taryn cocked a brow Shelby's way. "Am I imagining it, or is Dex coming across as clucky, too?"

"Since looking after Tate these past weeks, he can't stop talking about having kids. We're really gonna miss that little guy if Guthrie decides he can stay." She sent Grace an apologetic look. "Sorry. We're leaving you out, running off at the mouth here."

Grace waved the apology away. She'd anticipated talk focusing on happily-ever-afters and babies. "I'm really glad for you both."

"Cole says you all knew each other as kids," Taryn said.

Grace glanced toward the pool. The three older brothers were play-wrestling, strong bodies glistening, muscles rippling, while Tate sat on the pool's edge, laughing and clapping his hands.

Grace admitted, "We've all changed a lot since then. I didn't recognize Wynn."

Leaning forward, Shelby straightened her bikini-top tie. Dex's fiancée had a presence—tall with striking features; she might have been a catwalk model rather than the nanny Dex had employed when he'd needed a sitter for Tate.

"They sure are big boys now," Shelby said. "What was Wynn like twenty years ago?"

"Earnest. Intense. He certainly didn't like girls. At least he didn't like me."

"And you?" Taryn asked. "Did you think he was cute even back then?"

"I had a tiny crush," Grace admitted. "A couple of times

I pinched his arm and ran away. The way he remembers it though, I harbored evil plans to ruin his life."

Taryn laughed. "True love," she said, while Shelby exclaimed, "It was meant to be, just like Dex and me. When we met, I was so off men. We took a long route round, but now I can't imagine life without him."

"I thought Cole was an arrogant jerk. He was so, my way or the highway." When Taryn came back from a memory that made her cheeks glow, she asked Grace, "How did you and Wynn meet up again?"

Grace cleared her throat and reinvented the truth.

"At a wedding," she said. "We talked, danced. He was leaving when the bride threw the bouquet. The flowers landed at my feet then skated across the floor right up to him. He brought them back and kissed me right in front of the crowd."

The words were out before Grace could think twice; she hadn't meant to reveal so much. Now Shelby was swooning while Taryn swirled her drink.

"A sentimental streak runs deep in the Hunter boys," Taryn said, "no matter how much they try to hide it at first. No question, they're all into family."

Grace focused on Wynn again. His arms out, he was encouraging Tate to dive back into the pool. Yes, she thought. If he ever got over the ex, Wynn would do well with a family of his own at some stage, and perhaps Taryn and Shelby were wondering if it might be with her. Still, this conversation didn't make Grace feel as uncomfortable as she'd thought it might. Rather she felt included—part of the club—even if the gist wasn't relevant to her.

While the three women discussed plans for the wedding as well as Taryn's dress, which sounded amazing, Grace spotted Teagan emerging from the house. Looking superfit in a black and neon-orange tankini, Teagan glanced around. Rising from her chair, Grace excused herself and waved her friend's way.

"What say we fill up some water bombs," Teagan said as Grace moved closer. "We can set off a full-scale attack."

Grace laughed. "You mean against the guys in the pool?"

"Who else?" Teagan took a fruit skewer from the nearby table filled with food. "I still can't believe you're here and Cole's getting married." Teagan's eyes sparkled. "It would be nosey to ask whether you and Wynn are headed that way, wouldn't it? It's just so bizarre thinking of you two together."

Grace's stomach gave a kick. "We're not really together, Tea. Not in the way, say, Shelby is with Dex."

"Oh. Sure." Teagan waved her skewer. "Nothing wrong with cool and casual. Totally understand."

Grace wasn't sure that she did.

She and Teagan hadn't communicated since those pen-pal letters years ago. Even so, Grace now felt that same connection—the trust. It seemed like only yesterday they had shared and talked about everything. Grace wanted to fill her friend in a little on her previous relationship but it wasn't for everyone's ears.

While the others were occupied with wedding talk, she told Teagan about Sam—what a great guy he'd been, how he'd died and how she should have let him go much sooner. She omitted what had transpired thirty minutes before the accident. No one knew the truth about that; she hadn't even written it down in her notebook yet. She finished by saying that whatever she and Wynn shared, it was with a view to having fun in the now rather than till death do them part.

"I'm in a similar kind of relationship," Teagan admitted. "On the surface, we're great together. Underneath, it's complicated."

"Is he coming to the wedding?"

"No. Like I said. Complicated." Teagan slid a grape off

the skewer. "He comes from a big family. His brothers and sisters are all already married. Damon is eager to follow in his siblings' footsteps, which includes heaps of kids."

"How many kids?"

"He's mentioned six."

Grace let out a long whistle. "I was thinking maybe three."

"Maybe none."

Grace's head went back. A couple having a half dozen children wasn't that common nowadays, was it? But none? Was it because Teagan thought it was too soon to be discussing having a family with this man? Maybe his many family members could be nosey and interfering.

Teagan was about to say more when Guthrie and Eloise strolled out of the house. As Guthrie helped his wife into a chair near the pool, Teagan nudged Grace.

"I should go see if they need anything."

Grace was about to follow when a pair of cold, strong arms coiled around her, hauling her back against a hard, equally chilly chest. Yelping, she jumped and tried to spin around, but Wynn wouldn't let go.

"Struggle is futile," he said while his sister laughed.

"Told you," Teagan said. "You should have bombed him while you had the chance."

Two hours later, Tate was in bed and Guthrie stood at the head of the outdoor table, preparing to say a few words. His smile was sincere, but also weary, as if he'd been on a long journey and knew that soon he could rest.

"I don't need to tell anyone how pleased I am to have you all together, to see you happy, particularly, of course, Cole and the soon-to-be bride, our dear Taryn."

While Cole lifted Taryn's hand to his mouth for a kiss, the rest of the gathering put their hands together in a light round of applause.

"Next Sunday will be a special day," Guthrie went on. "I've taken measures to be certain nothing is, well, spoiled." He lowered back into his chair. "Brandon is still working hard to track down information that will lead to the unmasking of the unknown parties who have caused us so much grief these past months. I want you all to be assured that security will be the top priority on the day."

"We've kept the announcement from the press," Cole said. "The invitation list is at bare-bones."

"No red carpet and blowing of horns," Dex pointed out, linking his arm through Shelby's.

"So, who did make the cut?" Teagan asked.

"You guys, of course," Cole said. "Taryn's aunt and a handful of our closest friends."

Wynn remembered Cole mentioning that Taryn's aunt was the only family she had.

"Your Aunt Leeanne and Uncle Stuart." Guthrie began his own list.

"Your sister and her husband? Nice," Teagan said. "We haven't seen them in ages."

"Talbot and Sarah," Guthrie continued, which raised a few eyebrows; until recently, when the attacks had started, the two older Hunter brothers hadn't spoken in years. "And Talbot's son."

Dex sat up. "Slow down. Talbot doesn't have any kids."

Flinching, Eloise pushed lightly on the top of her pregnant belly. "Seems one's worked his way out from the woodwork."

While Guthrie bowed his head as if restraining himself from reacting to the snide remark, Wynn got his mind around the statement—Uncle Talbot had a son? Was he the result of a previous relationship, or had Talbot at some stage strayed from the marriage bed?

Cole's comment was supportive. "I look forward to meeting him."

Guthrie sent a grateful smile. "There are a few people from Hunter Broadcasting. A couple of family friends." He flicked a look Wynn's way before addressing the table again. "Including a longtime friend and his wife, the Riggses."

Wynn sat up. Christopher Riggs's parents? Guess he'd be fielding questions relating to how their boy was doing in New York, not that there was much to report at this early stage.

Dex brought the conversation back to a more serious subject. "So, no new leads on the case?"

"Whoever's responsible," Guthrie said, "seems to have vanished off the face of the earth."

"And hopefully," Eloise added, "that'll be the end of that."

Cole growled. "I won't give up looking for that SOB until he's caught. Neither will Brandon."

Shelby agreed. "If you don't finish it, these kinds of things have an ugly habit of creeping back into your lives." She and Dex shared a look.

Taryn spoke up. "Sometimes troublemakers move to another country. Some simply pass away."

Grace's stomach was knotted as she listened intently to all the back and forths.

If she were Taryn, she would pray for that last scenario. Not only would Taryn want the wedding to unfold without a hitch. She'd want her future children to be immune to these kinds of dangers. All the Hunters wanted to keep Tate free from the possibility of coming to any future harm. One day soon, God willing, Taryn and Cole would have children of their own. Dex and Shelby, too. How could any one of them feel relaxed about having their son or daughter visit this home or spend time with their grandfather with this maniac still on the loose?

Wynn's ex must be grateful she didn't have to deal with

that dilemma. He had said that once he'd wanted to have a family with her. Although now Wynn was steering clear of commitment, which suited this situation just fine.

Wynn reached for her hand.

"You okay?" he said only loud enough for her to hear. The others were still discussing the stalker. "You really don't have to worry," he went on. "I don't know if we'll ever get to the bottom of all this, but those first three incidents were close together. After all this time, I don't think we'll hear from him again."

"So you'd be okay with Tate coming back here to stay?"

Wynn blinked. "He's not my son to say."

"If it were your son," she asked, "what would you do?"

Wynn's jaw tightened as he gave a tight grin. "That's a question I doubt I'll ever need to answer."

Grace watched as a recent-model pickup, boasting the name of a construction firm on its side panel, drove up to the Hunter estate and two privately uniformed men stepped forward to check it at the gate. At the side entrance, which led to the Hunters' vast manicured back lawn, another man waited, constantly running his eye over the zone.

Grace quietly took it all in while waiting for Wynn by their rental car parked on the drive. They'd stayed on for two days, picnicking, boating and generally catching up with his family. She'd been made to feel so welcome; she'd enjoyed every minute, particularly her chance to chill with Teagan, though Tea's idea of relaxation was a ten-mile jog followed by a protein shake. The words cheesecake and alcohol weren't in her vocabulary.

Apparently neither was "kids." Not that Teagan had brought that subject up again.

This morning Wynn had told her it was time to unveil his vacation surprise. They were in for a bit of a drive, he'd explained, but that was all part of the experience.

At breakfast, she and Wynn had said farewell for now to the rest of the clan. A moment ago, packed and about to jump in the car, Wynn had asked if she could wait a second while he gave his little brother another goodbye hug; Guthrie and Cole were in the side yard, teaching Tate to throw a pass.

From the side yard, Taryn spotted her and wandered over.

"The guys are sure enjoying being all together again," Taryn said as she joined her. Wynn had taken the ball and was executing a controlled toss to Tate. Taryn laughed. "You might need to go over and physically drag him away if you want to be on the road by noon."

"I don't mind." Grace straightened her hat; the sun Down Under had a real bite. "This is his time, not mine. I think he misses seeing Tate more than he knows."

"Tate is everyone's favorite, particularly when we all came so close to losing him that day."

Grace shuddered at the thought of seeing a loved one assaulted and then barely escaping an abduction. She couldn't imagine how a child would interpret and internalize all that. As if reading her thoughts, Taryn explained.

"He's spoken with counselors and doesn't appear to have nightmares, thank God. Cole was pretty shaken up over it, though. Not long after that incident, Cole took Tate to a park to toss a ball, like they're doing now. When Cole took his eyes off him for a minute, Tate vanished."

Grace held her sick stomach. "But Cole must have found him."

"Safe and sound. Cole told me later those few moments turned his world upside down. For the first time he understood what he truly wanted from life."

Grace surmised. "A family of his own."

"To protect. To love." Watching her fiancé swing Tate up onto his shoulders, happiness shone in Taryn's eyes.

"Not long after that ordeal, with Brandon Powell on the case, we set sail and got away for a few weeks. That time only brought me and Cole closer together. There hasn't been any trouble since."

"So, maybe Eloise is right," Grace said. "Perhaps the stalker's given up, gone away."

"Doesn't mean the Hunters will give up their search. Whoever's responsible needs to be behind bars."

Eloise appeared in the side yard. Guthrie crossed over to offer a chair to his pregnant wife. Grace couldn't help but notice Cole's reaction to his stepmother's appearance. He seemed to stiffen and his expression cooled before he swung Tate down from his shoulders. When Tate ran to join his mother and father, both Cole and Wynn headed over, too.

Although the men were well out of earshot, Taryn lowered her voice. "I'm sure you've guessed. Eloise isn't Cole's favorite person."

"Wynn mentioned something about how Cole and Dex think she married their father for his money."

"If only that were the worst of it."

Before Taryn could say more, Cole and Wynn were upon them. Cole acknowledged Grace with a big smile before leveling his hands on Taryn's hips and stealing a quick kiss. "What say we see how things are going out back?"

"Sounds good," Taryn replied.

Wynn opened the passenger door of their rental car for Grace. "We'll see you guys in a couple of days."

A moment later, when the convertible passed through the opened gates, both security guards threw them casual salutes. Grace wondered if they were wearing guns, and then whether they would need to use them while they were on this assignment. But everyone seemed so confident. All this security was only a precaution.

Wynn changed gears then reached to hold her hand.

"Ready for an adventure?"

Grace sat straighter and looked ahead.

"Maestro, lead the way."

Nine

By the time they reached the Blue Mountains west of Sydney, Grace had put her questions and concerns regarding the wedding's security out of her mind. Instead, as she slid out of the passenger seat, she focused on the magnificent retreat where Wynn had booked accommodation. With the sash windows and gothic-inspired pointed arches, the hotel reminded her of the Elephant Tea Rooms in London. Then there were the pure, eucalyptus-scented air and serene, top-of-the-world views…

And apparently Wynn had something even more amazing planned.

At the hotel reception counter, a man around Wynn's age lowered his magazine as they approached.

"Morning," the man said. "You have a reservation, sir?"

Wynn gave his name and the man—Mick, according to his badge—studied his computer screen.

"You don't appear to have a booking, Mr. Hunter."

Wynn's eyebrows hiked. "Look again."

A few seconds later, Mick shook his head. "We do have a room available. Ground floor. No view, I'm afraid."

When Wynn's expression hardened and he pulled out his cell phone, Grace cast a look around. A few guests were mulling over brochures. A few more were headed out the door to sight-see, she assumed. She looked back at Mick, who gave her a thin smile before Wynn disconnected. His voice was low and unyielding.

"My assistant assures me a reservation was made. She received a confirmation for a deluxe suite with views. She spoke with you personally, Mick."

Rubbing a palm over his shirt, Mick analyzed the screen again, and then his shoulders bounced with a "can't help you" shrug. "I apologize, sir."

Wynn rapped a set of fingertips on the counter. "Is your manager in?"

A little girl, around April's age, had wandered out from a room adjoining the reception area. She tugged on Mick's sleeve. "Daddy, wanna help me color?"

Mick called the manager before combing a palm over his daughter's wispy fair hair. "Hang on, peaches."

After a three-hour drive, Grace was simply happy to be here. She didn't care what kind of room they had. She certainly didn't want to upset that little girl.

Setting a forearm on the counter, Mick leaned closer. "I can do a great deal on that room, but all the suites are taken."

Another man strolled out. Introducing himself as the manager, he enquired, "Is there a problem?"

As Mick explained and Wynn put his objection forward, Grace stepped back. The manager was apologetic. Then, when he realized who Wynn was—the Hunter family was legendary in Australia—he was doubly so. When Mick got tongue-tied—he couldn't explain the missing email or botched booking—the little girl crept back and hid behind

that door. Her chocolate-brown eyes were wide. She had
no idea what the problem was, why her daddy was upset.

Wynn saw her too and held up his hands. "Don't worry,"
he said. "We'll take that room."

"I'm so sorry, Mr. Hunter," the manager said again.

Wynn took the key card. When they reached their com-
pact double room on the ground floor, Grace was curious.

Wynn dropped his cell phone on a table. "Not what I
had in mind."

"You weren't happy."

"I'm not a fan of incompetence."

"You wanted to tell them both that."

"I think I had a right."

"But you didn't." She moved over. "Why not?"

He shrugged. "No point."

"It was because of that little girl, wasn't it? You saw her
watching so you dropped it."

"It wasn't that big of a deal, Grace."

Grinning, she trailed a fingertip around his scratchy
jaw. "You backed off."

He narrowed his eyes at her. "You like a man who backs
down?"

"For those kinds of reasons, absolutely." She circled her
finger around the warm hollow at the base of his throat.
"You can be quite chivalrous, do you know that?"

"As opposed to what you thought of me as a kid." His
hands skimmed down her sides. "You didn't think that I was
behaving in a gentlemanly fashion back then, remember?"

"Except whenever I teased you, no matter how much you
wanted to belt me, you always walked away."

His lips twitched as he moved in closer. "I remember at
least one time when Cole needed to hold me back."

Standing on her toes, she brushed the tip of her nose
against his. "Face it, Wynn Hunter. You're one of the good
guys."

"Uh-uh." He angled his head to nip her lower lip. "I'm bad to the bone."

Before she let him kiss her, she admitted, "But in a very good way."

Two hours later, Grace was gazing upon the most incredible site she could ever have imagined. And this place was used for wedding ceremonies? *Wow.*

Wynn had bought tickets for a tour of the Lucas Cave, the most popular of the three hundred forty million-year-old Jenolan Caves, which were within walking distance of the hotel. After climbing hundreds of steps, they entered an anteroom and then the Cathedral Chamber, which soared to a staggering fifty-four meters at its highest point. It reminded her of that scene out of *The Adventures of Tom Sawyer.*

Grace instantly forgot the muscle burn from the climb as she stood in the midst of such amazing limestone formations. Some looked like stained glass windows. The guide pointed out a limestone bell tower and a pulpit, too.

The chamber could accommodate up to one hundred guests and the acoustics were apparently perfect; orchestras and a local Aboriginal band regularly entertained audiences here. When the guide wanted to show how disorientating the caves could become without electricity, she turned out the lights. As they were dropped into darkness, Grace gripped Wynn's arm while he chuckled and held her tight.

Farther along the flights of narrow stairs that wove through the caverns, the temperature dropped and they were introduced to formations that looked like sheets of white lace, as well as ribbons of stalactites that flared with reddish-orange hues. In another cave, pure white calcite formations looked like icicles dripping from the ceiling and snow-dusted firs sprouting up from the ground.

When they emerged from the cave and were greeted by

warm sunshine again, they walked hand in hand around the fern-bordered Blue Lake, which was, indeed, a heavenly, untouched deep blue. They spotted a platypus; Grace stood spellbound as the mammal, which looked like a cross between a duck and an otter, wiggled around the bank, foraging for food. As they approached a group of wallabies, she expected them all to hop away. One actually let her brush a palm over its supersoft fur and look into those liquid black eyes. Later, however, she was more than a little hesitant, skirting around the frozen, guarded posture of a dragon lizard.

She flicked on her phone's camera, snapped a few shots of the wildlife and sent them straight through to April via her mom's cell. Grace got a reply back a minute later. April wanted to know if her auntie could bring home a wallaby.

Back at the hotel, she and Wynn showered and changed for dinner at a nearby first-class restaurant. Thankfully there weren't any hiccups with reservations this time.

They were halfway through their meal when conversation turned to work. Wynn had asked about her studies.

"Before getting my masters," she said, "I had dreams of starting my own practice."

"What does a person need to study to get a license for speech therapy?"

"Speech-language pathology. I learned about anatomy, physiology, the development of the areas of the body involved in language, speech and swallowing."

"Did you say swallowing?"

"People don't tend to realize how important it is."

He grinned. "I've always been a fan."

Setting down his cutlery, Wynn reached for his glass. He'd chosen a wine produced in Victoria—an exquisite light white. After forking more of the creamy scalloped potato into her mouth, Grace picked up the thread of their conversation.

"We studied the nature of disorders, acoustics, as well as the psychological side of things. Then we explored how to evaluate and treat problems."

"I knew a boy who stuttered. Aaron Fenway could barely get his name out. It must have been tough. But it didn't seem to faze him. He was always top of the class at math."

"Sounds like my younger sister. A head for figures."

"Aaron owns a huge dot-com now."

"Bruce Willis and Nicole Kidman stuttered. Winston Churchill and Shaquille O'Neal, too."

"I'm trying to imagine anyone being brave enough to tease Shaquille."

"Apparently, when Shaquille was a kid, he'd sit in class, sweating over whether the teacher would ask him a question. He knew he wouldn't be able to get the words out."

"Must make you feel good, helping." Wynn set down his glass. "The business I'm in doesn't have that kind of reputation, I'm afraid."

"News needs to be told. It's a noble profession."

"It can be. Lots of challenges ahead of us there, though. More and more readers are getting their news off the Net."

"So, what's the future?"

"Keep our eyes open to all the options. Change is the one constant. We need to look at cutting costs on the print side. Factory and distribution overheads. I'm talking with someone at the moment."

"To share those costs?"

"More than that. We're looking to merge parts of our companies."

"Ooh, sounds very highflier."

"And very confidential. Not even my father knows."

She studied his expression and put down her fork. "You don't look as if you're punching the air about telling him."

"Guthrie's idea of building success is to buy out the opposition or run them out of business. He doesn't *merge*."

"Isn't that your decision? You run Hunter Publishing now."

"For things to go smoothly, I need his approval." He pushed his plate aside. "And I need it soon. Better to explain face-to-face."

"Sometime this week?" He nodded. "Maybe keep it for after the wedding."

"My thoughts exactly."

After the meal, the young waitress served coffee and asked if they'd enjoyed the tours.

"I saw you this afternoon," the waitress explained, "wandering back from the Grand Arch."

Grace well remembered the Arch. According to the guide, while that particular cave had collapsed many centuries ago, the giant rock arch of the original structure remained—a truly awe-inspiring sight.

Grace sighed. "It was all amazing."

"Did anyone mention the ghosts?" the waitress asked, setting down the cups.

Wynn's lips twitched. "We missed that tour."

But Grace remembered seeing a mysteries and ghosts tour outlined on a brochure.

"There's evidence of strange things happening down there—photographs and videos." The waitress lowered her voice. "There's even supposed to be a ghost living right here, in this restaurant."

"Does she float around the town, as well," Wynn asked, "rattling her teapot?"

"If she does," the waitress said, "don't worry. She's friendly."

Later, when Grace and Wynn were back at their hotel and entering their room, Wynn suddenly grabbed her from behind, around the waist. Grace's heart leapt to the ceiling before, spinning around, she smacked his shoulder and, heart pounding, turned on the lights. Why did guys think stuff like that was funny? It wasn't—or at least not when she'd imagined the sound of footfalls following them up the street. She might have heard a teapot rattle, too.

"You're such a child."

He laughed as she strode off. "Oh, *I'm* a child? Will we leave on a night-light tonight?"

"I'd love to see how smart you'd be if a ghost sailed through that door right now and poured cold tea all over your head."

He followed her. "So you believe all that haunted house woo-ha." Lashing an arm around her middle, he growled against her lips, "Good thing I'm here to protect you."

Refusing to grin, she set her palms on his chest, which seemed to have grown harder and broader since the last time they'd made this kind of contact.

"I have an open mind. I can also look after myself."

"Just letting you know," he said, lowering his head to nuzzle her neck, "I'm here if you need me." He nuzzled lower. "For anything." His hand curved over her behind. "Anything at all."

Her eyes had drifted shut. Damn the man. She couldn't stay mad.

"You want to help?" she asked.

"Want me to order a medium? Organize a séance? Sprinkle some salt on the threshold?"

She grabbed his shirt and tugged him toward the cozy double bed. "You're going to help me with a whole lot more than that."

Ten

"Promise me one thing," Grace said.

Wynn squeezed her hand. "Anything?"

"No stunt today like the one you pulled at that other wedding."

When she and Wynn had returned from their magical stay at the Blue Mountains with a hundred snaps and a thousand memories, the final preparations for Cole and Taryn's big day were in full swing. They'd watched the extensive back lawn and gardens being pruned to perfection. A giant fairy-tale marquee had shot up and the furnishings had been arranged both inside and out.

Now Grace looked around at the marquee's ceiling draped with white silk swags and the fountains of flowers, as the sixty or so guests took their seats on either side of a red-carpeted aisle.

Beside her, Wynn wore a tuxedo in a way that would impress James Bond. Now, responding to her request that he behave himself, he sent her a wicked grin and stage whispered, "No surprise kiss in front of the multitudes? Why? Can't handle it?"

She tugged his ear. "Mister, I can handle anything you care to dish out."

"Except letting people know that there might be more."

"More of what?"

"More to us."

That took her aback. What did he mean *more*? They were here in Australia, doing exactly as he'd suggested: relaxing and enjoying themselves. There wasn't any *more* to it.

Or she was reading too much into his words. That tease was more likely a warning that she shouldn't become too complacent. He just might shock the crowd again. She had news for him.

"Just remember whose show this is, okay?"

"Yep." The corners of his smoldering eyes crinkled. "Can't handle it."

When he leaned closer, she put on a business-only face and dusted imaginary lint from his broad shoulders. "Time you went and joined your brothers at the altar."

He gave her a curious look. "You think so?"

She hesitated before laughing. He was acting so strangely today.

"You look amazing in that dress," he said.

"You told me," she grinned. "Maybe ten times."

He tipped close and took a light but lingering kiss that brought a mist to her eyes. His warm palm curved around her cheek. "You'll be here when I get back?"

She wanted to laugh again, but his gaze was suddenly so serious.

"Yes," she said and softly smiled. "I'll be right here. I promise."

On Wynn's way to the platform where Cole and Dex waited, Guthrie pulled him aside to introduce a couple who seemed familiar, in more ways than one.

"Son, you remember Vincent and Kirsty Riggs," Guthrie said with his father-of-the-groom smile firmly in place.

"Of course." Wynn shook Vincent's hand and nodded a greeting at the wife. "Nice to see you both again."

Mr. Riggs's expression was humble. "Christopher's so pleased that you've allowed him this chance in New York."

"I'm sure he'll be an asset to the company," Wynn replied.

"We should catch up after the ceremony," Vincent went on. "I'd like to know what you have in store for him."

"But right now," Mrs. Riggs said, nodding at the altar, "you have an important job to do."

"Guthrie mentioned that Dex will be joining his older brother soon," Vincent said, "tying the knot."

When Vincent flicked a glance Grace's way and waited for some kind of response, Wynn only grinned and replied, "It's true. Dex will soon be a married man. Another reason to celebrate." Wynn bowed off. "Please excuse me."

Strolling up to the platform, Wynn concentrated on the task ahead. He and Dex were to stand beside the oldest Hunter brother as he took this important step in his life. But another related thought kept knocking around in his brain.

After that initial hiccup with their booking, he and Grace had enjoyed every second of their time away in the mountains. They'd explored, eaten out, talked a lot and when they weren't otherwise engaged, made love. He had assumed the constant physical desire would, in some way, slack off. Anything but. His need to feel her curled up around him, have his mouth working together with hers, had been a constant. He understood sexual attraction, but he and Grace seemed to have created their own higher meaning.

Ever since he'd been here, when he and Cole and Dex sat down at the end of the day with a beer, he listened to their banter about how much they looked forward to settling down, and the ache he'd suffered after that bust-up with Heather had begun to fester again. In the past, whenever he'd looked ahead, Heather had been there, standing alongside him. But seeing Grace tonight in that knockout strapless red gown with the sweetest of all sweetheart necklines, silver bangles jangling on both wrists and her eyes filled with sass and life...

He didn't want a relationship, and yet he and Grace were doing a darn fine imitation of having one. A moment ago, after he'd hinted at perhaps wanting more, for just a second, he'd meant it. But he didn't need to go down that track again. Why rock a perfectly happy boat?

He was nearing the platform when another guest stopped him—a tall, well-built man in his twenties.

"You're Wynn, right?" the man asked.

"We've met?"

"I'm Sebastian Styles."

Wynn thought back and then apologized. "No light bulb, I'm afraid."

"Talbot's son."

Wynn had known to expect his long-lost cousin today, but no one had passed on a name. And while the brothers had speculated, no one seemed to know the story behind this surprise addition to the Hunter line. Which wasn't a problem. Sebastian Styles was family now and more than welcome.

As the men shook hands, Wynn confirmed, "Good to meet you."

"I wasn't sure whether Guthrie had explained my sudden arrival on the scene."

"Only that you'd caught up with your father."

The rest really wasn't any of Wynn's business. He glanced toward the platform—he needed to take his place alongside his brothers right now.

"I've heard plenty about you," Sebastian was saying,

"and your brothers. Can I join you for a drink after the ceremony?"

"I look forward to it."

Wynn skirted around the front section of chairs, which were filling with guests, and came to stand alongside Dex— three Hunter brothers all in a row.

Assuming the apparently obligatory "hands clasped in front" stance, he asked the others, "We set to go?"

Dex dug into a breast pocket and flicked out a clean white handkerchief for Cole. "For when the perspiration starts coursing down your face."

"I'm not nervous." Cole straightened his bow tie. "This is the best day of my life."

"When you know it's right, you know," Dex said, and the two older brothers bumped shoulders before remembering themselves. They were happy, settled. Wynn was not.

Oh, for pity's sake.

"I wish you two would stop going all goofy on me," Wynn growled. "I thought you'd know by now—I'm over that other stuff."

"Grace is a special woman," Cole said sagely.

Dex followed up with, "You two give off some pretty intense sparks. As long as you're both having fun. Right, Cole?"

But Cole's attention was elsewhere. He straightened his tie again.

"My master of ceremonies just gave the signal. Taryn's ready to come out." Cole sent his brothers a fortifying wink. "See you on the other side, boys."

Grace was figuring out the seating arrangements.

The only person she recognized in the first row, which was set aside for family, was a put-upon Eloise, who was draped in yellow chiffon and nursing a baby bump that looked more like a balloon ready to pop. Teagan was a bridesmaid and Tate, a page boy. Shelby wasn't anywhere to be seen. Without Wynn to sit beside, Grace didn't want to crash. Perhaps she ought to sit more toward the middle—neutral territory.

She was deciding on a row when, looking breathtaking in a glamorous single-shoulder, emerald-green gown, Shelby came rushing up.

"You're sitting with me," she said, indicating the second row before continuing on her way. "I'll be back in a shake. Just want to give one of the best men a big kiss for good luck."

Lowering onto the outermost chair of the row Shelby had indicated, Grace was perusing the leather-bound order of service when a man appeared at her side—the man Grace had seen Wynn speak with before taking his place beside his brothers on the platform.

"Is there room for one more?" the man asked.

He had a presence about him, Grace decided, which complemented his smooth baritone and kind hazel-colored eyes.

"Of course." Grace moved over.

Settling in, the man rubbed both palms down his suit's thighs before he glanced at her. "I'm feeling a little out of the circle."

She returned his awkward smile. "Me, too."

"I'm Sebastian Styles, by the way. The long-lost cousin."

"Grace Munroe." She added, "Third brother's date."

"I didn't feel as if I should intrude today. It's such a private affair. Smaller guest list than I'd even imagined."

It wasn't her place to ask how much Sebastian knew about the stalker business, so she merely agreed with his last point.

"At first, I declined the invite," Sebastian said. "But Talbot and, apparently, Guthrie insisted."

She nodded toward a couple in the front row. "Are they your parents?"

"That's Leeanne—Talbot and Guthrie's sister—and her husband, Stuart Somersby. Sitting alongside them are Josh and Naomi, their grown kids."

From this vantage point, Josh looked to be in his early twenties with sandy-colored hair and strong Hunter features, including a hawkish nose. Biting her lip she was so excited, Naomi was younger and extremely attractive. Her tumble of pale blond hair was dotted with diamantés.

Perhaps having heard her name, Leeanne—a slender, stylish brunette—glanced over her shoulder and wiggled her fingers, *hi*. Sebastian and Grace wiggled back before he nodded toward a magnificent display of flowers where two men were discussing some obviously serious matter.

"That's Talbot, my father, speaking with Guthrie."

"Neither one looks happy."

"I'm guessing it's about the security. My father was none too pleased about being frisked so thoroughly at the door." Sebastian's brow creased before he hung his head and smiled. "My father. Still sounds weird."

"I know everyone's looking forward to meeting you." She turned a little toward him. "Do you have a partner?"

His expression changed before he straightened in his seat. "No. Nothing like that."

The music morphed into a moving tune that Cole and Taryn had chosen to kick off this all-important part of the day. When the bride appeared, on the arm of the woman who must be her Aunt Vi, a rush of happy tears sprang to Grace's eyes. Who didn't love a wedding?

Shelby appeared and Sebastian and Grace both shifted one seat over in the row.

Pressing a palm to her heart, Shelby whispered to them both. "What a gorgeous dress. She's the most beautiful bride I've ever seen."

Then Tate, in a tiny tux, and Teagan and another brides-maid started off down the aisle and Grace sat back.

This was bound to be an amazing day.

Hours after the ceremony, during the reception that was also held inside the marquee, Grace caught a glimpse of Teagan. She stood behind a massive, decorative column, a cell phone pressed to her ear. Biting a nail, she looked upset enough to cry.

The music filtered through the sound system, drawing lots of couples onto the dance floor. Grace had just finished speaking with a couple—Christopher Riggs's parents, as a matter of fact—lovely people who seemed pleased their son was moving forward with his life in New York.

Grace had been ready to join Wynn, who appeared to be enjoying his conversation with his new cousin. Now, Grace hurried over to Teagan.

"You're upset," she said as Teagan disconnected her call.

"That guy I've been telling you about…" Teagan tacked up a weak smile. "He's missing me."

Grace let out a sigh of relief. That wasn't bad. That was *sweet*. Grace had wanted to learn more about Teagan's guy but when her friend hadn't brought the subject up again, Grace didn't want to prod.

Now she said, "Looks like you're missing him, too."

Beneath the marquee's slow-spinning lights, Teagan's gaze grew distant and her jaw tensed, as if she were try-ing to keep from frowning.

"Guess I've gotten used to having him around. Except… I can't see things working out between us. Not in the long term."

"Because he wants lots of children?"

Teagan nodded.

Teagan's guy sounded a lot like Sam, Grace thought.

Difference was that Teagan obviously cared deeply for this man in the way a future wife should.

"So, he's proposed?" Grace asked.

"Not yet. And I don't want him to. Like I said, it's complicated. I was going to talk with you more about it, but…"

"You don't have to explain—"

"I want to." She took Grace's champagne flute and downed half the glass—a big deal, given that Teagan didn't usually drink.

After a visible shudder, Teagan handed the glass back. "That accident I had all those years ago…"

They'd spoken about that, too, these past days. "You were in and out of hospital."

"I missed so much school. Mom and Dad tried to make it up to me. I had every material thing a girl would wish for. I think they knew pretty much from the start. I found out later." Her lips pressed together and, staring off at the people dancing, she blinked several times. "I can't have children."

The words hung in the air between them before Grace's heart sank to her knees. She gripped her friend's hand. She'd never dream for one minute…

"Oh, Tea…"

"It's okay," she said quickly. "I'm used to the idea. There's plenty of other things in life to keep a person focused and busy."

"Maybe if you spoke to him. There are options."

"Sure. Great ones. But you'd have to meet him, Grace. I look at him and know he's destined to have boys with his strong chin and the same sparkling blue eyes." Her wistful expression hardened. "He deserves everything he wants from life."

"Speak with him," Grace implored.

Teagan's chin lifted even as she smiled. "I'm fine with who I am. I don't want anyone's pity. I've had enough of that in my life. I certainly don't want to put him in a position where he feels he has to choose."

Between marrying the woman he loved and marrying someone else who could bear his children?

Grace remembered those hours she and Teagan had spent as kids playing with baby dolls, pretending to feed and rock and diaper change. Grace took for granted that when she was happily settled and tried to get pregnant, she wouldn't have trouble. Of course, adoption and surrogates had proven wonderful alternatives for so many couples who couldn't conceive. Although Teagan said she was used to the idea of being unable to conceive, something in her eyes said that this minute, she found acceptance hard.

When the music faded, both women's attentions were drawn by some commotion playing out on the marquee's platform. Taryn was getting ready to toss her bouquet. So Grace put her conversation with Teagan aside. If her friend ever wanted to talk more, Grace would be available, even from halfway around the world.

Having composed herself, Teagan tipped her head toward the gathering and put on a brave face. "Are you having a go?"

"Last time I was involved with a bouquet, I got way more than I bargained for."

Teagan grinned. Grace had told her about that kiss at the reception.

"I'm rooting for Shelby," Teagan said. "But I'll help make up the numbers."

When Teagan and the other eligible women were positioned on the dance floor, Taryn spun around and then threw her bouquet. The flowers sailed a few yards before Shelby, using her height advantage, snatched them out of the air. As people cheered, Dex marched up to her. Pride shining from his face, he dipped his fiancée in a dramatic pose before kissing her. All the wedding crowd sighed, including Grace.

Those two seemed so right for each other. It was as if all their edges and emotions were two halves of a whole.

At first, Grace had been hesitant about coming to Australia, to this event. She'd worried she might need to defend the fact that she and Wynn weren't serious the way Cole and Taryn were. The way people had assumed she and Sam had been.

And yet, with all these sentimental feelings surrounding her now, Grace felt as if she were falling into that very trap herself. In these couple of weeks, she felt so connected to Wynn.

From the platform, the DJ asked the women to move aside. Cole was preparing to throw the bride's garter.

Wynn stood at the back of the pack. When he caught sight of her, he sent over a wave an instant before Dex grabbed both his brother's arms and, fooling around, struggled to hold them behind Wynn's back. Grace laughed even as her chest tightened. Like the bouquet, tradition said that the person who caught the garter was meant to marry next. Dex would want to catch the garter and slip it on his fiancée's leg. But, as he wrangled free of Dex's hold and prepared to leap, Wynn seemed just as determined. A competitive spirit.

Or something more?

Teagan joined her. No one would guess that she'd been close to tears a few minutes ago.

"Look at those brothers of mine." When Dex tried to body block Wynn, Wynn elbowed his way in front again and Teagan laughed. "I've never seen Wynn have so much fun as he has this trip. These past months, whenever we've spoken on the phone, he's been so distant." Teagan wound her arm through Grace's. "Then you came along."

Grace looked at her twice. Right there was the kind of

comment she hadn't wanted to deal with during this trip. Wynn had lost the woman he had wanted to marry. Grace hadn't wanted to come across as anyone's replacement. She was still working through her own past.

And yet, something inside her had shifted. Something had changed.

Up on the stage, the groom knelt before his new bride and slipped the garter off her leg. As he held it above his head, the bullpen erupted with calls to begin.

The DJ revved them up more. "Guys, are you ready?"

A roar went up, the groom about-faced, and then the garter went flying at the same time as Wynn's heels grew wings. He caught the garter on a single finger. Feet back on the ground, he accepted slaps on the back from his peers. Meanwhile, out of the corner of her eye, she noticed Tate scooting through the pack and climbing the steps to the platform. He'd been having a blast dancing up there most of the night.

Wynn ambled over to her and dropped to one knee. The room hushed and all eyes fell upon them. Grace shrank back. This all had a familiar ring to it.

"Heel up here," Wynn demanded and slapped his raised thigh.

And have everyone ask later whether they'd set a date? That was going too far. She shook her head.

He sent her a devilish smile. "Guess I could always wear it as a headband." When he widened the garter and threatened to fit it around his crown, the crowd exploded with laughter. "You can't disappoint everyone." His voice lowered and gaze deepened. "Don't disappoint me."

The DJ stepped in, egging her on, and the crowd got on board. Wynn's expression wasn't teasing now. It was… solemn.

Grace's heart was booming in her chest, in her ears. This display was sending the wrong message.

Or was it just a bit of fun? With all the room smiling at them, she couldn't help but smile herself.

She placed one shoe on his knee. He slipped the garter up over her toes to just above the knee and then, holding her gaze with his, pushed to his feet. Rather than applaud, their audience was hushed. Were the guests aware of the energy pulsating between the two of them?

"Know what this calls for?" he asked.

She felt almost giddy. "A modest bow?"

Of course, his arms wound around her, and when his lips touched hers, any urge she might have had to push away, tell him to behave, faded into longing. She hadn't wanted to be the center of attention. She didn't want people to peg her into yet another hole. And yet…

Sensations gathered, vibrating through her body and spilling out like ripples from the sweetest sounding bell. For the slightest fragment in time, she believed that the fireworks going off in her mind and through her blood were so powerful that they physically shook the room.

Then a different reality struck, and the crowd began to scream.

Eleven

The force from the blast almost knocked Wynn over.

With the noise from the explosion ringing in his ears, he spun around. A piece of debris smacked his cheek as a haze of dark smoke erupted from somewhere near the platform. He remembered who had been standing there a second earlier and his stomach crashed to his knees.

He turned to Grace. "Get out of here. *Run!*"

With a hacking cough, she gripped his arm. "Tate's over there."

He knew it. He spun her around.

"Go!"

He headed toward the smoke by the platform, at the same time checking out the rest of the area. Guests smeared with dust and debris were charging toward the exit. He couldn't see Cole or Dex but, glancing over his shoulder, he caught sight of Taryn and Shelby helping Grace outside. Chances were his brothers were somewhere searching in this smoke, too.

With sparks spitting against his face, his nostrils burning and surrounded by the smell of his own singed hair, he leapt onto the platform. A pint-size silhouette—Tate?—stood frozen off to one side. If he'd been knocked down, he was on his feet again now. He'd be disorientated, possibly injured.

Wynn was bolting across when another explosion went off—different from the first. It was the electrical equipment shorting. Catching fire. Flames spewed out from the area where the DJ had set up. Heat radiated from the fire, searing Wynn's back as Tate's smudged, frightened face appeared in the smoke. His little hands were covering his ears. His eyes were clamped shut. Lunging, Wynn heaved Tate up against his chest, holding him close with one arm.

He was jumping off the creaking platform when Brandon materialized out of the chaos, holding an extinguisher. Brandon acknowledged Tate before disappearing back into the haze.

A moment later, Wynn was out in the sunshine, legs pumping toward the house where many of the startled guests had gathered. Security men were herding them back. Teagan was on her cell, presumably to emergency services, although he was certain one of Brandon's men would have sent up the alarm already. Teagan was also consoling Eloise, who was visibly shaken. When Teagan saw Tate, she covered her mouth to catch a gasp of relief. Dropping her phone, she put out her arms.

As Wynn passed the boy over, he did a quick check. Tate's little dress shirt was gray from the smoke, but Wynn didn't see any blood. The child's eyes were still closed, his face slack. Poor kid must have fainted.

While Teagan cradled Tate, Eloise seemed to emerge from her stupor. She brought both Teagan and Tate close, hugging them as much as her belly would allow. Wynn spun away, searching for Grace. And then, familiar arms were around him and she was saying, "Thank God you're out. Thank God you're safe."

He pulled her back, looked into her eyes. Grace was shaken but unhurt.

The screams of sirens bled in over the noise of the fire that had eaten through the marquee's ceiling. He gripped her arms. "I'm going back in."

As he pulled away, she tried to hold him back. Her eyes were as wide as saucers. They said, *Please, please, don't go.* During that beat in time, he remembered her ex had been a firefighter; if he had died in an accident, Wynn guessed it had been a blaze. But today he had no choice.

He couldn't see his father anywhere. Cole and Dex must be inside that trap, too. Engines were on their way, but there were extinguishers in there; Brandon had gone through safety procedures thoroughly with them before the guests had arrived and now his team needed help.

As Wynn sprinted back through the entrance, shock subsided into rage. When they found whoever was responsible, he wanted just five minutes alone with the son of a bitch. He wanted a fight?

This meant war.

"This time yesterday, champagne corks were flying down there." Grace turned from the window as Wynn entered the bedroom. "Hard to believe it's all cordoned off now with police tape."

Brandon Powell and his team, along with Wynn and his brothers, had extinguished the majority of flames before emergency services had arrived. Consequently, most of the marquee still stood, but the air outside reeked with the stench of charred debris. As Wynn joined her, Grace turned again to the view. This side of the crime scene tape, Brandon stood, arms crossed, as he spoke with a detective. A few feet away from them lay a bunch of flowers—Taryn's bouquet?—dirty and trampled.

"Teagan's with Tate." Wynn's arms wound around her middle as he pressed his chest snug against her back. "I can't believe he came out of it all with nothing more than a couple of scratches." He rested his chin on her crown. "He can't remember anything between the time I caught the garter and when he came to outside."

"Will he ever remember?"

"No one knows."

Hearing the screams and feeling the heat of the flames again, Grace winced and, pressing back against Wynn more, hugged his arms all the tighter. She hoped Tate never remembered.

Wynn turned her around to face him. "Cole followed up on his guests. Other than still being a little shell-shocked, everyone's fine."

"I guess the authorities will be in touch with them all."

"Brandon, too. If anyone saw anything that didn't fit, it'll come out. No one's going to let up until we track down whoever's responsible. In the meantime, Dad's been offered protective custody. He's considering it."

The Hunter clan had spent the night in a nearby hotel with security. After the grounds and house had been swept by the bomb team and cleared, they'd returned this morning. But questions remained: Would that madman try to strike again here? When? How?

The public was curious, too.

"Is the media still out front?" she asked.

"It's news," he groaned, before leading her to the bed and coaxing her to lie down next to him. Studying her expression, he brushed some hair away from her cheek.

"Did you get ahold of your family?" he asked.

"Mom says she wants me back right away."

"I'll speak with your father myself. Pass on my apologies."

"This isn't your fault."

"I'm still responsible. Cole doesn't want Taryn anywhere near this place. He's stepped up the security at the Hunter Broadcasting building, too."

"And Dex?"

"He wants Tate to go back to L.A. with him and Shelby. Makes sense, but Tate is clinging to his mom." He cursed. "Christ, this is a mess."

"And you?"

He held her chin and told her firmly, "I agree with your mother. I need to get you out of here."

He brushed his lips over hers and it didn't matter what had gone before—she felt nothing but safe.

"Did you get an update from Brandon?" she asked.

"He's adamant that every workman and hospitality person was checked coming in and going out. They've bagged some evidence that'll help determine the sophistication of the device, although bets are it was small and crude. No suspicion of high-grade explosive material."

He pressed a soft kiss to her brow. The warm tingles fell away as he pushed up off the bed and onto his feet.

"We have seats booked on an evening flight to New York," he said, moving to pour a glass of water from a carafe. "And you'll be flying on to Florida a few days after that."

It was a statement. And she did need to get back to Florida. She'd just expected to be here a couple more days. It was all ending so quickly.

"I've told Teagan we need to keep in touch," she said. "Either she'll come out to the East Coast or I'll visit her in Seattle."

He moved to the window to gaze out over the debris in silence.

She swung her feet over the edge of the mattress onto the floor. If she was ever going to know, she might as well ask now.

"What was she like?"

"What was who like?"

"The woman in that hotel foyer that night." *The woman you used to love. Perhaps still love.* "What was her name?"

When he faced her, his jaw was tight. She thought he was going to say he didn't want to talk about her, not ever. But then his chin lifted and clearly, calmly, he said, "Her name is Heather Matthews."

Grace crossed over to join him at the window. "I met Sam at a local baseball game. I dropped my hot dog. He offered to buy me another one."

Wynn considered her for a long moment.

"I met Heather at a gallery opening. She's a photographer. Inventive. Artistic. My perfect foil." He frowned to himself. "That's what I'd thought."

"Sam asked for my number," she said. "He asked me out the next week. A movie and hamburger afterward. Not long after that, I met his parents and he met mine."

"Cole and Dex were the devout bachelors," he said. "Too busy with other things to worry about that kind of commitment. But me…"

"You proposed."

"After two years."

"Sam and I were together for five years before…"

"He asked you to be his wife. And you said yes."

They were talking so openly, feeding off each other's stories. Now she opened her mouth to correct him. She hadn't accepted Sam's proposal. She'd turned him down. But the words stuck in her throat. If she admitted that— told him the truth about that, wouldn't he view her as another Heather? A woman who gave a man in love some hope only to wrench it away.

What would he think about her if he knew the rest of the story?

He set his glass on the window ledge and held her. "I didn't lose what you lost. *How* you lost."

Her stomach turned over. If he only knew…

"It was hard for you, too. Although…" She said the rest before she could stop herself. "Heather was only being honest with you."

He cocked his head as his mouth twisted into an uncertain grin. "Are you defending her?"

Grace was defending herself.

"The truth is," he said, "that when we met, I had industry connections. Two years on, she didn't need them anymore."

The urge swelled up inside Grace like a big bubble of hot air. She had to be honest with him, even if he could never understand.

"Wynn, I need to tell you something."

His face warmed with a smile that she imagined he kept only for her. "You don't need to tell me anything."

"I do."

"If it's something more about Sam, you don't have to explain. That explosion, those flames—yesterday would have shaken you up maybe more than any of us. I was cut when Heather and I broke up, but I didn't lose her in a fire—"

"Wynn, Sam didn't die in a fire."

His brows snapped together. "He was a firefighter." She nodded. "When your father mentioned an accident, I assumed…"

"Sam died in a car crash."

She wanted to tell him more, tell him everything, how she'd felt about Sam, how the years they'd spent together as a couple had just seemed to pass and drift by. She wanted to tell him about the secret that she had yet to describe even in that notebook. But now she couldn't bear to think of how quickly that thoughtful look Wynn was sharing with her now would turn into a sneer.

He led her over to a sofa. They sat together, his arm around her, her cheek resting against his chest. After a time, he dropped a kiss on her brow and asked, "Will you be okay alone for a while? I need to speak with my father. I need to get something off my chest before we leave."

"About that merger deal?" she asked.

"I'm not looking forward to it. Especially not after yesterday."

She held his hand. "You'll still be his son."

He sent her a crooked grin. "Fingers crossed."

Wynn found Eloise reclining on a chaise lounge, lamenting over the images in a swimwear catalogue. Seeing him, she seemed to deflate even more.

"Honey, could you bring me some ice tea from the bar?" She fanned herself with the catalogue. "I feel so parched. Must be all that ash floatin' around."

Wynn dropped some ice in a highball glass and then filled it from a pitcher in the bar fridge. Handing it over, he asked, "Where's Dad?"

"In his study, last I heard, worrying over insurance."

Soon, he'd be worrying about even more than that.

Wynn turned to leave, but Eloise called him back. She had a certain look on her face. He thought it might be sincerity.

"Wynn, I need to thank you."

Was this about how he'd rescued Tate from the burning marquee? He waved it off. "You've already done that."

Everybody had, but no one needed to. In his place, anyone would have done the same.

Eloise dragged herself to a sitting position. "I want to thank you for supporting us—my family. Supporting *me*."

Her chin went down and her gaze dropped. "I'm ashamed to say, I haven't always deserved it."

"There's no need to—"

"No. There is." Her palm caressed her big belly. "I may not be a fairy-tale mother, but I do love Tate. With him being away so much this year, with us almost losing him yesterday…" Her eyes glistened and her mouth formed what Wynn knew was a genuine smile. "I don't know what I'd do without you all."

Wynn allowed a smile of his own before he headed out. In a place he rarely visited, he knew the truth: some time ago, Eloise had propositioned Cole. Before this stalker trouble had begun, Tate had lived here in Sydney. Cole had had the benefit of seeing their father and Tate regularly, but he also had to contend with those issues surrounding his stepmother. Not pleasant.

Wynn arrived at his father's study and knocked on the door. He waited before knocking again. When there was no response, he opened the door and edged inside. Guthrie sat in a corner, staring into space. His hair looked grayer and thinner. The frustration and despair showed in every line on his face. As Wynn drew nearer, his father roused himself—even tried to paste on a smile.

"Take a seat, son."

"I wanted to let you know," Wynn began, "Grace and I are flying out this evening."

"Understood. Only sensible."

"If there's anything I can do… If you need me to come back for any reason—"

"You need to get back to New York. They'll be missing you there."

Wynn rubbed the scar on his temple. "There's a lot going on. Lots of industry changes."

"How do they put it? The death of print. We simply need

to find ways to work around it. Diversify. Make sure we're the last man standing."

"Actually, I have something in the pipeline. Something I'm afraid you won't like."

A keen look flashed in his father's eyes. "Go on."

"I've had discussions with Paul Lumos from Episode Features. My attorneys have drafted up a merger agreement."

His father's face hardened, but he didn't seem surprised. "You went behind my back."

"You assigned me to run our publishing operations in New York. I'm doing what I feel is best. Frankly, I don't see any option. Together, Hunter Enterprises and EF can save on overheads that are threatening to kill us both. And I want to act now. Eighteen months down the track, it could be too late."

"You know, it's not the way I do business."

"Then, I'm sorry, but you need to change."

"I'm too old to change."

"Which is why you put me in charge."

Pushing to his feet, Guthrie crossed to the window, which overlooked the peaceful southern side of the property. As boys, Wynn and his brothers had pitched balls there, and roughhoused with Foxy, their terrier who had long since passed on. Wynn's mother had always brought out freshly made lemonade. She'd never gotten involved with the business side of things. Her talent had lain in cementing family values, keeping their nucleus safe and strong. When she'd passed away, the momentum of everything surrounding her had begun to warp—to keel off balance.

His father had remarried, then had needed heart surgery. The company had been split up among "the boys," and the siblings had gone off to live thousands of miles apart. Wynn's decision to mount this merger was just another turn in the road.

He waited for his father to argue more or, hopefully, see reason and acquiesce.

Guthrie turned to face him. "Now I have something I need to say."

Wynn sat down. "Go ahead."

"Christopher Riggs..."

Wynn waited. "What about Christopher?"

Guthrie pushed out a weary breath. "Vincent Riggs and I were having lunch a couple of months ago. His son joined us. Of course, I'd met Christopher before, but he's grown into such a focused man. Afterward, Vincent confirmed that Chris was extremely thorough—a dog with a bone when he got his teeth into a task. His background is investigative reporting."

When his father seemed to clam up, Wynn urged him on.

"I know Christopher's background." What was it that Guthrie wanted to say?

One of his father's hands clenched at his side. "I employed him," Guthrie said. "I gave him a job."

"You mean you had *me* give him a job."

"Son, I gave him the task of being my eyes and ears in New York."

Wynn sat back. He didn't like the feeling rippling up his spine.

"Why would you need him to do that?"

Before he'd finished asking, however, Wynn had guessed the answer. The righteous look on his father's face confirmed it. And then all the chips began to stack up. His insides curled into a tight, sick ball.

"Despite your objections to a merger, you suspected." Wynn ground out. "You knew I'd go ahead and put the deal together."

When Guthrie nodded, Wynn's pulse rate spiked before

he bowed forward, holding his spinning head in his hands. His throat convulsed. He had to swallow twice before he could speak.

"You hired that man to *spy* on me?"

"You mentioned mergers months ago. I needed to know what was going on." He moved closer. "Christopher admires you. It took a good deal to convince him."

"I'm sure a fat transfer into his checking account helped."

"I knew, out of all my boys, you would have the most trouble accepting why I would need to do something like this."

Understatement. Wynn felt it like a blunt ax landing on the back of his neck. "Who else have you got over in New York, sharpening their knives, waiting for the chance to stab me in the back?"

"This was a special circumstance. I needed to be able to step in. Defuse anything before promises were made I couldn't keep."

"Do Cole or Dex know?"

"No one knows."

Wynn swallowed against the bile rising at the back of his throat. His lip curled. "Guess we're even."

"We can move on from this."

"Until the next time you decide to go behind my back."

"Or you behind mine."

"I could go ahead without your approval," Wynn pointed out. He had the necessary authority.

His father slowly shook his head in warning. "You don't want to try that."

Wynn shot to his feet and headed for the door.

His father called after him. "You're more like me than you know."

"Yeah. We're both suckers." He slammed the door behind him.

He was striding down the hall when he ran into Dex.

"What the hell is wrong with you?" Dex asked, physically stopping Wynn as he tried to push around him.

"It's between me and the old man."

"Whatever it is, it couldn't be any worse than what we all went through yesterday."

"It's up there."

Wynn told Dex everything—about the merger plan, about the lowlife corporate spy, Christopher freaking Riggs. When Wynn had finished, his brother looked uncomfortable. Dex ran a hand through his hair.

"Geez, I wonder if he's ever sent anyone over to spy on me."

He'd needed his sons to take over the reins. None of them was perfect, but at least each brother was nothing but loyal to the family.

"He'd be better off sending someone to spy on his wife," Wynn growled under his breath. "If he thinks I betrayed him organizing a company merger, what the hell would he think of Eloise throwing herself at Cole, and God knows how many others?"

Dex gripped Wynn's arm and hissed, *"Shut up."*

"Why?" Wynn shook himself free. "You know the story better than me."

Dex was looking over his shoulder. Wynn paused and then an ice-cold sensation crept down his spine. He shut his eyes and spat out a curse at the same time his father's strained voice came from behind.

"Seems everyone knew the story but me."

With a sick feeling curdling inside, Wynn edged around. His father stood a few yards away. Leaning against the wall as if for support, his skin had a deathly pallor.

Wynn felt his own blood pressure drop. *What the hell have I done?*

From behind, he heard footfalls sounding on the polished wooden floor. As he stared at his father, he heard Cole exclaim, "Eloise's water just broke. Dad, she's having the baby."

Twelve

Grace was headed downstairs when she heard a commotion. A woman was crying out as if she were in pain. Grace clutched the rail. What the hell was going on? Had that maniac stalker somehow struck again?

Below her in the vast foyer, Teagan appeared. Wynn's sister was helping Eloise to the front door. The older woman supported the weight of her big belly with both hands. Her stance was stooped and the grimace on the beautifully made-up face pointed to only one thing.

Grace fled down the stairs. She had not expected to be around for this. Wynn would want to stay longer now. It wasn't every day a person got to meet their new little brother or sister.

"Is there anything I can do?" Grace asked as she reached Teagan.

At that moment, Cole appeared. Rushing up, he let them know, "I just told Dad. He's on his way."

Eloise groaned, a guttural, involuntary, in-labor sound.

"Oh, *God*. We need to hurry." After another grimace, she started to pant.

"You'll be fine," Teagan told her. "Just try to relax. And nice deep breaths."

"I'll bring the car up," Cole said, flinging open one half of the double doors. "And where the hell is Dex?"

Suddenly Guthrie was there. The older man's expression was harried but not excited. His pallor, his shuffling gait…Wynn's father looked almost stricken. Wynn, who was coming up behind him, didn't look much better.

As Guthrie and Teagan escorted poor ambling Eloise out the door, Grace crossed over to Wynn. Worried, she cupped his bristled cheek.

"You look like you're ready to collapse."

He waited until everyone else was out the door, out of earshot, before he replied in a gravelly voice.

"I spoke with my father."

About the merger deal. "Guess he took the news badly."

Under her palm, a muscle in his jaw flexed twice. "He already knew."

Confused, she shook her head. "How?"

"And now he knows something else," Wynn muttered before wincing and rubbing his brow as if massaging the mother of all headaches. "I'm the world's biggest ass. I should have kept my freaking mouth shut," he groaned, clamping his eyes shut.

Grace tried to make sense of what he was saying but couldn't. "Wynn, Eloise is having the baby. You're going to be a brother again very soon."

He was shaking his head as if he wanted to block something out. Either they were staying or returning to New York. But if they were going to make that flight, they needed to think about getting to the airport.

"I opened my stupid mouth and now—" Resigned, he

exhaled and shrugged his broad shoulders. "Guess now I have to live with it."

Grace's heart was thumping high in her chest. "Wynn, please tell me what you're talking about."

His gaze—vacant and resigned now—met hers. He tried to tack up a tired smile. "There's no point dragging you into all this. You can't help. No one can."

As he grabbed her hand and they headed up the stairs, it took Grace all her willpower not to grill him again. But he was right. Whatever had happened between Wynn and his father, she couldn't help, no matter how much she might like to.

She and Wynn shared a certain spark. Aside from yesterday's near tragedy, these past days had been fun. But they were two individuals who had agreed to come together for a short time to enjoy a diversion. With bombs going off, things had gotten complicated enough. She shouldn't expect to get any more involved.

More to the point…Wynn clearly didn't want her involvement, either.

Later that evening, as Grace followed Wynn into Eloise's private hospital suite, she wished she were someplace else.

He'd decided they should stay and cancelled the flights. A couple of hours ago, when they'd received word that Eloise had given birth and both mother and child were doing well, Wynn had seemed less than enthusiastic.

Looking around the hospital suite now, the first thing Grace saw was a big white teddy bear with pink balloons and a sign that read, It's a Girl. Sitting up in bed, wearing a midnight blue nightgown set, Eloise looked radiant as she gazed down at her sleeping baby, who was wrapped in a pale pink blanket. Despite her complaints about being uncomfortable and "over it," she obviously adored this child.

While Shelby and Taryn were close enough to sigh over

the miniature fingers and that perfect baby face, Wynn's back remained glued to the wall. Dex looked uncomfortable, too. Guthrie stood on the opposite side of the room by a window, gazing upon the family scene from afar. No smile. Certainly he'd been through a lot these past hours, but Grace couldn't keep Wynn's earlier comment from her thoughts.

And now he knows something else.

Before coming to the hospital, she and Wynn, along with Dex and Shelby, had spent a quiet time with Tate. Wynn hadn't provided any more information about what had transpired between father and son that afternoon. She had vowed not to dig any more than she already had. But this situation, seeing Wynn so distant and cold, was cutting her to the quick.

Eloise was running a gentle fingertip around the baby's plump cheek. "Isn't she a honey? In fact, Honey would be a fine name." She glanced across at her husband. "Guthrie, darlin', you haven't had a hold. You know she looks just like you."

Wynn flinched. Muttering "Excuse me," he headed out the door.

Grace found him at the far end of the corridor. He seemed oblivious to the activity buzzing around him— nurses checking trays, mothers being wheeled to birthing suites. Gripping the wall behind his back, he looked haunted, as if he'd met a monster from his worst nightmare. She strode up to him.

Wynn wiped a palm down his face. Then, taking her arm, he led her into a small unoccupied waiting room.

Sitting together, he inhaled a fortifying breath.

"I didn't mean for him to hear," he began to explain. "I was blowing off steam. He must have followed me out of the study. I had no idea he was coming up behind me."

Blowing off steam. Grace's scalp began to tingle. "You mean your father? What did you say, Wynn?

"I said if anyone needed to be spied on, it was his wife." He angled toward her. "Can't you guess the reason Cole would rather avoid his beautiful, attention-seeking stepmother?"

When a thought crept in, too vile to contemplate, Grace shivered. She felt too stunned to breathe.

"Are you sure?"

"One holiday here in Australia, Eloise cornered Cole. Dex walked in and witnessed the tail end. Eloise had been trying to kiss Cole, caress him. She'd been drinking...." Wynn shuddered. "I never wanted to believe it. Now my father can't even look at me, or his wife, or his baby. After keeping it quiet all this time, Cole will be pissed when he finds out that Dad knows. He never wanted to be the bearer of that news. And Tate..."

Cringing, Wynn held his head in his hands. After a long tense moment, he sat back. His expression blistered with contempt.

"If I were Guthrie, I'd want to know. I'd want to know everything, straight up." He hung his head and then coughed out a humorless laugh. "You're probably thinking I wanted to give as good as I got."

That he'd meant to hurt his father through Eloise the same way he'd been hurt by Heather? God, no.

"I think there are times when lines get blurred."

"Between truth and deception? I'm not that naive." He found a grin. "Neither are you."

"I said that sometimes lines blur. Sometimes a person can unintentionally, well, *mislead*. Mislead themselves."

He thought about it and finally nodded. "Sure. I've convinced myself of things that turned out to be a lie."

"Me, too." She pulled down a breath. "The night Sam died," she said, "he proposed to me."

Wynn groaned and reached out to squeeze her hand with such tenderness, Grace could barely stand it.

"Wynn…" She swallowed. "I said no."

Wynn's expression stilled before doubt faded up to gleam in his eyes. "But…you *loved* Sam."

"I did love Sam." Her throat convulsed. "But more like a friend."

His brows swooped down. The grip on her hand tightened and then grew slack. "I'm confused."

"Sam and I dated for years. Everyone expected us to marry one day. I don't know if we started out in the same place and I grew in another direction, or if I was just too young to understand what I was getting myself into." Feeling heat burn her cheeks, she took a breath. "One minute we were kids, having fun. The next, people were asking when we were planning our big day."

Grace waited as the information sank in and Wynn slowly nodded.

"So, you turned Sam down," Wynn said, "he left, upset I imagine. And you never saw him again."

He paused and his eyes narrowed. "Did Sam say anything before he went?"

"Like what?"

"Like, I wish I was dead."

She recoiled. *Oh, God.* "Don't say that."

"But that's what's behind this confession, isn't it? What you've been thinking all these months after his accident. That you might have pushed him to it."

"I couldn't stop him from charging off," she explained, "getting in his truck. When I got word of the crash…"

The same raw regrets wound through her mind again. *If only I'd told him sooner. If only he hadn't taken the news so hard. If only I could have loved him the way that he'd loved me.*

"I never wanted to hurt Sam." She hesitated. "I'm not sure that Heather ever wanted to hurt you, either."

Wynn's face broke with a sardonic grin. "Hell, that's part of the attraction here, isn't it? Part of our bond. Only I didn't know it until now. Sam's tortured soul might be gone but I'm still here. You can't ask Sam just how bad it was, but you can ask me."

Before she could deny it, or admit he was right, Wynn went on.

"Well, I can tell you that the hours after Heather left me were the worst in my life. Jesus, I didn't *want* a life. My world was black, meaningless, and I couldn't see a way past it. So, if you're after some kind of absolution from me, I'm sorry, Grace. I just can't give it."

A tear spilled down her cheek. Wynn didn't have to forgive her. She hadn't expected that he would. The question was: would she ever forgive herself?

"I wish I could go back," she said. "Somehow make it right."

"There's no way back. All we can do is move forward. Call the truth the truth when we see it." He reached for her hand. "Avoid making the same mistakes."

Those words seemed to echo in her ears.

"That first night we met again," he went on after a moment, "we were clear on what we wanted. What we didn't want."

Grace remembered. She'd told him, *I'm not after a relationship...of any kind.*

"I'd always wanted a family of my own," he said. "When Tate came along, I decided I wanted a kid just like him." Taking a breath, he seemed to gather himself as he sat up straighter. "I don't want that anymore. None of it. I don't want to worry about infidelity or divorce or seeing my children every other weekend. I don't want permanent. No broken hearts. That's the God's honest truth."

A sound near the door drew their attention. A man walked in. His hair was rumpled like his shirt, but his smile was clear and wide; it spread more when he saw them sitting there.

"Hey, I have a boy!" he exclaimed as if he'd known them for years. "He's one hundred percent healthy." The man held his nose, as if he were trying to stem tears of joy. "He even looks like me. Same wing nut ears."

As the man headed for the coffee machine, Grace noticed someone else standing in the doorway. His head was hanging and a plastic dinosaur lay on its side near his sneakers. As she pushed to her feet, Wynn strode over and swung his little brother up on his hip.

"What are you doing here all by yourself, little man?"

"I ran down." Tate laid his head on Wynn's shoulder. "Teagan's coming."

A second later, Teagan appeared. She ruffled Tate's hair. "You're as fast as a cat, you know that?"

Putting on a brave face, Wynn hitched Tate higher. "Your baby sister's cute, huh?"

Tate rubbed a finger under his nose. "I guess."

Teagan dropped a kiss on Tate's cheek. "Doesn't mean we won't all love you just the same."

When Wynn pressed his lips to his brother's brow, a rush of emotion filled Grace's chest. Once he'd wanted a little boy just like Tate, but not anymore. At that wedding in New York, she'd told him that she wasn't after a relationship. She'd been clear. That had been *her* truth.

But now…

She didn't want to worry about infidelity or divorce, either. But one day she did want to get married. One day she wanted a child. A husband and family of her own. And she wanted to be closer to the family she had. She wanted to be near at hand to support Rochelle and April through the hard times ahead. Foremost, she wanted to truly get over the past, not just play at it. She thought she might finally be getting there.

No surprise. As much as that might hurt now, that meant a future without Wynn.

Thirteen

Two days after Eloise gave birth, Grace and Wynn landed back in New York. Wynn said she could stay at his place before she went back to Florida. She kept mum about her decision not to return there for good. Rather she said that she'd stay on with him an extra couple of nights.

He wanted to negotiate and they settled on five nights; after that explosion, they'd cut their stay in Australia short anyway. He'd have to make appearances at the office, he said. But Grace figured, with evenings all their own, five days would be enough for a proper goodbye.

When they arrived from the airport at Wynn's apartment, Grace headed for the attached bathroom where she ditched her travel clothes and slipped on a bathrobe. A few minutes later, she found Wynn, minus his shirt, standing in the middle of the master suite. He was studying his cell phone as if it might hold some answers.

"That was Cole," he said, looking up. "Apparently since we left, my father hasn't come out of his study."

Grace edged closer. Before leaving for the airport, Wynn had told his brother about his ill-timed slip regarding Eloise. "Does your stepmother know that Guthrie knows?"

"If she doesn't yet, my guess is she will soon." With a mirthless grin, Wynn rubbed his jaw. "My father's not the type to let a conflict go unresolved."

His young wife had sexually propositioned his oldest son—a humiliating kick in the gut. Guthrie would have suffered a complete loss of faith in Eloise—in his marriage. Still, some relationships could be repaired.

"Do you think they'll work it out?" she asked.

"Christ, I hope so. For the kids' sake."

That brand new baby, Honey, and, of course, Tate. When she and Wynn had left the Hunter mansion, his little brother had clung to Teagan's hand, a toy dinosaur clamped under his other arm. His chin had wobbled. He'd tried so hard not to cry.

"How's Tate?" she asked.

"Cole said he's missing us."

Missing Wynn. The Hunters didn't all get together often. Studies had proven that children benefited in so many ways from regular contact with extended family. That situation made her decision about being closer to her own family not only clearer but also vital. She'd made friends in Florida, in and outside of the practice. But when she'd left New York a year ago, Florida had merely been a means to escape.

She'd licked her wounds long enough. It was time to come home and, perhaps, start up her own practice. Years ago, when she'd decided on her college degree, that was the original plan. But she didn't want Wynn to think her decision to come home to stay, whenever he found out, had anything to do with *him*. It didn't. He'd told her—and in plain terms—he wasn't after "permanent." So, no need to further complicate this time together with info that didn't concern him. Wynn wouldn't want complications, either.

Now when he lifted her wrist and his mouth brushed the skin, a stream of longing tingled through her system. For these remaining days, she had every intention of acting on that physical desire. Then she would set those feelings aside. It made no sense to hang on to those emotions and fall in love with someone who would never love her back.

His arm wound around her at the same time his lips met hers. He kissed her until she was giddy and kneading his bare chest. By the time his lips left hers, her limbs were limp. This might not be forever but it was real and comforting and, for now, utterly right.

He swung her up into his arms and carried her over to the bed. When they lay naked on the sheet, he kissed her again—lazy and deep. Then his mouth made love to each of her breasts, her belly and then her thighs. She was coiling a leg around his hip, getting ready for his incredible icing on their cake, when he shifted and maneuvered her over onto one side.

The warm ruts of his abdomen met her back at the same time his tongue traveled in a mesmerizing line between her shoulder blades and up one side of her neck. As his palm sailed over her hip toward her navel, then her sex, her heightened physical need rushed to heat her blood. He explored her, delving and stroking until mad desire quivered and twisted inside of her.

Then he moved again, swinging her over. With her straddling him, he shifted her into position, aligned himself, and then thrust up, forcefully enough to send air hissing back through her teeth. Unsteady, she tipped forward, planting both palms on his pecs before his hands gripped her hips and she gave herself over to the heat and magic of his skill.

The strokes grew deeper, stronger, until each time he filled her, she pushed back and told herself never in her lifetime would she ever feel this good again. She'd never felt so connected, had never felt closer to anyone, to anything—

Her climax hit at the same time Wynn groaned and dragged her off him. Her fingers and toes were still curling when, out of breath, he gathered her close and buried his face in her hair. He ground out the words.

"I forgot."

Forgot what?

Then her eyes sprang open. She'd forgotten, too. They hadn't used protection. But he hadn't spilled inside of her.

"You pulled away in time," she said.

Which didn't mean a whole lot. Even with contraception, no one was a hundred percent safe. Every freshman knew a couple should never rely on withdrawal.

"We both got carried away," he said, urging her closer.

So true. But, no matter how carried away they'd both gotten, this was inexcusable.

"Wynn, that can never happen again."

He pressed a kiss to her brow. "You read my mind."

Which ought to have been the right response. No thinking person wanted an unplanned pregnancy, particularly between two people who had zero intention of spending their lifetimes together. And yet there was a part of her that felt—*disappointment?* Or, more simply, a sense of sadness.

One day she would find Mr. Right. Have a family. But she wasn't so sure about Wynn anymore. He was fun to be around. On so many levels he was caring, thoughtful. He was a good brother. An excellent lover.

But, deep at his core, Wynn could be cynical. Even bitter. He didn't believe in love—not for himself, in any case.

And it wasn't her place to convince him.

"In Greek mythology, Prometheus had returned the gift of fire to mankind. As far as Zeus was concerned, he'd overreached. The immortal was sentenced to an eternity of torment. A lifetime in hell."

Hunching into her winter coat, Grace listened in as a

local explained the story behind the famous Rockefeller Center statue to his tourist friend. Then he related how an engineer from Cleveland was contracted in the winter of 1936 to build a temporary ice-skating rink that had become a permanent fixture. Sometimes a bold idea panned out.

Sometimes it didn't.

Beside her, Wynn was on a call. Each time he spoke, vaporous clouds puffed out from his mouth. His black wool overcoat made his tall, muscular frame look even more enticing. When his gaze jumped across to her and he sent her a slanted smile, heat swam all the way through to her bones.

This afternoon, they'd strolled along Fifth Avenue, checking out the window displays at Saks, listening to carolers; Wynn's favorite Christmas song was "Winter Wonderland," and hers was "Silver Bells." No pressure. And yet, oftentimes Grace caught herself wondering where the two of them would be next holiday season—or five seasons from now.

Wynn finished the call and, with an apology, pulled her close.

"I'm taking you home, out of the cold," he said. "We can wrap presents." His lips grazed her cheek. "Do some *un*wrapping, too." His mouth grazed hers again. "I'll call Daphne and tell her I'm not coming back into the office."

"But you have a meeting about the merger this afternoon."

"That was Lumos. He postponed." He stole another feathery kiss. "I'm all yours."

Hand in hand, they headed down the Channel Gardens, a pedestrian street that linked to Fifth Avenue.

"Did you ever hear back from Christopher Riggs?" she asked, as the sound of carolers and the smell of roasting chestnuts wafted around them.

She'd been floored when Wynn had explained how

Guthrie had employed Riggs as a plant to feed back information regarding the possibility of a merger.

"Not a word," he said. "I figure, since he hasn't shown up at the office since I got back to town, my father must have gotten in touch and told him that his services were no longer needed."

"But you're going ahead with the merger. What if your father won't agree?"

"Then I'll have to reconsider my position here." He shoved his hands deeper into his coat pockets. "Times have changed. Are still changing, and fast. Business needs to keep ahead. I know a merger is the right way to go, and I can't twiddle my thumbs about it. I have to act now. If Hunter Publishing ever goes down, it won't be because I was a coward and didn't push forward."

So, he was willing to step down from his role at Hunter Publishing? She hoped this stalemate between father and son wouldn't come to that. And yet she saw in Wynn's expression now something that told her he wouldn't back down. Not because he was being stubborn but because he thought he was right. Typical Wynn.

But what was the alternative? He was convinced his company needed to evolve in order to survive and, hopefully, grow. If he couldn't make this deal happen—if a drastic change wasn't made—to his mind, he'd be knowingly committing corporate suicide.

She shunted those thoughts aside as he wrapped an arm around her waist.

"So," he leaned in toward her, "about that unwrapping…"

Her stomach swooped. He knew very well what day it was. Their agreement had been for her to stay at his place five nights. She'd made plans and, however much it cut her up inside, she needed to stick to them.

"I'm staying at Rochelle and April's tonight. We're putting a new star on their tree." Her heart squeezed for her sister and niece's situation. "Trey's not coming home for Christmas."

"Poor kid." His mouth tightened. "Another marriage bites the dust."

Grace understood the attitude, but his tone made her wince. He'd had his heart broken. Hell, Grace had broken someone's heart, too. But a man and a woman *could* build a happy life together. If they met at the right time, if they shared similar values, were prepared to commit—if they believed in their love, in their future, marriage could absolutely work out.

"So, you're staying at your sister's place tonight."

She nodded. "Flying to Florida tomorrow."

To formally resign and make arrangements to sublet her apartment there. In the New Year she would be back in New York and find a new door to hang her speech therapist sign on.

"But you'll be spending Christmas with your family, won't you?" he said as they turned onto Fifth Avenue.

"I thought I'd fly back up a couple of days beforehand." And stay—at her parents' home initially—until she found a place of her own.

"An invitation came through this morning," he said. "A Christmas Eve masquerade ball. All monies raised go to the Robin Hood Foundation."

Grace knew the charity. She supported their work helping all kinds of people in need. But she couldn't accept Wynn's invitation.

"You go." He would be generous with his donation either way. "I've already let my family know. I'm staying in with them Christmas Eve."

"You can change your mind."

"No, Wynn. I can't."

He didn't respond other than to tighten his grip on her hand.

When they passed a window display featuring a well-dressed snowman, she tried to edge the uneasiness aside. She wanted to enjoy what little time they had left together.

"Whenever I see a snowman," she said, "I think of that Christmas in Colorado."

When he didn't reply, she glanced across at him. Preoccupied, he was looking dead ahead. Fitting a smile into her voice, she tried again.

"You were the snottiest boy I'd ever met. You were always so serious."

"I've been thinking," he said. "This doesn't have to end. You and me. Not completely. I could fly down to Florida. You'll be up here to see family. And we can always get away again. Maybe to the Bahamas next time."

Grace hung her head.

She'd anticipated this moment. Wynn didn't want to say goodbye. Not completely. But *she* didn't want to risk this affair going on any longer. Every day she felt herself drawn all the more. Breaking off now, for good, was hard. One of the most difficult things she'd ever had to do.

But how much more difficult would it be if they went on and on until she had to admit to herself, and to Wynn, she wanted more. It might not have started out that way but, ultimately, she would be after a commitment that he couldn't give.

He thought they could get away again sometime...

She tried to keep her tone light. "I don't think that'll work."

His frown was quickly interrupted by a persuasive smile. "Sure it can."

"No, Wynn." *I'm sorry.* "It can't."

When he stopped walking, she stopped, too. His gaze had narrowed on hers, as if he were contemplating the best way to convince her. To *win*. Finally, his chin kicked up and he took her other hand, too.

"Let's go home and we'll talk—"

"Your apartment isn't my home, Wynn, it's yours. I was only a guest." She hadn't even unpacked her bags properly.

"You can come and stay any time you like," he said.

"For how long? One month? One year? As long as it's not permanent, right?"

Her heart was thumping against her ribs. As she drew her hand from his, his brow creased even more.

"Where did all that come from?"

"We had an agreement. We extended it. Now it's over."

"Just like that?"

"Tell me the alternative."

He shrugged. "We go on seeing each other."

"When we can. Until it ends."

Her throat was aching. She didn't want to have this discussion. Wynn had been burned—now he was staying the hell away from those flames. His choice. But she had to do what was best for her. She had to protect her heart. She had to get on with her life.

Her phone rang. Needing a time out, Grace drew her cell from her bag and answered.

"I wanted you to know," Rochelle began, sounding concise but also breathy. "It was scary at the time, but everything's fine now."

Grace pushed a finger against her ear to block the noise of nearby traffic as Wynn, hands back in pockets, frowned off into the distance.

"What was scary?" she asked.

"April was admitted to the hospital this morning."

Grace's heart dropped. She pressed the phone harder to her ear.

"What for? What happened?"

"She was on a play date," Rochelle said. "Cindy's mother knew about the allergies. No nuts. Not a hint. Apparently an older sister had a friend over who'd brought some cookies…"

Rochelle explained that when April had begun to wheeze and complain of a stomachache, the mother had called Rochelle right away. April's knapsack always carried an epinephrine auto-injector in case of just this kind of emergency. Her niece had spent the next few hours in the E.R. of a local hospital under observation. Sometimes there was a second reaction hours later. Not this time, thank God.

"We're at Mom and Dad's now," Rochelle finished.

"I'll come straight over."

"You don't have to do that. I just wanted you to know." Rochelle paused. "But if you can make it, I know April would love to see you. Me, too."

When Grace disconnected, Wynn's expression had eased into mild concern. He cupped her cheek.

"Everything okay?"

Grace passed on Rochelle's news. "I need to go and give them both a big hug."

Wynn strode to the curb and hailed a cab in record time. But when he opened the back passenger-side door, Grace set a hand on his chest.

"You don't need to come," she said.

"Of course I'll come."

An avalanche of emotion swelled, poised to crash over the edge. She shook her head. "Please. Don't."

As traffic streamed by one side of them and pedestrians pushed past on the other, Wynn's gaze probed hers. For a moment, she thought he was going to insist and then she would have to find even more strength to stay firm when all she really wanted to do was surrender and let him comfort her. But that was only delaying the inevitable.

His look eventually faded beneath a glint of understanding. She could almost feel awareness melt over him, and see the consequences of "what comes next" pop into his head. In his heart, Wynn knew this was best.

"What about your bags?" he asked.

"I'll arrange to have them picked up."

"No. I'll send them on. I've got your father's address."

Leaning in through the passenger doorway, he spoke to the driver. "The lady's in a hurry," he said before stepping back.

On suddenly shaky legs, she slid into the cab. Before Wynn could close the door, she angled to peer up at him.

"I really did have the best time," she said.

His jaw flexed and nostrils flared before his shoulders came down and he nodded. "Me, too."

And then it was done. The door closed. The cab pulled away from the curb and she rode out of Wynn Hunter's life for good.

Fourteen

The next day, Wynn sat in his office, staring blankly at an email message his father had sent. He'd read it countless times.

Son, you have my blessing.

His eyes stinging, Wynn's focus shifted to the final merger document waiting on his desk. All the *i*'s were dotted. Every *t* crossed. Bean counters were happy and public-relations folks were beaming over the positive spin they could generate. In an hour, signatures would be down and the deal would be done.

Thank God.

He had his father's consent, but did he really have his approval? Did Guthrie understand that his son had acted only in the best interests of Hunter Publishing? Of the family? Which brought to mind that other predicament. The issue surrounding his father's marriage. The question of infidelity. Of trust. And desire.

He glared at his cell phone and finally broke. A moment later, he was waiting for Grace to pick up. When the phone continued to ring, he thought back and analyzed the situation.

There was no reason for her to be upset with him. After her niece's allergic reaction scare, Grace had been told that the little girl was home and fully recovered. Nevertheless, naturally he'd wanted to jump in that cab and keep her company—offer his support.

Yes, he'd wanted her to come to that charity ball Christmas Eve. If at all possible, he'd wanted her to stay a few more nights. Sure, the vacation was over but he wanted to see her again. Way more than he could have ever imagined. He cared for Grace a great deal.

Enough to continue to push the point?

He hadn't changed his mind about relationships, particularly after pondering the future of his father's second marriage. And it seemed Grace hadn't changed her mind about not wanting a serious relationship, either. Yesterday she'd been blunt. They'd had an arrangement. Now it was over. She didn't want the tie.

The line connected. Grace said hello.

"Hi." He cleared his throat. "Just making sure your niece is okay."

"April's fine. Thank God."

He closed his eyes. Just her voice… The withdrawal factor after only twenty-four hours was even worse than he'd thought.

"Did your bags get to your parents' address?"

"Yes. Thanks. I really appreciate it."

A few seconds of silence passed before he asked the question. "So, you're leaving for Florida today?"

"On my way to the airport now."

Wynn paused to indulge in a vision: him jumping in a cab and cutting her off at the pass. Crazy-ass stuff. Better to simply let her know his thoughts. His—*feelings*.

"Wynn, you there?"

"I'm here."

"I need to pay the driver. I'm at the airport."

"Oh. When's your flight?"

"Soon."

He heard a muffled voice—the driver, Wynn presumed.

"Sorry," she said. "I really have to go."

The line went dead. Wynn dropped the phone from his ear and rewound the brief conversation in his head. Then he stared at that merger contract again. He was about to sit back, rub his brow, when his cell phone chimed. Jerking forward, he snatched it up.

"Grace?"

A familiar voice came down the line. "Hey, buddy."

Wynn slumped. "Hey, Cole."

"Before I start, I want you to know that no one, including Dad, blames you for the fallout from your slip last week."

Cold comfort.

"Where is he with it?" Wynn grunted. "Filing for divorce?"

"*No*. He and Eloise have spoken. Are speaking."

Well, that was something.

"I'll keep you up to date," Cole said.

If only he could take it back. Of course, he didn't condone Eloise's behavior. He simply hadn't wanted to be the unwitting messenger, particularly when things in Sydney were crap enough for his father as it was.

"How's the investigation going?" Wynn asked.

"No one's easing up. Surveillance footage hasn't turned up any leads. Crime investigation is still tracking down possible links with the device's components. They're looking into DNA."

"And Brandon?"

"Everyone's in his sights, even his own men."

Off the job, Brandon Powell exuded a laid-back air, but beneath the cool sat a steely nerve. With his black belt in martial arts, a man would have to be nuts to pick a fight with that guy.

"Is there still a battery of security guards around the place?" Wynn asked.

"Twenty-four seven."

"And Tate?"

"When Tate begged to stay with his parents a bit longer, Dex and Shelby stayed on, too. Tate knows his parents are either avoiding each other or quarrelling. We all try to shelter him from it as much as we can, but Eloise isn't good with conflict."

Cole was being kind there.

Wynn was concerned about Tate coping with this situation, but none of this could be good for that baby—his half sister—either.

Wynn loosened his tie. Thank God he'd never have to go through anything like this. This whole situation sucked so bad, discussing it made him feel physically ill.

"I have something to ask," Cole said.

"Anything."

"Could you have Tate come for Christmas?"

Wynn blinked several times. "Where exactly is this coming from? How's Tate going to take that?"

"Tate's the one asking."

"And he asked to stay with me? Not Dex or Teagan or you?"

"He must want to spread the love. Or maybe he feels particularly safe with you. The way you rescued him that day—"

"He doesn't remember that."

"Maybe he does." Cole took a breath. "Can I put him on a flight next week?"

"Of course." *If that's what Tate really wants.* "Let me know the details when they're locked in." Dates, times, and obviously Tate would need a chaperone on the flight.

There were two beats of silence before Cole asked, "How's Grace?"

Wynn explained yesterday's conversation—how she wanted to end it and how he had complied.

Cole grunted. "How do you feel about that?"

"I feel...well, pretty crappy about it, actually."

"Because?"

He needed to ask? "Because we had a good time together."

"And?"

"And, I *like* her. But, Cole, she's right. We had an arrangement."

"What's that?"

Wynn hesitated a moment and then spilled it all—about Grace's ex, his proposal, the accident and how she wasn't interested in getting serious with anyone right now.

"What about you?" Cole asked.

"Of course, I was on board."

"Because of your bust-up with Heather."

Wynn ran his fingers through his hair. This wasn't rocket science. "Yes, because of my bust-up. I planned to marry the woman."

"Now you plan to stay single."

"Yes, sir, I do."

"And you told Grace that."

Wynn narrowed his eyes. "I told her. But you're missing the point. Cole, *she* was the one who wanted to end it."

"Smart girl."

Wynn cocked a brow. "I think I should feel insulted."

"Ask yourself something, and answer it truthfully. Are you falling in love with Grace Munroe?"

Wynn opened his mouth and then shut it again before he decided on a defense. "Just because you're happily married now—"

"Wynn, it doesn't have to be Grace, but I'd hate to see you lose someone meant for you because you're too damn stubborn and stuck to see what's right in front of your nose."

When they disconnected, Wynn was hot around the gills. Cole didn't understand. Wynn didn't need anyone second-guessing his life, his decisions, or telling him what he should or should not feel.

Five minutes on, Wynn had cooled down, not that it made him feel any better. His relationship with his father had been resurrected. The merger deal would go through. And yet, with all that he had…irrespective of all that "being right"…none of it seemed to matter alongside one simple, complicated truth.

He'd lost Grace.

Fifteen

A few days after Grace had flown down to Florida to re-sign her position, she was back in New York for the holidays. Back in New York to stay, although she had yet to find a place of her own. Not that Wynn could know any of that.

When he sent a text to say his little brother was visiting for the holidays, naturally Grace was curious. Were Guthrie, Eloise and the baby here in the States, too? She doubted it. She'd responded, How cool! Tate would always have a very special place in her heart. Then a second text had mentioned that Tate loved to visit Rockefeller Center—every day at around two.

She knew she probably shouldn't. But she decided to go anyway.

Five minutes ago, she'd arrived at the Center and immediately spotted her boys. Dressed for chilly weather, the Hunter brothers were checking out skaters, laughing whenever Santa slid around with a conga line of kids hanging off the back of his red suit. The giant tree towered over the crowd, rewarding everyone with glowing, festive thoughts. Like streams of sparkling atoms filling the air, on Christmas Eve, magic seemed to be everywhere.

As if he sensed her nearby, Wynn pulled up tall and scanned the crowd. When their gazes connected, a spark zapped all the way up her spine. His expression shut down before a smile tugged the corners of his beautiful mouth.

He didn't call her over. Rather he simply waited, drinking her in as if he worried that, should he look away, she might disappear. Then Tate tugged his brother's windbreaker and his little red beanie tipped back. Wynn crouched down.

Tate seemed to know that his big brother was distracted. When he spotted her, Tate jumped into the air, so high she thought his feet must have grown springs. Wynn placed a hand on his shoulder, but Tate refused to calm down. Grace heard his squeals for her to join them.

He was such a good kid, going through such a hard time. His family might have wealth but, no doubt, he would trade everything, and in a heartbeat, for a safe and settled home.

As she came closer, Tate broke away. In a bright blue parka and boots, he scampered up and flung his arms around her hips.

"This is a really big city," Tate said, still hugging her tight. "You found us anyway." He pulled back and looked up with the familiar tawny-colored eyes that stole her heart away. "The Empire State Building has a hundred and two stories."

She laughed. "Pretty high, huh?"

"Didja see the snowman in that window?" He pointed toward the avenue before he flapped his arms against his thighs and shrugged. "Santa's coming tonight. We need to finish the tree."

Wynn had strolled up. "And we need to get to bed before those reindeer swing their bells on into New York."

Grace's stomach fluttered at the sound of his voice—the

white flash of his smile. She had to dig her hands deeper into her pockets to stop them from reaching out.

"Mommy takes my picture when I put cookies out for Santa, but Wynn's gonna do it this year."

When Tate took his brother's leather-gloved hand, the picture, its setting, just seemed to fit.

Grace schooled her features. She was getting misty, damn it.

"Not going to that masquerade ball?" she asked Wynn.

"They have my donation." He winked at his little brother. "Tate and I have important things to do."

Tate gave a big nod. "Can Grace come over?"

Wynn arched a brow. "I think she already has plans."

"I'm staying with my parents," she told Tate. "My sisters will be there tonight. My niece, too. April's almost your age."

Tate's mouth hooked to one side, not in a happy way. "A girl?"

"Like Honey," Wynn said, "only older." Then he checked out the sky, which was heavy with the promise of snow. "We were getting ready to go for a hot chocolate—"

"Oh, sure," she slipped in. "I won't hold you up."

"I like mine with marshmallows on top," Tate said. "Wynn likes chocolate curls."

Grace jerked a thumb toward the street. "I really have to go. But I have something for you, Tate." She drew a wrapped gift from beneath her coat. Accepting it, Tate looked to Wynn. "He can open it now," she said.

Tate peeled the wrapping and eased out the gift. His legs seemed to buckle before he whooped with delight.

"A Yankees triceratops! His horn goes right through the cap!" Tate gave her an earnest look. "Santa can't beat this."

Grace held her throat. Her heart felt so full and at the same time so empty. She wished she could stay longer. But a fast, clean break would be best.

"After the holidays, Wynn's gonna take me to his office." Tate tugged his brother's coat. "Can I go see the skaters?"

"Sure, pal." When Tate was out of earshot, Wynn stepped closer. His gaze swept over her face, lingered on her lips.

"You look great," he said.

"You look—relaxed. Did your father come out with Tate?"

"Cole chaperoned him over on the flight. Tate had asked if he could come out."

Wynn didn't need to explain more. Grace thought she understood.

"Dad let me know he was okay with the merger going through," he went on.

"*Wow.* That's great. Congratulations."

"He and Eloise are trying to work things out."

She eased out a grateful breath. "I'll pray that they do."

He looked back at Tate standing a short distance away, checking out Santa, who was performing one very fine axel jump.

"It's good having Tate over," he said, "even if the circumstances aren't the best."

"Any progress on who was behind that explosion?"

"Not yet. But I'm sure they'll find something soon." He adjusted one leather glove then the other. "Dex and Shelby are flying over tomorrow afternoon. They're staying with her father in Oklahoma tonight. In fact, Mr. Scott is flying out here with them."

"A real family affair."

"He and Tate got to be chums when Dex took him out there for a stay."

"What are Cole and Taryn doing tomorrow?"

"Visiting Dad and the new baby. And Eloise, I suppose."

Awkward. "And Teagan? Is she flying out to be with Tate, too?"

"She says she isn't. When I spoke to her, I got the feeling it might have something to do with a man."

The man who wanted a big family? "Did she sound okay?"

"She sounded preoccupied."

As soon as she left here, Grace decided, she'd phone Teagan. She hoped her friend hadn't broken up with the guy she'd been seeing. If he was in love with her, and Teagan felt the same way, there had to be a way to sort everything out.

"I was wondering," Wynn said, crossing his arms, "whether you might like to come over tomorrow, too. I know you'd have all the traditional stuff in the morning with your family. And lunch. But if you're free for dinner, Tate would love to have you over. Dex and Shelby, too."

As he made the invitation, the ache in Grace's throat grew and grew. But she'd been prepared for something like this. Wynn didn't give in easily. Neither did she.

Over these past few days, with being away from Wynn and missing him so much, she'd come to a solid conclusion. She loved this man. Loved most everything about him. But she wasn't about to do anything foolish like admit it and set herself up for a gigantic fall. She'd seen firsthand how a move like that could destroy a person.

"Thanks for the invite," she said, proud of herself for holding his gaze. "But I can't. I'm sorry."

"No. It's fine. *I'm* sorry. Just had to ask. You know. For Tate."

Tate was gazing up at the big tree in wonder, holding his new dinosaur under his arm. So cute and innocent.

She swallowed.

God, her throat was tight. Clogged.

She really had to go.

"I'll just say goodbye," she said.

Wynn tried to smile. "You've only been here a minute."

She began to skirt her way around him.

"Stay a little longer," he said.

"I have to go."

"Grace." He caught her arm and her eyes finally locked with his. A soft smile touched the corners of his mouth. "Grace. I don't want to lose you."

She held her stomach. How blunt did she need to be? "Wynn, you don't want what I want."

"I want you."

"And I want *love.*"

Her heart was thumping in her ears. She felt weak and emotional and, hell, it was *true.* And now, in a single heartbeat, it was out.

She watched understanding sink in and then resistance darken his eyes. Meanwhile, Tate had run back and was tugging on his big brother's coat again.

"Wynn, where's the hot chocolate shop? I'm cold."

Grace crouched down. She prayed Tate didn't see that she was trembling or that tears edged her eyes.

"You'll have a great Christmas with everyone, won't you, hon?"

"Are you gonna come, too?" Tate asked.

"Afraid not," she said.

Tate studied the Yankees dinosaur she'd given him. "Well," he said, "maybe next time."

When she looked up at Wynn, he was taking Tate's hand.

"Come on, buddy," he said. "Don't want that hot chocolate going cold."

They started off and then Wynn stopped, turned back around.

"Have a good day tomorrow, Grace," he said.

Forcing a smile, she nodded but couldn't say the words. *Merry Christmas.*
Happy New Year.

It was past eight that night when Grace edged inside the room her niece used whenever she stayed at Grandma and

Grandpa's. The night-light was on, casting stars around the ceiling and walls.

"Is she asleep?" she whispered.

With a children's Christmas book closed on her lap, Rochelle had been gazing at her daughter.

"I thought I'd need to read *'Twas the Night Before Christmas* at least twice through." Rochelle eased to her feet. "April was counting sugar plums after the third verse." Crossing over, Rochelle saw the notebook Grace held. "You're working on exercises tonight?"

"Not the kind you think."

The women tiptoed out of the room. Downstairs, their mother was finalizing tomorrow's menu with Jenn. Dad would be reading in his chair. Tilly was out with friends, due home soon, or at least not late.

Grace led Rochelle into her room. The fire she'd lit earlier was crackling with low yellow flames while snow piled up on the windowpane outside. A gift she'd bought April that afternoon lay on the bed. When she and Rochelle sat on the quilt, Grace rapped her knuckles against the notebook's cover.

"I had something I needed to work through," Grace explained. "I thought writing it all down might help. It's about Sam." She bowed her head. "A year after the funeral, I still felt responsible."

"Because you didn't love him?"

"The night Sam died, he asked me to marry him." Everyone knew that he had planned to sometime very soon. "Rochelle, I said no. I turned him away."

Rochelle froze. "Okay, wait. You think he took his own life, or maybe he was so upset that he lost control of the vehicle?"

"Not anymore." Wincing, Grace gripped the book. "I mean, I don't know."

"He'd just gotten off a long shift. It was deemed an accident."

Grace finished for her. "Authorities surmised he'd fallen asleep at the wheel. But I couldn't put it to rest."

"So you kept it bottled up inside of you all this time?" Rochelle's hand covered hers. "Grace, you're not responsible for what happened to Sam. Just like I'm not responsible for Trey's actions."

"Yeah. I know, but…"

"Sam was taken away from us too soon. We were all lucky to have known him. But you can't change the past, and you can't change how you feel. If Sam were here now, he'd want you to let it go and really get on with your life."

Grace expelled a breath. Of course, Rochelle was right. Tonight, missing Wynn and wondering about the future, Grace had only needed to hear it, and from someone she trusted, despite any past sisterly spats.

That story finished, Grace slid the notebook into her bedside drawer and then eyed the velvet box containing April's gift. "What time's Trey collecting April tomorrow?"

"He isn't. Says it'll be too awkward for her." Rochelle rolled her eyes. "Makes me all the more determined. This Christmas is going to be extra special—with plenty of family and love to go around. Every kid deserves that."

Grace picked up April's gift and flipped open the lid. A huge crystal ring shone out. "Think she'll like it?"

"April?" Rochelle gave a low whistle. "Heck, I want it myself."

Grace cut the paper while Rochelle ripped off some tape.

"Have you heard from Wynn?" Rochelle asked, pressing a glossy pink bow on top.

Grace had confided in Rochelle about that afternoon when she'd called after April's allergy scare. She spilled all about her tormented feelings toward Wynn as well as her decision to stay clear. To protect her heart.

"I saw him today." Grace set aside the wrapped gift. "His little brother's out for the holidays."

"I thought you said you two were through."

"We are. But Tate asked to see me. After all that kid's been through, I wasn't going to stand him up."

"Oh, Grace, are you sure you want to end it? You had such a great time in Australia."

"Aside from the explosion."

"Aside from that." Rochelle leaned forward. "The way you feel about each other…the things he says and does…"

"Are all *incredible*. Addictive is the word. But Wynn isn't interested in strings." She fell back on the bed and stared at the ceiling. "He doesn't want the hassle."

"He might change his mind."

No. "I need to get on with my life."

Grace's cheeks were hot, her throat thick. She sucked down a breath and, determined, pulled herself up. She was moving on.

"For now," she said, calm again, "that means helping you bring Santa's presents in from the garage." Swiping April's gift from the quilt, she headed for the door. "One extra-special Christmas coming up."

Wynn jingled the ornament at the overdecorated tree, which was set up in a prime corner of his apartment's living room.

"This is the very last bell."

Tate pointed to a spot on a lower branch. "Here."

After securing the bell in place, Wynn pushed to his feet, flicked a switch and the tree's colored lights blinked on, flashing red and green and blue.

Tate squealed. "We did it!"

"Of course we did! We can do *anything*."

They jumped into a "dice roll" move and finished with a noisy high five.

"Now, we need to put out those cookies for Santa," Wynn said, shepherding Tate toward the open-plan kitchen.

"And take a picture to send to Mommy."

Tate dropped some red tinsel on the special Santa plate while Wynn broke open a new batch of cookies. When the milk was poured, they moved to the dining table and set the snack up. They took a photo and sent it through to Australia. Within seconds, they got a reply.

Looks delicious! Love you, baby.

Tate read the message ten times over. When he said, "Send it to Grace," Wynn hesitated. He'd sent her a couple of messages during the week and when she'd shown up that afternoon at the rink, frankly, he'd almost begged her to stay. And then things had gone a little far afield. At first he hadn't been sure what she'd said. He'd only known the word *love* was involved.

She'd put it out there. What she'd wanted had changed. Or shifted one hell of a lot forward. At Cole's wedding, before that explosion, he might have been swayed. Knowing he was at least in part responsible for the possibility of his father's marriage ending—knowing the added crap this small boy would need to endure if that union ultimately broke down for good... Why the hell would he, would anyone, knowingly risk that much? When things went south, it just freaking *hurt* too much.

His jaw clenched tight and he lowered the phone. "How about we send the snap to Grace in the morning?"

Hopefully, with everything else happening and their visitors arriving, Tate would forget about it.

"Won't Grace like the picture?"

"Well, sure. She'd love it. It's just getting late. She's probably already in bed."

"She could still find it in the morning when she wakes up."

"Which is why we ought to send it then."

"We might forget."

"No way."

Tate blinked. "Please, Wynn."

Wynn took in his brother's uncertain expression, the mistrust building in his eyes. "You're right," he said, thumbing a few keys. "There. Sent."

They waited. No reply came through. But Wynn simply explained, "See. Told you she'd be asleep by now. We should be, too."

Picking up Tate, he swirled him through the air until his brother was giggling madly. Then they moved to the guest bathroom, where Tate brushed his teeth. After Wynn had bundled his brother into bed, he saw the distant look in Tate's eyes. Was he thinking of his home?

"Do you miss your Mom, Tate?"

He fluffed the covers. "Daddy, too. But I'm kinda used to it."

"Being away?"

Tate nodded. "I had lots of fun with Dex and Shelby. With Teagan and Damon, too."

"Damon's Tea's friend, right?"

"He likes Tea a lot. Like you and Grace. They hold hands and laugh."

Wynn cleared the thickness from his throat. "Sounds good."

Tate's head slanted sideways on the pillow. "Why didn't Grace want to come home with us?"

"It's Christmas Eve. Grace is with her family."

Tate flashed a gappy grin. "I'm glad I'm here with you."

"Things must seem a little...mixed up back home."

"That's not why I wanted to come. I thought you'd be lonely. I thought we could hang."

Wynn smiled but then sobered. "Why did you think I'd be lonely?"

Tate frowned but didn't say anything.

"Things aren't as good as they could be back home," Wynn said. "But you need to remember that everyone loves you very much—your parents, your brothers, Tea. Me. Family's very important."

"If that's right, Wynn, why don't you want a little boy of your own?"

Wynn stopped breathing. "Why would you say that?"

"You said so. You don't want to have a son like me, or family, or anything."

"Did you hear that at the hospital?"

"Tea wanted something hot to drink. I ran ahead. You and Grace were there, talking." He fluffed the covers again. "It's okay. I don't want to be a dad, either. Kids only get in the way. Mommies only ever sleep or cry." His voice lowered. "Mommy says it's all your fault. Don't know why."

Wynn did. If he'd kept his big mouth shut, Guthrie wouldn't have overheard his bleating to Dex about Eloise coming on to Cole.

Tate pushed out a sigh. "I'm pretty sure it's my fault though. That's the other reason we should have Christmas together. No one else has to feel mad or sad when we're around."

It felt as if a giant hand was squeezing the life from his windpipe. Tate thought it was *his* fault?

Wynn's voice cracked as he said, "I'm so sorry about what's happening at home." He'd never been more sorry about anything in his life.

"Aw, Wynn. Don't cry." Tate reached to cup his big brother's face. "You're perfect."

A serrated knife twisted high in Wynn's gut. He ran a hand over his little brother's head. So soft and sweet and unreservedly worthwhile. His own childhood had been great. He'd known he was loved and adored by both parents. That's why he'd been so sure about having a family of his own. Then Heather had done him in and all of that no longer mattered. Except…

Now, looking deeper, that *hadn't* changed. In this moment, that dream seemed like the only thing that *did* matter. What the hell was the point of being here if he couldn't be with the person that he—?

That he what exactly? Just how deeply did he feel about Grace?

"I want you to know that if ever I had a boy of my own," he croaked out, "I'd want him to be just like you."

"That's not what you said. You said if you never had a family of your own, you wouldn't miss it."

"You're wrong." Drawing back, Wynn shook his head. "No. *I* was wrong. I was sad and confused. I haven't, well, been myself lately. But I do want a son."

Tate touched his big brother's cheek. "I think Grace is mad at you, too."

"I don't blame her." Wynn found Tate's hand on his cheek and set his jaw to stem the emotion. "We're just going to have to fix it, is all."

"Do you think that we can?"

"Of course we can. Remember?" Wynn smiled. "You and I can do anything."

Sixteen

Early the next morning, with all the presents opened, April was twirling around the Munroe's twelve-foot tree showing off the new pink princess costume that Santa had brought. There were coloring books and puzzles and a bike with training wheels, too. Grace liked to think her niece's favorite gift was the big crystal ring she'd received from her aunt. When she'd opened the box, April's eyes had bugged out. The ring hadn't left her finger since.

Now Grace sat on a couch sampling a perfume that Tilly had hoped she would like—sweet and sassy, just like her younger sister. Her father stood by the window that overlooked the vast backyard and, beyond that, a park. Children had constructed a snowman there—hardly anything new for this time of year. Still, this morning the sight created a giant lump in Grace's throat.

Wynn and that long-ago Christmas were in her thoughts constantly. After seeing him with Tate yesterday, she'd barely been able to sleep. She imagined she heard his laugh.

She closed her eyes and saw his sexy, slanted smile. She felt so filled with memories, she wondered if her family could see them mirrored in her eyes. Smell them on her skin.

April twirled over and presented a large gold and crimson Christmas bonbon.

"I'll let you win," April said.

Grace grabbed an end and angled her wrist just so, but when April tugged hard, the gold paper ripped and she won the prize—a green party hat and tiny baby doll.

Rochelle was checking out the foot spa Grace had given her. "My toes can't wait to use this," she said, wiggling her slippered feet.

"And I can't wait to wear these." Her mom was showing off a silk scarf and sapphire drop earrings.

Grace forged her way through a sea of crumpled paper to join her dad. He had three new ties slung around his neck.

"More snow's on the way," he said, surveying the low, gray sky.

April's voice came from behind. "Didn't stop Santa last night. Mommy, can I ride my bike?"

Rochelle was studying the titles on a CD, a gift from Tillie who, earphones in, was tapping her foot to a tune belting out of her new iPod.

"It might be too slippery." Rochelle pushed up and crossed over to the duo parked by the window. Then she poked her nose closer to the pane. "That's a mighty fine looking snowman."

April squealed. "Can I go see?"

Grace turned around and tapped April's tiara. "I'll take you. I want to see him, too." She crouched before her niece. "But our guy looks as if he's missing a hat and pipe."

"That's my job." Grandpa headed off. "I put them away in the same place every year."

She and April pulled on their boots, shrugged into coats and worked their fingers into mittens or gloves. April took the hat from Grandpa, Grace the pipe, and together they headed out down a shoveled path rimmed with glistening snow. As they passed through the side gate, April scooted on ahead.

"Be careful!" Grace called out. "Don't slip. You don't want to get your princess skirt wet."

When Grace caught up, April was skipping about the snowman.

"He's so tall!" Her niece held out the hat. "I'll put it on."

Grace lifted April high and she very carefully positioned the battered fedora on the snowman's head. When Grace put April down, the little girl stood back. With her mittened hands clasped under her chin, she inspected her work.

"It's crooked."

"I think it lends him character."

"What's that?"

"It means snowmen are more fun when their hats don't sit straight."

But if Wynn were here, Grace thought, he would want to straighten it, too.

"You can do the pipe." Examining the snowman, April tilted her head and her beanie's pink pom-poms swung around her neck. "Put it in crooked."

Grace slid the pipe in on one side of the snowman's mouth, and then flicked it up a tad.

April danced around the snowman again, her pink princess skirt floating out above her leggings while she sang. Then she stopped and trudged closer to their man.

"Something's up there." April pointed. "On his broom." She gasped. "Presents!"

Grace trod around and looked. Sure enough, two wrapped gifts were dangling from the rear of the snowman's broom. She leaned in closer. Were they tied to shoelaces?

"Whatever they are, we should leave them be." Grace

took April's hand as she reached for the gifts. "They don't belong to us."

"They do, too. Santa left them." April glanced around. "Maybe he left more."

"They're for decoration."

April wouldn't listen. Only her eyes appeared to be working—they were wide, amazed. Grace sighed. If April was disappointed when those boxes ended up being empty, perhaps Aunt Gracie could leave something special out here later to compensate.

Grace untied the gifts and handed them over. April would accept only one.

"That one's for you," April said.

Grace peeled off her wrapping while she kept an eye on April. They both got to their boxes at the same time and flipped open the lids. April let out a sigh filled with wonder.

"It a Christmas watch!"

When April tried to slide the white leather band off its looped holder, Grace helped. April slipped the oversize watch over one mitten, and then held her arm out to admire it.

"It has a Christmas tree," April murmured.

"And Christmas balls at the ends of the hands."

"What about yours?"

Wondering now if they ought not to have opened the boxes—clearly these were meant for someone else, perhaps the neighbors—Grace examined her watch face. "Mine has a snowman—" she blinked, looked harder "—with a crooked hat."

"Why did Santa leave them out here?"

Grace was about to admit she had no idea when a voice replied for her.

"He wanted to let us know that it's time to count our blessings—past, present and, hopefully, future."

On suddenly wobbly legs, Grace turned around while April crept forward.

"Gracie, someone's standing behind our snowman."

Wynn stepped into view. He wore a black sweater and windbreaker and pale blue jeans. With his dark hair ruffling in the breeze, he'd never looked so handsome.

When April whispered *"Who is he?"* Grace was brought back to the moment and replied, "I think he must be lost."

Wynn stepped forward and his one-in-a-million energy radiated out. The wind was cool and yet she might have been standing on a hot plate.

"I don't feel lost. Not anymore." He glanced at the sky. "Snow's coming—any minute, I reckon."

Smooth. He was after an invitation. "I'd invite you in, but—"

"I brought someone with me," he cut in, and nodded toward a vehicle Grace hadn't noticed until now. Tate was waiting by the hood. All bundled up for the weather, he arced an arm over his head, waving.

April tugged her aunt's jacket. "Do you know him? Is he nice? Can I say hi?"

Wynn answered April. "I'm sure he'd like that."

Still, April looked to her aunt with pleading eyes. Giving in, Grace straightened April's beanie.

"Sure. Go ahead."

Her tiny boots crunching in the snow, April trundled away. When she stopped before Tate, April hesitated before extending her hand to give him a look at what Santa had left.

Grace had put it together. "You built this snowman."

"Me and Tate."

"How did you know I'd come out to have a look?"

"I'd like to think I know you pretty well."

When he edged closer and reached out, Grace was ready to push him away—no matter how much she might want to, she wouldn't change her mind about rebooting their affair. But he only gestured at the watch.

"You like it?" he asked. "They're matching *his* and *hers*."

As in *you* and *me?* "You're not going to get that watch back from April."

His crooked grin said, of course not. "Tate brought a gift especially for your niece."

Near the vehicle, Tate was holding the watch, inspecting the face, while April ogled a necklace decorated with huge sparkling blue and clear "jewels." The two kids began to talk, and then laugh.

"That's a good sound," Wynn said. "Reminds me of when we were kids."

"I don't remember you laughing very often."

"Perhaps because I expected too much."

She crossed her arms over her coat. "I don't expect too much." She only knew what she needed. What she'd accept.

She didn't want to sound harsh but neither would she back down. What they had shared had been a wonderful but also brief journey. He wanted the fun times to go on. She'd made herself a promise. She needed to get on with her life. And Wynn didn't want to be a part of that. Not in the long term.

Wynn was studying the snowman. "Tate and I had a talk last night. It opened my eyes to a lot of things. Honesty can slog you between the eyes," Wynn said. "But we get back up. A couple of months ago, my truth was that I needed some release. Some fun. A connection. I found that with you. And I found a lot more."

Nearby, snow crunched as if someone had fallen, and then a little cry ripped out. A few feet away, Tate lay face down. Without missing a beat, April shot out her hand. Tate wrenched himself up and then they set off, running around again.

"I wonder if they'll remember this day," she said, watching as the kids stopped to pat together two snowballs.

"My bet is, as clearly as I remember that day in Colorado when I tripped over my lace."

She narrowed her eyes at him. "After all these years, now you remember it that way?"

"I remember that I'd agonized over whether or not to give you a gift."

"A poke in the eye?"

"A bunch of flowers, plastic, lifted from a vase in one of the chalet's back rooms. But then I thought you might want to hug me or something gross like that, and it seemed easier to pretend I didn't like you."

Her smile faded. "We're not kids playing games anymore."

"No. We're not."

He leaned forward just as a snowball smashed against his shoulder. Tate stood a short distance away; given his expression, he didn't know whether to run or laugh or fastball another one. Beside him, April's pom-poms were dancing around her neck, she was giggling that hard. She pitched her baby snowball and bolted in the other direction. Tate followed.

Grinning, Wynn swiped snow off his jacket. "Naughty and nice."

"Is Tate missing his folks?"

"He knows they're arguing. He's not sure why. He thinks it's his fault. Well, his and mine. That's why he wanted to come over from Sydney. So we pariahs could hang together."

Her heart clutched and twisted. "That's so sad."

"We'll work through it, me and Tate—and the rest of the family. Sometime in the New Year, I'm going back to... well, face it all."

Grace cast a glance toward the house. Her father was

peering out the window again. She thought of all the food and warmth and company inside that house. She could hear Tate and April playing some game together and, after listening to what poor Tate was going through, it seemed wrong not to ask.

"Wynn, would you and Tate like to have breakfast with us?"

His somber expression faded into a soft smile. "We'd like that very much. There's something else I'd like even more." His eyes searched hers. *"You."*

She shivered with longing, with need, but she wanted more than "just for now," and she refused to feel guilty because of it.

"Wynn, we don't need to go through this again."

"We really do."

The knot high in her stomach wrenched tighter. He was making this so hard. "I want a family of my own, Wynn. Don't you get it?"

"Me, too. So, we need to get married. The sooner the better."

She'd come to terms with him showing up unannounced, organizing the snowman, the gifts. But this? A proposal? She wanted to be hopeful, excited. But a man didn't change his mind about something like that overnight.

"I didn't believe it," he went on, "that it could happen that fast. Falling in love, I mean."

Her back went up. "I can't help how I feel."

"Not you. *Me*." His gloved hand slid around the back of her waist. "I love you," he said, and then broke out into a big smile. "Damn, that felt good."

Time seemed to stop. She set her palm against his chest to steady herself as her head began to spin.

"This isn't happening," she said.

"Close your eyes and I'll prove that it is."

When his mouth slanted over hers, her eyes automati-

cally drifted shut and, in an instant, she was filled up with
his warmth—with his strength. And then the kiss deepened
and a million tiny stars showered down through her system—her head and her belly. Most of all, her heart. When
he drew her closer, she stood on the toes of her boots and
curled her arms around the padded collar at his neck. He
tilted his head at a greater angle and urged her closer with
a palm on her back until they were pressed together like
two pages in a book.

When his lips finally left hers, she couldn't shake herself from the daze. His face was close and had a contented
expression. In his eyes she saw every shade of "I'm certain." And the way he was holding her… No matter what
she said, he wasn't about to let her go.

"I love you, Grace. The kind of love that can't take no
for an answer. The kind that just has to win out."

While deepest emotion prickled behind her eyes, snow
began to fall, dusting their hair and their shoulders. A snow-
flake landed on the tip of his nose at the same time a hot
tear rolled down her cheek.

"Marry me," he said in a low, steady voice. "Be my wife.
My love forever."

She swallowed deeply. Tried to speak.

"This isn't a rebound, is it?" she asked.

He only grinned. "Not a chance. I want you to have my
name. Grace Hunter. Mrs. Wynn Hunter. I want to have
babies with you and work through all those ups and downs
families face. The challenges and triumphs that will make
us even stronger."

Two little voices drifted over.

"He's gonna kiss her again."

"Gracie's gonna be a princess bride."

When she and Wynn both looked over, the kids darted
away. Wynn's voice rumbled near her ear. "Smart kids."

He kissed her again, working it until she was mindless,

boneless—completely, unreservedly his. When his mouth gradually left her, she had to grip his windbreaker while her brain tried again to catch up.

"Can you see the future?" he asked. "Me in a tuxedo, Dex and Cole standing at my side. Your father is walking you down the aisle and our guests are sighing, you look so beautiful. So happy."

A breath caught in her throat. And then she realized. He was right. She could see it, too. Their families were there—all of them.

"Tate will be a ring bearer," she murmured, as another drop slid down her cheek, "and April the flower girl."

"And?"

"And..." She cupped his jaw then ran fingers over that faint scar on his temple. He was waiting for her answer. It seemed the *only* choice.

"I love you," she said. "I can't wait to marry you."

The snow was falling harder, catching on his lashes, in the stubble on his jaw, and as he kissed her again, everything in their world—everything in her heart—felt incredible. Amazing. Just the way it ought to.

"Would you believe," he said as his lips slipped from hers, "I don't have a ring."

A little hand tugged Grace's coat. One of April's mittens was off and she was offering up her crystal solitaire.

Grace laughed she was so touched, and Wynn cocked his head. "Wow. April, are you sure? That looks like a lot of carats."

Tate held April's hand. "I'll get her another one."

A call came from the house—it was Grace's father telling everyone to come in. When Tate looked up at his brother, Wynn said, "Go ahead, buddy."

As they watched the young couple trot toward the path, Grace linked her arms around her fiancé's neck.

"Guess we ought to go in, too," she said. "Snow's coming down pretty fast."

"Let it snow," he said. "I *love* the snow. I love you." Cupping her cheek, he smiled adoringly into her eyes. "Today all my Christmases have come at once."

Epilogue

Meanwhile in Seattle...

Crouched on her bathroom floor, Teagan Hunter hugged herself tight, and then groaning, doubled over more. Her stomach was filled with barbed wire knots, but the pain went way beyond physical. It was memories. It was regrets. They circled her thoughts like a pack of vultures waiting to drop.

The High Tea Gym had barely seen her all week, and that had to change. She had a business to run, bills to pay, staff to supervise and clients to inspire. But then those vultures swooped again and Teagan only had the strength to lower her brow to her knee.

Her determined side said this was a case of mind over matter. She'd be fine. She would endure. No. She would *flourish*. God knew, up until now, she'd coped with a lot in her life. Still, she couldn't shake another voice gnawing at her ear, telling her that what she had lost this time was immeasurable—impossible to have, or try to protect, ever again.

As she dragged herself into the kitchen, her cell phone sounded on the counter. It could be Cole with some news about their father's ongoing stalker situation, she thought. But, checking the ID, tears sprang to her eyes. Her finger itched to swipe the screen, accept the call. But what if she lost it and broke down?

Finally, she pushed the phone aside and crossed to the pantry. She forced down a protein shake—vanilla with blueberries, usually her favorite, although this morning it went down like gobs of tasteless sludge. After tying her shoes, she stretched her calves while trying to project positive thoughts for the coming day. Thought dictated behavior, which in turn determined mood. Picking yourself up and moving forward was without question the best way.

And yet this minute she only wanted to curl up and cry.

When her phone sounded again, Teagan set her hands over her ears and headed for her rowing machine. She didn't have any answers for Damon. He would simply have to accept it. She didn't want to—couldn't bear to—see him ever again.

Three days ago, she'd sat behind her desk and had calmly passed on her decision. His eyes had gone wide. Then an amused smile had flickered at one side of the mouth she had come to adore. But when she'd stood her ground—had asked him to leave—his jaw had tensed and his brows had drawn together.

"Tell me what's going on, Tea," he'd said. "I won't leave until you do."

Now, as she positioned herself on the machine, strapped in her feet, grabbed the ropes and eased into the flow—sliding forward, easing back, pushing with her legs, holding in her belly…already firm and flat and *empty*—

She dropped the handles. The ropes flew back and, shaking, she covered her face. She'd already cried so much, surely she was done, and yet the salty streams coursing down her cheeks wouldn't stop.

It must pass *sometime*—the constant praying and begging that she could have that chance again. Because she didn't know how much longer she could bear it…the images from that night when her greatest dream came true had turned into a nightmare. It all seemed so pointless, so gut-wrenchingly cruel. She'd been told she would never conceive. She'd learned to live with that fact. She'd pushed on and had come to accept it.

But how could she ever accept that she'd miscarried a child—Damon's baby—because now…

Nothing in the world seemed to matter.

* * * * *

IT HAPPENED
ONE NIGHT

KATHIE DENOSKY

*This book is dedicated to the authors of the
Texas Cattleman's Club: The Missing Mogul.
Working with you all was a real pleasure.*

Kathie DeNosky lives in her native Southern
Illinois on the land her family settled in 1839.
Her books have appeared on the *USA TODAY*
bestseller list and received numerous awards,
including two National Reader's Choice Awards.
Readers may contact Kathie by emailing Kathie@
kathiedenosky.com They can also visit her web-
site, www.kathiedenosky.com, or find her on
Facebook, www.facebook.com/Kathie-DeNosky-
Author/278166445536145.

Prologue

When Josh Gordon let himself into his girlfriend's apartment, he wanted two things—to make love to Lori and get some much-needed sleep. He'd spent a long day preparing job bids for Gordon Construction and an even longer evening wining and dining a potential client, who couldn't seem to make up his mind whether to give the contract for his new office building to the construction business Josh and his twin brother, Sam, co-owned or to one of their competitors.

Josh wasn't overly proud or happy about it, but they'd had enough to drink to float a fleet of ships before the man finally gave the nod to Gordon Construction. That's why Josh had made the decision to spend the night with Lori. The wine had dulled his normally sharp senses and he didn't think his being behind the steering wheel of a car was in anyone's best interest.

Since she had given him a key to her apartment a few weeks back and it was only a couple of blocks from the restaurant, walking to Lori's place had seemed wiser than trying to drive the five miles to his ranch outside of town. Besides, he hadn't seen her in a few days and missed losing himself in her soft charms.

The fact that their relationship was more of a physical connection than it was an emotional attachment should have bothered him. But neither he nor Lori wanted anything more, and he couldn't see any harm in two consenting adults spending their time enjoying each other for as long as the attraction lasted.

As he made his way across the dark living room and headed down the hall toward her bedroom, he decided not to turn on a lamp. The headache that had developed during the last few rounds of drinks already had his head feeling like his brain had outgrown his skull. The harsh glare of a light certainly wouldn't make it feel any better.

Loosening his tie, he removed his suit jacket as he quietly opened the bedroom door and, stripping off the rest of his clothes, climbed into bed with the feminine form he could just make out beneath the covers. Without thinking twice he took her in his arms and teased her lips with his to wake her.

He thought he heard her murmur something a moment before she began to kiss him back, but Josh didn't give her a chance to say more. He was too captivated by her. Lori had never tasted as sweet and the scent of whatever new shampoo she had used caused him to ache with the urgent need to sink himself deep inside of her.

When she ran her hands over his shoulders, then

tangled her fingers in the hair at the nape of his neck as she kissed him with a passion that robbed him of breath, a shaft of longing coursed through him. She needed him as badly as he needed her. He didn't hesitate to slide his hand down her side to her knee, then, catching the hem of her nightshirt, he brought it up to her waist. Never breaking the kiss, he made quick work of removing the scrap of silk and lace covering her feminine secrets and nudged her knees apart.

His heart felt like it might jump right out of his chest when he rose over her and she reached to guide him to her. Her desire for him to join their bodies was as strong as his and, giving them what they both wanted, he entered her in one smooth stroke.

Setting an urgent pace, he marveled at how much tighter she felt, how her body seemed to cling to his. But the white-hot haze of passion was stronger than his ability to reason and he dismissed his confusion as a result of too much wine.

When she clenched her tiny feminine muscles, he knew she was poised on the edge, and deepening his strokes, Josh pushed them both over the edge. As he emptied himself deep inside of her, her moan indicated that she was experiencing the same mind-blowing pleasure that pulsed through him, and feeling drained of energy, he collapsed on top of her.

"Oh, Mark, that was incredible."

Josh went completely still as his mind tried to process what he had heard. The woman he had just made love with had called him Mark. If that wasn't enough to send a cold sense of dread knifing through him, the fact that it wasn't Lori's voice sure as hell was.

What had he done? Where was Lori? And who was the woman he had just made love with?

Sobering faster than he could blink, Josh levered himself to her side, then quickly sat up on the side of the bed to reach for his discarded clothes. "I…um… oh, hell. I'm really sorry. I thought…you were Lori."

The woman was silent for a moment before she gasped and he heard her jump to her feet on the other side of the bed. "Oh, dear God! No, this can't be… We didn't… You must be—"

"Josh," he finished for her, since she seemed to be having problems conveying her thoughts.

He kept his back to her as he pulled on his pants and shirt. Not that she could see in the dark any more than he could. But all things considered, it just seemed like the right thing to do.

"I really am sorry." He knew his apologies weren't nearly adequate enough for the circumstances, but then he wasn't sure anything he could say or do would make the situation any less humiliating for either of them. "I swear to God, I thought you were Lori."

"I'm her…sister," the woman said, sounding like she might be recovering her ability to speak in a complete sentence.

He knew Lori had a sister, but since their relationship was mostly physical, he and Lori hadn't delved too deeply into the details of each other's lives. And if she had mentioned her sister by name, he'd be damned if he could think of it now.

"I'd give anything if this hadn't—"

"Please, don't," she said, cutting him off. "Just leave…Josh."

He hesitated, then, deciding that it was probably

the best—the only—thing he could do, he walked to the front door and let himself out of the apartment. He had no sooner pulled the door shut than he heard her set the dead bolt and slide the chain into place.

His heart stalled for a moment, then began to beat double time. He had been just drunk enough and she apparently had been sleepy enough for both of them to forget the use of a condom. It was something he had never forgotten before and he couldn't believe that he'd done so this time.

Completely sober now, he shook his head as he walked the short distance to his Mercedes still sitting in the restaurant's parking lot. He was going to drive home and when he woke up in the morning, he hoped to discover that he'd dreamed the entire incident.

But as he got into the car and started the engine, he knew as surely as the sun rose in the east each morning that wasn't going to be the case. Nothing was going to change the fact that he had done the unthinkable. He had made love to his girlfriend's sister—the most exciting, responsive woman he had ever met. And what was even worse, he had no clue what she looked like and didn't even know her name.

One

Three years later

Standing in the hallway outside the meeting rooms at the Texas Cattleman's Club, Kiley Roberts sighed heavily. If she hadn't had enough problems dealing with the vandalism of the club's new day care center a few months ago, now she was about to face the funding committee to ask for an increase in funds to run it. Unfortunately, from everything she had heard, she was facing an uphill battle. Several of the committeemen had been extremely vocal about not seeing the need to provide child care for club members, and among them was the chairman of the funding committee, Josh Gordon.

They had never been formally introduced and she didn't even know if he knew who she was. But she knew him and just the thought of having to deal with the man made her cringe with embarrassment.

Every detail of what happened that night three years ago had played through her mind since discovering that Josh was a member of the club. But when she learned he was chairman of the funding committee—the very committee that controlled the money to run the day care center—she felt as if she'd been kicked in the stomach. Being the center's director, she had to go to the committee for approval on everything outside of the budget they had set for it. That meant she would frequently have to deal with him.

She took a deep fortifying breath. How could fate be so cruel?

If she hadn't been half-asleep and wanting so badly to believe that Mark—her then-boyfriend and now ex-husband—had followed her to her sister's apartment to apologize for the argument they'd had, the incident three years ago would have never taken place. She would have realized right away that Josh wasn't Mark and stopped him before things went too far.

Kiley shook her head at her own foolishness. She should have known when Josh kissed her with such passion that the man in bed with her wasn't Mark. The only thing Mark had ever been passionate about was himself.

Sighing, she straightened her shoulders. There was nothing she could do about it now, and there was no sense in dwelling on something she couldn't change. She just wished anyone other than Josh Gordon was heading up the funding committee. Aside from the humiliating incident, he had broken her sister's heart when he abruptly ended things between them a month or so after that fateful night, and Kiley simply didn't trust him.

When the door to the meeting room opened, interrupting her tumultuous thoughts, a man she assumed to be one of the members motioned toward her. "Ms. Roberts, the committee is ready to hear from you now."

Nodding, Kiley took a deep breath and forced her feet to move forward when what she really wanted to do was turn around and head in the opposite direction. "Thank you."

As she walked toward the long table at the head of the room where Josh sat with three men and a woman, she focused on them instead of Josh. The only two she recognized were Beau Hacket and Paul Windsor. Great. They seemed to be the unofficial leaders of those opposed to the day care center and it was just her luck that they both happened to be on the funding committee. Kiley's only hope was to appeal to the lone female member and the man sitting next to her.

"Good afternoon," she said, forcing herself to give them all a cheerful smile when she was feeling anything but optimistic.

"What can we do for you today…" Josh glanced at the papers on the table in front of him as if checking for her name "…Ms. Roberts?"

When their gazes finally met, she felt a little better. She had been hired by the club's personnel director and had managed to avoid coming face-to-face with Josh in the short time she had been working at the Texas Cattleman's Club. But now, she realized her nervousness had been unfounded. Apparently Lori had never mentioned her by name and thanks to the blackout curtains her sister preferred, neither of them had been able to see the other that night. Deciding he was either a good enough actor to deserve an Academy Award or he had no idea who she was, her confidence returned.

"As the director, I'm here to ask the committee to consider appropriating additional funds for the day care center," she stated, surprised her voice sounded strong and steady in spite of her earlier case of jangled nerves.

"What for?" Beau Hacket demanded. "We've already budgeted more than is necessary to babysit a bunch of little kids."

"I can't believe you just said that," the middle-aged woman seated to Josh's right said, glaring at Beau.

Kiley watched Josh give the man a disapproving glare before he turned his attention back to her. "What do you think you need the additional funds for, Ms. Roberts?"

"The club members' response to the day care center has been so positive, we have more children than we first anticipated," she answered, already knowing from the negative expression on his face how Beau Hacket would be voting on the matter.

"All you're doing is watching a handful of little kids for a couple of hours," Beau spoke up. "I don't see where you need more money for that. Sit them down with a crayon and a piece of paper and they'll be happy."

"Beau."

There was a warning in Josh's tone, but Kiley knew it was more a rule of order than any kind of support for her. Josh Gordon had been almost as vocal in his objections to the day care center as Beau Hacket and Paul Windsor had. Since the club started admitting female members a few years ago, the TCC had experienced quite a few growing pains as it made changes to accommodate the needs of women in its ranks, the most recent change being the addition of the day care center.

Focusing her attention on the others seated at the conference table and off the committee chairman, she decided it was time to set them straight. "I think some of you have a few misconceptions about the day care center. Yes, we do provide a safe environment for the members to leave their children while they attend meetings or events at the clubhouse, but we're more than just a babysitting service. Some of the members depend on us for early childhood education, as well."

"My granddaughter is one of your students and in the short time she's been attending, we've all been amazed at how much she's learned," the woman seated beside Josh said, smiling.

"Why can't they teach their own kids how to finger-paint at home?" Beau demanded, his disapproval evident in the tone of his voice as he glared at her.

"I'm trained in early childhood education," Kiley explained, hoping to convince the man of the importance of day care, but knowing she probably wouldn't. "The center's programs are age appropriate and structured so that the children are engaged in learning activities for their level of development." When the committee members frowned in obvious confusion, she rushed on to keep one of them from cutting her off. "For example, the toddlers learn how to interact and share with other children, as well as begin to develop friendships and basic social skills. The preschool class learns to recognize and print the letters of the alphabet, as well as their names. And in addition to teaching them how to count, my assistant and I play learning games with both groups designed to pique their interest in things like science and nature." She shook her head. "The list is endless and I could stay here all day outlining the importance of early childhood education and the benefits to a child."

When Kiley stopped to take a breath, the woman on the committee nodded. "My granddaughter has not only learned a lot, she's conquered some of her shyness and has become more outgoing, as well."

Appreciative of the woman's support, Kiley smiled. At least she had one advocate on the committee.

Josh glanced down at the papers on the table in front of him. "You're not asking for more space, just additional money for the center?"

"No, the size of the room isn't a problem. We have enough room for the children we have now, as well as many more." She could tell he wasn't paying much attention to what she had to say and would probably like to deny her outright. But protocol called for the committee to hear her out, discuss her request, then take a vote on the issue. "All I'm asking for is additional money for the day-to-day operation of the center."

"Since you don't have utilities or rent to worry about, what specifically would the funds be used for?" Paul Windsor asked, giving her a charming smile. A ladies' man if there ever was one, the older gentleman's flirtatious smile didn't fool Kiley one bit. He was just as opposed to the day care center as Beau Hacket.

"Some of the children are with us for the entire day, instead of a half day or just a few hours, Mr. Windsor," she answered, relieved she wasn't having to focus on Josh, even though she didn't like Paul Windsor. "We need the extra money for the materials for their activities, as well as the additional lunches and snacks. We also need to hire an extra worker for the infants we occasionally have when their mothers have a tennis match or engage in some of the other activities here at the clubhouse."

"We wouldn't have this problem if we hadn't let women into the club," Beau muttered as he sat back in his chair to glare at her.

"What was that, Beau?" the woman demanded, looking as if she was ready to do battle.

Beau shook his head as he belligerently folded his arms across his barrel chest. "I didn't say a damned thing, Nadine."

Kiley wasn't the least bit surprised at the man's comment or the woman's reaction. Beau Hacket was one of the men still resentful of women being permitted membership into the prestigious club, and the female members had quickly learned to stand up to the "good old boy network" and demand the respect they deserved.

"Is there anything else you'd like to add?" Josh asked, clearly ready to dismiss her and move on to the discussion phase.

"No, I believe I've adequately outlined the purpose of the day care center and the reasons we need the extra funds," she said, knowing in her heart that her plea had fallen on deaf ears—at least where the male members of the committee were concerned.

He nodded. "I think we have more than enough information to consider your request. Thank you for your time and detailed explanation, Ms. Roberts."

Looking up at her, he smiled and Kiley felt as if

the floor moved beneath her feet. His bright blue eyes and engaging smile sent a shiver of awareness coursing from the top of her head to the soles of her feet and, as much as she would have liked to forget, she couldn't stop thinking about what happened that night three years ago.

"I'll drop by the center later this afternoon to let you know the outcome of our vote," Josh finished, oblivious to her reaction.

Feeling as if having to listen to her had been an inconvenience for them, Kiley nodded and walked from the meeting room. There was nothing left for her to do now but await the committee's decision. She wished she felt more positive about the results of their vote. Unfortunately, with three of the center's biggest opponents on the committee, a favorable outcome was highly unlikely.

But as much as she feared hearing their decision, Kiley dreaded having to see Josh again even more. Why couldn't he send one of the other members to let her know what had been decided? Didn't she already have enough on her plate without having to worry about seeing him again?

She had a two-year-old daughter to care for and a house that seemed to be in constant need of one repair or another, and, if the additional money for the day care didn't come through, the center might have to close due to a clause in the club's amended bylaws assuring that no member's child would be turned away, and she would be out of a job. And even if he didn't know who she was, she certainly didn't need the added stress of being reminded of the most embarrassing incident of her entire life.

* * *

As Josh walked down the hall toward the day care center, he couldn't for the life of him figure out why he felt as though he knew Kiley Roberts. He didn't think they had met before she walked into the meeting room earlier in the afternoon. If they had, he knew for certain he would have remembered her. A woman that attractive would be damned near impossible to forget.

Normally he preferred his women tall, willowy and with an air of mystery about them. But Kiley made petite and curvy look good—real good. With her chin-length, dark blond hair and the prettiest brown eyes he had ever seen, she looked soft, sexy and very approachable.

He frowned as he tried to remember if he'd even seen her before this afternoon. She might have been at Beau Hacket's barbecue a few months back. It seemed that Hacket had invited the entire membership of the Texas Cattleman's Club, as well as most of the residents of Royal. Or more likely he'd seen her somewhere around the clubhouse, maybe in the restaurant or the bar. But he couldn't shake the feeling that there was more to it than that.

When he reached the door to the old billiard room—now renovated to house the day care center—he shrugged. It really didn't matter. Once he gave her the news that she wouldn't be getting any more money from the club, he would go straight to the top of her Grinch list and that would be the end of that.

Looking through the window in the door, he noticed that the room looked much nicer now than it had a couple of months ago when vandals broke in and tore up the place. They still hadn't caught who was behind the destruction or their motive for doing it, but Josh felt sure the culprits would eventually be caught and dealt with accordingly. Royal, Texas, wasn't that big of a town, and many of its residents were members of the TCC. It was just a matter of time before someone remembered seeing or hearing something that would lead the authorities to make an arrest.

He would hate to be in the vandals' shoes when that happened, he thought as he opened the day care center's door. Whether the place was wanted by all of the members or not, nobody came in and destroyed any part of their clubhouse without the entire membership taking great exception to it.

"I'll be right with you, Mr. Gordon," Kiley said from across the room.

"Take your time," he said, looking around. Several children sat in pint-size chairs at tables that were just as small. He couldn't imagine ever being little enough to fit into furniture that size.

As he watched, Russ and Winnie Bartlett's youngest little girl got out of her chair and walked over to hold up a paper with crayon scribbles for Kiley's inspection. She acted as if the kid had just drawn the *Mona Lisa,* causing the toddler to beam with pride.

Josh had never taken much to little kids. For one thing, he had never been around them and didn't have a clue how to relate to them. But he found himself smiling as he watched Kiley talk to the child as she pinned the drawing to a bulletin board. Only a coldhearted bastard would ignore the fact that she had just made the little girl's day.

"Carrie, could you take over for me for a few minutes?" she asked a young woman Josh assumed to be the day care worker Kiley had hired not long after the center opened. When the woman nodded, Kiley walked over to him and motioned toward a door on the far side of the room. "Why don't we go into my office? Otherwise, I can't guarantee we won't be interrupted."

As he followed her to her office, he found himself fascinated by the slight sway of her hips. He had to force himself to keep his eyes trained on her slender shoulders. But that only drew his attention to the exposed skin between the collar of her red sweater and the bottom of her short blond hair—a spot that looked extremely kissable.

His heart thumped hard against his rib cage and heat began to fill his lower belly. What the hell was wrong with him? Had it been that long since he and his last girlfriend parted ways?

"Please have a seat, Mr. Gordon," Kiley said, walking behind the small desk to sit down in an old wooden chair.

He recognized both the desk and the chair as having been in the storage room for as long as he had been a member of the club and probably for decades before that. If circumstances had been different, he might have felt guilty about the funding committee insisting her office be furnished with the club's castoffs. But considering none of the members on the panel, with maybe the exception of Nadine Capshaw, expected the center to remain open past spring, it had been decided that the used furniture would be good enough.

"Call me Josh," he said, sitting in a metal folding chair across the desk from her.

"I assume you've come to tell me the funding committee's decision on my request...Josh?" she asked, sounding as if she already knew the outcome of the vote.

There was something about the sound of her voice saying his name that caused him to frown. "Before we get into the committee's decision, could I ask you something?"

"I...uh, suppose so." He could tell by the hesitation in her voice and her wary expression that she didn't trust him.

"Do we know each other?" he asked, realizing immediately from the slight widening of her expressive brown eyes that they did.

"No," she said a little too quickly.

"Are you sure?" he pressed, determined to find out what she knew that he didn't.

"Well, we...um, don't know each other formally," she said, suddenly taking great interest in her tightly clasped hands resting on top of the desk.

She was hiding something, and he intended to find out what it was. "So we have met?" he continued.

"In a way...I guess you could say that." Her knuckles had turned white from her tight grip and he knew whatever she hid was extremely stressful for her. "It was quite by accident."

Every hair follicle on his head felt as if it stood straight up, and he suddenly wasn't so sure he wanted to know what she obviously didn't want to tell him. "Where would that have been?" he heard himself ask in spite of his reservations.

Getting up, she closed her office door, then slowly lowered herself into the chair when she returned to the desk. "You used to date my sister."

A cold, clammy feeling snaked its way up his spine. "I did?"

When she finally raised her head to meet his gaze head-on, a knot the size of his fist began to twist his gut. "I'm Lori Miller's sister. Her *only* sister."

Josh opened his mouth, then snapped it shut. For the first time in his adult life, he couldn't think of a thing to say. But his unusual reaction to her suddenly started to make sense. From the moment she'd walked into the meeting room to plead her case to the funding committee, he had been fighting to keep his libido under control. Now he knew why. He might not have realized who she was, but apparently his body had. The chemistry between them that night three years ago had been undeniable and it appeared that it was just as powerful now. Unless he missed his guess, her nervousness had just as much to do with the magnetic pull between them as it did with her reluctance to admit what had taken place.

As he stared at her, it occurred to him why Kiley seemed familiar to him. Although it had been too dark to tell what she looked like that night, he could see the resemblance between her and her sister now. Kiley had the same extraordinary brown eyes and flawless alabaster skin that Lori had. But that seemed to be where the similarities between the two women ended. While Lori was considerably taller and had auburn hair, Kiley was shorter and had dark blond hair that looked so silky it practically begged a man to tangle his fingers in it as he made love to her. When his lower body began to tighten, he swallowed hard and tried to think of something—anything—to get his mind back on track.

"Your last name is different," he stated the obvious.

She straightened her shoulders and took a deep breath. "I was married briefly."

"But not anymore?" he couldn't stop himself from asking.

"No."

He swallowed hard as a thought suddenly occurred to him. "You weren't married—"

"No. Not then."

Relieved that he hadn't crossed that particular line, Josh released the breath he hadn't been aware of holding. "That's good."

"Look, I'm not any happier than you are about having to work with you on the day care center's funding," she said, her cheeks coloring a pretty pink. "But this isn't the time or the place to get into what happened that night. I think it would be for the best if we forgot the incident ever happened and concentrate on my request for the day care center and the committee's decision not to give me the extra money I need to keep it running."

He knew she was right. A day care center full of little kids certainly wasn't the place to talk over his mistakenly making love to her. And she had a valid point about forgetting that night. It would definitely be the prudent thing to do. But some perverse part of him resented her wanting to dismiss what had arguably been the most exciting night of his life. He'd never been with a woman, either before or since, as responsive and passionate as Kiley had been.

"I agree," he finally said. "We can take a trip down memory lane another time." He could tell his choice of words and the fact that he thought they should revisit the past wasn't what she wanted to hear.

She folded her arms beneath her breasts, causing his mouth to go dry. "Mr. Gordon—"

"I prefer you call me Josh," he reminded her.

"Josh, I think you'd better—"

"I have good news and bad news," he said, thinking quickly. If her body language was any indication, she was about two seconds away from throwing him out of her office.

Whether it was due to the lingering guilt he still harbored over his part in the incident or the distrust he detected in her big brown eyes, he wasn't sure. But he suddenly felt the need to prove to her that she had the wrong opinion of him.

"I'm going to give you a month's worth of the funding you requested in order for you to convince me that the day care center is worthwhile and a needed addition to the services the club provides to the TCC membership," he stated, before she could interrupt.

She frowned. "That isn't what the committee decided, is it?"

"Not exactly," he said honestly. "The committee voted four to one to deny you the extra money. But after seeing the way you were with the Bartletts' little girl, you've got my attention. I'll be checking in periodically to see for myself that the money was needed and put to good use."

If anything, she looked even more skeptical. "What happens at the end of that time?"

"If I determine that you do need the additional funding, at our meeting just before Christmas I'll give my personal recommendation to the committee that we add the amount you asked for to your yearly budget," he finished.

"If my request was turned down, where is this money going to come from?" she asked, looking more suspicious by the second.

"You let me worry about that," he said, rising to his feet. "I'll see that the appropriate amount is added to the day care's account as of this afternoon. It should be accessible for whatever you need by tomorrow morning."

Before she could question him further, he opened her office door and left to go to the TCC's main office to make arrangements for the funding to be put into the day care's account. He was going to be taking the money out of his own pocket to subsidize the center for the next month, but it would be worth it. For one thing, he wanted to prove to her that he wasn't the nefarious SOB she apparently thought him to be. And for another, it was the only thing he could think of that might come close to atoning for his role in what happened three years ago.

Two

Kiley spent most of the next day jumping every time the door to the day care center opened. True to his word, Josh had added money to the center's account and she did appreciate that. But it was his promised visits to observe how she ran things and to see what the funds were being used for that had her nerves stretched to the breaking point. She didn't want to see him again or have to jump through hoops to get the money the center needed. Besides, every time she looked into his blue eyes, it reminded her that they shared a very intimate secret—one that, try as she might, she couldn't forget.

"The children have put away the toys and I've finished reading them a story. Would you like for me to take them outside to the play area for a bit before we start practicing their songs?" Carrie Kramer asked, walking over to where Kiley had finished putting stars by the names of the children who had remembered to wash their hands before their afternoon snack.

"That would be great." Kiley smiled at the young woman she'd hired to be her assistant after meeting her at the Royal Diner. "While they expend some of their excess energy outside, I'll get things ready for us to practice their songs before they go home."

As she watched Carrie help the children get their coats on and form a single line by the exit to the play yard, Kiley turned to go into her office for the things they would be using for the holiday program they were putting on for the parents the week before Christmas. Gathering the props, she decided she would have to make two trips as she turned to retrace her steps back into the main room. Distracted as she tried to remember everything they would need, she ran headlong into Josh standing just inside the doorway to her office.

"Oh, my dear heavens!" The giant jingle bells in the box she carried jangled loudly as she struggled to hang on to it.

Placing his hands on her shoulders to steady her, he frowned. "I didn't mean to frighten you. I called your name when I found the other room empty."

The warmth of his hands seemed to burn through her pink silk blouse. Kiley quickly took a step back. "I must not have heard it over the sound of these bells."

"Let me help you with these," he said, taking the box from her. "Where are the kids?"

"My assistant took them outside for playtime before we start practicing for their Christmas program," she said, picking up her CD player and several large plastic candy canes.

Their arms brushed as she walked past him, and an awareness she hadn't felt in a very long time caused her heart to skip several beats. She did her best to ignore it.

"I intended to stop by earlier in the day, but I got tied up at one of our construction sites and it took longer than I anticipated," he said, following her over to the brightly colored carpet where the children gathered for story time. "I wasn't sure anyone would still be here. When do the kids go home?"

"Normally, all of the children get picked up by five-thirty," she answered, setting the candy canes and the CD player on a small table. "But Gil Addison sometimes gets detained by club business and runs a few minutes late picking up his son, Cade." A single father, the current president of the TCC had been one of the first to enroll his four-year-old son in the preschool class. Unlike the members of the funding committee, Gil seemed extremely enthusiastic about having the center at the clubhouse. "No matter what time it is, I stay until every child is safely in the care of their parents or someone they've designated to pick up the child."

"So this isn't just a nine-to-five job, then?" he asked, placing the box on the carpet.

"Not hardly." Shaking her head, she removed a disc from its case to put in the player. "I have to be here at seven each morning to get things ready for the children's arrival."

"When is that?" he asked, his brow furrowing.

"A couple of them get here a few minutes after I do, but they're all here between eight and eight-thirty," she said, wondering why he was so interested in the hours the day care center operated. "Why do you ask?"

He ran his hand through his short, light brown hair. "I realize you're working on contract with the club and aren't paid overtime, no matter how many hours you work, but doesn't that make for a pretty long day?"

She couldn't help but smile. Being able to be with her daughter while she did her job was well worth any extra time she had to put in at the center. "I don't mind. This is my dream job."

"I guess if that's what makes you happy," he said, looking as if he couldn't understand anyone feeling that way about working those kinds of hours with a group of small children.

When the children began filing into the room from outside, Kiley breathed a sigh of relief. It wasn't that she was afraid of Josh. But being alone with him made her feel jumpy and she welcomed the distraction of a roomful of toddlers and preschoolers. She wasn't at all happy about the effect he had on her and refused to think about why he made her feel that way. She was almost certain she wouldn't like the answer.

"After you've hung up your coats, I want you all to come over to the carpet and sit down, please," she announced to the children. "We're going to practice our songs for your Christmas program before you go home this afternoon."

Her daughter ran over to wrap her arms around one of Kiley's legs, then looked up at her and giggled. "Me sing."

"That's right, Emmie," Kiley said, stroking her daughter's dark blond hair as she smiled down at the only good to come out of her brief marriage. "Can you go over and sit with Elaina and Bobby so we can get started, please?"

Emmie nodded, then hurried over to join her two friends where they sat with the rest of the toddlers.

"Miss Kiley, Jimmy Joe Harper pulled my hair," Sarah Bartlett accused, glaring at the little boy seated beside her.

"Jimmy Joe, did you pull Sarah's hair again?" Even before he nodded, one look at the impish grin on the child's face told Kiley that he had. "I'm sorry, but I told you that if you pulled Sarah's pigtails again you'd have to sit in the 'time out' corner for five minutes."

Without further instruction, the child obediently got to his feet and walked over to sit in a chair by himself in the far corner of the room. When she noticed Josh glancing from her to Jimmy Joe in the "time out" corner, Kiley raised an eyebrow. "Is there something wrong?"

"You didn't even have to tell him to go over there," he said, sounding as if he couldn't quite believe a child would willingly accept his punishment. "And he didn't protest at all."

"Jimmy Joe is no stranger to the 'time out' corner," Kiley answered, smiling fondly at the adorable red-haired little boy. "He loves aggravating Sarah."

Josh looked confused. "Why?"

"Because he likes her." Kiley turned to her assistant. "Could you please pass out the bells and candy canes, Carrie?"

"I see," Josh said as a slow grin curved the corners of his mouth. "In other words, he's teasing her to keep her attention focused on him."

"Something…like that," Kiley said, her breath

catching at how handsome Josh looked when he smiled.

As her assistant finished handing each child an oversize bell or a giant plastic candy cane, Kiley queued up the music on her CD player and purposely avoided looking at Josh. He made her nervous and she wished he would leave. But it appeared as if he intended to stay for a while.

Deciding that as long as he was there, he might as well participate, she picked up one of the bells and shoved it into his hand. "I assume you know the words to 'Jingle Bells'?"

He looked surprised, then determined as he shook his head. "Yes, I'm familiar with the song, but I'm afraid I can't stay. I promised a friend I would stop by his place this afternoon and I'm already running late."

"That's a shame," she lied. She had accomplished what she set out to do. He was going to leave. She couldn't help but smile. "Maybe another time."

"Yeah, maybe," he said, sounding doubtful. He reached out and, taking her hand in his, placed the bell in the center of her palm, then gently folded her fingers around it with his other hand. "Will you be free tomorrow evening?"

Startled by his unexpected question and the warmth of his hands holding hers, she stared at him a moment before she managed to find her voice. "Wh-why?"

"I'd like to discuss a couple of things with you," he said evasively. He gave her a smile that made her insides flutter. "Unfortunately, I don't have time to talk to you about it now. I'll come by here around five-thirty on Friday evening and we'll have dinner in the club's restaurant. They have an excellent menu and we'll be able to talk without interruption."

Kiley opened her mouth to refuse, but when he tenderly caressed her hand with his, she forgot anything she was about to say. As she watched him walk across the room to the door, she shook her head in an effort to regain her equilibrium.

What was Josh up to? And what did he think they needed to discuss? She had been quite clear when she spoke to the funding committee about the use of the extra money for the day care center. Surely he couldn't want to talk about what happened that night....

"Miss Kiley, can I go back to the carpet now?" Jimmy Joe asked from the "time out" corner.

"'May I go back to the carpet,'" Kiley automatically corrected.

"May I?" the little boy asked, flashing his charming grin.

"Yes, you may," she said, deciding that she could give more thought to Josh and his dinner invitation after the children had gone home for the day.

Kiley went through the motions of rehearsing the Christmas show the children would put on for their parents in a few weeks. But her mind kept straying back to Josh and his ridiculous invitation. Even if she were willing to go to dinner with him—which she wasn't—she didn't think he would be all that enthusiastic about dining with a two-year-old.

It wasn't that Emmie wasn't well-behaved. She was. But by the end of the day, she was tired and wanted nothing more than dinner, a bath and to go to bed. Besides, there was absolutely nothing Kiley felt the need to discuss with Josh. Now or in the foreseeable future.

* * *

As Josh drove his Mercedes through the gates of Pine Valley, the exclusive golf course community where several of the TCC members had built mansions, he couldn't help but wonder what he'd been thinking when he asked Kiley to dinner. Why couldn't he just drop what had happened that night three years ago?

He knew that would be the smartest thing to do and what Kiley wanted. But for reasons he didn't want to delve into, some perverse part of him wanted her to admit that, although the circumstances that brought them together that night might have been an unfortunate accident, their lovemaking had been nothing short of amazing.

"You've lost your mind, Gordon," he muttered as he steered his car onto Alex Santiago's private drive.

Doing his best to forget the matter, he parked in front of the palatial home, got out of the car and climbed the steps to the front door. Before he could ring the doorbell, the door opened.

"Hello, Señor Gordon," a round-faced older woman with kind brown eyes said, stepping back for Josh to enter. "Señor Alex is in the sunroom."

"How's he feeling today, Maria?" Josh asked as the housekeeper whom Alex's fiancée, Cara Windsor, had recently hired led the way toward the back of the elegant home.

Maria stopped, then, turning to face him, gave Josh a worried look. "Señor Alex still has headaches and can't remember anything before he was found."

"I'm sure it's just a matter of time before he recovers his memory." Josh wasn't entirely sure who he was trying to reassure—the housekeeper or himself.

Alex had been missing for several months before being found, suffering a head injury, in the back of a truck with a group of migrant farm workers smuggled across the border from Mexico. No one seemed to know how he wound up across the border or how he got into the back of the truck with the workers, and he couldn't tell the authorities anything. There was strong evidence that he had been beaten several times and one theory was that he had been kidnapped. But no matter what had happened, Alex still had amnesia. It had only been recently that he'd been released from Royal Memorial Hospital. With Cara's encouragement, Alex's friends from the TCC had been taking turns dropping by to check on his progress. No one had said as much, but Josh knew they all hoped to help him recover his memory so they could find whoever had done this to him.

"How are you feeling today, Alex?" he asked, walking into the sunroom where his friend sat reading a book.

Alex smiled and slowly rose to his feet to extend his hand. "Josh, isn't it?"

Nodding, Josh shook Alex's hand. The man's grip was firm and Josh took that as a good sign that his friend was regaining some of his strength. But he was still cautious about making sure he called his friends by the correct name, which indicated his memory wasn't much better.

"I wanted to stop by and let you know that we're all hoping to see you and Cara at the Christmas Ball." Before his disappearance in the summer, Alex had been on the planning committee for the annual holiday gala. Josh hoped that referring to the event might spark a memory.

"Yes, Cara and I discussed it and we're hoping that being at the Texas Cattleman's Club with all of my acquaintances will help me remember something," Alex answered. He sighed heavily. "It's damned irritating not being able to remember anything about my life before waking up in the back of that truck."

"I'm sure there will be a break in the case soon," Josh said, hoping he was right. "The Royal Police Department's detective unit is one of the best in the entire state and they're letting Britt Collins, the state investigator, take the lead. With her FBI training and specialty in kidnapping cases, they'll have whoever did this to you behind bars in no time."

"I was told this morning they intend to send my picture to the national television networks in an attempt to find anyone who might have seen who I was with while I was missing. It might also help locate any family I have," Alex added. "Apparently none of them live close by, because there haven't been any family members respond to the local news reports about me."

Josh smiled. "I'm sure the news of all this going national will help to escalate the investigation."

As they continued to discuss Alex's frustration with his lack of memory and the possibility of the police turning up something that would give them a clue who had beaten him, Josh's mind kept straying back to Kiley and his invitation to dinner the following evening. It suddenly occurred to him that she hadn't said no.

Of course, she hadn't exactly accepted his invitation either. But he decided not to give that a second thought. As far as he was concerned they were having dinner tomorrow evening and he fully intended to discuss that night three years ago. He needed for her to understand that he wasn't in the habit of making love to a woman he didn't know, then leaving her like some kind of thief in the night. He also wanted her to admit that she had played a part in the incident when she had been so receptive to him. Then, as far as he was concerned, the matter would be closed for good.

Satisfied that he had a viable plan, he filled Alex in on things that were going on at the clubhouse. "The day care center is open and has quite a few kids attending."

"I am sure the female members are happy about that," Alex said, smiling. "But Cara tells me her father and a few others are less supportive."

Josh nodded. "I wasn't entirely sure it's needed, but after the director's request for more money to operate the center I'm taking the time to learn more about it before I make up my mind."

"It is always good to keep an open mind and get the facts before one passes judgment," Alex said, nodding.

As Josh listened to Alex, he appreciated the wisdom in his friend's quietly spoken observation. "Thanks for the advice. I'll be sure to do just that." Rising to leave, he shook Alex's hand. "You know if you need anything, all you have to do is give me a call."

"I appreciate that, Josh," Alex said, following him to the front door. "I will certainly keep that in mind."

As Josh descended the front steps, he noticed a car coming up the long drive. When it pulled to a stop behind his and the driver got out, he recognized Alex's former housekeeper, Mia Hughes.

She waved. "Hi, Josh. How is Alex doing today?"

"He's frustrated with his lack of memory, but that's to be expected." He smiled. "I hear that congratulations are in order."

The pretty young woman beamed. "You heard about my engagement to Dave Firestone?"

"Yes." He laughed. "News like that travels through the TCC like a flash fire through a wood pile."

She laughed. "Thank you, Josh. I've never been happier."

"If the smile on Firestone's face these days is any indication, I'd say he's just as happy," Josh said.

"It was nice seeing you again, Josh," Mia said as she started up the steps to the front door.

Josh nodded. "I'll see you in a few weeks at the Christmas Ball."

Getting into the car, he drove away from the Santiago mansion feeling pretty good about the day. He had successfully straightened out a problem with the work crew on one of the Gordon Construction job sites, had a nice visit with his friend and had set up dinner with Kiley Roberts for tomorrow evening.

"A very good day," he said aloud as he drove across town to his ranch just outside Royal.

The next afternoon, Kiley tried to remain focused and not think about Josh stopping by, expecting her to go to dinner with him. But try as she might, every time the door opened, she looked up expectantly. So far, it had been parents arriving to pick up their children, but she knew it was just a matter of time before she looked up to find Josh entering the day care center.

Of course, she had no intention of going anywhere

with him. But how could she anticipate and dread him stopping by all at the same time?

"Kiley, would you mind if I leave now?" Carrie asked, looking hopeful. "There are only two more children to be picked up by their parents and I have an appointment at the hair salon in fifteen minutes."

"Do you have a date with Ron tonight?" Kiley asked. From the time the young woman started working for her, Carrie had chattered nonstop about her boyfriend and Kiley expected any day to hear that they had become engaged.

Her assistant nodded. "He's taking me out to dinner and then we're going to see the new Channing Tatum movie."

"You can only leave early on one condition."

"What's that?" her assistant asked cautiously.

Kiley grinned. "You have to tell me all about the movie and how many times Channing takes his shirt off."

Carrie laughed as she grabbed her coat and purse from the closet by the door. "I can do that."

"Have a nice evening, and I'll see you tomorrow morning, Carrie."

As her assistant rushed out the door to get her hair done for her date, Kiley's heart skipped a beat when Josh walked in. Dressed in a black suit, pale blue shirt and navy tie, he looked more handsome than any man had the right to look outside the pages of *GQ*.

"Instead of making a reservation for us in the restaurant here at the club, I thought we might try that new place on the west side of town," Josh said, flashing her a smile that sent goose bumps shimmering up her arms. "Have all of the kids gone home?"

"Not yet." She collected the Santa Claus faces made of construction paper and cotton balls that the pre-school class had made during their craft time. "But I'm afraid I won't be able to…" She let her voice trail off when Russ and Winnie Bartlett entered the day care center to pick up their two little girls.

While Josh shook hands with Russ and talked about the upcoming meeting of the general membership, Kiley and Winnie chatted about the children's holi-day program.

"It's all Sarah can talk about," Winnie said, smiling at her little girl. As she helped her youngest daughter into her jacket, she laughed and smoothed her toddler's straight dark hair. "And Elaina tells me she's going to be one of the 'kidney' canes."

Grinning, Kiley nodded. "She calls them 'kidney' canes and Emmie calls them 'kitty' canes."

"Isn't it fun deciphering what a two-year-old means as they learn new words?" Winnie asked.

"Oh, yes." When Emmie toddled over to give Elaina a goodbye hug, Kiley smiled fondly at her beautiful little girl. "At times it feels like they speak a foreign language."

After the Bartletts bid them a good evening, Kiley and Emmie were left alone with Josh. Turning toward her office to retrieve her purse, Kiley heard Emmie start chattering about her toy ponies. Glancing over her shoulder, she almost laughed out loud at Josh's perplexed expression.

"Me pony," Emmie said, reaching up to wrap her little hand around one of Josh's fingers to tug him in the direction of the play area.

"What does she want?" Josh asked, sounding a little

alarmed. He might have been bewildered about what Emmie wanted, but to his credit, he followed her over to the toy box on the other side of the room.

"She wants to show you her favorite toys," Kiley said, quickly grabbing her things and switching off the office light.

"That's nice." Josh smiled when Emmie held up a purple pony with a flowing white mane and tail. "How much longer before one of her parents arrives to get her?"

"Emmie goes home with me," Kiley said, taking their coats from the closet. "She's my daughter."

"I didn't realize you had a child," he said, glancing down at Emmie digging through the toys to find more ponies.

When he looked back at her, Kiley could tell by his expression that Josh realized her going to dinner with him wasn't going to happen. But as they continued to stare at each other, a mischievous spark lit his brilliant blue eyes.

"So you like ponies and horses, Emmie?" he asked.

Emmie vigorously nodded her little blond head. "Yes."

Squatting down to her level, he handed the toy pony back to her. "I like horses, too. I have several of them at my ranch."

Emmie's little face lit up. "Me wanna see."

"I think that can be arranged," Josh said, giving Kiley a triumphant grin.

Kiley didn't like the idea in the least. "I don't think that would be—"

"Why don't you ask your mother to bring you over to my ranch on Saturday afternoon so I can show you my horses?" he asked before Kiley could stop him from making the offer.

"Pease, Mommy?" Emmie asked, skipping over to her. "Pease. Wanna see ponies. Wanna see ponies."

Kiley was fit to be tied. Josh had deliberately manipulated the situation and now her daughter looked so hopeful, she hated to refuse. But on the other hand, she didn't want to spend more time with Josh than she had to. Nor was she overly happy about his taking control of the situation.

"Is this retaliation for not going to dinner with you?" she asked, delaying her answer. A thought suddenly occurred to her. "You aren't going to let this influence your decision about the funding for the day care center, are you?"

"Not at all." A frown creased his forehead as he rose to his full height and walked over to her and Emmie. "I just thought your little girl might like to see a real horse."

"You knew she would," Kiley accused.

"Not really," Josh said, rocking back on his heels. "I don't know enough about little kids to know whether she would or not."

She wasn't buying his innocent expression for a minute. "This is punishment for not going to dinner with you and we both know it."

"Oh, I wouldn't go so far as to call it that." Standing closer than she was comfortable with, he leaned over to whisper, "And no. I won't let this influence my recommendation to the funding committee. Although you could have told me sooner that dinner wasn't really an option."

"You didn't give me a chance yesterday afternoon,"

she said defensively. "And you didn't come by the center earlier for me to tell you."

"We both know you could have called my office or left a message for me here at the clubhouse," he reminded, his voice so intimate it sent a tiny shiver of awareness straight up her spine. "So what do you say?" he asked, smiling. "You just said yourself that Emmie would like seeing the horses."

The woodsy scent of his cologne and the fact that he stood so close were playing havoc with her equilibrium. Taking a step away from him, she looked down at Emmie. Her daughter looked so excited and happy, how could Kiley possibly disappoint her?

"Oh, all right," she finally conceded. "But we'll only stop by for a few minutes."

"Good." Josh gave her directions to his ranch just outside of town. "I'll expect you and Emmie around one." Bending down, he smiled at her daughter. "I'll see you in a few days, Emmie." Straightening, he lightly touched her cheek with his index finger. "Have a nice evening, Kiley."

As she watched him stroll to the door, a shiver coursed through her at his light touch and the sound of his rich baritone saying her name. She shook her head to clear it.

"This is ridiculous," she muttered as she put Emmie's coat on her, then stuffed her arms into the sleeves of her own.

Josh Gordon was the very last man she should be shivering over. He couldn't be trusted. He might have given her a month's worth of extra funds for the day care center, but that didn't fool her for a second. She had overheard enough comments from some of the other members to know that he would like to see it fail—almost as much as Beau Hacket and Paul Windsor did.

So what was he up to? And why?

When Josh entered the bar, he looked around to see
if any of his friends had stopped by for happy hour

Three

When Josh entered the bar, he looked around to see
if any of his friends had stopped by for happy hour
since it appeared he was going to be spending his evening hanging out with the guys. Not exactly what he
had planned. He had intended to have an early dinner with Kiley at the exclusive new restaurant across
town, lay to rest what happened that night three years
ago and convince her that he fully intended to give her
day care center a fair evaluation.

Why her opinion of him mattered was still a mystery to him. He had never before cared one way or the
other what others thought of him. As long as he based
his decisions on what he knew was right, he could
sleep at night. But for some reason it bothered him
that Kiley obviously had such little faith in his integrity. Why would she think he would stoop so low as

to let her not going to dinner with him influence his recommendations to the funding committee? More importantly, why couldn't he just let it go?

Normally once he discovered a woman had a child, his interest in her took a nosedive and he moved on. But for some strange reason, Kiley and her daughter piqued his curiosity. Why would any man in his right mind willingly walk away from either of them?

"Hey, Josh," someone called, drawing him out of his introspection.

Spotting the current TCC president, Gil Addison, seated on the far side of the room, Josh threaded his way through the crowd. "I didn't expect to see you here, Gil," he said when he reached the table.

"Cade was invited to have dinner with one of his friends from the day care center." Gil shrugged. "I was just trying to decide whether to go home and raid the refrigerator or stay here and order something."

"Mind if I join you?" Josh asked. "My plans for dinner fell through at the last minute."

Grinning, Gil motioned toward the empty chair across from him. "Have a seat. I can't remember how long it's been since I had a meal that wasn't business-related or kid-dominated."

"You've had a pretty full plate since becoming president," Josh agreed, pulling out the chair to sit down.

A single father, Gil Addison was totally devoted to his small son, and he wasn't often seen having a beer with other members in the club's bar just for fun. It was nice to see his friend enjoying a little downtime for a change.

"Hi, I'm Ginny. I'll be your server tonight. What can I get for you two?" a tall, dark-haired waitress asked, placing cocktail napkins in front of them in anticipation of a drink order. "We have a steak and fries plate that's out of this world, it's so good."

"I'll have that and a beer," Josh spoke up.

"Might as well double that order," Gil added.

"Great choice," Ginny said, jotting their orders on a pad of paper. "I'll be right back with your beer."

While they waited on Ginny to return with their drinks, Josh and Gil talked about how the club membership had grown with the addition of women to its roster.

"I know some of the older members have a problem with it," Gil said, shrugging. "But the Texas Cattleman's Club needs to be progressive in its thinking and recognize that this isn't the same club Tex Langley founded around the turn of the last century. The 'good old boy network' was fine a hundred-plus years ago, but it just isn't practical in today's world."

"I have to admit, I've had my share of misgivings about women belonging to the club," Josh said honestly. "But after working with Nadine Capshaw since she was appointed to the funding committee last month, it's given me a new perspective on the issue. I think my main concerns now revolve around some of the changes the women are lobbying for. It seems at times that the TCC is heading toward becoming more of a country club than an organization that has always set the bar with its dedication to serving the needs of the community of Royal."

They both fell silent when the waitress brought them mugs of beer.

"I understand your and some of the other members' concerns," Gil said when Ginny moved away to serve another table. "And I know that some of the additions being made to the club's services for our members are viewed as unnecessary. But the way I see it, the more opportunities we offer, the better the chance our membership will stay strong and enable us to continue assisting the community."

"I guess you have a point," Josh conceded. He waited until Ginny had set their plates of food in front of them before he continued. "Speaking of our services, how do you like the new day care center? Is it living up to your expectations for your son?"

"It's exceeded them," Gil answered, cutting into his steak. "Cade looks forward to being with his friends each day and it's a load off my mind, knowing that while I conduct TCC business, he's being looked after right down the hall."

"The director seems to be pretty good with kids," Josh said, taking a bite of his steak.

Gil nodded. "Kiley Roberts is amazing. I can't believe some of the things Cade has learned since starting at the day care center last month." He smiled fondly as he talked about his son. "He can tie his own shoes now and is able to recognize a few basic words when he sees them."

"That's pretty good for a four-year-old, isn't it?" Josh asked. He really didn't know if it was or not. But then he didn't know much about what little kids learned at any age.

"Kiley has a real way with kids. She makes a game out of learning and they soak it up like sponges." Gil grinned. "Even getting Cade to go to bed is easier because she told them how important it is to get plenty of rest at night so they can play with their friends the next day."

Josh finished his dinner and took a drink of his beer. "She's asked for more money from the funding committee and I've been stopping by the center to see what the funds would be used for, and to determine whether I should recommend increasing the day care's yearly budget."

"Yeah, I heard Beau grousing about it the other day." Gil paused for a moment. "I know the decision to appropriate more money to the day care center's budget is entirely up to the funding committee. But for what it's worth, I think it would be money well spent." Something on one of the many televisions around the bar suddenly caught his attention. "Damn!"

Josh looked up to see a picture of Alex Santiago on one of the national evening news broadcasts. The anchorman reported that although Alex had been found, the investigation into his mysterious disappearance was ongoing. The reporter asked that anyone having seen Alex during the months he had been missing to please contact the state investigator, Britt Collins. He wrapped up the segment with a statement that all leads were being followed and that several members of the prestigious Texas Cattleman's Club had been questioned as persons of interest in the case.

Clearly angered by the report, Gil shook his head. "I don't like that the TCC is being disparaged by any of this. Our reputation has always been impeccable and every member of the club is carefully screened before they're granted membership. This Collins woman has already interrogated Chance McDaniel, Dave Firestone and myself. Who's she going to single out next?"

"It's my guess she'll investigate every one of us if she has to," Josh said, finishing his beer. "I've heard she's quite thorough."

"She'd do well to look elsewhere for possible suspects," Gil stated flatly.

Josh motioned for the waitress to bring their checks. "I wouldn't worry too much about the TCC's reputation. We've always been above reproach. We can weather this and anything else that casts a shadow of doubt over our integrity."

"You're right, but the club has been the subject of more than one negative news report lately," Gil reminded.

"Have there been any more leads in the vandalism of the day care center?" Josh asked, picking up the slip of paper the waitress placed facedown in front of him. "The last I heard the police think it might have been teenagers."

"That's what I heard, too." Gil reached for his check. "They're the only ones I can think of that might be stupid enough to mess with the TCC. The lead detective did tell me they found a partial fingerprint, but when they ran it through the national database there weren't any matches. He thinks it might be one of the members' kids."

Josh nodded as he removed his wallet from the inside pocket of his suit coat and tossed several dollars on the table to cover his dinner and a generous tip. "Kids are the only ones stupid enough to do something like this. Anyone else knows better than to come into our house and destroy any part of it. But you'd think a kid of one of our members wouldn't even think about it."

"Well, whoever it is, they've bit off more than they realize," Gil agreed. "I personally can't think of a single member, no matter what they think of the day care center, who doesn't want them held accountable for what they've done." Checking his watch, he rose to leave. "I guess I'd better get over to the Whelans' and pick up Cade. Thanks for sharing dinner with me, Josh."

Rising to his feet, Josh followed his friend out of the bar and walked to his car in favor of having the valet bring it to him. On the drive home, he thought a lot on what Gil had said about the day care center. It was true that the more the TCC had to offer, the better the chances of maintaining a full roster of members. And after seeing the way Kiley dealt with the kids, he knew firsthand that she was good at her job and the day care center was top-notch. Had he been looking at the club's need for a child care facility through jaded eyes?

Josh had to admit it was highly possible. He and his twin brother, Sam, had been raised by a man who made no secret that he thought a woman's place was in the home taking care of her own children and not outside of it working a job or playing tennis while someone else looked after her kids. For the most part, he had agreed with their father and it wasn't until he'd watched Kiley work with the kids that he was starting to question his steadfast opinion.

Maybe his thinking would have been different if his mother had lived long enough to really have an influence on his and Sam's lives. But other than what he saw from the pictures his dad had shown him,

Josh couldn't honestly say he recalled much about his mother.

Turning his car up the long drive leading to his ranch house, he decided to take Alex's advice and not make any rash decisions about his recommendation to the funding committee. He had the rest of the month to observe what went on at the day care center and he owed it to Kiley, as well as the members of the TCC, to give it a fair evaluation before he decided one way or the other.

On Saturday afternoon when Kiley parked in front of Josh's barn, her pulse sped up as she watched him walk toward her car. If she had thought he looked good yesterday when he stopped by the day care center, it couldn't compare to the way he looked today. In a suit and tie the man looked very handsome. In worn jeans, a blue chambray shirt, boots and a wide-brimmed black cowboy hat, he was downright devastating. Who knew he had been hiding such wide shoulders and narrow hips beneath the expensive fabric of those Armani suits?

"Right on time," he said, smiling as he opened her car door for her. "Good, you're wearing jeans."

Silently chastising herself for her wayward thoughts about the man, she took a deep breath and got out of the car. "You didn't think I'd wear heels and a dress to walk through a feedlot, did you?"

He laughed. "You wore a dress the other day."

"That's because I was going before your committee to ask for more money for the day care center," she said, turning to open the back door of the car. "You've seen me in slacks and a blouse every time since then."

The look in his blue gaze stole her breath. "And you've looked very nice in everything I've seen you in."

Surprised by the compliment, she didn't even think to protest when he gently moved her out of the way, opened the rear door, then unbuckled the safety straps and lifted her daughter from the car seat. "Are you ready to ride a horse, Emmie?" he asked.

Seated on his forearm, Emmie clapped her little hands together. "Me wide ponies."

"You didn't say anything about riding," Kiley accused, glaring at him. He knew she hadn't wanted to pay him a visit to begin with, let alone spend more time with him by going for a horseback ride.

"I didn't think of it until just a short while ago." He smiled at her happy daughter. "I thought this little lady might enjoy it."

"I'm sure she would," Kiley said without thinking. As soon as the words passed her lips, she knew she'd made a huge mistake and played right into his hands.

Josh gave her a triumphant grin as he placed his free hand to the small of her back. "Then it's settled."

"You're manipulating the situation, the same as you did yesterday afternoon," she said tightly as he guided her toward the corral where two saddled horses stood, their reins tied to the top rail of the fence.

"Not really." He opened the gate to the corral and led her over to a pinto mare. "I wasn't sure how experienced you are with horses, so I had my foreman saddle Daisy. She's the most gentle horse I own. You can ride, can't you?"

"Yes, but it's been a while since I've had the opportunity," Kiley admitted, patting the horse's neck.

"Do you need help mounting?" Josh asked from behind her.

She shook her head as she untied the reins and raised her leg to mount up. "I think I can manage."

Unfortunately, she was short and the horse was quite tall. When she put her foot in the stirrup, her knee was even with her chin and made it all but impossible to pull herself up into the saddle.

"Here, let me help," Josh said.

Before she realized what he intended, she felt his hand cup her backside and, as if she weighed nothing, he gave her the boost she needed to mount the mare. Her cheeks felt as if they were on fire when she settled herself in the saddle. Thankfully her daughter provided the distraction Kiley needed to regain her composure.

"Pony," Emmie said delightedly, touching the mare's mane.

When Kiley reached for her, Emmie stubbornly shook her head and put her arms around Josh's neck. "Wide a pony."

"You're going to ride a pony with me," Kiley explained.

Her daughter's blond pigtails swayed as she shook her head. "No!"

"Emmie," Kiley warned, keeping her tone firm but gentle.

Her little chin began to wobble and tears filled her big brown eyes. "No, pease."

"She can ride with me," Josh offered softly.

Emmie nodded her head. "Wide."

Kiley wasn't happy, but she finally nodded her consent. It wasn't that she didn't think Josh would keep her daughter safe. It was a matter of Emmie becoming too attached to him. She had watched her little girl's reaction when some of the children's fathers arrived at the end of the day to take them home and it was clear Emmie missed a paternal influence in her life.

As Kiley watched Josh untie the reins of the bay gelding and effortlessly swing up into the saddle while still holding Emmie, her heart ached. Her daughter deserved to have two parents, but it hadn't worked out that way and there was no sense lamenting the fact that she didn't.

"Me wide pony," Emmie said happily when Josh settled her on his lap and nudged his horse into a slow walk.

By the time they rode through the gate into the pasture beyond, Kiley had to admit that although she had been against the outing and still resented the way Josh had controlled everything, she wouldn't have missed the excitement on Emmie's face for anything. Her little girl was having the time of her life.

"She seems to be enjoying herself," Josh said, smiling when Emmie braced both hands on the saddle horn and grinned over her shoulder at him.

Kiley nodded. "She's always loved animals, but horses and ponies are her favorites. Even before she could sit up on her own, she had a stuffed pony that she wouldn't let out of her sight."

"Does her dad like horses?" he asked. "Maybe that's where she gets it from."

"No, he hasn't been in the picture since right after she was born," Kiley said, shrugging.

"I'm sorry," Josh said, sounding sincere.

"Don't be." She stared off into the distance. "Emmie and I are better off without him."

"He doesn't have any contact at all with you and Emmie?" He sounded disapproving.

Shaking her head, she smiled. "No. Mark signed over all legal rights to her so he wouldn't have to pay child support."

Josh stopped the bay gelding to turn and look at her. "And you're okay with that?"

"Actually, I'm just as glad I don't have to deal with him," she said honestly, reining in the mare. "But it breaks my heart for Emmie. When she gets a little older she'll start wondering why her dad didn't want anything to do with her."

"It's his loss," Josh stated flatly. "He's the one missing out and it sounds to me like the bast—" he stopped, looked down at Emmie, then, grinning, finished "—the jerk doesn't have the sense to know it."

She didn't know why she had opened up to Josh, but it was no secret in Royal that Mark Roberts cared little or nothing for anyone but himself. Of course, he wasn't a part of the same social set as Josh and his friends, so she doubted Josh had ever heard of Mark or his reputation for being his own number one fan.

"I know it's none of my business, but why did you marry him?" Josh asked, frowning.

"You're holding her." Kiley smiled fondly at her pride and joy. "I became pregnant and his grandfather insisted that he had to do the 'right thing' and marry me."

"You didn't have to go along with it," he pointed out.

"It appears that my sister isn't the only one in the

Miller family who makes poor choices when it comes to the men she gets involved with," Kiley said without thinking.

"Ouch."

"Oh, I'm sorry," she said, realizing that Josh thought she meant him. It was true that he had broken Lori's heart, but he was just one of a long list of men Lori had fallen for over the years. "I didn't mean you in particular," she hurried to add. "I just meant Lori seems to always fall for men who are all wrong for her."

He shrugged. "Lori's a great girl. But her attention span isn't all that long."

When he didn't say more, Kiley wondered what he meant by that comment. Lori wasn't known for seeing anyone for very long, but he made it sound as if she was the one who'd dumped him instead of the other way around. But Lori had said...

"That's why you said the day care center was your dream job," he said, drawing Kiley back to the present. "As long as you have to work to support yourself and Emmie, it's better to have her with you."

"By having her with me, I don't have to worry about missing any of her childhood milestones or wonder if someone else is taking good care of her," Kiley said, nodding.

He looked thoughtful, as if mulling over what she had told him before glancing down at Emmie. "Uh-oh. It looks like this little cowgirl is going to miss part of the ride."

When she looked over at her daughter leaning back against Josh, she smiled. Emmie was fast asleep.

"I think it was probably the rhythmic movement of the gelding's slow walk and the fact that she has been extremely excited about seeing the horses. When the adrenaline level starts to drop off, the little ones are usually asleep in no time." She stopped the mare. "Do you want me to take her?"

Smiling, he shook his head. "No, she's fine. Besides, I'd hate to wake her."

They fell silent as they rode along a creek on the far side of the pasture before turning back. Maybe Josh wasn't such a bad guy after all, Kiley decided.

As they rode across the wide pasture, Kiley found herself glancing at Josh holding her daughter securely to his wide chest and a warm feeling began to fill her. Was there ever a more endearing sight than a man tenderly holding a child?

When she remembered how surrounded she'd felt with his chest pressed to hers and the latent strength of his arms holding her close as he made love to her that night, a streak of longing coursed through her at the speed of light. Her heart skipped a beat and she had to remind herself to breathe. Where had that come from? And what on earth was wrong with her?

Josh Gordon was the very last man her heart should be fluttering over. If he and some of the other funding committee members had their way about it, the day care center would close and she would be out of a job—her dream job. She would be much better off focusing on that than to be thinking about how passionate he had been or how cherished she'd felt when he'd made love to her.

When he and Kiley rode the horses back into the corral, Josh was careful not to wake Emmie as he dismounted the bay. He had never before noticed how cute a little kid was when they were sleeping. Of course, he hadn't been around kids enough to know whether they all looked innocent and sweet or if it was just Emmie.

How in the name of hell could Roberts have walked away from her and Kiley? Why hadn't he at least wanted to be a big part of his kid's life?

Josh shook his head as he turned to help Kiley down from the mare. "Emmie's going to be disappointed that she slept through most of her first horseback ride."

Kiley nodded as she took Emmie from him and lifted her daughter to her shoulder. "Thank you, Josh. She really enjoyed it while she was awake and she'll be talking about petting the horses for days."

The sound of her soft voice saying his name and the sweet smile she gave him caused a warmth like nothing he had ever known to rush through him. He had to clear his throat before he could speak. "It was my pleasure, Kiley. We'll have to do it again soon. Maybe Emmie will be able to stay awake through the entire ride next time."

Emmie stirred against Kiley's shoulder and, raising her head, sleepily looked around. "Ponies." When she realized the ride was over, tears filled her eyes and she looked as if her heart had been broken. "Wide... a pony."

Josh felt like he'd taken a piece of candy or a favorite toy from her. "Do you mind if I hold her on the saddle while I lead the horses into the barn?" he asked Kiley. "You know, give her a little more riding time?"

"No, I don't mind," she said, wiping a big tear from Emmie's round little cheek. "Would you like for Josh to give you another ride on the pony?"

Emmie nodded and held both of her arms out for him to take her. "Wide a pony."

Without a moment's hesitation, he took her from her mother and set her on the gelding's saddle. "Hold on to the saddle horn," he instructed, showing her where to put her hands. Emmie gave him a smile that he wouldn't have missed for anything. "We'll come back for the mare," he said, turning to Kiley. "That way, she'll get to ride twice."

Putting his arm around Emmie to make sure she didn't slide off the saddle, Josh loosely held the reins as he urged the gelding into a slow walk. All of his horses had been well-trained and he was confident the animal wouldn't just take off. But he wasn't taking any chances, either.

Once the bay was tied to a grooming post inside the barn, Josh and Emmie returned to the corral to get the mare. From the look on Emmie's face, he had made some major points with her. The child was grinning from ear to ear by the time the mare was tied beside the gelding.

"Bobby Ray, would you start grooming the mare?" Josh called to his foreman at the far end of the barn. "I'll be back in a few minutes to take care of the bay." Lifting Emmie from the saddle, he walked back out to where Kiley stood by the corral gate, talking to Bobby Ray's wife. "I see you've met my housekeeper, Martha," he said, smiling at the two women.

"Oh, my word," Martha said, her face splitting into a wide grin when she spotted Emmie. "What a beautiful little angel!"

"Would you like for Martha to show you her new kittens?" Josh whispered to Emmie as if they were sharing a big secret. For reasons he didn't want to dwell on, he wanted to prolong her and Kiley's departure.

"Wanna see kitties," Emmie said happily.

"Is it all right to take her to see the two kittens we adopted from the animal shelter?" Martha asked Kiley.

"That would be fine," Kiley answered, smiling. "I'm sure she would like that."

When Josh set Emmie on her feet, she readily took Martha's hand and waved at him and her mother. "Bye."

"She's a great kid," Josh said, watching his housekeeper and Emmie walk back into the barn.

"Thanks."

"I feel like I should be the one thanking you," he said truthfully. "I've really enjoyed getting to see the wonder on her face."

Kiley nodded. "Every day is a big adventure for a two-year-old."

"I'm sure it can be an adventure for you, as well," he said, thinking about how difficult it had to be, raising a child with no help.

She laughed. "Well, there have been a couple of times when her adventures have turned into my disasters."

The delightful sound of Kiley's laughter did strange things to his insides and he didn't think twice about reaching out to pull her into his arms. "Thank you for letting me share in Emmie's latest adventure," he said, hugging her close.

Her body pressed to his felt wonderful even through the many layers of their clothing. When she leaned back to look up at him with her luminous brown eyes,

Josh couldn't have stopped himself from kissing her if his life depended on it.

Slowly lowering his head, he gave her the chance to call a halt to things. To his relief, her eyes fluttered shut as his mouth covered hers. Soft and sweet, her lips clung to his, reminding him of that night in her sister's apartment. A spark ignited in his belly and his lower body began to tighten predictably. He had suspected part of the reason that night had gone as far as it did was because of an undeniable chemistry between them. Now he knew for certain he was right. The reality of her response surpassed his memory of that night, and he knew absolutely that a force of nature was at work drawing them together.

Forcing himself to keep the kiss brief and non-threatening, he eased away from the caress instead of deepening it as he would have liked. "I've been wanting to do that for the past few days," he said, smiling down at her.

Kiley took a quick step back. "Th-that shouldn't… have happened."

"I'll be damned if I'm sorry it did."

"I… We should go," she said, looking a little flustered. Unless he missed his guess, she felt the magnetic pull as strongly as he did and it scared her senseless.

Before either of them could say anything more, Martha and Emmie returned from the barn.

"Me petted kitties," Emmie said excitedly.

"Tell Mr. Gordon thank you for inviting us to see the ponies and the kitties," Kiley said, her gaze not quite meeting his.

"Tank you," Emmie said politely.

Taking the little girl by the hand to lead her to the

car, he smiled. "You're very welcome, Emmie. We'll go for another ride the next time you come back to my ranch. Would you like that?"

The toddler nodded until her curly pigtails bounced. "Yes."

He opened the back door of Kiley's car and lifted Emmie into the car seat. Stepping back, he waited until Kiley buckled the safety straps and closed the car door before he reached up to brush a strand of blond hair from her smooth cheek.

"Drive safe."

She nodded as she hurriedly turned to get in behind the steering wheel. "I'll see you next week at the day care center."

"Yeah," he said, smiling confidently as he watched her turn the car around and start back up the drive to the main road. "You'll see me before then, too."

He had forgotten to tell Kiley about the partial fingerprint the detectives had found when they investigated the vandalism at the day care center and that after running it through their database, they had concluded the perpetrator didn't have a criminal record. It wasn't anything that couldn't wait until he saw her at the day care center, but as far as he was concerned it was reason enough to pay her a visit that evening. Besides, they still had yet to discuss their night together, and she might be more inclined to talk about what happened in the privacy of her own home.

Whistling a tune, he walked back to the barn to help his ranch foreman finish grooming the horses. Now that he had plans for the evening, he suddenly couldn't wait to get them started.

Four

Driving across town after picking up a pizza, Josh thought about what Kiley had told him earlier that afternoon while they were riding his horses. She had never received help from her ex-husband. As chairman of the funding committee, he knew exactly what her salary was. The TCC paid her the going rate for a day care center director, but it wasn't something she would ever get rich from. In fact, he wouldn't be the least bit surprised if she was struggling to make ends meet.

Suddenly several things became quite clear, causing a knot to form in his gut. Kiley had called working at the day care center her dream job. But aside from being able to be with Emmie, she needed to keep her position for two very important reasons. She needed to provide for herself and Emmie, and she probably couldn't afford the rising cost of child care if she worked any other job.

Now he felt guilty as hell for being so closed-minded about the day care center. To a certain degree he had been on the same page with Beau Hacket and Paul Windsor. His father had raised him and his twin with the misguided belief that a woman's place was in the home, taking care of her own kids. Period.

But what they had all failed to take into consideration was the fact that women not only had the right to enjoy recreational activities the same as men, but that some women didn't have a choice but to be out in the workforce. They had to hold a job to help their families make ends meet or, as was Kiley's case, be her family's only support.

Determined to be more open-minded in the future, he turned into the entrance of a subdivision and started watching street signs for Cottonwood Lane. It seemed to be a nice enough neighborhood, but he could tell that it was older and some of the houses were in desperate need of repairs, if not a complete renovation.

When he turned onto Kiley's street, he hadn't gone far when he spotted her older Ford sedan parked in the driveway of a small bungalow. He pulled his Mercedes in behind her car. The lights were on inside the house and he would bet that she and Emmie were probably getting ready for dinner.

"Right on time," he said, grabbing the pizza box and getting out of his car.

Walking up to the front door, he rang the bell and waited. When Kiley opened the door, his heart stalled and he couldn't believe how hard it was to take in his next breath. Dressed in a pink T-shirt that gave him a pretty fair idea of the size and shape of her breasts, and black leggings that hugged her slender legs like a second skin, she could easily tempt a saint to sin.

He forced himself to give her what he hoped was an innocent smile as he presented the pizza. "Dinner is served."

She looked confused. "Josh, what are you doing here?"

"I thought you'd be tired after today's outing and might not feel like cooking," he said suddenly, wondering if he'd lost his mind. It was clear Kiley was trying to keep him at arm's length. Why couldn't he accept that?

Emmie peeked out from behind her mother's legs. As soon as she recognized him, she started looking around the yard. "Ponies. Wanna wide ponies."

"I'm sorry, Emmie. The horses were tired and I left them at my ranch to rest," he said, hoping it was a good enough explanation for a two-year-old. He held out the box for her to see. "But I brought pizza for dinner."

The temptation of pizza worked its magic and, grinning, the little girl clapped her tiny hands. "Petza."

Kiley didn't look happy. "I normally make sure she has a more healthy dinner."

"I thought of that," he said, rocking back on his heels. "That's why I ordered the vegetable pizza with real cheese on a hand-tossed, whole-grain crust."

He was actually pretty proud of himself for thinking of the nutritional value for a change. Normally, when he had pizza it was loaded with meat, there wasn't the hint of a vegetable on it and the crust was as thick as a slice of Texas toast.

"Petza, Mommy," Emmie said, tugging on the tail of Kiley's T-shirt.

"Oh, all right," she finally said, stepping back.

When he entered the house, Josh looked around. It was exactly as he thought it would be—very warm and homey. The furniture was older and a bit worn, but everything was neat and clean, and looked very comfortable.

Noticing a couple of place mats on the coffee table, he raised an eyebrow. "Dinner in front of the TV?"

"Saturday is movie night for Emmie and me," Kiley explained. "I was just about to make tuna sandwiches." Walking into the kitchen, she returned to put another place mat down on the coffee table along with three small plates. "Would you like a glass of iced tea? I'm sorry I don't have anything stronger."

"I'll have whatever you're having," he said, placing the pizza box on the table with the plates. He waited until she returned with two glasses of iced tea and a small cup of milk with a straw built into the lid. "What are we watching this evening?"

"A classic cartoon about a mermaid princess who wants to be a real girl," Kiley said, dishing up slices of pizza. "It's one of Emmie's favorites."

Their fingers brushed when she handed him his plate, and it felt like a jolt of electric current traveled up his arm and exploded somewhere around his solar plexus. As quickly as she jerked her hand back, Josh knew beyond a shadow of doubt that she had felt it, too.

"Me pincess," Emmie said, nodding as Kiley fastened a bib around her neck to protect her pink footed pajamas with fairy-tale princesses on them. It was obvious the toddler was ready for bed and Josh would bet his last dollar that she fell asleep well before the movie was over.

While her mother cut the slice of pizza on her plate into little pieces, Emmie suddenly took off running down the hall.

"Where did she go?" he asked, confused.

Kiley smiled. "She's going to show you that she's a real princess."

When the little girl returned, she was wearing a gold-colored plastic crown with jewels painted on it. It was a little too large for her head and it kept sliding to one side, but she wore it as proudly as if it were the Crown Jewels.

"Me pincess," she said again as she picked up one of the bite-size pieces of pizza and put it into her mouth.

"Yes, you are," Josh said, unable to stop smiling. For some reason, he found everything the kid did to be cute as hell, and he was fascinated by her enthusiasm and delight in the simplest of things.

When he caught Kiley staring at him, he frowned. "What?"

"N-nothing," she said, picking up the remote control. Pushing a couple of buttons, she started the DVD and in no time Emmie became completely engrossed in the cartoon.

As they ate, he noticed Kiley glancing at him and then Emmie several times, but she remained strangely silent. Before he could ask her what was wrong, she paused the DVD player.

"If you'll excuse us, I need to finish getting her ready for bed," she said, taking Emmie by the hand.

While she took her daughter down the hall to the bathroom to wash her face and hands and brush her teeth, Josh took their plates and the empty pizza box into the kitchen. When he returned to the living room, he had barely settled himself on the couch when Emmie came running in to climb up on the cushion beside him.

Grinning up at him, she jabbered something that he assumed meant she wanted him to start the movie again. Fortunately Kiley was right behind her. Maybe she could translate toddler speak.

"Does she want me to start the movie again?" he asked, wondering why Kiley had stopped just inside the room. She looked as if she'd seen a ghost. "Is something wrong?"

His question seemed to snap her out of whatever she'd been thinking and, giving him a slight smile, she shook her head. "Please go ahead and take the player off Pause."

When Kiley started to sit in the armchair, Emmie shook her head and, getting down, took hold of her mother's hand. "Mommy," she said determinedly, tugging Kiley toward the couch.

"I think she wants you to sit with us," Josh said, deciding he owed the kid a debt of gratitude.

Kiley didn't look all that happy about it, but she did as her daughter wanted, and after Emmie climbed up beside him, she sat down on the other side of the little girl to finish watching the cartoon. Within ten minutes, Emmie surprised him yet again when she crawled over to sit on his lap and lean back against his chest.

Kiley started to move to the opposite end of the couch, but Josh put his arm around her shoulders to stop her. "The princess is about to go to sleep. If you move, it might disturb her," he whispered close to her ear.

He felt a tremor course through her before she gave him an exasperated look. "What are you doing, Josh?"

"Watching the movie with you and Emmie."

"You know what I mean," she said, shaking her head.

"Could we discuss this after she goes to sleep?" he asked, stalling.

The truth was, he didn't know why he felt the need to get close to Kiley. Normally women with little kids were the last females he wanted to get close to. But that wasn't the case with Kiley. Maybe it was that night three years ago that compelled him, or it could be the fact that the more he learned about her and her daughter, the more he wanted to know. He wasn't sure. But he had always followed his gut instinct and it was telling him not to be too hasty—to take his time and explore what was drawing him to them.

"She's asleep," Kiley said quietly as she reached for Emmie.

"If you'll lead the way, I'll carry her for you," Josh said, cradling the toddler to him as he rose to his feet. "She's as limp as cooked spaghetti."

Kiley's soft laughter caused a warm feeling to spread throughout his chest. "Children don't have the stress adults have. When they fall asleep they're completely relaxed."

Following her down the hall to Emmie's room, he placed the little girl on the smallest bed he had ever seen. He waited for Kiley out in the hall while she pulled the covers over Emmie and kissed her goodnight.

"I didn't know they made beds that little," he said when they walked back into the living room.

"It's a toddler bed." She turned off the DVD player

and removed the disk. "Emmie is too old for a crib and too little for a twin-size bed."

"That makes sense."

Staring at him for a moment, she finally asked, "Why did you come by tonight, Josh?"

"I forgot to mention this afternoon that the detective in charge of the vandalism case told Gil Addison that they analyzed a fingerprint found at the day care center," he stated.

"Were they able to find out who it belonged to?"

He shook his head. "It didn't match anyone in their database, so whoever was behind the destruction doesn't have a criminal record."

Kiley straightened the afghan on the back of the couch. "I was hoping by now the authorities would have someone in custody or at least have an idea of who the person was."

"From all indications, they think it might be a couple of the TCC members' kids," Josh said from behind her.

"And this couldn't have waited until Monday?" When Kiley turned to face him, her heart skipped a beat. He was way too close for comfort.

His slow grin sent goose bumps shimmering over her skin. "It probably could have, but I wanted to see you again."

"We spent the afternoon with you. Wasn't that enough?" she asked, wishing her voice didn't sound so darned breathless.

Slowly reaching out, he put his arms around her. She knew he was intentionally giving her a chance to back away, but for the life of her, she couldn't seem to get her feet to move.

"No, it wasn't enough," he said, smiling. "I wasn't able to give you a proper goodbye kiss this afternoon."

"Josh, it wasn't a good idea then and it's an even worse idea now." Why couldn't she make her tone sound more convincing?

"Why do you say that, Kiley?" he asked, brushing his mouth over hers.

"I… Well…it just…is," she said, sounding anything but sure. She needed time to think, but he was making it impossible.

As she stared up into his darkening blue eyes, he lowered his mouth to hers and any protest she was about to make went right out the window. She had tried for the past three years to forget how his lips felt moving over hers, how masterful his kiss was. It had been a subtle reminder when he'd kissed her earlier that afternoon at his ranch. But that paled in comparison to the way he was kissing her now.

Tasting and teasing, he traced her mouth with his tongue until she parted her lips on a soft sigh. When he slipped inside to gently explore her inner recesses, a delicious heat began to slowly glide its way through her and her knees suddenly felt as if they were made of rubber. When she raised her arms to his shoulders, he caught her to him, and the feel of his hard masculine body pressed against her softer form felt absolutely wonderful. It had been so very long since she'd been held by a man, felt the carefully controlled strength of his caress and the excitement of his lips claiming hers.

Lost in the delicious feelings, it took a moment for her to realize that Josh had brought his hand up to cup her breast. Even through her clothing the feel of his thumb chafing the tight tip caused a tingling sensation to travel straight to the most feminine part of her. A longing like nothing she'd ever known threatened to swamp her.

The ringing of her phone suddenly broke through the sensual haze Josh had created and helped to restore some of her sanity. Pulling from his arms, her hand trembled when she reached to pick up the cordless unit. She immediately recognized her sister's number on the caller ID.

"I-It's…Lori. I'll…call her back…in a few minutes," she said, struggling to catch her breath. "You should probably…go, Josh."

Josh stared at her for several long seconds before he finally nodded. "Tell Lori I said hello." He started for the door, then, turning back, reached up to run his index finger along her cheek. "I know that you're reluctant to acknowledge that it even exists, but whatever this is between us hasn't diminished. If anything, it's stronger now than it was that night."

"Josh—"

Giving her a quick kiss, he opened the front door. "I'll see you Monday afternoon."

Unable to form a coherent sentence, Kiley watched him leave before she sank down on the couch. Her head was still spinning from his kiss, but it was what she had noticed when she watched him and Emmie together that made her feel as if the rug had been pulled out from under her.

She had always thought that Emmie looked like her. They both had the same hair and eye color. But watching Josh and her daughter together, Kiley had noticed several similarities that had her questioning everything she thought she was sure of. Emmie had the same smile as Josh, the same patrician nose, and although her eyes were brown instead of blue, they were the same shape as his.

Shaking her head to clear it, Kiley rose from the couch and wandered into the spare bedroom she used for an office. Sitting down at the desk, she booted up her laptop and brought up a website that she hoped would prove that she'd lost her mind.

A half hour later, Kiley stared off into space as the gravity of her findings sank in. She had calculated everything twice and there was no way to deny it. There was a very real possibility that, instead of her ex-husband, Josh Gordon was Emmie's father.

Kiley waited until the following morning to call her sister back. She was still trying to come to terms with the probability of Josh being Emmie's father. But the more she thought about it, the more it explained.

Emmie looked absolutely nothing like Mark. He had an olive complexion, black hair and a distinct Roman nose. Nothing like her daughter's facial features. And then there were the numbers that added up against Mark being her father.

Kiley had always thought she became pregnant a few weeks later, when she and Mark patched things up after that night in her sister's apartment. But the more she thought about it, the less likely that was the date she had conceived. If she calculated Emmie's birth by that, Emmie had been born three weeks early. But when she calculated it by the night she and Josh made love, Emmie had arrived right on time.

She knew that wasn't conclusive proof. Only a DNA test would be proof positive. But everything added up to suggest that Josh was more likely Emmie's father than Mark.

Deciding that she would end up completely overwhelmed by it all if she didn't distract herself, she dialed her sister's number. "Hi, Lori," Kiley said when her sister answered the phone. "I'm sorry I missed your call last night. I was…um, busy."

"No problem," Lori said cheerfully. "I figured you were probably having trouble getting my adorable niece tucked in for the night."

"Saturday nights are easy. Emmie always falls asleep during the movie and it's just a matter of carrying her to bed," Kiley said, wondering how she was going to bring up the subject of Lori's relationship with Josh. From what he had said about Lori being a great girl, it didn't sound like the breakup had been as disastrous as her sister had described at the time.

"I tried calling yesterday afternoon to see if you wanted to go help me start my Christmas shopping, but you weren't home." Lori laughed. "You know me. I always wait until the last minute to buy gifts for everyone and I need your opinion. Otherwise, I go into panic mode and buy something completely inappropriate for everyone." It was so typical of Lori. She had procrastination down to an art form.

"I put all of the gifts I'm giving into layaway this past fall." Kiley smiled. "It doesn't feel as expensive when I pay a little out of each paycheck and I'm able to put a little more thought into what I'm giving."

"You always were the smart one of the Miller girls," Lori said, laughing.

"There are only two of us," Kiley reminded.

"Just ask Mom and Dad, they'll tell you I'm not the

brightest bulb in the chandelier," Lori said. "Especially when it comes to men."

"Did you break up with your latest boyfriend?" Kiley asked, not at all surprised. Lori's relationships never seemed to last more than a few months.

"No, Sean and I are actually doing quite well," Lori said, sounding amazed. "We've even started talking about moving in together."

"Maybe he's Mr. Right," Kiley said, hoping her sister could find someone who loved her in spite of her flightiness.

"I'm actually thinking he might be," Lori said, sounding extremely hopeful.

"By the way, you'll never guess who I've been having to work with on funding for the day care center," Kiley said, hoping Lori would volunteer some information about her breakup with Josh.

"Who?" Lori asked, her interest obviously piqued.

"Josh Gordon," Kiley stated, awaiting her sister's reaction.

"Oh, Josh is very nice," Lori said, sounding sincere. She laughed suddenly. "In fact, he's one of Royal's most eligible bachelors. I think the two of you should get together. You'd make a really great couple and you need to start dating again."

"I'm not in the market to be part of a couple now or in the future," Kiley said, shaking her head. She knew her sister was teasing her, but she wasn't in the mood.

"That's a shame, because Josh really is a terrific guy," Lori stated.

Kiley frowned. "Now, hold it. Didn't you tell Mom and Dad that he broke your heart when he ended things with you?"

There was a long pause before her sister answered. "Well, it didn't exactly happen the way I told Mom and Dad. You know they're convinced that I make some pretty poor choices in my relationships."

"It must run in the family," Kiley muttered, unable to stop herself.

"Hey, Mark Roberts was the only guy you dated that they didn't approve of," Lori reminded her. "And we both know they were right about him."

Kiley took a deep breath. She didn't want to discuss her brief marriage. "Tell me the real story behind your breakup with Josh."

"We had been dating for a couple of months, but there were times when we'd go for a week or so without seeing each other." Lori paused, then went on. "You know me. I got bored. I sort of started going out with someone else and everything was going great. I saw Josh when we could get together and the other guy when we couldn't." She sighed audibly. "At least, everything was going great until Josh caught us."

"Lori!"

"I know, it was a dumb thing to do," her sister said, sounding contrite. "When Josh found out I was seeing this other guy, I begged him to let me tell Mom and Dad that he was the one who lost interest and ended things between us."

"Why?"

"Because I didn't want to listen to them tell me that I'd screwed up again." Lori sighed. "Josh and I both knew it wasn't a forever kind of relationship from the beginning. When I asked him to help me save face by going along with me telling everyone that he'd found someone else and dumped me, he was really nice and agreed."

Kiley couldn't believe what she'd just heard. "So all this time, we've been thinking that he's a snake in an Armani suit, when in fact he was innocent of doing anything wrong?"

"That just about sums it up," Lori admitted. "Please don't tell Mom and Dad. Things are going great with Sean and I and I'd rather not have strained relations with them when I take him to meet them at the end of this week."

"Don't worry. It's your place to tell them what really happened—not mine," Kiley assured her sister. "I've never been a tattletale and I'm not going to start now. But Josh doesn't deserve their condemnation and they deserve to know the truth. You really should set the record straight." She didn't like lying to anyone, but especially not to their parents.

"I know, and I promise I'll confess soon." She paused. "I'd better go. Sean is here to take me to brunch. Give Emmie hugs and kisses for me."

"I will," Kiley said absently as she ended the call.

How could everything that she'd been so certain about change so quickly?

She had never questioned that Mark was Emmie's father. Hadn't even given it a second thought. But now she knew there was every likelihood that he wasn't. She had also never doubted, until recently, that Josh was the unfeeling jerk who had broken her sister's heart. Finding out that he had been the innocent party in their breakup, yet he'd been generous enough to allow Lori to make him out to be the bad guy in order to save face with their parents, was almost more than Kiley could comprehend.

What else had she been wrong about? And why was she so darned relieved to hear that Josh wasn't a heartbreaking reptile after all?

Five

Josh cursed the weather as he made his way across the ice-covered mud at the job site for the new Duncan Brothers Western Wear store. Hot one week, cold the next, it had been nothing short of bizarre for the past several weeks. But today it had taken a particularly nasty turn. It had been raining since before daylight, but it had only been in the past hour that it started sleeting. With the temperature steadily dropping all day, it had finally reached the freezing point and conditions were deteriorating rapidly. Deciding it was just too dangerous for his men to walk the iron girders of the structure, he'd made the decision to shut the job down for the day and send the crew home. No building was worth risking a man's life.

Climbing into his SUV, he quickly dialed the Gordon Construction offices. "Sam, I've shut down the

Duncan job site and I'm heading home," he said without preamble.

"I figured that was going to happen," his twin brother agreed. "I'm getting ready to go by the clubhouse and pick up Lila, then head home. She had a yoga class at the gym for pregnant mothers and as bad as the roads are getting, I don't want her trying to drive."

Josh didn't blame his brother. Sam's wife, Lila, was only a few months away from having their twins and if Josh had a pregnant wife, he knew he'd be just as cautious.

A sudden thought occurred to him that sent apprehension knifing through him. Kiley and Emmie were at the day care center and wouldn't be able to leave until all of the other kids had been picked up. By that time the roads would be so slick he didn't want to think about what might happen.

"I may see you at the clubhouse," he said, starting his Navigator's powerful engine. It was his work truck and for the first time since he bought it, he was glad it had all-wheel drive. "The day care center's director and her little girl are going to need help getting home."

"Oh…really?" His brother drawled the words. "I didn't think you went for women with kids."

"Can it, bro," Josh said, irritated with his twin. "She lives over in the Herndon subdivision and you know how winding the highway is out that way."

"Yeah, I think the engineer who laid out that road must have been part sidewinder," Sam said, his tone disgusted. "It's bad enough driving that way when the weather's clear, but on days like this it's pure suicide."

"I know. That's why I'm taking them home with

me," he said, instantly making the decision. Just the thought of Kiley and Emmie sliding off into a ditch or, worse yet, into the path of an oncoming car had a knot the size of his fist twisting his gut. "You and Lila be careful getting home."

"We will and the same to you and your new family, Josh," Sam teased.

"Sam, Kiley and I—"

His brother laughed, cutting him off. "Liar. The fact that you're defensive about it tells me these two mean more to you than you're willing to admit."

"Smart-ass," Josh muttered as he ended the call.

He forgot about his brother's observations and concentrated on driving to the clubhouse as fast as it was safe to get there. He wasn't sure, but he would bet anything that parents were picking up their kids early and that Kiley would head home as soon as she could.

Turning on the radio for a weather report, he gritted his teeth at the forecast. The sleet and freezing rain were expected to continue into tomorrow and there were already reports of power outages throughout the region. Kiley's subdivision was one of the areas with no electricity.

He briefly thought about calling her, but decided against it. For one thing, he needed total concentration to keep the truck on the road. And for another, he had a feeling Kiley was going to need some convincing to get her to agree to go to his place.

It seemed as though he'd been on the road for hours by the time he finally made the normally short drive from the job site to the TCC clubhouse. His heart pounded hard against his ribs when he turned into the parking area and it was almost deserted. Had Kiley and Emmie already left?

Looking around for her older sedan, he breathed a sigh of relief when he spotted it on the far side of the parking lot. Hell, just trying to walk on the ice from the front doors of the club all the way over to her car would be more dangerous than it was worth. With a little kid in tow it would be impossible without someone getting hurt.

Josh quickly parked the truck close to the front entrance without blocking it and gingerly walked the short distance across the icy glaze to the doors. Once inside the clubhouse, he quickened his pace and made a beeline down the hall to the day care center.

"How many more kids are left to be picked up?" he asked as he entered the room and found her looking nervously out the window at the coating of ice forming on the children's play area.

"Josh? Why aren't you on your way home? I've heard the roads are really getting treacherous," Kiley said, frowning.

"They are," he answered, looking around. The only other child in the center besides Emmie was Cade Addison. "How long before you're able to leave?"

"Gil is on the way from the president's office to get Cade now," Kiley answered. "I intend to leave as soon as he gets here. Why?"

"I came by to get you and Emmie," he answered, checking his watch. "I'd say we have just enough time to get to my ranch before the highway department closes the roads."

Kiley shook her head. "We're going home."

"This is nonnegotiable, Kiley," he stated flatly. "I

can't in good conscience allow you to drive on the road out to your subdivision."

"Excuse me?" When she turned on him, he realized he'd made a huge mistake. "You can't *allow* me to drive home?"

"Maybe I should rephrase that," he added hastily. "I'm not at all comfortable with the idea of you and Emmie traveling that particular road coated with ice. I'd feel much better about it if you'd let me take you and Emmie to my ranch. It's a lot closer and we'll be off the roads that much sooner."

She shook her head. "I can't do that, Josh."

"Why not?" he demanded, becoming irritated with her stubbornness.

Gil Addison chose that moment to enter the center to get his son, interrupting them. "I hope you both have plans to take off for home as soon as Cade and I leave," he said, helping his son into his coat. "I heard the police are advising people to get off the roads and stay off until the ice storm is over and the highway department gets the roads cleared off."

Josh nodded. "Kiley and I were just discussing that."

"Don't worry about trying to get here to open the day care center for the next couple of days, Kiley," Gil said as he ushered his son toward the door. "I'm closing the clubhouse until the roads are clear, and I anticipate that won't be until closer to the end of the week."

"Thanks for letting me know," she answered. "Please be careful on your way home."

When Gil left, Josh waited until Kiley turned off the lights in her office, grabbed her tote bag and retrieved their coats from the closet. He wasn't about to give up. She would be going home with him.

"On the way over here, I heard that your area of town has already lost power," he reported, hoping he could make her see reason. "Aside from the probability of having an accident on the way home, how are you going to keep Emmie warm for the next several days, provided you could even get there?"

"We would be in the same predicament if you lose electricity," she insisted, looking a little less sure of herself as she zipped up Emmie's coat and tied the hood.

"No, we wouldn't. When I built the house, I had an emergency generator installed. It runs on propane and supplies enough power for the entire house." Deciding they could move faster if he carried her, he reached down to pick up Emmie. "Would you like for me to take you and your mommy home with me to the ranch where the ponies are, Emmie?" he asked the little girl.

It would probably be considered underhanded to use Emmie's love of ponies to get Kiley to go along with him, but so be it. The way he saw it, keeping them safe was a lot more important than playing fair.

"Wanna see ponies," Emmie said, nodding. "Pease!"

Kiley glared at him a moment before she caught her lower lip between her teeth and he could tell she was reviewing her options. "Josh, I'm just not sure it's a good idea. We might be stuck there for several days."

"How many times have you driven on ice?" he asked as they walked out of the day care center and she turned to lock the door.

Making their way down the hall toward the clubhouse's main entrance, she shook her head. "Since it's extremely rare for us to get weather like this, I can't remember ever driving on it."

"I have and I can tell you that it's no picnic." When they reached the doors, he set Emmie on her feet. "Stay here. I'll go get my SUV and pull it under the canopy so you both stay dry."

"I need to get Emmie's car seat," she said, digging in her tote bag for her car keys.

"There's no sense in either of us breaking our necks trying to walk across a sheet of ice. After I get my truck, I'll drive over to your car and get the car seat." He took her keys from her. "When I come back for you and Emmie, I'll park under the canopy and you can show me how to install it in the backseat."

He had to go so slow that it took several minutes to get to his Navigator and drive over to the other side of the lot in order to retrieve the car seat, then get back to the clubhouse entrance. The SUV kept wanting to fishtail and Josh was more certain than ever that he'd made the right decision to come after Kiley and Emmie.

When he finally drove from under the canopy at the club's front entrance and headed for home, the car seat had been installed, and Kiley and Emmie were safely buckled into their seats. Gripping the steering wheel with both hands, Josh hoped the truck was heavy enough to get at least a little traction, but he wasn't counting on it. Just beyond the TCC's parking lot, a semi hauling a tanker had slid through the intersection and into a deep ravine on the opposite side of the road. If a rig that size had trouble with skidding, what chance did his much lighter SUV have?

Slowly steering the truck out onto the street, Josh didn't draw another breath until he had it straightened out and headed down the highway toward his ranch. The streets were completely deserted, and as they passed car after car off in the ditches lining the road, he decided that although he'd made the right decision about taking Kiley and Emmie to the ranch, it was going to be one hell of a long drive home.

As Josh slowly steered his SUV onto the lane leading up to his ranch house, Kiley finally relaxed enough to unclench her fists. The five-mile trip from the TCC clubhouse to his ranch had taken the better part of an hour and had been more than a little nerve-racking. She had lost count of the vehicles they'd passed that had slid off the road, and there were several times it felt as if the Navigator was going to join them. Fortunately, Josh was an excellent driver and managed to control the truck.

Although she was reluctant to admit it even to herself, she was glad he had insisted that she and Emmie go home with him. There was no way she'd have made it to her subdivision without having an accident. The highway had too many curves, and combined with her inexperience driving on ice, it would have made it impossible not to end up in a ditch. The thought that Emmie might have been hurt caused a chill to snake up her spine.

"Are you cold?" Josh asked, reaching for the heater. "We're almost at the house, but I can turn the heat up if you need me to."

She shook her head. "Thank you, but I'll be fine."

When Josh finally parked the SUV in the attached four-car garage and shut off the engine, he pushed a button on the remote clipped to the driver's sun visor to close the door behind them. "It may have taken a while to get here, but we made it safe and sound."

"Thank you," she said, meaning it. "I can't believe how bad the roads are."

He nodded. "I'm afraid we'll have to make our own dinner. I called Martha earlier this afternoon when the weather started to fall apart and told her and Bobby Ray to go on home. They have a ten-mile drive to their place and I wanted to make sure they got there before the roads got too bad."

Kiley stared at him for a moment. The fact that he was concerned for his housekeeper's and foreman's safety caused her opinion of him to go up several notches.

"I make dinner for Emmie and myself every evening," she said, smiling. "I think I can manage making dinner for the three of us."

He grinned. "Good. I'm afraid my culinary skills only extend as far as boiling water for ramen noodles or packaged macaroni and cheese."

"I thought most Texas men were born knowing how to grill," she teased as she reached for the door handle.

"Wait," he said, getting out of the truck to walk around to her side. Opening the door, he extended his hand to help her down from the seat. "I do know how to grill, but I'm not going to risk life and limb in this weather to walk out to the barbecue pit to burn a couple of steaks."

She laughed. "Where's your sense of adventure?"

"I used it up on that drive home," he said, his smile fading. He reached up to thread his fingers through her hair. "I'm glad you made the decision to come home with me." He leaned down to brush her lips with his.

"I couldn't stand the thought of you trying to navigate all those curves."

Her pulse sped up. "Josh—"

He placed his finger to her mouth to silence her. "I don't want you to worry. Contrary to what happened three years ago, I swear I can be trusted."

Before she could respond, he turned to open the Navigator's back door and reached in to unbuckle Emmie. "She's sound asleep," he whispered, gently lifting her daughter from the car seat.

Kiley's breath caught when Emmie roused, saw who held her, then put her arms around his neck and trustingly laid her head on his shoulder. Her daughter was friendly by nature, but she had never taken to anyone as quickly as she had Josh. Did Emmie somehow sense that he was supposed to be someone special in her life?

Following Josh as he led the way into the house, she couldn't help but wonder what she was going to do about her suspicions that Josh might be Emmie's real father. How was she supposed to even start that conversation? She couldn't very well say, "Oh, by the way, I suspect the child you're holding might be your daughter." That wasn't something just thrown out as a casual comment.

Deciding to keep her silence for the time being in hopes an opportunity presented itself, Kiley followed Josh through the mudroom into the spacious kitchen. When he turned on the lights, she caught her breath as she looked around. The black marble countertops and white custom-made cabinets were gorgeous, but it was the restaurant-size stainless-steel appliances that really caught her eye. They would make cooking an absolute joy.

"This kitchen is a dream come true for anyone who loves to cook," she stated as they continued down a hall to the front foyer. "Do you entertain a lot?"

"I always have our employee Fourth of July barbecue here because I have a bigger yard than my brother." He held Emmie while Kiley removed her sleeping daughter's jacket. "And Sam is in charge of hosting the company Christmas party." He waited until she removed her coat, then handed Emmie to her to take off his. "We sometimes take turns having a couple of dinner parties throughout the year for clients, but that's about it."

While he hung up their coats in a closet close to the front door, Kiley admired the cream-colored marble floor in the foyer and the sweeping staircase leading to the upper level. Everything about Josh's house indicated that he had spared no expense when he'd had it built.

"Hungee," Emmie murmured, waking up to look around.

"Hey there, princess," Josh said, smiling as he closed the closet door.

"Ponies," Emmie said with a shy smile.

Josh laughed and the rich sound did strange things to Kiley's insides. "The ponies are in the barn having their dinner now, but I promise when the weather gets better I'll take you to see them again. Will that be okay?"

Emmie nodded, then put her arms around Kiley's neck. "Hungee, Mommy."

"Then I suppose I'd better find something to make

for dinner," Kiley said, tickling her daughter's tummy. When Emmie dissolved into giggles, she turned to Josh. "Is there anything special you were planning to have Martha make, or should I just search to see what you have?"

"Martha always keeps the refrigerator and pantry fully stocked, so whatever you want to fix is fine with me," he answered. He led the way back to the kitchen. "If you'll tell me what to do, I can probably help a little." He grinned. "And if you need boiling water, I'm your man."

Kiley laughed as she set her tote bag on the kitchen island and reached inside for one of Emmie's ponies. "I'll be sure to remember that." Handing her daughter the toy, she asked, "Could you keep an eye on her while I get started?"

"Do you think she'd like to watch something on TV?" he asked. "I have satellite, as well as access to all kinds of movies and television shows on demand. I'm sure I can find something suitable."

She didn't normally allow Emmie to watch a lot of television, but these weren't normal circumstances. "There is a pony cartoon that I let her watch on occasion."

"I'll find it," Josh promised. Turning to Emmie, he asked, "Would you like to go into the family room with me to see if we can find the pony show on TV?"

"Yes, pease," Emmie said, nodding until her blond pigtails bobbed up and down.

When she watched her child put her little hand in Josh's and walk into the family room with him, Kiley bit her lower lip to keep it from trembling. Her little girl deserved to have a daddy. But how was she going to work up the nerve to share her suspicions with Josh? And if she did manage to find the courage, how receptive would he be? Mark had rejected Emmie, even though he thought she was his child. Would Josh do the same?

"Don't go there," she muttered, shaking her head.

There was one more thing she needed to do that might possibly help her with her decision about talking to Josh. As soon as the weather cleared and things got back to normal, she would call to ask Mark about his blood type. If that ruled out any possibility of him being Emmie's biological father, then she would somehow find the courage to talk to Josh. Until then it would be better to remain silent and turn her attention to a more pressing matter—finding something to make for dinner.

"You're a great cook," Josh said, sitting back from the dining room table. "That was fantastic."

Kiley gave him a smile that sent heat racing through his veins. "I'm glad you liked it, but a simple chicken casserole and some steamed vegetables isn't exactly gourmet fare."

"Would you like to know a little secret about most men?" he asked, grinning.

"Oh, this should be good," she said, laughing. "By all means, please tell me."

Standing, he picked up their plates to carry them to the kitchen, then leaned down to whisper close to her ear. "Most guys really don't care what we eat as long as it's good and there's plenty of it."

She smiled as she wiped off Emmie's face and

hands. "There should be an addendum to that statement."

He arched one eyebrow. "Oh, yeah? What's that?"

"Men really don't care as long as they don't have
to cook it," she shot back.

He laughed. "That's a given, honey."

While he put their dishes in the dishwasher, Kiley
got Emmie ready for bed. He wasn't sure how other
women were with their kids, but Kiley was nothing
short of amazing with hers. He couldn't believe how
prepared she was. She not only carried toys to entertain Emmie in that tote bag, she also had a change of
clothes for her daughter, toddler-size cutlery and an
array of healthy snacks.

He decided right then and there that if he ever found
himself in a survival situation, he wanted Kiley and
her magic tote bag with him. She was prepared for
every contingency and managed to get it all in a nice,
neat little canvas bag about the size of a large box of
cereal.

Walking into the family room to sit down on the
couch, he wasn't at all surprised when the lights
blinked a couple of times, then went off completely.
The generator kicked on automatically and the lights
immediately came back on, making him glad that he
had thought to add the auxiliary power source when he
built the house. The three of them might be stranded
until the ice melted, but they would be warm and
wouldn't go hungry.

Emmie suddenly came running into the family
room as fast as her little legs would carry her. Dressed
in the smallest pair of pink sweats he'd ever seen, the
little girl's hair was a cloud of damp blond curls around

her shoulders and her eyes were wide. She was clearly excited about something. Jumping into this lap, she waved her hands and her big brown eyes sparkled as she jabbered for all she was worth.

"What's she saying?" he asked when Kiley walked in and sat down in the armchair.

Kiley smiled. "She's trying to tell you about the lights going out while she was in the bathtub."

"I promise we won't have to worry about the lights going out again," Josh assured the little girl. He didn't know if she was frightened or just trying to tell him about the experience, but he figured a little reassurance wouldn't hurt.

"Is the house on auxiliary power now?" Kiley asked, putting the clothes Emmie'd had on earlier in the tote bag.

He nodded as he picked up the television's remote control. "I was just getting ready to see if the local news has a report on how widespread the outages are."

As they watched the news, they learned that Royal and the surrounding area had been virtually shut down by the ice storm. There were only a few pockets of people who still had electricity, but as the ice brought down more trees and power lines, the utility company expected those to be without power by morning.

When the news program ended, Kiley got up and walked over to him and Emmie. "She's asleep."

"Do you want me to carry her to bed for you?" he asked, careful to keep his voice low.

She shook her head. "It might frighten her if she wakes up by herself in a strange place." She lifted her daughter to her shoulder. "I'll just lay her down on the love seat until I go to bed."

After laying Emmie on the love seat, Kiley started to sit back down in the armchair, but he caught her hand in his. "Sit here."

"Josh, I'm not overly comfortable—"

"It will be easier to talk without disturbing Emmie," he reasoned, interrupting her.

She stared at him for several long seconds before she slowly lowered herself to the cushion. "I suppose you're right. She normally isn't a light sleeper, but that's at home in her own bed."

"I've been thinking about the sleeping arrangements," he said, nodding.

"And just what about them?" she demanded, looking suspicious.

He couldn't keep from chuckling. "Calm down. There are two master suites—the one down here that you used to give Emmie a bath, and one upstairs. There are also four more bedrooms upstairs. I thought you could take your pick of where you and Emmie are going to sleep. But common sense tells me that little kids and stairs aren't always a good mix."

"Oh." She paused for a moment. "Thank you. That's very considerate. But since your things are in the master suite down here, I assume it's your room?"

He nodded. "Martha has a bad knee and it's easier for her to clean and make the bed if she doesn't have to go up and down the stairs all the time."

Her slow smile sent heat straight to the pit of his belly. "You're one surprise after another, Josh Gordon."

He frowned. "Why do you say that?"

"Not everyone would be that considerate of their housekeeper," she answered.

"I've known Martha and Bobby Ray all my life," he said, shrugging. "When they had to sell off their herds because of the drought, they were in danger of losing their ranch. I offered them jobs because I knew they wouldn't accept help otherwise."

"I can understand that. It's a matter of pride." She seemed to visibly relax as they continued to talk. "Were they able to keep their land?"

He nodded. "They didn't have the money to start over, but since the ranch has been in Bobby Ray's family for over five generations, they wanted to keep it for their grandson. By working for me, they have enough money for their needs, as well as being able to keep the ranch."

"And you make adjustments in your life, so they're able to continue doing that," she said softly.

"Something like that," he answered, feeling a little uncomfortable. He hadn't thought about it as anything more than what it was—the right thing to do.

Deciding it was time to change the focus of their conversation, he grinned. "You know what we need to do tomorrow?"

"I can't imagine," she said, giving him the smile that never failed to send his hormones racing.

"We need to decorate this place for Christmas." He pointed to the corner beside the stone fireplace. "That's where I put the tree the first holiday after I moved in."

"You haven't decorated since then?" she asked, frowning.

"I haven't really had the time." He had, but he hadn't seen any reason to decorate since he was the only one around to appreciate it. "Do you think the tree should go there or somewhere else?"

"By the fireplace is fine," Kiley agreed, hiding a yawn behind her delicate hand. "Emmie and I put ours up on Sunday afternoon. She's going to love getting to decorate another one. But where are you going to get one in this weather?"

"I have a seven-foot artificial tree stored in the garage. But we can talk more about it tomorrow. You're tired," he said, rising to his feet. Holding out his hand to help her up from the couch, he pulled her into his arms. "I'm going to give you a good-night kiss, Kiley." When she started to protest, he put his index finger to her lips. "Just a kiss. Then I'm going to go upstairs—"

"We can sleep—"

He reached up to lightly run the pad of his thumb over her full lower lip, interrupting her protest. "It's all right. I'll take the suite upstairs."

He felt a slight tremor course through her at his touch and without hesitation brought his mouth down to replace his thumb. Careful to keep the kiss non-threatening, Josh barely brushed her lips with his as he waited for an indication from Kiley that she wanted him to take the caress to the next level. When she slowly raised her arms to his shoulders and leaned into him, he felt a moment of triumph. She wanted more, but teasing her with a featherlight touch, he continued to wait. He wanted an indication of her eagerness for his kiss, wanted to know she was impatient for him to give her the kiss she deserved.

Nibbling at her perfect mouth, Josh sensed her increased frustration when a tiny moan escaped her slightly parted lips and she pressed herself closer. "Do you want me to kiss you, Kiley?"

"I...shouldn't," she said, sounding delightfully breathless.

He leaned back to look down at her. "But you do."

"Yes."

It was all he needed to hear, and lowering his head, he covered her mouth with his to give them both what they wanted. Soft and yielding, Kiley had the sweetest lips. Coaxing her to open for him, he deepened the kiss, sending a shaft of heat straight to the region south of his belt buckle.

When she sagged against him, Josh caught her to him. He had no idea why, but even with several inches' difference in their heights, no other woman had ever felt as perfect in his arms as Kiley did. Thinking about how flawlessly they fit together reminded him of that night three years ago and caused his body to harden with need so fast it left him feeling light-headed.

Pulling her more fully against him, he knew the moment Kiley felt his arousal pressed firmly to her. Her breathing quickened and instead of pulling away as he thought she might, she tightened her arms around his shoulders and seemed to melt into him.

The knowledge that she wanted him as much as he wanted her sent his blood pressure sky-high and he sensed that it wouldn't take much for either of them to throw caution to the wind and give in to the explosive chemistry between them. But that wasn't what Josh wanted. When they made love that night in her sister's apartment, their coming together had been frenzied and desperate. And they had both thought they were making love with someone else.

When they made love again—and there wasn't a doubt in his mind that was exactly what was going to eventually happen—he wanted them to take their time. He wanted them to explore each other thoroughly and completely until there was no doubt in either of their minds whom they were making love with.

Slowly easing away from the kiss, Josh took a deep breath. Looking down into her pretty brown eyes still glazed with desire, it was all he could do to keep from resuming the kiss and letting the chips fall where they may.

"J-Josh, I—"

"Shh, honey," he interrupted, kissing the tip of her nose. He released her to walk over to the love seat and pick up her daughter. "Let's get you and Emmie settled in my bedroom. Then I'm going to go upstairs and take a shower cold enough to freeze the balls off a pool table."

Six

The following afternoon, Kiley sat on the couch watching as Josh let Emmie help him put a seven-foot artificial tree together in the corner by the fireplace. It was taking twice as long as it should to assemble the tree because of his "helper." But he didn't seem to mind and patiently waited for her daughter to bring him each branch from the piles he had sorted by length earlier that morning.

Yawning, Kiley laid her head back against the back of the couch. She was completely exhausted and it wasn't hard to figure out why. The kiss they'd shared last night had made her feel as if she would go into total meltdown, and if that hadn't been enough to keep her eyes wide open the entire night, Josh's insistence that she and Emmie sleep in his room was.

The entire suite had that clean, masculine scent

she'd come to associate with him, but when she'd crawled under the covers of his king-size bed, she'd had the sense of being surrounded by him. That had triggered memories of the night he had accidently made love to her, and an accompanying restlessness stronger than anything she could have ever imagined kept her tossing and turning the rest of the night.

"Mommy, see," Emmie said, climbing up on the couch beside her.

Opening her eyes, Kiley smiled at her beautiful little girl. "What do you want me to see, sweetie?"

Emmie beamed as she pointed to the corner by the fireplace. "Twee."

"It's beautiful," Kiley said as she watched Josh plug in the multicolored lights. "You did a really good job helping put it together."

When the tree's branches seemed to instantly come alive with hundreds of twinkling stars, Emmie's eyes widened and she clapped her little hands. "Pwetty."

"It does look pretty good, doesn't it?" Josh grinned. "Would you like to put the angel on the top, Emmie?"

Nodding, Emmie scrambled down from the couch to hurry over to him. As they searched the boxes of ornaments for the tree topper, Kiley couldn't help but notice once again the similarities between them. She had already noticed they had the same eyes and nose, but she now realized that Emmie's hair was closer to Josh's light brown shade than her own dark blonde.

As she watched, Josh lifted Emmie to place the angel on the top of the tree. When they turned to get her opinion, Kiley sucked in a sharp breath. Even their smiles were the same.

She still intended to go through the motion of calling Mark to ask about his blood type, but there was no longer any doubt who had fathered her precious little girl. Emmie looked just like Josh. Confirming the fact was just a matter of formality.

"How does it look?" Josh asked.

"Other than being a bit crooked, it looks fine," she answered automatically.

Setting Emmie on her feet, he walked over to stand in front of her. "Are you feeling all right?"

"Y-yes. Why do you ask?"

"You just looked so—" he paused as if searching for the right word "—preoccupied."

Shaking her head, she forced a smile. "I'm just a little tired. That's all."

He stared at her for several long seconds before nodding. "I didn't sleep all that well myself." He smiled. "I couldn't seem to stop thinking about that kiss and—"

"I didn't say I wasn't able to sleep last night," she interrupted, reluctant to admit to him that she had suffered the same problem.

"You didn't have to, honey," he said, reaching out to tenderly caress her cheek with his calloused palm. "The dark circles under your eyes told me that much."

She wasn't sure she liked Josh's knowing that he had been the reason for her exhaustion. Thinking quickly, she grasped the first excuse that came to mind. "Children tend to be restless sleepers."

Josh stared at her a moment longer. "If you say so," he finally said, turning back toward the boxes of ornaments. She could tell he didn't believe her for a minute, but at least he hadn't pressed the issue.

By the time they finished decorating the tree, Emmie had started rubbing her eyes sleepily and

Kiley knew it was time for her daughter to take a nap. "Emmie, would you like for me to read one of your books to you?"

"Ponies," Emmie said, reaching into Kiley's tote bag.

While she read her daughter's favorite book, Kiley noticed that Josh collected the empty ornament boxes, then, setting one aside, took the others back out to the storage area of the garage. When he came back in, he sat down in the armchair next to the couch. Every time she glanced up, he was staring at her, and she wondered what was running through his mind.

"She's asleep," he finally said, getting up to walk over and lift her daughter from Kiley's lap. Carrying her over to the love seat, she watched him cover Emmie with a colorful Native American blanket. "Would you like a cup of coffee? I made a fresh pot while you were reading to the pony princess," he said, chuckling.

"A cup of coffee sounds wonderful." Maybe the caffeine would help chase away some of her fatigue. "How do you take yours?" she asked, rising to her feet.

"I'll get it." He grinned. "You cooked dinner yesterday evening and, unless a tropical heat wave sweeps through the area to melt all this ice off the roads, you'll probably be cooking again this evening and maybe tomorrow evening. The least I can do is bring you a cup of coffee."

Telling him how she liked her coffee, Kiley sat back down on the couch. For the past few years she had thought of him as a man who couldn't be trusted—an unfeeling jerk who had broken her sister's heart. And in the past several months, she'd come to think of him as the uncaring chairman of the TCC funding committee who, along with some of his fellow committee members, wanted nothing more than to see the day care center fail and her be out of a job.

But the more she got to know him, the more she had to admit that Josh was different than she had perceived him to be. Even before her sister finally confessed that their breakup hadn't gone quite the way she'd told everyone, Kiley had started to realize that he wasn't such a bad guy after all.

If he was as heartless as she'd first thought, he wouldn't have given her a month's worth of the extra money she had asked for and the chance to prove to him that it was needed for the day care center. Nor would he have been concerned for her and Emmie's safety and insisted on driving them to his ranch, rather than her trying to get them home on a treacherous, ice-glazed road.

"Here you go." Laughing, Josh handed her a steaming mug. "Coffee-flavored milk with a little sweetener."

She smiled. "I suppose you're one of the coffee purists?"

He nodded as he sat down beside her. "I like it black, and the stronger the better."

"Aside from the taste, if I drank it like that, I'd never go to sleep." She set her cup on a coaster on the end table. "I didn't even start drinking coffee until after I had Emmie. It was the only way I could stay awake during the day after staying up all night with a colicky baby."

"So when you told me that your ex-husband left

right after Emmie was born, you meant immediately after?" he asked, frowning.

"Mark moved out four days after she was born." Kiley shrugged. "Looking back on it, I'm just as glad that he did. Taking care of a baby was enough to keep me busy. I didn't need a demanding, immature male to deal with at the same time."

"What about your mom or your sister?" Josh asked, sounding genuinely interested. "Surely they helped out."

She nodded. "They were there for me as much as they could be. But they both had to work. Besides, Emmie was my baby to take care of."

He seemed to think over what she had just told him before he finally nodded. "I can understand your sense of responsibility, but it couldn't have been easy. What about some time for yourself?"

"If by that you're asking if I've seen anyone since she was born, the answer is no." She smiled lovingly at her little girl sleeping so peacefully on the love seat. "It might have been extremely difficult at times, but there isn't a single second of it that I regret. I don't need a social life—I have my daughter. Nothing is more important to me than being her mother."

Setting his coffee on the end table, Josh moved closer to her. "You're a great mom and Emmie is a great kid," he said, pulling her into his arms.

"Josh, what are you doing?" she asked, wishing her tone had been a bit more demanding.

"I'm trying to remind you that besides being a great mom, you're a beautiful, desirable woman." He brushed her mouth with his. "You want to know what I think?"

"Probably not," she said, wondering why she couldn't be more assertive. All he had to do was take her into his arms and she seemed to lose every ounce of common sense she'd ever possessed.

He rested his forehead against hers. "I think you need to hear that on a regular basis." Kissing his way down her cheek, she could feel his smile against her skin. "I know you'd rather not think about it, but I know firsthand just how passionate and desirable you are."

A shiver of awareness streaked up her spine and for the first time in years, she was keenly aware of how long it had been since she'd felt anything even close to passion and desire. "You're right," she said, meaning it. "I'd rather not think about that night."

"But it's something neither of us will ever forget, honey." He kissed his way down the side of her neck. "I know every time I look at you, it's just about all I'm able to think about," he admitted as he nibbled at the rapidly beating pulse at the base of her throat. "We might have made love by mistake, but I can't say I'm sorry about it."

"I—I…thought you…were Mark," she said defensively.

"And I thought you were Lori." He cupped her cheeks with his hands and lifted her gaze to meet his. "But that doesn't negate the fact that something happened between us that night that was nothing short of amazing."

As she stared into his remarkable blue eyes, Kiley knew what he said was true. She had never felt anything even close to the connection, the intimacy she had experienced with Josh. It was as if their souls had touched.

"You felt it, too," he stated. It wasn't a question, and she knew by the look on his handsome face that it would be futile to deny it.

Instead of waiting for her response, he lowered his head. The moment their lips met, Kiley felt as if stars burst behind her closed eyes and it seemed that time came to a halt. The awareness she felt whenever she was around him became a magnetic pull that she found impossible to resist, and she couldn't have kept herself from melting against him if her life depended on it.

When he traced her lips with his tongue, she automatically parted them on a soft sigh, inviting him to deepen the caress. As he tenderly stroked her inner recesses, Kiley marveled at how exciting and arousing it was each time he kissed her. Josh Gordon was an expert, and there wasn't a doubt in her mind that he could seduce a marble statue with nothing more than his talented mouth.

Sliding his hand from her back along her side, when he cupped her breast and teased the puckered tip with the pad of his thumb, Kiley thought she would be swamped by the seemingly endless waves of heat sweeping over her. The sensations were so exquisite, she felt branded by his gentle touch.

"Kiley...honey, there's something...going on between us," he said, sounding as out of breath as she felt. "It started that night in your sister's apartment... and it's just as strong now, if not stronger, than it was then." He gave her a kiss so tender it brought tears to her eyes. "All I'm asking is that you acknowledge that."

She couldn't deny that there was something drawing them together much like a bee was drawn to a field of wildflowers. But she wasn't altogether sure she was ready to admit it either.

"We do seem to share an awareness of sorts," she said, choosing her words carefully. She tried to be honest without revealing the full impact of his effect on her.

To her surprise, instead of arguing with her to try to get her to admit that it was more than a mild attraction between them, Josh kissed her soundly, then, releasing her, stood up. "That's all I needed to hear." He took her hand in his and, pulling her to her feet, handed her the box he had set aside earlier. "Could you do me a favor and decorate the mantel, while I take care of hanging a few lights around the front door?"

Relieved and much more comfortable with his shift of focus, she nodded. "After I finish, I'll start dinner."

"Sounds like a plan," he said, giving her a lingering kiss that caused her toes to curl into the plush carpet.

As she watched him turn and stroll down the hall toward the front door, she sighed. How could life become so complicated in such a short span of time?

Opening the box he'd handed her, she placed holly and pinecones along the top of the mantel. It had been so much easier to think of Josh as the heartbreaking Ebenezer Scrooge of the TCC funding committee. She almost wished that she still could. It would be a lot less stressful than the reality of the kind, thoughtful man that he had turned out to be.

On Wednesday afternoon, Josh stood in his family room, staring at the Christmas tree he and Emmie had put up the day before. When had his house become so damned big and empty? He had lived in the place for over five years and in all that time, he couldn't think of a single time that he had felt as alone as he did at that moment.

After the morning news reported that the roads were clear and that power had been restored to the subdivision where Kiley lived, they'd gone to the TCC clubhouse to get Kiley's car, then he'd come home to work. But he hadn't expected to find himself listening for Kiley as she moved around in the kitchen cooking or the sound of Emmie's delightful giggles as she played with her toy ponies.

"You're losing it, Gordon," he muttered as he walked down the hall to his office.

He liked being a bachelor—liked living alone. He could do what he wanted, when he wanted, and there wasn't anyone but himself to worry about. Besides, he had work to do and didn't have time for anything else.

An hour later, he uttered a heartfelt curse and turned off his computer. He had been working on the same bid sheet since he'd sat down and gotten absolutely nowhere with it. All he had been able to do was sit there wondering what Kiley and Emmie were doing.

Had the house been warm enough when they arrived home? Did she need him to check out the plumbing to make sure the water pipes hadn't frozen from the low temperatures and caused a leak? What were they planning to have for dinner? Did they miss having him around?

Rising from his desk chair, he walked out of his office and straight through the house to the door leading to the garage. He grabbed a jacket on the way through the mudroom and within minutes, Josh was driving down the highway toward Royal.

By the time he knocked on Kiley's door, he was confident his plans for the evening were set. He would see if she needed anything, then he fully intended to pick up takeout at his favorite Chinese restaurant, go back home and work on the bid sheet he needed to turn in for the new addition to the women's crisis center over in Somerset.

"Josh, I didn't expect to see you again until Monday afternoon," Kiley said, looking confused when she let him in. "Is something wrong?"

"No, I just wanted to check in and make sure you and Emmie made it home all right." He realized how lame his excuse sounded. Picking up the phone and giving her a call would have accomplished the same thing.

"Hi," Emmie said, grinning as she ran up to him and held up her arms.

"Hi," he said, picking her up. "How's the pony princess?"

She surprised him when she put her little arms around his neck to give him a big hug, then started jabbering excitedly. He looked to Kiley for a translation.

"Emmie thinks you're here for dinner and a movie," Kiley said, smiling. "She wants you to stay."

"And what does her mom want?" he asked, lightly running his index finger along her smooth cheek.

As she stared up at him, he felt her turn ever so slightly into his touch. It was almost imperceptible, but there was no denying it had happened.

"I was going to pick up Chinese on the way home,"

he said, trailing his finger over her lower lip. "Why don't we have it delivered here?"

"Okay," she said, suddenly taking her daughter from him and backing away. "I'll give Emmie a bath and get her ready for bed. That way she can go to sleep while we watch the movie."

He had a good idea why she had retreated. Unless he missed his guess, she was frightened by the strength of the chemistry between them. Hell, it was pretty unsettling for him as well. But he knew beyond a shadow of doubt that if they didn't explore it further, he would end up regretting it for the rest of his life. He had a feeling she would, too.

Two hours later, Josh couldn't help but smile as he sat on Kiley's couch, waiting for her to finish getting Emmie tucked in for the night. They had stuffed themselves on lo mein and egg rolls, then watched the movie about the little mermaid princess again. And if anyone had told him a week ago that he would be happy staying in, watching a kids' cartoon for the second time in less than a week, he would have told them they were in serious need of psychiatric evaluation.

It wasn't that he was a player or ever had been. But his idea of a good time had always been taking a woman to dinner, maybe a little dancing afterward, and seeing where the evening led them.

He suddenly sat up straight as the realization set in that he hadn't even asked Kiley out on a date. They had spent a week and a half seeing each other as often as he could arrange, shared some extremely passionate kisses and, even though it had been three years ago and due to a case of mistaken identity, they had made love. But he hadn't taken her out for a night on the town.

Deciding to remedy that oversight, he waited for her to walk back into her living room. "Kiley, come over here and sit down. I have something I need to ask you."

"What would that be?" she asked, looking as if she dreaded what he might want to know.

When she sank down on the cushion beside him, he put his arms around her. "I know this is short notice, but would you be my date for the TCC's Christmas Ball on Saturday night?"

"That's all?" she asked, visibly relaxing.

Nodding, Josh frowned. "What did you think I wanted to ask you?"

She stared at him for a moment before she finally shook her head and smiled. "I...wasn't sure."

Pulling her closer, he lowered his mouth to hers to nibble and nip at her lower lip. "As much as I enjoy spending time with Emmie watching the mermaid cartoon, I'd like to take her mother out for dinner and an evening of dancing."

He felt a shiver course through her. "Josh, I don't usually...go out."

"How long has it been since you went dancing?" he asked, kissing his way to the slight hollow at the base of her throat.

"I...uh...before Emmie was born," she said, sounding distracted.

"You're joking." He leaned back to look at her. "You haven't gone out since your divorce?"

"No."

"Surely you've enjoyed an evening with some of your friends," he said, having a hard time believing that she hadn't at least had a girls' night out.

She shook her head. "All of my friends are married

and most of them have children. We're all too busy. Besides, going to clubs is expensive."

He pulled her back against his chest for a comforting hug. She had just confirmed his suspicion that she struggled to make ends meet, and he suddenly wanted to find her ex-husband and give him a lesson in facing up to his responsibilities that the man wouldn't soon forget.

"Having kids doesn't mean you can't get out and socialize." He kissed her forehead. "I'm not an expert by any means, but I think interaction with other adults would be a necessity after dealing with kids all the time."

"I didn't say I don't spend time with my friends," she said, defensively. "We sometimes get together on Saturday afternoons for shopping trips to the mall. And tomorrow I'm going to lunch with Piper Kindred."

"I think that's great, honey." He cupped her cheek with his palm and, staring into her warm brown eyes, he smiled. "But I want to take you out on a date. I want to hold you in my arms when we dance and remind you of what a beautiful, desirable woman you are."

"I'd have to find a dress and arrange for someone to watch Emmie," she said, her tone uncertain. "And I'm not sure that it isn't frowned on for employees of the Texas Cattleman's Club to attend special events like the Christmas Ball."

Frowning, Josh shook his head. "Let's clear up something right now. Members of the TCC might be affluent, but we aren't snobs. I can't think of anyone who would have a problem with you being my date for the evening."

"Not even Beau Hacket or Paul Windsor?" she

asked, arching one perfect eyebrow. "I'm sure one of them would have something to say."

"Beau Hacket will be too busy bragging about his son Hack's latest accomplishments to think of anything else. And the biggest issue with Paul Windsor would be him trying to put the moves on you." Grinning, he shook his head. "That's an opportunity I don't intend to give Windsor or anyone else."

"I don't know, Josh. It's been so long since—"

"Just say yes, Kiley."

"I probably wouldn't be able to get a sitter on such short notice," she hedged.

He pulled his cell phone from his shirt pocket and handed it to her. "Call your parents and see if they can keep Emmie for the night."

"Why?"

"It's going to be late by the time we leave the ball, then we would have to drive the fifty miles up to Midland and back to get her," he answered. "I just figured you might not want to disturb her sleep."

Kiley stared at him for several seconds before she nodded and handed his phone back to him. "I'll use the phone in my office."

While she went to make the call to ask her parents about keeping Emmie Saturday evening, Josh thought of something else he needed to do. Kiley had mentioned she would need to find a dress for the ball, and he could imagine just what a dent the price of an evening gown would make in her budget. If she'd let him, he would like nothing more than to make things easier for her by giving her one of his credit cards to use. But if there was one thing he had learned in the past week and a half, it was how fiercely independent she was. She would no doubt tell him where he could put his card, as well as tell him to find someone else to go to the ball with him.

Deciding that he could use a little assistance with his idea, he made a mental note to call Piper Kindred first thing tomorrow. He had heard that she and Kiley had become friends when Piper taught a CPR class at the TCC clubhouse, and he had known Piper for years. He knew he could count on her to help him out.

"What did they say?" he asked when Kiley walked back into the living room.

"They're thrilled that I'm going to the ball," she said, frowning as she sat back down on the couch beside him. "My mother even told me it's past time that I started dating again."

"Your mom sounds like a wise woman," he said, pulling Kiley to him. He was a bit surprised that her mother approved of Kiley going to the ball with him, considering the story Lori had planned on telling them after they broke up. Either Kiley's mother had forgotten who he was or, at some point in the past three years, Lori had come clean and told them the truth about how their brief relationship had ended.

Deciding it didn't matter, he gave Kiley a kiss that sent his blood pressure sky-high and caused his jeans to feel as if they were a few sizes too small. "I'm sure she just wants you to be happy."

"I know, but I'm so…out of practice at the whole dating thing," she said, shrugging one slender shoulder.

"The ball may be our first date, but it's not like we haven't spent a lot of time together in the past couple of weeks," he said, kissing her temple. "And let me assure you that I plan on spending a lot more with you in the future."

"Josh, I have Emmie…to think about." She melted against him. "I have to think of what's best for her."

He knew Kiley's reluctance stemmed from her concern that Emmie might become too attached to him and end up being hurt, not to mention the possibility of being rejected herself. The way that bastard of an ex-husband had walked out on her and Emmie, it was no wonder she was afraid of taking a chance on another relationship.

His heart came to a screeching halt and he had to take a deep breath. What the hell was he thinking? He wasn't looking for anything long-term, was he?

It was true that he had been relentless in getting close to Kiley because he wanted her to admit there was an overwhelming chemistry between them. And she had done that. But beyond that, he hadn't given it much thought. Did he want to try exploring something exclusive with her?

He wasn't sure. But he was certain of one thing. Just the thought of anyone, himself included, causing her or Emmie any kind of distress was more than he could tolerate. Nor could he stand the thought of Kiley in the arms of another man.

"Honey, I give you my word that I will gladly walk through hell and back before I hurt you or Emmie in any way," he assured her.

Needing to make sure she understood that he meant every word he said, Josh lowered his mouth to hers. For reasons he didn't care to analyze too closely, all he wanted to do was make Kiley happy, to show her how special she was to him and to make things easier for her and her delightful little girl.

When Kiley placed her hand over his heart, the warmth of her palm and the feel of her caressing his chest through the fabric of his chambray shirt set off little electric charges throughout his being. Heat rushed through his veins and his body hardened with an urgency that left him feeling light-headed.

At that moment, nothing would have pleased him more than to remove both of their clothes and make love to her right there on her couch. But Kiley wasn't ready and he didn't care how many cold showers he had to endure, he wasn't going to rush her. When they made love again, it would be because it was what they both wanted, what they could no longer resist.

"I think I'd better leave," he said, breaking the kiss.

As he gazed down at her, he came close to losing his resolve. The passion and desire in her luminous brown eyes was breathtaking and he knew as surely as he knew his own name, they would be making love soon.

"If you and Emmie need anything, don't hesitate to let me know," he said, standing up. He took her hand to help her to her feet, then led her over to the door. Brushing her perfect lips with his, he smiled. "I'll see you when I drop by the day care center on Friday afternoon, Kiley."

Seven

The following day, when Kiley parked her car outside the Royal Diner, she checked the time on her cell phone. She was running a little late and she hoped that Piper had already found them a booth.

"Over here, Kiley," Piper called to her.

Spotting her friend, Kiley smiled and made her way toward the back of the newly renovated diner. A paramedic working out of Royal Memorial Hospital, Piper had been the instructor for the first-aid and CPR classes Kiley had arranged for the TCC employees. She had wanted to make sure that in case of an emergency with the children at the day care center, everyone knew exactly what to do and how to administer aid if it was needed.

"Sorry I'm late," she said, sliding into the booth on the opposite side of the table from her friend. "I had to wait for one of my volunteers to arrive to help Carrie with the children's afternoon activities."

Piper shook her head. "Don't worry about it. I just got here myself."

"So what's up?" Kiley asked, picking up the plastic-covered menu. "When you called the other day you sounded a little panicked."

"I need your help," Piper said, looking a bit uncomfortable. "I know I've probably put it off way too long, but I need a dress for the Christmas Ball and we both know I'm a lot more comfortable in jeans and a flannel shirt than I am in an evening gown." She grinned. "I was hoping you'd go with me this afternoon to help pick it out."

"Of course I'll go with you," Kiley answered, relieved that nothing was seriously wrong. "In fact, I was going to look for a dress for the ball myself this afternoon. Josh Gordon asked me to be his date."

Piper grinned. "Keep your friends close and your enemies closer?"

Kiley grinned sheepishly. "Something like that."

"I knew there had to be something going on between the two of you," Piper said, nodding. "Your reaction to him a few weeks back was just a little too strong for there not to be."

"Well, at that time I thought he was about as trustworthy as a snake," she said, laughing. "But I've recently discovered that he isn't all that bad." Even her parents had revised their opinion of Josh and didn't seem to question her decision to start seeing him after her sister confessed her role in their breakup three years ago.

"Josh is a really nice guy," Piper agreed. "In fact,

most of the members of the TCC are basically good guys. Some of them might have a few rough edges, but they really do try to live by the TCC code."

As they continued to chat about who they thought would be attending the ball and the type of dresses they wanted to look for, Kiley noticed a woman with dark brown hair sitting at a table close by. She had finished her lunch, but seemed to be taking great interest in what they had to say. So much so that Kiley could tell she was delaying her departure. Only when the conversation turned to the shopping trip they were planning to find dresses for the event did the woman get up to go pay her bill and leave.

"Did you notice that woman eavesdropping?" Piper asked as they watched her walk up to the counter to pay for her meal.

Kiley nodded. "I wonder who she is."

"I don't know, but I intend to find out," Piper said, motioning for Amanda Battle, the manager of the diner, to come over to their booth.

"How can I help you two?" Amanda asked, smiling.

"Who was that woman sitting at the table next to us?" Piper asked, cutting right to the heart of the matter.

Amanda glanced toward the front of the diner where the woman was just leaving. "That was Britt Collins, the detective in charge of investigating Alex Santiago's kidnapping."

"That explains why she was so interested when we started talking about the TCC," Kiley commented.

Suddenly distracted by the tall, dark-haired man entering the diner, Kiley placed her napkin on the table. She had tried to phone her ex-husband the day before to inquire about his blood type, but he hadn't returned her call. She wasn't going to let him get away without answering her question now.

"If you two will excuse me, I see someone I need to talk to," she said. "I'll be right back."

Walking over to his table, Kiley wasn't surprised when he looked around as if trying to find a way to escape.

"What do you want?" he asked, clearly unhappy about seeing her again. "I figured when I didn't call you back yesterday that you'd get the idea that I don't want to have anything to do with you or the brat."

"You couldn't possibly want to avoid having to talk to me as much as I want to avoid talking to you," Kiley said, wondering what she'd ever seen in the man. "I only called yesterday because I need to know your blood type."

"What do you need that for?" he demanded as if she'd asked him to reveal some deep, dark secret.

"It's for Emmie's medical records," she said, thinking quickly.

"Is that it?" he asked, looking suspicious.

"That's it," she assured him. When he told her his blood type, she nodded. "Thank you."

Without another word, she turned to walk back to the booth where Piper still sat talking to Amanda. Kiley had known in her heart that her suspicions were well-founded, but to have them confirmed was almost more than she could come to terms with.

She had done enough research on blood types and establishing paternity by that method to know that for the past three years the man she had thought to be Emmie's father, wasn't. Now all she had to do was

find the right time and way to tell Josh Gordon that
the little girl he fondly called the "pony princess" was
his daughter.

Driving across Royal, Josh went through four traffic lights on yellow and, looking both ways, rolled
through two stop signs as he sped toward Kiley's.
When she'd called, she wouldn't tell him what was
wrong, only that it was urgent that she see him right
away.

When he finally pulled into her driveway, he barely
had the engine turned off before he was out of the car
and sprinting his way up to her door. Not bothering to
knock before he entered the house, he stopped short
when he spotted Kiley sitting in the armchair beside
the couch, glaring at him.

"Are you and Emmie all right?"

"We're just fine," she answered. "But you're not."

A strong sense of relief washed over him. She was
upset, but otherwise, she and Emmie were okay. "So
what's wrong?"

"You know what's wrong," she accused, her brown
eyes sparkling with anger. "How dare you?"

"How dare I what?" He feigned ignorance, but he
had a good idea why she was in a snit.

"You used my friendship with Piper to steer me to
the dress shop where you had made arrangements to
pay for my dress," she accused.

He glanced at the garment bag from one of Royal's
exclusive boutiques draped over the back of the couch.
He'd figured she wouldn't be overly happy with him,
but he hadn't counted on her being downright furi-

ous that he had arranged to buy the dress she would be wearing to the Christmas Ball.

Slowly closing the door, he looked around as he walked farther into the living room. "Have you already got Emmie in bed for the night?"

"Yes. Why?"

He nodded. "That's good. I'd hate for her to have to listen to us argue. It might upset her."

"There isn't going to be an argument," Kiley insisted. "You're going to take your dress and leave."

"Sorry, honey, you're going to have to keep it," he said, grinning. "It isn't my size." He knew immediately that a flippant remark was the wrong thing to say.

Her eyes narrowed and her cheeks turned crimson as her obvious anger rose. "You bought it. You can keep it, take it back or stick it where the sun never shines." She shook her head. "It really doesn't matter to me. Just take it and go."

"Now, honey—"

"Don't you 'now, honey' me, Josh Gordon." She stood up and came to stand in front of him. "Let's get something straight right now," she said, poking him in the chest with her index finger. "I'm not a charity case. I pay my own way."

After her reaction to his glib comment, he knew better than to grin. But damn she was cute when she was all fired up about something.

"I understand that you want to be independent and I respect that, Kiley," he said, reaching out to put his arms around her. When she tried to push herself free, he tightened his arms and pulled her more fully against him. "But I also know an evening gown wasn't something you planned to buy." He brought his hand up to lift her chin until their gazes met. "I asked you to go with me to the ball because I wanted you to have a good time, not to wreck your budget."

"I could have charged it," she insisted.

"I know that," he said, nodding. "But the point I'm trying to make is this—when I take a woman out for the evening, I want her to relax and enjoy herself. I don't want her having to worry about how she's going to pay for the dress she's wearing."

Before she could argue with him further, Josh lowered his mouth to hers. Unyielding at first, he moved his lips over hers until she melted against him. Then, using his tongue, he sought entry to lightly stroke and tease her inner recesses. No other woman had ever tasted sweeter and he knew without question that if he wasn't already, he could quickly become addicted to kissing her.

Bringing his hand up under the hem of her sweatshirt, he released the front clasp of her bra to cup her breast with his palm. Caressing the soft, full mound, he grazed the beaded tip with the pad of his thumb, causing a tiny moan to escape her parted lips. His body responded instantly and he didn't think twice about pressing himself to her. He wanted her to feel what she did to him, how she made him want her.

As he eased away from the kiss, he stared down into her passion-glazed brown eyes. "I'm still angry with you," she said stubbornly.

"I know, honey." Nodding, he removed his hand from her shirt. "But please believe me when I tell you it was never my intention to upset you. All I wanted to do was make it easier on you." He kissed her until they both gasped for breath. "Now, I'm going to go back home because if I don't, I'm going to take you into the bedroom and spend the rest of the night making love to you."

She worried her lower lip for a moment before she spoke. "Josh, we need to talk."

"Is it something that can wait?" he asked, knowing that if he didn't put distance between them, and damned quick, he wouldn't have the strength to leave.

"I suppose so," she said, nodding.

"Good." He pressed his lips to hers for a quick kiss, then, setting her away from him, walked to the door. "Because right now, I have to get back to my place. I have an ice-cold shower waiting on me and a sleepless night ahead." He laughed in an attempt to release some of the tension gripping him. "I think it's about time for me to get started on it."

As Kiley watched Josh close the door behind him, she caught her lower lip between her teeth. She had started to tell him that Emmie was his daughter. But when he stopped her, she had readily gone along with putting off the inevitable for just a bit longer. She couldn't decide if she was being a coward for not insisting that he listen to her, or just being cautious.

For one thing, she wasn't quite sure how to start the conversation, nor was she looking forward to his reaction to the news. There was no doubt he would be shocked. But there was also the possibility that he would think she was trying to use her daughter to sway his recommendation to the funding committee. He knew how important her job was to her and how much it meant to be able to be with Emmie while she still made a living to support them.

Unfortunately, time was not on her side. The more

he was around Emmie the greater the chance he would realize she not only looked like him, the timeline for her birth supported that he had fathered her.

Kiley took a deep breath as she reached for the garment bag with her new evening gown and walked down the hall to hang it in her closet. The funding committee would be meeting next week and unless something happened to further complicate the matter or the perfect opportunity presented itself, she might do well to wait until the day care center's fate had been decided.

Then she had every intention of making him listen to her whether he wanted to hear what she had to say or not.

On Saturday evening when Kiley opened the door, her breath caught. Josh looked utterly devastating in his tailored black tuxedo. But it was the look of appreciation in his blue eyes that caused her heart to skip several beats.

"You look so beautiful, Kiley." He stepped just inside the door to take her in his arms and give her a soft, lingering kiss. "I'll be the envy of every man at the ball."

"I was just thinking something very similar about you and the women attending the ball," she said, smiling.

They hadn't seen each other since their argument over the evening gown. He had been busy working up bids for construction jobs, as well as overseeing several Gordon Construction job sites. But that wasn't to say that they hadn't had contact. He'd had flowers delivered to her at the day care center the day before, and he'd called her last night to ask about her day and see that she and Emmie were doing all right.

"Is the pony princess okay with staying at your folks'?" he asked, as he helped her with her evening wrap.

Nodding, Kiley picked up her sequined clutch. "I don't know who was more excited about her spending the night with them, Emmie or my parents. She has them wrapped around her little finger."

Josh laughed as he placed his hand to her elbow and guided her out to his car. "She has that effect on just about everyone. She's an adorable little girl."

"Thank you," Kiley said, hoping she had made the right decision to wait until after the funding commit-tee meeting to tell him that Emmie was his daughter.

Kiley jumped when Josh kissed her forehead. "I don't know what's running through that pretty head of yours," he said, helping her into the passenger seat of his Mercedes. "But frowning isn't allowed this eve-ning. Only smiles."

As he drove them to the TCC clubhouse for the club's biggest event of the year, Kiley decided he was right. Even if she hadn't made the decision to wait to tell him about Emmie, tonight wasn't a good time. When they talked, they would need privacy and plenty of time to sort everything out.

When Josh stopped the car at the front entrance, he handed his keys to a valet, then came around the front of the car and opened the passenger door for her. "This is beautiful, Josh," she said, looking around as she got out of the car.

The TCC's maintenance crew had strung white twinkle lights into an arched tunnel over the entrance for the ball's attendees to walk through. Complemented by big red velvet bows, the effect was magical.

"Haven't you attended one of these in the past?" he asked, tucking her hand into the crook of his arm as they started to walk through the tunnel of lights.

"No, I didn't move to Royal until I graduated from college and Mark wasn't a member of the club," she answered as she looked at all the pretty decorations.

"Wait until you see how they've decorated inside," he said, smiling as the doorman opened the big ornate oak entrance door for them. "The club spares no expense in making this *the* event of the year."

Inside the foyer gorgeous red and white poinsettias had replaced the usual flower arrangements on the hall tables, and big bows adorned the tops of every doorway. "This is absolutely beautiful," she said, taking it all in. "How long will they leave it this way?"

"They'll take everything down the day after New Year's," he said as they walked past several groups of couples greeting each other just outside the Grand Ballroom.

"I'm glad it will be like this the day of the children's Christmas program," she commented. "It will make everything so much more festive."

His smile sent a delicious warmth spreading throughout her body. "What day is the program?"

"This coming Tuesday."

"I'll make sure I'm free," he promised, kissing her temple.

"To check up on the use of the extra funds?" she asked.

"No." He stopped to gaze down at her from his much taller height. "I'll be there because Emmie is in the program and her beautiful mother will be directing it."

His low, intimate tone caused her knees to wobble and a delightful little flutter to stir in the pit of her stomach. But it was the spark of desire she detected in his intense gaze that stole her breath and sent a shiver of need streaking up her spine.

To distract herself from the sudden tension gripping her, she pointed toward a couple standing by the doors to the Grand Ballroom. "There's Piper and her fiancé, Ryan Grant." Concentrating on the emerald-green gown her friend had chosen the day they went shopping, Kiley walked over to hug her. "You look beautiful, Piper. The gown complements your red hair perfectly."

"Thank you." Piper smiled. "I was thinking the same thing about you. I know I told you the other day, but that black dress is gorgeous and looks like it was made just for you."

While Josh and Ryan talked about the new Western wear store Gordon Construction was building, Kiley smiled at Piper. "Are you feeling a little more confident?"

Piper grinned. "If by that you mean, do I still feel like a fish out of water in a dress, the answer is yes." She laughed. "But the look on Ryan's face when he saw me in it for the first time was well worth it."

Kiley knew what her friend meant. The look of appreciation in Josh's eyes had been absolutely breathtaking and she knew for certain it was one she would never forget.

As the conversation wound down, they walked into the ballroom and Kiley continued to marvel at the elaborate decorations. Dark green holly ringed gold-and-silver tapers that served as centerpieces on the round banquet tables, which were covered with pristine white tablecloths. But it was the fifteen-foot Douglas fir Christmas tree in one corner at the front of the room that caused her to catch her breath. It was huge, perfectly shaped and decorated with thousands of blue twinkle lights. A huge silver loopy bow served as a tree topper, its wide ribbon streamers cascading elegantly down over the branches. The effect was stunning.

Kiley enjoyed listening to the conversation at their table throughout dinner. They were seated with Piper and Ryan, Alex Santiago and his fiancée, Cara Windsor, and Josh's twin, Sam, and his wife, Lila. The brothers entertained them all with stories of how they had traded places in a variety of situations and the many pranks they pulled on their friends. And Ryan shared some humorous anecdotes about his days on the rodeo circuit. Alex seemed rather quiet throughout the evening, but that was understandable. He still suffered from amnesia and had no memory of his childhood or past events, but he did seem to enjoy listening to his friends tell about their antics.

Sitting beside her, Piper leaned close. "Are you enjoying yourself?"

"Absolutely," Kiley answered. "I love my daughter more than life itself, but I hadn't realized how much I missed social situations and adult conversation." Smiling, she asked, "How about you? Still feeling like a fish out of water?"

Piper laughed. "I've never been a 'girlie' girl by any

stretch of the imagination, but dressing up and pretending to be one isn't as bad as I thought it would be."

When Ryan claimed Piper's attention, Alex Santiago smiled at her from across the table. "I hear you are doing amazing things at the day care center."

"I'm not sure how amazing it is, but I love what I do," Kiley answered, smiling back. "The children's Christmas program is next week. We'd love to have you join us if you're feeling up to it."

"I think I would like that," Alex said, looking thoughtful.

As Alex turned to greet a fellow TCC member, Josh's twin brother, Sam, spoke up. "In a couple of years we'll be needing the services of the day care center for our twins."

"Even if I decide I'm not going to go back to work, I'll probably need the respite." Lila laughed. "Especially if they're anything like Sam."

When the band started playing, Kiley and Josh sat in companionable silence for a time as they listened to the music. But when the singer introduced a slow song, Josh smiled as he rose to his feet and held out his hand. "Would you like to dance, honey?"

"I haven't danced in so long, I've probably forgotten how," she answered, laughing as she placed her hand in his.

"It's just like riding a bicycle," he said, leading her out onto the dance floor. "Once you learn, you never forget."

As he took her in his arms and placed his hand at her back, Kiley's heart skipped a beat and her knees threatened to give way. The feel of his warm palm caressing the skin exposed by the low-cut back of her gown was intoxicating and caused a longing within her stronger than anything she could have ever imagined.

"We'll have to do this again sometime." He pulled her close to whisper in her ear. "Although I have recently discovered there's a lot to be said for staying in on Saturday nights."

His breath feathering over her ear and the heat from his hand on her back reminded her of just how long it had been since she'd been held by a man as they danced, how much she missed the closeness. She briefly wondered if anyone watched them, but everything around them seemed to fade into nothingness as she stared into Josh's heated gaze.

"Y-You really like eating in front of the television and watching cartoon movies?" she asked, hoping to distract herself from the heat swirling throughout her body.

Shrugging, he smiled. "Watching the show with the pony princess is a lot of fun. But it really starts to get interesting after she's gone to bed and I get to hold and kiss her enticing mother."

The evidence of his rapidly hardening body pressed to her stomach made her feel as if her insides had been turned to warm pudding and she found herself clinging to him for support. "Josh—"

"I'm not going to lie to you, Kiley," he said, his expression turning serious. "I want you and nothing would please me more than to take you home, get you out of this slinky black dress and sink myself so deep inside of you that we both forget where you end and I begin. But that isn't going to happen unless it's what you want, too."

Staring up into his smoldering blue eyes, her heart

began to beat double time and her breathing became shallow. Before they took such an important step, she really needed to tell him about being Emmie's father. "Josh, I…want you, too. But—"

Pressed tightly against her, she felt his body surge at her admission. "There's no 'buts' about it. Do you want me, Kiley?"

"Yes, but we need to talk about something first," she said, wondering why she couldn't sound more insistent.

"Honey, we can talk as much as you want later on," he said, leading her off the dance floor. They stopped by their table for her clutch and evening wrap and came face-to-face with Sam as they turned toward the exit.

"Hey, where are you two going? The night's still young," he said, his eyes twinkling mischievously.

"Can it, bro," Josh said, glaring at his twin.

Seemingly unaffected by his brother's displeasure, Sam turned to her. "It was very nice to meet you, Kiley. If this boneheaded brother of mine gives you any problems, you just let me know."

Kiley smiled and nodded. "I enjoyed meeting you and Lila, as well."

"You and Lila have a nice evening and I'll see you at work on Monday, Sam," Josh said over his shoulder as he hurried her toward the exit. Fortunately the other couples were out on the dance floor and they didn't have to explain their early departure to anyone else.

As they stood beneath the twinkling white lights as they waited for the valet to bring Josh's Mercedes to the front entrance, she felt compelled to try again to tell him about Emmie before things between them went any further. "Josh, please. It's really important that I talk to you about—"

He cut her off with a deep, lingering kiss, then, lightly running his finger along her jaw, he smiled. "I give you my word that we'll discuss whatever is on your mind tomorrow. But tonight is all about us, Kiley. This thing—this need—between us has been building since you walked into the meeting room to address the funding committee, and it's past time we explored it."

Her pulse raced as he helped her into the car, then drove away from the TCC clubhouse. There was no question that the chemistry between them was explosive, but was she ready to take what seemed like the next natural step with Josh? She still hadn't managed to tell him that he was Emmie's real father.

"We aren't going back to my house?" she asked when he steered the Mercedes toward his ranch.

The look he gave her sent heat sweeping throughout her entire body and she forgot anything else she was about to say. "You've slept in my bed without me," he said, his voice low and intimate. "But not tonight." Reaching across the car's console, he took her hand in his and raised it to his mouth to kiss. "Tonight I'm going to hold you and make love to you the way you were meant to be loved. And I'm not about to let anything interrupt that."

The promise in his words and the look on his handsome face caused her to shiver with anticipation, and by the time they reached his ranch, she knew she really didn't have any choice in the matter. Heaven help her, she wanted to once again experience the power of his lovemaking, needed to feel as cherished as when he'd made love to her that night three years ago.

Eight

When they reached his place, Josh led her directly into his bedroom, closed the door and turned on the bedside lamp. Taking her wrap and sequined clutch from her, he placed them on the dresser, then, turning back, he took her in his arms. Any second thoughts she might have had evaporated like the morning mist on a warm summer's day when he lowered his head to capture her lips with his.

His firm mouth moved over hers with an expertise that left her breathless, and she realized that no other man's kiss had ever caused her to react quite the way Josh's did. With sudden clarity, she knew no other man's kiss ever would.

Running his hands along her sides, he nibbled his way down the side of her neck to the base of her throat. "Honey, would you like to know what I've been thinking ever since you opened your door this evening and I saw you in this slinky black dress?"

"I—I'm not sure," she admitted. She shivered with anticipation when he brought his hand up and trailed his index finger along the V neckline of her gown.

"All I've been able to do is think of ways to take it off you," he whispered, kissing her collarbone and the valley between her breasts. "And when we were dancing I wasn't sure I wouldn't lose my mind."

"Wh-why?" She had to concentrate hard to keep from melting into a puddle at his feet.

"When I put my hand to your bare back I couldn't help but imagine how it would feel to caress every inch of your soft skin." There was such passion in his deep baritone, a wave of heat streaked from the top of her head to the soles of her feet.

Her knees threatened to give way and Kiley placed her hands on his chest to steady herself. "I'd like to touch you, too."

The look in his eyes stole her breath a moment before he stepped away from her to remove his tuxedo jacket and tug his shirt from the waistband of his trousers. He held her gaze with his, and neither of them said a word as he unfastened the stud closures, then shrugged out of the shirt and tossed it aside.

Her hand trembled as she reached out to run her fingers over his padded pectoral muscles and the taut ridges of his abdomen and stomach. The light sprinkling of hair covering his hard flesh tickled her palm and reminded her of the marvelous contrasts between a man and a woman.

When he shuddered from her light touch, she smiled. "Your body is perfect, Josh."

He brought his hands up to brush the stretchy fabric from her shoulders, then kissed the newly exposed skin. "Having you explore my chest feels wonderful, honey. But I want to touch you, too." As he pushed the evening gown down her arms, then over her hips into a shimmery black pool at her feet, Kiley's pulse raced at the look of appreciation in his smoldering blue eyes. When he discovered that she wasn't wearing a bra, his sharp intake of breath caused an interesting little flutter deep in the pit of her stomach. "You're beautiful, Kiley."

Cupping her breasts with his hands, he alternated kissing and teasing her beaded nipples, sending waves of heat sweeping over her. But when he took one of the tight buds into his mouth to explore her with his tongue, the sensations coursing through her were so intense, she felt as if she might faint.

"J-Josh... Oh, my."

"Does that feel good, Kiley?"

Unable to form a coherent thought, all she could do was nod.

"Do you want me to take off the rest of our clothes?" he asked, continuing to taunt the overly sensitive tip.

"Y-yes."

Dressed in nothing but her panties and high heels, she stepped out of the dress at her feet and braced her hands on his shoulders for him to remove her black velvet shoes. When he straightened, she watched him quickly kick off his own shoes, then unzip his tuxedo trousers to shove them and his boxer briefs down his legs. He tossed them and his socks onto the rapidly growing pile of their clothing. When he turned to face her, Kiley's breath lodged in her throat.

She'd been right. Josh's body was—in a word—perfect. His shoulders were impossibly wide, his muscles well-defined and his torso lean. But as her gaze traveled lower, her eyes widened. Josh wasn't just perfect, he was magnificent.

Fully aroused and looking at her as if she were the most desirable creature on earth, he stepped forward to hook his thumbs in the waistband of her lace panties. "I want to feel all of you against me," he said, his intimate tone sending another flash of heat flowing through her.

Once the scrap of silk and lace had been added to the pile of clothes, he took her back into his arms, and the feel of skin against skin caused her knees to give way. He caught her to him and Kiley thought she might go into complete meltdown. His firm, hair-roughened flesh pressed to her smooth feminine skin, the hard length of his erection nestled against her soft belly, set off tiny little sparks skipping over every nerve in her body.

"Honey, I think it would probably be a good idea if we get into bed while we both still have the strength to get there," he said, his warm breath feathering the hair at her temple.

He led her over to the bed and while she pulled back the navy satin duvet and got into bed, he reached into the drawer of the bedside table. Tucking a small foil packet under his pillow, he stretched out beside her and pulled her to him.

"I'm going to try to go slow, honey," he said, giving her a kiss so tender it brought tears to her eyes. "But I've wanted you again for so damned long, I'm not sure that's going to be possible."

"A couple of weeks isn't…all that long," she said, trying to catch her breath.

"I'm not referring to seeing you at the meeting of the funding committee," he said, skimming his hand down her side to her hip. Caressing her thigh, his movements were slow and steady. "I'm talking about how long it's been since we made love the first time. I haven't been able to forget that night three years ago. If I had known your name, I would have tried to find you. But I didn't think asking your sister was the right thing to do, especially since I started distancing myself from her after that night."

His impassioned words created a longing inside of her stronger than anything she had ever experienced before, and she knew that whether she had realized it or not, she had wanted him since that night, as well. But before she could tell him, he parted her to gently touch the tiny nub nestled within and she suddenly felt as if she would go up in flames. His light teasing strokes and the feel of him testing her readiness for him caused a coil of need to tighten deep in the most feminine part of her, and she couldn't stop herself from moving restlessly against him.

Wanting to touch him as he touched her, Kiley slowly slid her hand over his chest, then down his rippled abdomen and beyond. When she found him, her heart skipped several beats at the sheer strength of his need. His body went completely still and a groan rumbled up from deep in his chest as she measured his length and girth with her palm, then explored the softness below.

"Kiley…nothing would make me happier…than to have you touch me like this…for the rest of the night," he said haltingly. When he caught her hands in his, he sounded as if he couldn't take in enough air. "But I want you so damned much…I'm not going to last… if you keep that up."

The look in his eyes sent her temperature soaring, and her need for him grew with each passing second. If they didn't make love soon, she knew for certain she would be reduced to a cinder.

"P-please make love to me, Josh."

He reached under his pillow, quickly arranged their protection, then kissed her with a passion that caused her head to swim. Before she could fully recover, he held her gaze with his as he nudged her knees apart and rose over her.

"Show me where you want me, Kiley," he said, taking her hand in his to place it on his hardened body.

Her heart pounded as she guided him to her and she felt his blunt tip slowly begin to enter her. His gaze never wavered from hers as he eased himself forward and she knew she'd never felt more complete than she did at that moment.

"It feels so good to be inside of you," Josh whispered as he gathered her to him.

Before she could respond, he set a slow pace and Kiley felt as if she were being swept away by the exquisite sensations filling her entire being. Wrapping her arms around his wide shoulders, she held him to her as the coil of need deep within her tightened to the empty ache of unfulfilled desire. But all too soon, she found herself climbing toward the pinnacle, and apparently sensing that she was poised on the edge of finding the satisfaction they both sought, Josh quickened the pace of his lovemaking.

Heat and light flashed behind her tightly closed eyes as she was suddenly set free from the tension holding her captive. Waves of pleasure flowed over her and Kiley had to cling to Josh to keep from being consumed by the exquisite intensity of it all. He thrust into her one final time, then, groaning her name, he joined her in the all-encompassing pleasure of mutual release. As they slowly drifted back to reality it felt as if their souls had been united to become one, and she knew beyond a shadow of doubt that if she hadn't already done so, she was close to losing her heart to the man holding her so securely in his arms.

"You're amazing, honey," he said, kissing her until they both gasped for air.

"That was...breathtaking," she murmured, still trying to come to terms with her newfound realization.

Levering himself to her side, he pulled her close. "Are you all right?"

Deciding there would be plenty of time to analyze her feelings for him later, she kissed his chin. "'All right' doesn't begin to describe how incredible I feel right now, Josh."

She felt his body stir against her leg a moment before a wicked grin appeared on his handsome face. "That's good, because I'm going to spend the rest of the night reminding you of just how incredible we are together."

And to her utter delight, he did just that.

The following Monday afternoon, Kiley gathered some festive paper and a memory stick. "Carrie, will you and Lea be able to watch the children until I get back? I need to walk down to the administrative office to get the programs printed for the Christmas show tomorrow."

"Sure thing." Carrie nodded toward the children sleeping on colorful mats on the floor. "They should nap for another thirty minutes or so. Lea and I can just start story hour a little early if you aren't back when they wake up," she added, referring to the volunteer Kiley hoped to add as a paid staff member after the first of the year.

Nodding, Kiley headed for the door. "I shouldn't be too long."

As she walked down the hall, she couldn't stop thinking about her night with Josh. Never in all of her twenty-eight years had she experienced that level of passion or felt more cherished than she had in his arms. But as wonderful as her night with him had been, once he had taken her back to her place the following morning, reality had intruded as she remembered the unresolved issues between them.

She sighed. He had made it easy to forget that the funding committee would be meeting at the end of the week and she still had no indication if he would recommend additional funds for the day care or side with Beau Hacket and Paul Windsor in hopes of seeing the center close. And then there was the matter of finding the right words to tell him that he was Emmie's father.

If she told him now, how would he react? As fond as he seemed to be of Emmie, Kiley was almost positive he would accept and love her. But her main concern was that he might think she was trying to use her daughter to influence his recommendation to the funding committee. For that matter, it could cross his mind that she had made love with him for that same purpose.

She really didn't think he would consider her making love with him a ploy to keep her job. As if by unspoken agreement, neither of them mentioned the day care center's future when they were away from the TCC clubhouse. But she wasn't so sure he would take the news about Emmie being his child as well. That's why she had made the decision not to tell him until after the funding committee met. If she withheld the information, then there would be no question about her motives. And besides, it wasn't like a couple of days would make a difference. Josh was Emmie's biological father and there wasn't anything that would ever change that fact.

Lost in thought, she paid little attention to the group of teenage boys gathered in one of the alcoves she passed as she walked down the main hallway. At least, she didn't until she heard one of them mention her name.

"I'm telling you it's just a matter of time before that damned Roberts woman and her day care center full of rug rats are history," she heard one of the boys say.

Stopping just out of sight of the sitting area, she shamelessly listened to what the group had to say.

"What makes you think the day care center is going to close, Hack?" another boy asked. "From what I hear it's doing pretty good."

"Well, when it got torn up, my old man said whoever did it had done the club a big favor," Hack said, sounding smug. "He said he had enough influence on the funding committee to see that what the insurance didn't cover would be taken out of the center's budget and that it would run out of money by spring. He even told me he'd thank the vandal if he knew who he was." The boy laughed. "I told him he could just buy me a new truck and we'd call it even."

"You're full of it, Hack," one of the boys scoffed. "There's no way you're the vandal the police are looking for. And your dad wouldn't let you get away with doing something like that here at the TCC."

"Yeah, man, why would you say something like that?" another one asked.

"I know how to work the old fart. He thought I was joking with him." Laughing, the teenager added, "I wanted him in a good mood when I asked for my new ride."

"In other words, he got what he wanted, now you figure he owes you," the scoffer said slowly.

Kiley had heard enough. If what he boasted about was true, Beau Hacket's son had been responsible for the damage done to the day care center. But whether it turned out he was the vandal or not, his claim needed to be investigated.

The Christmas programs forgotten, Kiley walked straight to one of the house phones to have the switchboard operator page Josh. He had stopped by the day care center earlier on his way to lunch with Gil Addison and she hoped they were still in the restaurant or possibly in the bar.

"Josh Gordon here," he said, coming on the line a couple of minutes later.

"I know who vandalized the day care center," Kiley said, careful to keep her voice quiet.

"Kiley?"

"Yes. I just overheard someone bragging about it," she said, deciding not to say the culprit's name aloud for fear of alerting the boys that she had overheard their conversation.

"Where are you?" he asked.

"On the house phone in the main hallway," she answered, keeping an eye on the sitting area. The boys were still there. "Hurry, Josh. He's in a group of teenagers in the alcove across from the Grand Ballroom."

"Gil and I will be right there."

In no time, Josh and Gil came jogging down the hall toward her. "It's Beau Hacket's son," she whispered when they stopped beside her.

"Are you sure?" Josh asked.

She nodded. "The other boys called him Hack and he mentioned his father being on the funding committee."

"It really doesn't surprise me," Gil said, shaking his head. "Hack is a real smart-ass and there isn't a lot I would put past him."

Josh nodded. "And Beau has a blind spot when it comes to that kid. He never makes him face the consequences of his actions."

"Beau isn't going to have a choice this time," Gil said, pointing toward the two plainclothes detectives who had just entered the clubhouse.

"We phoned the police right after you called," Josh explained.

When the detectives joined them, Kiley relayed what she had heard. "They didn't realize I was eavesdropping," she finished.

"Do you know the boys' parents?" the older policeman asked. "They'll need to be called."

"From what he said, I think the Hacket boy acted alone," Kiley said, hoping the other boys weren't deemed guilty by association. They had sounded as appalled at the Hacket boy's claims as she had been.

"We need all of their parents present before we question them," the younger detective advised.

"Since the club has a policy of not allowing anyone underage on the premises without being accompanied by a parent, I'm pretty sure their dads are all here," Gil said, glancing into the alcove. He walked over to the house phone. "I'll have them paged."

While Gil called the switchboard, the police officers walked into the alcove and advised the boys that as soon as their parents arrived, they had some questions they wanted to ask them.

Putting his arm around her shoulders, Josh held Kiley to his side as they walked the short distance to the sitting area. "Are you doing okay, honey?"

"I'm fine," she said, nodding. "I'm just glad we found out who was behind the vandalism and why, even if it was a little disconcerting to hear him admit everything."

"I can't believe he did all that just to make points with his dad in hopes of getting the truck he wanted," Josh said, shaking his head. He grunted. "That kid needs a reality check."

"How do you think Beau will react when he finds out his son was behind all of the destruction?" she asked, checking her watch.

"Knowing Beau, he won't take the news well." Josh shrugged. "But it looks like we aren't going to have to wait to find out."

Looking up, Kiley watched Beau Hacket coming down the hall toward them like a charging bull. "What the hell's going on?" he demanded. If the scowl on his face was any indication, Josh was right about him not taking the news well.

"We know who was behind vandalizing the day care center," Josh answered.

"Who was it?" Beau asked, glancing into the sitting area. The blood drained from his face when he spotted his son among the four boys seated in the alcove. "This had better be some kind of joke."

As the detectives questioned the boys and sorted through the facts, they dismissed all of them but Hack. The teenager didn't look nearly as confident now as he had when the interrogation started.

"Who are you going to believe, Dad? Me or them?" Hack demanded, looking up at his father defiantly.

"Don't lie to me, son," Beau said firmly. "You know I'd never condone you breaking the law."

"I'm telling you, I didn't do it," the boy lied.

"We collected a partial fingerprint when we first investigated the vandalism," the younger policeman advised. "It's enough that once we take you down to the station and fingerprint you, we should be able to establish either your innocence or your guilt."

"I'm going to jail?" Hack asked, looking alarmed for the first time since the detectives arrived. "You're gonna get me out of this, aren't you, Dad? I did it for you," the boy said, unaware that he had just confessed.

"I don't know if I can, son." Beau looked from one detective to the other. "Is there any way to make this right without my boy having a criminal record?"

"It's up to the Texas Cattleman's Club if they want to press charges," the older detective advised. "But we're going to read him his rights and take him down to the station for further questioning. I would suggest you get in touch with your lawyer, Mr. Hacket. Your kid is facing charges of vandalism, criminal mischief and anything else we can think to charge him with." He gave Beau a pointed look. "Although this is the most serious, I don't have to tell you, this isn't the first time he's been in trouble."

Beau looked miserable when he turned to Josh and Gil. "What do you guys think? If I make full restitution for the damages do you think we can let this thing go?" he asked hopefully. "I give you my word I'll do whatever it takes to make this right."

"That's not up to us," Gil said, shaking his head. "This will have to be voted on by the executive board."

"While you all sort this out, we'll take Junior here down to the station." The younger police officer stepped behind Hack to put handcuffs around the teenager's wrists. "You have the right to remain silent...." The detectives led Hack toward the main exit as they continued to read him his rights.

"Can you call an emergency meeting of the board, Gil?" Beau asked, reaching for the cell phone clipped to his belt. Making a quick call to his lawyer, Beau turned back to Josh and Gil. "I can't tell you how much it would mean to me for Hack not to end up with a police record over this."

"Before this goes any further, I have a question for you, Beau," Josh said, folding his arms across his wide chest. "What are you going to do about your son? His complete lack of respect for people and property, as well as his self-discipline, are all but nonexistent. There's going to come a day when you can't pay his way out of the trouble he gets into."

Gil nodded. "I agree with Josh, Beau. I'll call an

emergency meeting for this evening, but if I recommend that the board let you do what you're proposing, we need an assurance from you that something like this won't happen again to us or anyone else in the community."

Surprisingly, instead of getting angry at Josh and Gil for pointing out that something needed to be done with his son, Beau nodded. "I give you my word that he won't be getting into any more trouble. I've threatened to send him to a military school in the past."

"You go on down to the police station with your son and we'll let you know what the board decides," Gil advised.

"There's one more thing that I want done," Josh said as Beau turned to leave.

"What's that?" the man asked, sounding as if he would agree to just about anything.

"When he vandalized the day care center, your son spray-painted a very derogatory word on the wall in reference to Ms. Roberts," Josh stated flatly. "I think an apology is in order. And it had better be sincere."

Beau nodded. "I can't tell you how sorry I am that this happened, Ms. Roberts. Believe me when I say I never intended for my objections to the day care center to cause my son to do something like this. I give you my word, I'll find a way to make this right."

"Apology accepted," Kiley said, suddenly uncomfortable at being the center of attention.

Beau nodded, then turned to Gil and Josh. "I'll be down at the police station. Could you let me know as soon as the board makes a decision?"

Gil nodded. "I'll call you one way or the other."

As they watched Beau hurry toward the exit, Josh

turned to Gil. "While you phone the executive board members, I'm going to walk Kiley back to the day care center," Josh said, putting his arm around her.

"Will you be there tonight for the meeting?" Gil asked as they walked out into the hallway.

Josh wasn't a member of the executive board, but unless it was a closed session, any member in good standing could attend. And since he had witnessed the police's questioning, Kiley wasn't sure he wouldn't be asked to give an account of what had taken place.

"I figure I'll throw my support behind Beau sending Hack off to military school," Josh said, nodding. "I think he could benefit from the discipline and structure of a military academy. It would probably be the best thing that ever happened to that kid."

"At this point, it sure won't hurt," Gil agreed. "And since his dad is one of our own, I'm pretty sure we can get the justice we want without leaving Hack with a criminal record." He smiled at Kiley. "I'll see you a little later this afternoon when I come to get Cade."

"Do you think the board will go along with what you and Gil have in mind?" Kiley asked when Gil left to go back to his office.

Josh nodded as they walked down the hall. "Every member of the TCC is sworn to live by its code— 'Leadership, Justice and Peace.' And we've got a long history of policing our own, as well as righting a lot of injustices for those outside of the club. This is something we can take care of ourselves."

"Hack will be taught a lesson without a criminal record and the club won't suffer further scandal," she guessed.

"That's it. He's seventeen and would have probably

been charged as an adult. This way he'll get the chance to clean up his act without the stigma of having been in trouble with the law." When they stopped at the day care center's door, he took her into his arms. "Thank you for catching him for us."

"I really didn't do anything but eavesdrop." She smiled. "But now that the mystery is solved, I'm glad I won't have to worry about coming in to work one morning and finding the place destroyed again."

He gave her a long, deep kiss. "Now that I have that meeting, I won't be able to see you until sometime tomorrow."

"Are you planning on attending the children's Christmas program tomorrow afternoon?" she asked, feeling the familiar flutter of desire begin deep in the pit of her belly.

"Of course." His deep chuckle caused the fluttering inside of her to go berserk. "I wouldn't think of missing the pony princess's singing debut."

Kiley's chest swelled with emotion. "She's going to be thrilled to see you there."

"I think Gil said the program is in the main ballroom?" he asked.

"Yes."

He nodded and gave her a quick kiss. "I'll call you this evening and let you know the outcome of the board's vote."

As she watched Josh walk away, Kiley caught her lower lip between her teeth to keep it from trembling. Any doubts she had about him accepting Emmie as his daughter had just been erased. Very few men would make sure they attended a toddler's Christmas program if they didn't care a great deal for the child. And once he learned he was Emmie's father, Kiley believed he would be the loving daddy that her daughter had always deserved.

But where did she fit into the equation?

Kiley knew that he liked kissing her and there was no doubt he desired her. But could he ever love her?

Her heart stalled and it suddenly became difficult to draw her next breath. She had known the night they made love that she was in danger of doing it, but had she actually fallen for him?

Knowing in her heart that was exactly what had happened, she slowly opened the door to the day care center. She wasn't comfortable with it and it certainly added another wrinkle to an already complicated situation. But there was no denying it, either.

Whether she liked it or not, she had fallen head over heels in love with Josh Gordon.

Nine

The next afternoon, Josh stopped his SUV at the TCC clubhouse entrance, got out and tossed the keys to one of the valets. He had just enough time to find himself a seat in the Grand Ballroom before the day care center's Christmas program started.

If anyone had told him a few weeks ago that he would be rushing to attend something put on by a bunch of little kids, he would have questioned their sanity. But now? He'd walk through hell if he had to in order to keep from disappointing one cute little girl and her beautiful mother.

He frowned as a woman standing by the door to the ballroom handed him a program with a brightly colored holiday design. When had Kiley and Emmie become so important to him? And how had it happened so quickly?

His mouth went as dry as a wad of cotton as he entered the ballroom and found himself a seat. Surely he hadn't fallen in love with Kiley. He knew he liked her a lot and the chemistry between them was nothing short of amazing. But love?

Giving himself a mental shake, he almost laughed out loud at his own foolishness. He had to be losing it. There wasn't any question that he was in lust with the woman. But that didn't mean he was in love with her.

And he could even understand his feelings for Emmie. She was a cute, friendly little girl and it would take a heartless bastard not to find her completely adorable.

He sat down next to an older couple close to the front of the portable stage that had been set up next to the Christmas tree. Seeing the decorated tree, he couldn't help but think about dancing with Kiley the night of the ball. That one dance had been all it took for them to decide to leave the gala and go back to his place for the most incredible night he'd spent in the past three years.

"We're here to see our grandson," the woman said, smiling. "And you?"

Before he could tell the beaming grandmother he was a friend of the day care center's director and her little girl, Christmas music filled the room and the kids began to take their places on the stage. When he spotted Emmie in her red velvet dress, pigtails bobbing as she skipped along, he couldn't stop grinning. She had to be the cutest kid ever.

As the program began, there were several times Josh found himself laughing out loud. Kiley and her helpers had to lead wandering kids back to their places, hand giant plastic candy canes back to the little ones who dropped theirs and take a giant bell away from one of the preschool boys when he used it to bop one of the little girls on the head. Josh enjoyed the program immensely and he was certain the rest of the crowd had, too.

When the kids sang the last song, Kiley thanked everyone for attending, told the parents that the day care was dismissed for the rest of the afternoon and then motioned for Josh to come up to the stage. "Would you mind watching Emmie for a moment while I get everything cleared up here?" she asked.

"No problem," he said, picking up the toddler. "We'll be over by the tree."

As he carried her over to look at the decorative ornaments on the tree, he marveled at the fact that he was actually watching after a kid and didn't mind it at all. "Did you see this ornament, Emmie?" he asked, pointing to Santa's sleigh with eight tiny reindeer hanging from one of the branches.

"Ponies," Emmie said, her little face beaming as she pointed at it.

Tickling her tummy, he laughed. "You've got a one-track mind, princess."

"Your daughter is very cute," the woman who had sat next to him throughout the program said as she and her husband walked over with their grandson in tow. "She looks just like you." Josh smiled and started to correct her, but the woman didn't give him the chance. "Do you have a cell phone?" she asked.

"Yes, do you need to use it?" He unclipped his phone from his belt and handed it to her.

"I'll use the camera on your phone to take your

picture with her here by the tree, if you'll return the favor and take one of us with our grandson," she said, pulling a digital camera from her purse.

"Sure," Josh agreed. He wouldn't mind having a picture of himself and Emmie, and if the woman wanted to think they looked alike, what would it hurt?

After the pictures had been taken and the couple moved on, he checked the gallery on his phone to see how the photo had turned out. He smiled at the image. Perched in the crook of his arm, Emmie had her hand resting on his cheek and the sweetest grin he had ever seen on her cute little face.

But his smile suddenly faded as he looked at his image and then Emmie's. He normally didn't pay any attention to who resembled who. He had a mirror image of himself in his twin brother, Sam, and didn't figure he looked like anyone else. Staring at the picture suddenly had him changing his mind.

He had never before seen himself and Emmie together—not in a mirror or a picture. And since he hadn't been looking for any similarities between the two of them, he hadn't given it so much as a fleeting thought. But there was no denying that Emmie looked a lot like him. He could see glimpses of Kiley in Emmie's big brown eyes and the delicate shape of her face, but the child had his nose and smile. And their hair color was almost exactly the same shade.

"Did you enjoy the program?" Kiley asked, walking up to them.

Looking up, he clipped the phone back on his belt as he nodded. "Are you finished for the day?"

"Yes. The children have all been turned over to their parents and the props have been stored in my office," she said as she took Emmie from him to set her on her feet. Helping the little girl into her coat, she zipped it up. "Would you like to come over and help us bake and decorate sugar cookies for the rest of the afternoon?"

Suddenly needing to put space between them, Josh shook his head. "I'll have to take a rain check on that. I need to get back to one of the job sites," he lied. What he needed was time to think.

"We'll save some for you," she said, oblivious to the turmoil beginning to roil through him.

He nodded. "I'll see you tomorrow."

"At the meeting of the funding committee?" she asked.

"Yeah." He kissed Kiley's cheek and the top of Emmie's head, then started toward the exit to the ballroom.

As he walked out of the clubhouse and got into his SUV, he sat there for several long minutes staring blindly at the steering wheel. He knew Kiley had expected him to at least drop by that evening after he finished with his duties at Gordon Construction. But he needed time to think, time to do some calculating and then decide what he was going to do.

Beyond learning how to protect himself and his partner when they made love, he hadn't paid much attention in sex education class. Hell, he couldn't think of a teenage boy who did. They all had more hormones than good sense and were too busy hoping to get lucky with one of the cheerleaders to give things like the gestation of a woman's pregnancy a lot of thought. But it didn't take a Rhodes scholar to figure out that there was more than just a possibility, there was a very real probability, that the cute little girl he called the pony princess was his daughter.

Standing in the hall outside of the meeting room, Kiley dried her sweaty palms on her khaki slacks as she tried to think of what she could say this time to convince the members to approve the increase in the day care center's budget that she hadn't gone over the last time they'd met. Of course, when Josh gave her the money to cover one month of the extra funds she'd asked for, he had promised that if he saw a need for the TCC day care center, he would personally recommend that the committee approve her request. But he hadn't mentioned making a decision and she hadn't asked.

"Ms. Roberts, the committee is ready to see you now." When she looked up, one of the members was holding the door for her to enter the meeting room.

As she walked up to the conference table, Josh was busy entering notes into his electronic tablet and barely raised his head to acknowledge her presence. A sinking feeling began to settle in the pit of her stomach.

"Ms. Roberts, have your needs for the day care center changed since our last meeting with you?" he asked, finally looking at her.

Confused by his all-business tone and cool demeanor, she shook her head. "No, I still need the extra money to supplement what the committee has already appropriated for the center."

Why was he acting so indifferent to the situation? He had stopped by the center enough times to know what the funds would be used for and that if she didn't get them the TCC day care center would have to close by spring.

He gave her a short nod. "I'm going to excuse myself from the discussion and vote because of our relationship, but I'll come down to the day care center after the meeting is over to let you know the outcome."

Effectively dismissed, there was nothing left for her to do but go back to the center and wait for Josh to explain himself. But as she walked back to the center she felt her cheeks heat as her anger rose.

She could understand that he had no choice but to excuse himself from the issue because of a conflict of interest. But surely he could have given his report on what he had observed of the day-to-day running of the center. And why was he acting so aloof? Was it his way of telling her that she had little or no chance for additional funding? If that was the case, the day care center would be closing down shortly after the first of the year.

"Merry Christmas, Kiley," she muttered sarcastically.

As soon as the holidays were over, she would have to start looking for another job. She had no doubt she could find something at another day care center, but she would have to accept whatever position they had open and she could only hope that it paid well enough for her to make ends meet for herself and Emmie.

By the time Josh opened the door and entered the day care center an hour later, Kiley wasn't certain she wanted to hear the official outcome of the vote. At least not until after the holidays were over.

"Let's go into your office," he suggested.

Nodding, she led the way to the former storage room that served as her office. When he closed the door behind them, she shook her head. "You don't have to tell me the outcome of the funding committee's vote," she said, sitting in the hard wooden desk chair. "I knew when I was summarily dismissed what the outcome would be." She took a deep breath in an effort to calm herself. "What I'd like to know is what these past few weeks have been about, since you clearly never intended to recommend additional funding for the day care center."

"The issue was tabled until a later date. But before we get into that, I have a couple of questions for you." His eyes narrowed. "Are you aware that I'm Emmie's father?"

Thrown off guard by his unexpected question, she slowly nodded. "Y-yes."

"Is that why your ex-husband refused to have anything to do with her? Did he know or suspect that she wasn't his child?" he demanded.

"No. As far as Mark is concerned, he still thinks he fathered her." Anticipating his next question, she met his angry gaze head-on. "And before you ask, I didn't realize it was even a possibility until you came by my house that first night with the pizza. That's when I noticed that Emmie looks a lot like you."

He rose to his feet to pace the small area in front of her desk. "Why didn't you tell me as soon as you suspected it was a possibility?"

"I wanted to confirm my suspicions before I talked to you about it," she defended herself.

His eyes narrowed. "And you've done that?"

She stood up to face him. "Yes."

"When?"

"The day I went to lunch with Piper, I saw my ex-husband in the Royal Diner and asked him about his blood type." She shook her head. "I had done enough research on the internet to know immediately that there was no way Mark could be her biological father."

Josh stopped pacing to glare at her. "That was a week ago, Kiley. What were you waiting on? Didn't you think I had the right to know I have a daughter?"

"Oh, no, you don't, buster," she fumed, walking up to stand toe to toe with him. "You're not going to make me feel guilty about not telling you right away that Emmie is your child. Not when I was doing every-thing I knew how to do to keep from making you think I was trying to use her to influence your recommenda-tion to the funding committee." She poked him in the chest with her finger. "But I shouldn't have bothered because you never intended to give the day care cen-ter a fair chance anyway, did you?" She turned away, then whirled back to add, "And just for the record, I intended to tell you as soon as the funding committee made a final decision and settled the day care center's fate once and for all. That way I couldn't be accused of something I wasn't guilty of."

"Let's leave the day care center out of this for the moment," he hissed. "I want to finish talking about my daughter."

"Our daughter," Kiley corrected. "And there's re-ally nothing to discuss. I won't try to stop you from being part of Emmie's life, if that's what you want. But I have two conditions before I'll agree to anything."

His expression was dark and guarded. "What kind of conditions?"

"I don't want your money to help support her. I'm perfectly capable of providing for my child."

"Our child," he reminded. "And let me make one

thing perfectly clear right now. It will be a cold day in hell before you tell me what I will or won't do to see that she's taken care of."

Kiley counted to ten as she tried to keep tears from welling in her eyes. How could she love him so much when she was so darned angry with him? So disillusioned?

"We can cover that another time," she finally managed to get out around the lump clogging her throat. "The most important stipulation I have is that you love her. Emmie deserves that and if you can't be the daddy she needs, I'd rather you not try to have a relationship with her at all."

A muscle worked furiously along his jaw. "I can't believe you think I would do otherwise." Staring hard at her for what seemed like an eternity, he finally turned and opened the door to her office. "We'll talk about this later when we're both thinking more clearly."

Through the office window looking out into the day care center, Kiley watched Josh march across the room and leave before she walked back around her desk on shaky legs. Sinking into her chair, she buried her face in her hands. Even before her sister had admitted that Josh wasn't the snake she'd led their family to believe, Kiley's instincts had told her that he wasn't a bad guy. Had she been wrong about him? Was she destined to be like her sister and see traits in a man that simply weren't there? Why hadn't he been able to see that she had handled the situation the best way she knew how?

A sudden thought had her sitting up straight in the chair. Could Josh have gotten the issue of the day care center tabled as a way of retaliation? Was he getting even with her for not telling him when she first suspected that he was Emmie's father?

She wasn't sure. But a day care center full of children wasn't the place to have an emotional meltdown. There would be plenty of time for that when she got home and let go of the tight grip she held on her emotions.

Feeling as if her heart had been shattered into a million pieces, Kiley did her best to pull herself together. Fate may have set her and Josh on a path three years ago with the conception of Emmie that would entwine their lives forever, but that didn't mean she was going to let it break her. She was a survivor. She had made it through the inevitable end of her disastrous marriage and the emotional pain of seeing her child rejected by the man she'd thought until recently was Emmie's father. She could certainly weather having her heart broken by Josh Gordon's deceit and betrayal.

She straightened her shoulders, stood up and with a smile firmly in place, walked out into the day care. She might be suffering from a broken heart that she was certain could never be mended, as well as facing the probability of losing her dream job in a few months, but until then, she had parents and children who were counting on her. And she wasn't going to let them down.

Sitting in his darkened family room, Josh took a swig from the half-empty beer bottle in his hand as he stared at the Christmas tree he and his daughter had put up during the ice storm. His daughter. He tightly closed his eyes as a wave of emotion surged through him. Dear God, he had a child.

The mere thought had him running his hand over his face in an attempt to wipe away the tangled feelings that had threatened to swamp him since discovering Emmie was his daughter. He had been crazy about the kid before. But now that he knew she belonged to him—that she was his own flesh and blood—it caused a tightness in his chest that was almost debilitating. He had never felt such love in his entire life and it had been almost instantaneous.

And then there were his feelings for her mother. What he had thought to be nothing more than a strong case of lust had turned out to be far more than he could have ever imagined.

His heart slammed into his rib cage with the force of a physical blow and he had to take several deep breaths as he gave in and acknowledged the emotion that he had avoided putting a name to. He'd fallen hopelessly in love with Kiley and he hadn't even seen it coming.

He'd known that he wanted to spend all of his time with her and that he desired her more than he had any woman in his entire life. But not once had it occurred to him that he was falling in love with her.

As the certainty of the emotion settled in, he knew he wanted to be the man to hold her while she slept at night, wanted to wake up with her each morning and spend the rest of his life spoiling her the way her jerk of an ex-husband never had. He wanted to help her raise Emmie and wanted to give her more babies for them to love and enjoy.

Unfortunately, he was almost positive he had destroyed any possibility of her ever allowing him to do that when he'd refused to talk to her about it further.

And he really couldn't say he blamed her. They had things they needed to work out and spending the past few days holed up in his house brooding about it all wasn't accomplishing anything.

"You blew it, Gordon," he muttered miserably as he opened his eyes to stare at the bottle in his hand.

Drinking the last of the beer, he set the empty bottle down on the end table next to the other three he had polished off earlier. He had overreacted to the entire situation when he'd confronted her at the day care center and driven the only woman he had ever loved—would ever love—from his life. Most likely for good.

Josh sighed heavily. Now that he'd had a few days to cool down and started looking at things rationally, he could understand Kiley's wanting to be positive about who had fathered Emmie before she approached him about it. It just made good sense to handle it that way.

He could even appreciate her reasoning for not wanting to tell him until after the funding committee decided on the additional funds for the day care center, too. She hadn't wanted there to be any question about her motives. He respected and admired that kind of integrity.

And although her fears were unfounded, he even got why she was afraid he wouldn't step up to the plate and be the father Emmie needed. She was trying to protect her child—their child—and there was no way in hell he would ever fault her for that. He would be disappointed in her if she didn't.

As he sat there staring at the twinkling lights on the tree, he thought back over the past few weeks. Spending time with her and Emmie had given him a glimpse of what his life with them could be like, and he wanted that more than he wanted his next breath.

He smiled through the mist of emotion gathering in his eyes. He'd enjoyed the nights they spent together eating in front of the television while they watched a movie, even if it had been the same cartoon both times. Then, after the pony princess was tucked into bed for the night, he loved sitting on the couch with Kiley, holding her close, talking to her and kissing her until they both gasped for breath.

He had even loved taking on the responsibility of being their protector. Initially, Kiley hadn't appreciated his insistence that he drive her and Emmie to his place to ride out the ice storm. But just the thought of her having an accident on the icy roads or either one of them being cold and uncomfortable in a house without heat and electricity had been more than he could bear.

Sighing heavily, he uttered a curse word that he only used around the guys or when he did something stupid like smash his thumb with a hammer. He loved them both unconditionally and that was something that would never change. But he was afraid he had come to that realization too late.

Unable to sit still, he stood up, gathered the beer bottles and went outside to the shed to toss them in the recycle bin. Standing in his backyard, he stared up at the star-studded night sky. He wanted it all—Kiley, Emmie and to be the best husband and father he could possibly be. But what could he do to get them back to where they had been, to make things right between him and Kiley?

He wasn't sure there was anything he could do to repair the damage he had caused to their relationship.

But the one thing he did know for certain was that he had to try. If he didn't, he knew as surely as the sun rose in the east each morning, he would regret it every second of every day for the rest of his life.

Ten

Two days before Christmas, Kiley sat in her living room watching Emmie play with the pony castle her grandparents had given her the night Kiley and Josh went to the Christmas Ball. She had spent a miserable few days wondering how she could have handled the situation with Josh any differently. After going over everything time and again, she had come to the conclusion that she couldn't.

Telling him about her suspicions before she had concrete evidence would have definitely made it appear as if she had some sort of agenda to use Emmie to keep the day care center open, as well as made her look utterly foolish if it had turned out he wasn't. Or he might have even thought she was somehow trying to extort money from him to support a child who wasn't his.

Sighing, she rose from the chair and walked into the kitchen to put her coffee cup in the dishwasher. To a point, she could understand Josh's angry reaction. Learning that he had a two-year-old child had to have been a huge shock. But that was no reason not to give her explanation serious consideration.

And then there was his promise to give the day care center a fair evaluation. Why hadn't he reported his observations and then excused himself from the vote for the additional funds for the facility? He knew that was the only chance the day care center had to survive. The only reasons she could think of to explain his actions were either he hadn't been impressed with the services she was providing to the children of the TCC members or he was retaliating against her for not telling him about Emmie. And that hurt almost as much as his unwillingness to listen to her.

Lost in thought, she jumped when the phone rang. It was probably her parents, asking her what time she thought she and Emmie would be arriving Christmas day to exchange gifts. But when she checked, the Texas Cattleman's Club number was displayed on the caller ID.

"Kiley, I'm sorry to bother you, but we need you here at the clubhouse," Gil Addison said when she answered.

"Is something wrong?" she asked. Now that Beau Hacket's son had been dealt with over the vandalism and was scheduled to attend a military school in central Texas immediately after the first of the year, she hoped nothing else had happened to the day care center.

"No," he assured her. "We just need to talk to you about your future employment here at the club."

Great, on top of everything else, they were going to fire her two days before Christmas. "I'll be there—" she glanced at the clock "—in about an hour."

"That will be great," he said, sounding cheerful. "We'll see you then."

When he hung up, she stared at the phone. She had thought Gil was quite happy with the job she was doing. Now it appeared he was happy to be rid of her.

Getting herself and Emmie ready to face the inevitable, she wondered why the TCC had decided to terminate her contract early, instead of waiting until it closed the day care center in the spring. "Your daddy probably had something to do with that," she said without thinking.

"Daddy?" Emmie asked, clearly confused. She looked around the room as if searching for something.

"No, sweetie," Kiley said, mentally chiding herself as they left the house and she strapped Emmie into her car seat. Two-year-olds tended to parrot everything they heard and since he hadn't come around them in the past few days, she had no idea if Josh intended to be a real father to Emmie or not. "Mommy made a mistake."

Twenty minutes later when she drove into the clubhouse parking lot, she recognized several cars and couldn't help but wonder why Piper and Ryan were at the club. She thought they were busy making final wedding arrangements. In fact, she thought everyone would be busy with last-minute shopping or traveling to spend the holidays with family.

"We might as well get this over with, Emmie," she said, lifting her daughter from the car seat to walk up to the front door.

The door opened before she could reach for the handle. "I'm glad you were able to make it on short notice," Piper said, grinning.

Kiley frowned. "What are you doing here?"

"They've called an emergency meeting of the funding committee," Piper said, hurrying her down the hall to the ballroom. "I'm here to give you moral support."

Before they entered the room, Kiley set Emmie on her feet to remove their coats. "Ryan isn't on the committee," she commented as she straightened. "What's really going on, Piper?"

"Ryan's here to support you, too." Her friend smiled mysteriously. "So are the majority of the parents who have kids in the day care center."

"Piper, I appreciate their support, but I doubt it will make a difference," she said tiredly. She hadn't slept well since arguing with Josh and didn't anticipate her insomnia getting better any time soon.

"Come on." Piper urged her toward the closed ballroom doors. "This won't take long. I promise."

Taking Emmie by the hand, Kiley opened the door to the big room, walked inside and looked around. Tables had been set up on the stage the day care had used and the funding committee members were seated behind them, looking at her expectantly.

Most of the parents and their children from the day care center sat in rows of chairs in front of the stage, and she was grateful for their support even though it probably wouldn't influence the committee's vote.

"Ms. Roberts, would you please approach the committee?" Josh asked, drawing her attention to him.

She had purposely avoided looking at him when she entered the room. But as she turned her attention his

way, her breath caught. Instead of a suit and tie like
the other male members on the panel were wearing, he
was dressed in boots, jeans and a chambray shirt. She
didn't think he had ever looked as handsome as he did
at that moment. But why was he dressed so casually?

Walking up to the front of the room, she was surprised when Josh grinned and stood up. "It would be
a conflict of interest for me to preside over this meeting, as well as vote on the future of the day care center.
For that reason, I'm excusing myself," he said, handing the gavel to Beau Hacket. "I do, however, retain
my right to report my observations on the center's operation and give my recommendation of action on the
issue." He walked to the end of the stage, descended
the steps and came to stand beside her.

"What's going on?" she demanded under her breath.

"Just wait," he whispered close to her ear.

"Can we at least sit down?" she asked. Why did
they have to humiliate her by firing her in front of
everyone?

"No. Just listen," he said, smiling at her. Her heart
skipped a beat at the warmth she detected in his brilliant blue eyes.

"Up," Emmie said, patting Josh's leg.

Without a moment's hesitation, he picked up their
daughter and held her close. "How's my little princess?" he asked, causing Kiley's chest to swell with
emotion. Even if he couldn't care for her, there was no
doubt how he felt about their daughter. It was easy to
see Josh loved their daughter with all his heart.

"It's been brought to our attention that the funding
committee needs to review our calculations for the
day care center's budget," Beau stated, drawing every-

one's attention back to the panel of men. "We've also been asked by Gil Addison to review Ms. Roberts's contract for the position of day care center operator."

Here it comes, Kiley thought. This was where they were going to terminate her contract. But why did they have to ruin Christmas for her and Emmie? Why couldn't they have waited until after the first of the year?

"I make a motion to start the discussion," Paul Windsor said when Beau gave him a nod.

When one of the other members seconded the motion, Beau looked directly at Josh. "I think you have something to report?"

Josh nodded and, with Emmie perched on his forearm, stepped forward. "After Ms. Roberts addressed the committee at the first of the month requesting additional funds for the day care center, I made periodic visits to see how she was running the operation and to determine if the money was actually needed."

"And what were your findings?" Beau asked, surprising Kiley with his even tone and pleasant expression. Apparently, his way of "making things right" for what his son had done was to at least appear interested and congenial.

"I've observed Ms. Roberts in several different situations at the day care center and I can honestly say I was extremely impressed by her dedication and how well she was able to relate to the kids," he said, making eye contact with every one of the panel members. "She gives each child individual attention and makes them all feel like everything they show or tell her is of the utmost importance. I've also observed her methods of discipline and I was amazed by the kindness and respect she showed." He chuckled. "The little boy in question happily accepted his 'time out' without protest or her having to raise her voice above normal." He turned to look at her and the expression on his handsome face was breathtaking. "And I doubt anyone could have done a better job of putting on an entertaining and enjoyable children's Christmas program."

The crowd of parents broke their silence with applause and several even called out words of encouragement and support.

When the parents quieted down, he continued, "In conclusion, I would like to add that the TCC has a top-notch day care center." His gaze never wavered from hers. "And we have the dedication and expertise of Kiley Roberts to thank for it. I recommend that you vote to keep the day care center open and appropriate the funds needed to keep it running."

"I would like to add that I think the TCC should renegotiate her contract to include a raise and a five-year extension," Gil Addison said, walking up to stand beside Josh.

The group of parents once again erupted in a round of applause and loud cheers.

Tears filled her eyes and Kiley couldn't have found her voice to save her soul. Josh's heartfelt endorsement was more than she could have possibly hoped for and proved that no matter what their differences were, he wasn't going to hold them against the club's day care center.

"Thank you," she mouthed, looking at the only man she would ever love. She just wished their problems could be resolved as easily as the fate of the day care center. Unfortunately, she wasn't sure that was going to be the case.

Beau banged the gavel to bring order back to the meeting. "Are there any other comments?"

"My son, Cade, has learned more at the TCC day care center in the past couple of months than he ever did at the child care facility he used to attend," Gil stated.

"All of the children love Miss Kiley," Winnie Bartlett added. "My daughters are disappointed on the weekends when they can't go to school."

"I move to adopt Josh Gordon's recommendations," the only female on the panel said, grinning.

"I second the motion," one of the men chimed in.

"Then I guess all there is left to do would be to bring it to a vote," Beau said, smiling. "All those in favor of the recommendations set forth by Josh Gordon and Gil Addison, please raise your hands."

When every member of the funding committee, including Beau and his cohort Paul Windsor, raised their hands high in the air, Beau nodded. "It's unanimous. The motion carries," he said, bringing down the gavel to seal the fate of the day care center.

Kiley couldn't believe what had just taken place. She had been summoned to the TCC clubhouse, expecting to be fired. Now she had job security for the next five years, as well as a raise.

Amid the thunderous cheers and standing ovation, Beau Hacket pounded the gavel on the table several times. "Order, please." He looked at Josh. "I think there's something else Josh wants to say."

She frowned. What on earth could he possibly have to add?

Still holding Emmie, Josh took Kiley by the hand and led her up onto the stage. Kiley's heart pounded so hard, she wasn't sure it wouldn't create a hole in her chest. What was he up to now?

"The reason I felt it would be a conflict of interest for me to preside over the meeting today was because, as many of you know, I've been seeing Kiley for the past few weeks," he stated, glancing down at her. His smile and the light she detected in his eyes caused her to feel warm all over. "I didn't feel I could vote without bias on an issue that involves the woman I love."

As the crowd clapped their approval, Kiley looked at Piper, standing with her fiancé, Ryan Grant. Smiling, tears filled her friend's eyes. "It's going to work out, Kiley," she mouthed. "I'm so happy for you."

Feeling as if she were in a bizarre dream, Kiley looked up at Josh. They still had problems. But for the first time in days, she felt there might be a glimmer of hope that things could work out between them, at least where Emmie was concerned.

"There's one more thing before we adjourn," Josh said, quieting the well-wishers. "I'd like to thank you all for coming to the club on such short notice to support Kiley and the day care center."

He grinned and whispered close to her ear, "Now let's get out of here. I have something at the ranch I want to show Emmie and we have some things we need to talk over."

They were silent as they made their way through the crowd to the clubhouse parking lot, and by the time they reached his SUV, Kiley felt as if she had regained some of her equilibrium. Josh had taken her by surprise when he made the recommendations for the day care center and his public announcement that he loved her had caused her head to spin. But now that she was able to think more clearly, her cautious nature took over. Just because he said he loved her didn't mean things would automatically work out for them.

Parking the truck by the corral gate, Josh looked over at the woman in the passenger seat beside him. Kiley was the only woman he had ever loved—would ever love. And he had to make things right between them.

"Thank you for allowing me to bring the two of you out here to the ranch," he said, reaching over to take her hand in his. "I wanted to give Emmie her Christmas present."

Kiley nodded, looking cautious. "I'm sure she'll love whatever you have for her."

He had hurt her emotionally and she was being careful. He could understand that and he didn't blame her one bit. He had been a complete jackass and he wasn't fool enough to think that telling her he loved her in front of a crowd was going to make everything okay. It was going to take some serious groveling on his part to make it up to her. He was prepared to do that and whatever else it took to get her to give him another chance.

"Wanna see ponies," Emmie chimed in from the backseat. Apparently she had recognized the barn when he stopped the truck.

"I think that can be arranged, princess," he said, smiling in the rearview mirror at the most precious little girl in the entire world. She and her mother were his whole world, and if Kiley would give him the chance, he would spend every minute of every day proving it to them.

Getting out of the Navigator, he came around the front to open Kiley's door and help her down from the seat. Then, getting Emmie from her car seat, he set her on her feet. "Are you ready to see the ponies?"

Emmie clapped her hands. "Pet a pony."

"You can do more than pet a pony," Josh said, smiling. "You can ride one."

Her little face lit up with glee as she nodded. "Wanna wide."

"We're not dressed for horseback riding," Kiley said, frowning. "Was that the reason you were dressed so casually for the meeting? You intended to go for a ride afterward?"

He shrugged. "I'm not going riding, but since a suit and tie aren't appropriate attire for a barnyard, I figured jeans were my best bet."

"I don't understand," Kiley said, looking confused.

"Emmie's Christmas present is in the barn," he said, grinning.

Kiley shook her head. "You didn't."

He nodded. "I sure did. My daughter likes ponies, she gets a pony."

"You're going to spoil her, Josh Gordon."

"That's my intention." He wanted to tell Kiley he intended to spoil her, too, but that would have to wait until a little later.

When Bobby Ray led the fat Shetland pony from the barn, already saddled and ready to ride, the look on Emmie's face was one Josh knew he would never forget. "Pony! Pony!" his daughter chanted excitedly.

"This is Rosy," he said, lifting Emmie to set her on the saddle. "She's your pony."

"Me pony?" The child's delight was priceless and he wouldn't have traded seeing it for the entire world.

Strapping a blue toddler-size riding helmet on her head, Josh walked beside the pony as he led her around the corral several times until he noticed Martha waiting at the corral fence. He had made arrangements in advance for his housekeeper to watch Emmie while he tried to straighten out things with Kiley.

Lifting his daughter down, he handed the lead rope back to Bobby Ray. "You can ride again a little later, princess. Do you think you could go with Martha now and have some lunch while I talk to your mommy?"

Grinning, Emmie waved as she and Martha walked toward the house. "Bye-bye."

"She's amazing, Kiley," he said, staring after their little girl. "You've done a wonderful job with her."

"She's my world," Kiley said, smiling for the first time since they left the TCC clubhouse.

"Do you have room in that world of yours for me?" he asked, gently touching her smooth cheek.

"Josh, please…" she said, starting to turn away from him. "I don't want to hear it if you don't mean it."

Reaching out, he pulled her into his arms. She tried to push away from him, but he locked his arms around her. He was determined to settle things between them. It was the only possible chance they had of building a future together.

"Kiley, don't just quit on us." Placing his finger beneath her chin, he tilted her head until their gazes met. "I know I hurt you, but hear me out before you make the decision to walk away from what we have together."

She stared at him for several long seconds before she spoke. "Besides Emmie, just what do you think we have, Josh?"

"Love," he answered. "I love you and you love me. And it's something I have every intention of fighting for. I meant it when I announced it at the meeting. I love you, Kiley."

"You didn't feel that way the other day." She shook her head. "You walked out in the middle of quite possibly the most important conversation we'll ever have—the one about our daughter."

The emotional pain and disappointment he saw in the depths of her pretty brown eyes made him feel as if he'd been punched in the gut. But it was no less than he deserved.

"I know I acted like a complete bastard, and I regret that more than you'll ever know," he said honestly. "I left because I needed time to come to grips with everything. I know it's no excuse for my behavior or the accusations I hurled at you, but it's the truth. I was never more shocked in my entire life than I was when I figured out Emmie is mine. But what angered me the most was that you knew and didn't tell me as soon as you suspected I could be her father."

"I didn't want to be an alarmist in case I was wrong," she said defensively. "Nor did I want you to think I was using Emmie to try to keep the day care open."

He nodded. "I understand that now that I've had time to think straight. And I admire you for handling it the way you did. But at the time, all I could think was that you'd deceived me."

"And I felt you had betrayed me when you put off the day care issue at the funding meeting," she shot back. "You had assured me you were going to give the day care center a fair evaluation. But that afternoon you acted like it was an inconvenience for me to even request the additional funds."

"To tell you the truth, the day care center was the last thing on my mind at that point," he said, meaning it. "I asked that the issue of additional funding be tabled because I figured with my state of mind, it was the only fair thing I could do."

"Why did you call an emergency meeting of the funding committee today to decide the day care's fate?" she asked, frowning. "Couldn't it have waited until after the first of the year?"

"I wanted to make sure that issue was dealt with and out of the way so I could concentrate on fixing the mess I had made with you." He brushed her lips with his. When she didn't protest, he took that as a positive sign and went on. "I love you, Kiley. And I take full responsibility for our argument." He kissed her forehead. "If you'll let me, I want to spend the rest of my life making it up to you for acting the way I did."

As she stared up at him, tears filled her eyes, and knowing he had caused her to cry made him feel as if someone tried to rip out his heart. "Josh, you don't have to say that." She shook her head. "I'm not going to try to stop you from being with Emmie."

"Honey, I know that." Giving her a kiss that had her clinging to him for support and him feeling as if his jeans had become too small in the stride, he smiled.

"What I'm trying to tell you is that I don't just want Emmie. I want you, too. I love you more than life itself. I want to marry you and raise a whole house full of kids just like our beautiful little girl."

"Josh, I don't know—"

"Do you love me, Kiley?"

Tears streamed down her cheeks as she nodded.

"Will you marry me?"

"I—I'm not sure—"

Kissing her again, he felt like he'd run a marathon by the time he raised his head. "Are you sure now?"

"I—I... You're not making it easy to think," she said, looking delightfully confused.

"Just say yes, Kiley," he commanded.

As she continued to look at him, he could tell the moment she gave in to what he knew they both wanted. "Y-yes."

"Thank God!" Releasing her, he reached into the front pocket of his jeans and pulled out the red velvet box he had carried with him since stopping by the jewelry store on the way to the TCC clubhouse earlier that morning. "Kiley, will you marry me?"

Laughing, she covered her mouth with both hands. "You already asked me that and I said yes."

"Say it again." He laughed as he opened the box, removed the one-carat solitaire diamond ring inside and slipped it on her finger. "And keep saying it until we celebrate our seventy-fifth wedding anniversary."

"Yes, I'll marry you, Josh Gordon," she said, throwing her arms around his neck.

"Good." He gave her a quick kiss, then, taking her by the hand, led her toward the house.

"Are we going to tell Emmie?" she asked.

"No. We can tell her later, after we've talked to your folks. I know they're going to have a lot of tough questions about my being Emmie's father and how that all came about." He kissed the top of her head. "But we'll do that together."

"Will you go with me to their place on Christmas Day?" she asked.

He nodded. "We can go to Midland to see your parents and on the way back home, we can stop by and tell my brother that we're going to be a family. But right now, I have something else in mind." He chuckled as he closed the corral gate behind them. "And standing in the middle of a barnyard isn't exactly the place I want to do it."

"You're incorrigible, Josh Gordon," she said, laughing with him.

"No, honey. I'm a man in love with the most desirable woman on the planet," he said, pulling her back into his arms for another kiss.

"I love you, Josh," she said softly.

"And I love you, Kiley." Grinning, he took her hand in his. "Now let's go inside the house and get started planning our life together."

* * * * *